T0149578

Until the Iris *Bloom*

A Novel

Tina Olton

iUniverse

UNTIL THE IRIS BLOOM

This is a work of fiction. As in most fiction, the literary perceptions and insights may be based on experience. In this work, all names, characters, places and incidents, however, are either products of the author's imagination or are used fictitiously. No reference to any real person is intended or should be inferred.

iUniverse books may be ordered through booksellers or by contacting:

iUniverse
1663 Liberty Drive
Bloomington, IN 47403
www.iuniverse.com
1-800-Authors (1-800-288-4677)

Because of the dynamic nature of the Internet, any web addresses or links contained in this book may have changed since publication and may no longer be valid. The views expressed in this work are solely those of the author and do not necessarily reflect the views of the publisher, and the publisher hereby disclaims any responsibility for them.

Any people depicted in stock imagery provided by Thinkstock are models, and such images are being used for illustrative purposes only. Certain stock imagery © Thinkstock.

ISBN: 978-1-5320-1237-2 (sc)
ISBN: 978-1-5320-1238-9 (e)

Library of Congress Control Number: 2017902272

Print information available on the last page.

iUniverse rev. date: 05/09/2017

For all elders who are struggling to maintain their physical and mental strength, their dignity, and their independence, including the scores I have met who inspired this story

———————

Prologue

She leaned on her cane as she looked out her window onto the street, watching the Mercury Grand Marquis pull up in front of her house. What? A Marquis? She put a hand to her face to confirm that her thick lenses were indeed covering her ninety-two-year-old eyes. It *was* a Marquis, her kind of car—big, tanklike. She had a tank car herself. People said she shouldn't drive it, but what did they know?

The Marquis driver exited his sedan and stood on the far side of the car, examining her house and adjacent property. He adjusted a dizzyingly bright blue-and-red herringbone tie, as if preparing for an important business meeting. But there was no business meeting at her house. Was there?

She squinted down at the man. Too young to be a business executive; a child, in a dark-gray suit and light-blue shirt with that horrible tie. His luxuriant, wavy brown hair, streaked by the sun (or something else), had the look of being combed often. *He thinks he's somebody, all puffed up.* What would Ivan think? Puffed up? A smile played at her lips.

No, Puffed Up's nothing to do with me. She thumped her cane as if to punctuate her thought.

Then again, when she'd woken that morning, she'd put on

her best white wool slacks, a fuzzy red sweater, and her black-and-red baseball cap. She usually dressed up when visitors came calling. Had Ivan told her about the visitor? No, she didn't think so; nobody that young, in that ghastly tie, could be coming her way.

She retreated from the window, shuffling with careful steps in her pink fluffy slippers, to a nearly threadbare couch.

Ivan should be here to remind her if things were happening. *Where the hell is he?* With a sulky sigh, she lowered her frail frame onto the lumpy cushions.

———

The white Marquis was not Reed Johnson's favorite wheels (he far preferred his girlfriend's canary-yellow Lexus two-seater), but in the real estate business you needed a car—plain, practical, but posh—for whizzing clients around in comfort from property to property.

This morning Reed was meeting the owner of the house before him, in hopes of becoming her agent. A prime asset on Main Street in the small town of Oakmont, the house had good sales potential and might land him a decent commission. Marilyn, of Green Tree Realty, had passed on the opportunity. As the owner's former agent, Marilyn had lined up several different buyers ready to grab the well-positioned property. But as soon as any deal had been negotiated, the owner had backed out. Frustrated, Marilyn had gladly handed the whole mess to Reed, who coveted a sale in the neighborhood.

The town of Oakmont was an unincorporated slice of the Northern California coast, sandwiched between two restless cities to the north and south. The waters of Perkins Bay kept the western boundary intact, and to the east, a regional park blocked the creeping fingers of development. The town, known for bars and brothels in its earlier days, now attracted more legitimate businesses, which in turn lured a broader base of residents.

Reed noted several properties on the block in the process of being renovated or rebuilt. On one side of his new interest, the construction of a two-story professional office building showed signs of completion, and on the other side, a mom-and-pop dry cleaner advertised its transformation into a Polish restaurant. He would find a buyer for the house in a flash, as it was the only remaining home in the area and the neighborhood was hot.

Marilyn had listed the house as a teardown, and as he exited the Marquis, Reed acknowledged her good judgment: the building was too small for a business, and as a residence—well, really, who'd want to live next to a Polish restaurant?

Marilyn had warned him about the owner. "Eccentric," she'd called her, and "unpredictable." Reed thought Marilyn tended to be too ladylike in her selling approach. *A little starch,* he thought, *that's what's needed.*

He finished fiddling with his tie, stepped around the car to the sidewalk, and almost gagged. What was with the green front porch? Bright green, spearmint green—the steps, the entire stoop, all painted a brilliant green. A blob of bubble gum stoop. "Definitely have to redo the entrance," he grumbled. The exterior paint, once white, was now dirty gray and blistered with old age. The whole facade presented as tacky. He was beginning to feel deflated from his earlier excitement about the property. Would he have to restage the entire house?

And herein lay the problem: if the house was a teardown, there was no reason to put any money into sprucing it up for a sale. But he'd have to face that issue when the time came; the time now was five minutes past his appointment.

On the green porch Reed punched the doorbell. A voice within—a screeching, not unlike a hawk, he mused—announced the owner's presence. "Quit your ringing. I'm coming."

Why it took so long, he didn't understand, but presently shrill words emanated from the other side of the door. "Hold on; I'm getting it." The latch clinked, and subsequent tugging eventually sprang the sticky door. A disembodied voice blasted at his chin, "Who the hell are you?"

Distracted by the green stoop, Reed had missed the all-but-opaque screen that now blocked his view of the woman inside. "Mrs. Bourbon." He felt suddenly unbalanced and didn't know why. "I'm Reed Johnson from Royal Realty. We have an appointment this morning, nine o'clock." Talking to a screen with a voice behind it—not his usual style.

"You're not exactly on time, but come in." Still through the screen, the voice said, "I'm Tidy," and from a farther distance, "Guessing you know that."

She's leaving me at the door, Reed raged. *What woman would do this to me?* He wrenched open the outer gate, stepped up into the house, and caught a first glimpse of his prospective client. He was seized by the sight.

Slight and stooped, she walked the bowlegged shuffle of old people afraid of falling and trying to keep their balance. Her costume (there was no other word for it) broadcast *old-fashioned,* and the incongruity of the baseball cap—well, it was laughable. And don't even mention the pink fluffy slippers. Eccentric was an understatement.

She had stopped her forward movement at the edge of the living room and, without turning, mumbled, "I'm old, and it's hard to know why I'm still here. Must be the Lord don't see fit to let me move on and can't figure out what to do with me. So I'm figuring it out for myself. Always have done. No one tells me what to do or messes with my life. If you're here to tell me what to do, you better think different." She stood immobile, her back to Reed, who was stuck behind her in the pocket-size front hall.

Reed drew in a long breath and wondered why the Lord hadn't seen fit to at least move her into the next room. "Mrs. Bourbon, I've come to talk about selling your house."

"What makes you think I want to sell my house?" Her voice had risen a pitch or two.

A bead of sweat sprouted on his forehead. The close space of the hall brought on a touch of claustrophobia. "You told me on the phone you did," Reed huffed. Her prattle and now the provoking challenge irritated him. "It's a good time to sell, Tidy, ah, Mrs. Bourbon … May I call you Tidy?" He reflected on which was more ridiculous: Tidy or Mrs. Bourbon?

"You call me anything you want. My mama named me Teresa Madeline Eugenia, but other folks been calling me Tidy since my girlhood down Louisiana way. I keep my room so neat, don't you see. My last name supposed to sound like the French snobs, *Bour-bon*." She pronounced the second syllable nasally. "Too much trouble to spell, so I just say Bourbon, like the drink. More likely be spelling Tidy now." She guffawed at her own humor and resumed her march into the living room, leaning heavily on her cane.

With a small gasp of relief, Reed escaped from the front hall. "Right, well, Tidy it is, then, and I don't mind telling you, Tidy, it's an excellent time to be selling, especially along Main Street." He doggedly carried on with something he understood better than dotty old ladies. "The neighborhood is heading for a major turnaround, and everyone will be wanting to buy in here." Reed warmed to his sales pitch.

They had progressed, if slowly, to the middle of Tidy's tiny living room. She had been trudging for the couch along the opposite wall, but at that moment she whirled to confront Reed, startling him to a standstill. "And just who is everybody?" she snapped.

Now eye to eye, he had his first full view of Tidy and, in particular, her relatively youthful face. She could be sixty—Marilyn had said ninety-two. High cheekbones, few wrinkles, bright eyes. Pale dark skin or dark white, he wasn't sure which it was. The baseball cap, askew, had no control over her uncombed gray wisps, which stuck out in disarray—so unlike his fastidiously managed mane.

"You realize you're the only residence left on this street." He wanted Tidy to understand the importance of her isolation. She lived alone here. Why not relocate?

Tidy resumed her trek across the living room, once again making for the graying couch. "Forgive me if I move slow," she said. "Have to watch every step I take so I don't fall. Still got my big feet from when I stood tall and straight, but I'm not tall anymore, and big feet can have me tripping, so I go slow."

Reed groaned, not quite audibly, and his shoulders drooped.

Tidy reached the end of the couch and turned, tiny step by tiny step, until she was positioned for sitting. But she didn't sit. Her head came up, and she stared at Reed standing before her. Her vacant expression momentarily unhinged Reed. She recovered quickly and plopped herself into the cushions long molded by her backside. She dropped her cane, and it crashed against the coffee table. "You sit on that ottoman so I can see your eyes," she said. "I know a man by his eyes."

The footstool lay squeezed between the TV and a heavy oak-and-steel coffee table that stretched the length of the couch. The furniture in the room was so … packed in, Reed noted, so unwieldy and … graceless. With some effort, he remembered his cause and straightened his back. *Starch,* he reminded himself, and he sat on the stool as instructed.

He scanned his surroundings. As the small structure was only one story, Reed could survey the entire floor from his perch on the stool. A few feet from where he sat was the bedroom, door open, revealing her bed, with lilac sheets, unmade. To the rear of the combined living and dining rooms, a short hall led to the back entrance. At the end of the hall were laundry machines. The whole of the inside was colorless, except for a comparatively new and outrageously purple carpet throughout. And somewhere along the way, Reed noticed, she'd lost the penchant to be tidy. Piles of newspapers, mail (opened and unopened), church bulletins, and calendars covered every horizontal surface apart from the floor, which was dotted with bits of who knew what. Some of it looked like oatmeal.

These hideous features—interior and exterior—would make pricing the property tough. Reed's forehead creased with a frown. Who would pay for a building they were going to demolish? He turned his attention back to Tidy and found her glaring at him, her dark eyes piercing, her expression resolute, the line of her thin lips straight and taut. She had been watching him make his inspection, he realized, and he sensed she didn't like it.

Not without some sensitivity, Reed imagined Tidy upset with the prospect of selling the house she had lived in for decades and decided to alter his approach. "You know, your property will sell for good money inside of a week. Right on Main Street, it's a prime spot for new retail."

"Just why I should stay. Keep them developers from turning around everything, like you saying. Who wants a downtown full of nail salons and swanky restaurants? The street surely needs some home life too." She sat straighter in defiance of the restaurants and nail salons. Her hands moved incessantly as she talked, plucking at her pant legs, ranging up the sweater sleeves to her shoulders.

Her constant motion unsettled Reed—again.

"Do you have a price in mind for your house, Tidy?" Reed asked, trying to get back on track.

"I'm not selling. I thought I told you."

"Mrs. Bourbon," he said, having trouble keeping a testy tone from his voice, "when I called the other day to ask if I could visit to talk about selling your house, you said yes."

"I said you could visit. I didn't say you could sell my house."

His hands, hanging limp on either side of the ottoman, curled into tight balls. "Tidy ..." he began, but a sudden rattling to the rear of the house interrupted him. He glanced up as the door of the back landing swung open to reveal a man of medium height and substantial bulk. Reed couldn't tell if the fellow staggered or swaggered as he turned to close the door.

Approaching the main room, the bulk appeared not young, not old. He moved with a peculiar gait, swinging left and right, like an elephant. Swagger. His badly cut black hair stuck out from his skull at odd angles. A thick black beard, trimmed short but nevertheless unkempt, filled his lower face. His rumpled clothing—ill-fitting pants, T-shirt, bomber jacket, all shades of black and gray—looked slept in. Heavy black glasses made him appear more like a distracted professor than the bum Reed presumed him to be.

"Ivan," Tidy squawked, "get in here. This man wants to sell my house. Just last week I'm telling you I'm too old to be moving. I'm ninety-two, and I'm staying in my house till the day I die."

On the ottoman, Reed slumped. This was worse than Marilyn had portrayed. And who was Ivan? Marilyn hadn't mentioned him.

"Ivan's my tenant, lives in the back room. Ivan, this here's ... What'd you say your name was, mister?"

"Ivan, I'm Reed Johnson, Royal Realty." He rose from the ottoman, extending his hand. Bum or not, he'd be polite.

"What you thinking, Tidy?" Ivan's voice, deep, with a thick Slavic accent, slushed his words together. "Why'd you let this man in? You no want to sell the house." He lunged forward into the room, his feet spread wide, not unlike Tidy's own gait, to keep from falling.

Stagger, Reed amended his former assessment and lowered his proffered hand. Bum was one thing, drunken bum quite another; apparent Russian drunken bum was not within his experience and might be cause for caution.

Tidy exploded, "Oh, Lord, you been drinking again. Here it is still morning. You sorry, no-good son of a bitch ... I can hardly talk you are so terrible." She rose from the couch and, ignoring her cane, teetered as she moved awkwardly around the coffee table toward the center of the small living room, which had grown smaller with the increase in population.

Reed stepped back toward the wall. He sensed these two characters were about to duke it out, but looking at the frail old lady and the drunken hulk, he wasn't sure what kind of duel it might be. To his astonishment, the rumpled Russian approached him instead. "You heard 'er. She not selling. You leaf now."

"Ivan, you're being rude. You don't tell people what to do in my house." Tidy's voice turned shrill. "My house! You think you're something here? You're nothing but shit and drunk, just plain drunk." The air of the room swirled with the vitriol.

Reed sensed the opportunity to advance his cause had ended and figured he might as well move on. Having backed himself against a wall, however, he had few escape routes available in the small space. Dodging to the right, he risked knocking Tidy off balance, but shifting to his left, he would face the Russian straight on. Being young and still ever so slightly chivalrous, Reed turned toward Ivan.

"Ivan, I'm glad to have met you, and I think—" Ivan's right fist came up more swiftly than Reed could have imagined. The impact, feeling something like a brick, landed just below his left eye. He heard the splintering of his cheekbone. The nerves of his facial skin seared as a couple of bulky finger rings inlaid with chiseled rocks coursed down toward the corner of his mouth. A warm, acidic liquid seeped into his lips. Although his vision to the left was now obscured, to his right he caught the blur of Tidy moving faster than her earlier shuffling would have suggested.

She swept up a clump of newspaper from the coffee table and flailed at Ivan's shoulder. "You goddamn drunk." Whack, whack, she flogged the debilitated hulk.

For all her weak demeanor and apparent frailty, Tidy in a rampage resembled a gray-haired dust devil. Within moments Ivan collapsed. In his inebriated state, he was the frail one, and he quickly succumbed to Tidy's barrage—at any rate, in turning to escape, he lost his balance and crumpled to the floor.

In the midst of the fracas, neither Tidy nor Ivan saw Reed reach for the phone.

"County Emergency Services …"

"I nee' schum hel'."

———————

The police arrived first, taking in the scene with amusement. Calls to Tidy's house were frequent and predictable. The sight before them, however, was curious. The drunk—usually ranting at the front door, locked out—was inside, on the floor. The old lady—usually screaming obscenities from behind the front door—was screaming obscenities over the drunk on the floor, kicking him in the ribs with fluffy pink feet.

Why the old lady allowed the drunk to live with her was a little obscure, although, over the years, the beat cops had come to understand that the Russian provided some degree of comfort and security for the old lady. Today, it appeared, their craziness had escalated.

The paperwork for this melee—a lot like the other scuffles they'd filed before—would be a nuisance. The cops couldn't ignore the punch, however, and one had to consider that the punch might have landed accidently on the old lady. Writing up the heightened action would at least make the report more interesting. And, not to forget the Realtor with the sunken left cheek—a casualty needing attention—they called an ambulance.

The officers picked three blades of dead grass from the browned front yard, one shorter than the other two. Officer Wilson pulled the stub and lifted the bracelets from his belt. His comrades hoisted Ivan off the floor and steadied him for the cuffing. They then led him out the door, down the spearmint-green porch, and into Wilson's patrol car, carefully guiding Ivan's large head so as to avoid any bumps.

Tidy watched the activity from the front window, her emotions moving in quick succession, irritated, amused, sad … so very sad. The flashing lights of the emergency vehicles were briefly startling, although the commotion generated by them was not unknown to her, given the number of times the police had been summoned to her home previously. Today, however, the fire truck and the ambulance and the three cop cars, all together, were annoying.

She thought about the pumped-up real estate agent, barging into her living room, carrying on about selling her home. He had left her home horizontal, with bloodied face and, oh my, that hair all a mess. A grin tugged at the corners of her mouth. Until her eyes followed Ivan into the police vehicle.

"You dumb bastard. What am I to do now?"

Chapter 1

Claire

This is a good case for you," Sergeant Jane Rios said crisply to Claire. "You're the best with these violations." Jane worked in the sheriff's elder-abuse department. The beat cops had figured one way to shorten the paperwork was to make an immediate verbal report to Sergeant Rios. The case warranted it, they'd announced to Rios; the threat of physical violence was too serious to ignore. Sergeant Rios had agreed and thus placed her call to Claire, a volunteer social worker for the county Senior Outreach Services. Claire and Jane worked together occasionally, so they were on familiar terms.

"Why is that? Because I have such a big heart?" Claire asked.

"You know what I mean. You're developing quite a reputation for getting our abuse cases resolved—and often enough into court, which makes us happy."

Claire smiled. Her work with the elderly was a new vocation, and she still doubted her effectiveness. Jane's praise pleased her. Claire had worked for family services until two years ago, when she'd turned sixty-two and chosen to retire. Her husband of thirty years had died shortly before, and after a period of grieving and adjusting, she'd concluded it was time for something different. The Senior Outreach Services program had seemed perfect for applying her skills to a new clientele.

"Okay, what's this one about?" she asked Jane.

"Vic's name is Tidy Bourbon."

"Tidy? T-i-d-y? Bourbon?"

"So her Social Security states."

Claire allowed a chuckle. "Who's the abuser?"

"Guy by the name of Ivan. He rents a room from her. An alcoholic, on disability. He's been in and out of our hands the last five or six years. I don't understand their relationship, but we've had several calls about them, usually relating to Ivan's alcoholism."

Jane explained that, over time, she'd read the files of Tidy and Ivan's escapades as the reports had found their way to her office. She'd noted occasional concern on the part of the responding cops, but mostly the pitch looked to them like Mutt and Jeff or Elmer Fudd and Bugs Bunny chasing a snit with one another—a variation of the odd couple. Seeing no reason to spend more department time and money on the hoot and the Russkie, in what everyone believed to be a verbal warfare, Jane had filed the reports away—until today.

"Why are you bothered enough to call me now?" Claire asked.

"Ivan has never shown any tendency to physical violence before, but the incident today involved an assault."

"On Tidy?" Claire blurted.

"No, thank goodness."

Jane relayed the information the patrol officer had radioed to her. "He stated Tidy was pretty adamant Ivan had never hit her," Jane said. "Still, the whole setup is strange. Even if the guy doesn't abuse Tidy physically, I wonder about other mistreatment—financial abuse, for instance. Ivan's unemployment, alcohol consumption, and their living arrangement make some sort of abuse a distinct possibility."

"Yes, peculiar … and curious."

Jane laughed. "I have your attention? You'll check it out?"

"What's the address?"

Jane repeated it for her.

"Good heavens, right smack in the middle of Oakmont!"

"Yup, and apparently peppermint green is the color of the year," Jane said, hanging up before Claire could ask what she meant.

Claire drove into Oakmont from the north, marveling at how well the town had maintained its charm—managing its development, retaining buildings at two stories, keeping out the housing tracts of nondescript, look-alike structures. The downtown main street was changing rapidly, she noticed. Several storefronts had been rehabilitated or razed, and the residences among the businesses had all but vanished, Tidy's tiny dwelling appearing to be the remaining exception.

By the time she arrived at the scene, the ambulance had left, and Wilson had driven Ivan away. Officer Rickerts had stayed behind as instructed by Sergeant Rios to wait for the social worker.

Claire walked slowly toward the patrolman standing at the end of the walkway and pulled a discreet picture ID from her pocket to identify herself. Claire's clients were often surprised to learn that she was, by some standards, old enough to be regarded "elderly" as well. Her parents' genes had given her smooth, unblemished Mediterranean skin. The only creases on her face were around her dark-brown eyes, which often crinkled with amusement. Claire liked to smile; in fact, she believed in humor as a restorative and said laughing made her feel younger.

The situation ahead, however, would not be particularly cheerful.

"Sergeant Rios called me with your request," Claire said to the officer. "She told me you often answer calls at this address. What prompted you to suggest I investigate Ms. Bourbon's circumstances?"

"Should have seen the guy in the ambulance—just left," Officer Dave Rickerts answered. He was young, tall, and well built with a thick neck, like an ex–football player. She'd want him on her side of an argument, Claire mused.

"Who was he?"

"A real estate agent, evidently. Ivan took a swing at him—a strong jab, I would say. Could be looking at assault and battery. Tidy was madder than hops, kicking Ivan—quite a sight."

Rickerts's nonchalance spoke of the frequency of these incidents. Jane had said the beat cops who answered the calls to Tidy's home thought the old lady and the Russian a little local color, worth a few laughs back at the station.

Claire was not entertained. "You mean Ivan laid the guy out?"

"More than that," Rickerts said. "We're talking blood and guts."

"Oh, come on."

"No, I'm not joking," he said, stiffening as if suddenly

remembering Claire's status. "The vic was decked, his face bashed in. Ivan had some lethal rocks on his fingers. They might constitute a weapon, and we could have a felony."

"Rocks?"

"Cut stones, big things, set in finger rings. Caused the lacerations."

"Rings, plural? More than one?"

"Two, nearly identical, maybe that means weapons, plural." Rickerts's laugh was silenced by a frown from Claire.

She tried not to show her annoyance with the attempt at humor. Violence constituted a dangerous environment for anyone, but for a frail elderly woman … And she didn't like the mention of *weapon*—one *or* two. "Okay, thanks for the account, and I appreciate you waiting for me."

Claire sighed and turned to approach Tidy's porch. Peppermint green. She hesitated and smiled, staring at the entrance. She looked forward to meeting the woman who had added such a remarkable decorative touch to her home.

At the peal of the doorbell, hawk-like cries came from within; Claire imagined a bird flapping sluggishly toward the entrance. The latch clonked several times. Grunting, interspersed with *shits*, could be heard before the door finally popped opened.

The hawk screeched in Claire's face, "Who're you? I've had enough messing in my life today."

Claire's reaction was not unlike Reed's: How do you deal with a voice, instead of a person? But Claire was more pragmatic; she was not unbalanced. "Ms. Bourbon, I'm Claire Richards from the county health services Senior Outreach Services program. The sheriff's elder-abuse department phoned me, concerned about what went on here. May I come in?"

Tidy snorted and paused. It was possible she even chuckled.

"I don't think that real estate man is old enough to be called an *elder*."

"No, Tidy, I'm here about you."

"Don't know why that'd be, but I always welcome visitors. You might as well come on in." Her voice, resigned, faded as she turned away.

Claire found the outer screen unlatched and let herself in. She caught a glimpse of Tidy, and her social worker routine took over, beginning with her physical assessment of the client. *Appropriately dressed,* she thought. Well, maybe the baseball cap was a little offbeat, and the pink fluffy slippers not quite up to the rest of the outfit, but Tidy was dressed. *Mobility issues,* Claire noted as Tidy clomped to the living room, feet spread wide, cane in hand.

Tidy led Claire into the main room of her home, heading straight for what Claire instantly perceived as Tidy's throne—a couch of formerly pale-gold damask material, now a yellowed beige, graying at the edges of the cushions where no one sat to clean off the dust.

"Sit down, sit down," Tidy said. "I'm sitting 'cause I'm worn out. That business with the cops was too much for me."

As Tidy plodded her way around the coffee table, Claire pushed a square ottoman closer to the couch. On the footstool she would have good eye contact, and in case Tidy's hearing was impaired, she wouldn't have to shout as they talked. Tidy eyed her suspiciously as she sat. Claire didn't blame her. When a social worker comes calling, seemingly without cause, anyone might be disturbed.

"The incident this morning … how distressing for you."

"What do you know about that?" Tidy flared.

"Not much," Claire said with near honesty. "It's why I'm

here, Tidy. The sheriff's department called me. It sounded as if Ivan was out of control, and we are concerned about his violent behavior."

"Violent!" Tidy chopped the air above her lap with her hands as if in demonstration but exclaimed stridently, "Ivan's *not* violent, never."

"Ms. Bourbon," Claire said slowly and evenly, "Ivan caused injury to the real estate broker, Mr. Johnson. The man's face was bloody. Ivan assaulted him." Claire repeated what she remembered of Rickerts's description, hoping her details were accurate.

"That estate man deserved it," Tidy said, but without much conviction. Her hands fell to her lap; her fingers fidgeted, picking at her sweater hem.

Claire, with the wisdom of experience, switched to another approach. "Has Ivan lived here with you for a while?"

"Been with me a long time—about ten years, maybe more. He drove a cab. One night he got beat up bad; they put him on disability. He can't afford much, so I rent him my extra room." She nodded down the hall, her hands now still. "He's a decent man. Helps me cleaning the house, pays his rent on time, quiet, good cook, drives me to the doctor if I need it. What went on today … he was trying to protect me. He didn't mean to hurt that man." Although her body had settled into the cushions, her eyes roved the room, away from Claire.

"Ms. Bourbon, has Ivan ever hit you?" Claire asked gently, worried Sergeant Rios might be right concerning physical abuse.

"No, goodness, no." Tidy sounded almost amused at the thought. Her eyes stopped their wandering and came to rest on Claire's shoes.

"What about a shove or a push?"

"Lordy, no, he never touches me unless I ask for help, like climbing the stairs or getting out of the car. Then he's quite the gentleman." Her eyes swept over Claire's, and their eyes locked momentarily.

"How often does he come home drunk?" Claire continued, trying to hold on to Tidy's gaze.

But with the new question, Tidy's attention dodged to the far wall of the room. "Off and on. He knows I don't like it. I throw him out when I can't stand his boozy ways anymore. But I take him back every time, 'cause it's too hard to live here without him. Ivan does so many helping things for me." She stared down at her hands patting one another in her lap.

Claire considered Tidy: lonely, living by herself at ninety-two … *any* companionship would be agreeable. *But a volatile Russian wouldn't be my choice,* she thought. Out loud Claire went on with more practical matters. "He pays you for the room?"

"Every month." Tidy spoke congenially now, seemingly pleased with this detail. "His disability check comes in the mail. Next day we go to the bank together to cash it. I get my money right there and put it into my account, holding out some for food. Then we go to the grocery store. Our routine every month."

"Do you pay for any of his needs?"

"What do you mean?" Tidy's dark eyes flashed.

"Do you ever pay for his food or medicine? Or do you ever give him money, if he asks?"

"What business is that of yours?" Tidy said a little too defiantly, which suggested to Claire she did.

Claire decided it was time for a more neutral topic—perhaps an inquiry about her client's odd name. "Tell me about your name, ah, Tidy … It's southern?

Tidy grinned. "Back in Louisiana my mama named me Teresa Madeline Eugenia Bourbon. Teresa's for her favorite saint, she told me. Eugenia was her mama's name, and Madeline, just a name she liked. She mostly called me Teresa, hoping I'd be saintly, I guess. When I'm not saintly, I got all three: 'Teresa Madeline Eugenia,' she'd yell. 'Get on over here,' or some such. Last name's one of those snobby French ones, supposed to be pronounced through the nose, my mama said. But I say it like the drink."

Claire smiled. "You're Cajun?"

"Only half, my daddy. He was gone by the time I turn two. My mama's quadroon. You know, some black. A man once called me ... what was it? Hi-bred! I said I didn't think I was so high as that."

Claire marveled at the change in the woman. Her face had cleared of worry, her eyes sparkled, and her grin was infectious.

"Mama passed after my eighth birthday, and Aunt Bessie took over. She's my mama's sister, but their daddies were different. Bessie's really black—not like me."

"And 'Tidy'?"

"Tidy's the name I've had since I was little. My mama used to say, 'No child ever had such a clean room all her child life.' Every night before I go to bed I put my books in their right place, every crayon back in the box, every doll on the shelf. When Mama went to buy another shelf for my things, the hardware store woman in Picouville names me Tidy." She laughed at the memory. "Picouville's the place where I was born, in southern Louisiana. Small town with nothin' much—feed store, grocery, hardware—for the rest we go on to Lafayette."

"When did you move to Oakmont, Tidy?"

"Nineteen forty-nine. I married my second husband, Mr. Browning, then. I'm living in this house fifty years and more."

"What became of, ah, Mr. Browning?"

"He was a good 'un, but he died after a few years, some kind of cancer. That's him over there," Tidy said, pointing to a sepia photo sitting on the top of a small secretary. The photo showed a middle-aged man with sparse, dark hair. He was wearing a suit and tie and glasses that made his face look pinched and narrow. Tidy nodded to the photo as if saying hello.

"Are there children?"

"No, none of them. Mr. Browning said our house would be good for one, with the extra room and all, but … Just as well." A sigh of regret seemed to escape her.

"I rent the room to Ivan now," Tidy resumed more sturdily. "Lord knows I need the money. Pays on the first, or his ass is out of here." She looked directly at Claire to signal this certainty. "Ivan's a good man when he's sober." She paused and slumped back into the couch cushions. "Lately he seems to be in jail more; that's bad, 'cause I need him here. He helps me—carries out the trash, gets my groceries, drives me to the hospital if it's necessary. When he's gone, I'm in a peck of trouble."

Claire wriggled on the ottoman with impatience. Tidy's repetitions, especially about Ivan, irritated her. *The guy's a jerk,* Claire thought. *Why sustain the relationship? Like in a bad marriage, hanging on is a waste. Tidy should be in an assisted-living facility, where her needs can be met and her welfare guaranteed.* Claire inhaled deeply, reprimanding herself for jumping to conclusions. She needed to do a thorough assessment of the situation. That was what a social worker was supposed to do before passing judgment.

"How long is Ivan usually in jail when he's been drinking?" she asked.

"A day, two or three. Doesn't matter; it's always bad for me," Tidy repeated yet again. Claire surreptitiously drummed her fingers on the side of the ottoman.

"I worry being alone," Tidy continued unbidden, "especially at night. I don't sleep well. Too many loud cars screeching up and down the street, dogs barking like they's hungry for meat. Little noises, scritchings, making me nervous."

Without thinking, Claire glanced at her watch and sank with the knowledge she was late for her next appointment. She considered whether she could leave Tidy unattended. Sergeant Rios had expressed concern about Tidy's judgment, and Claire wondered about leaving a ninety-two-year-old woman on her own in any case. She vacillated.

"You must be getting tired now, Tidy, and I should be on my way. If I may, I'd like to continue our visit tomorrow." Dodging the dilemma perhaps, but a practical solution.

"A visit tomorrow would be just fine." Tidy smiled. "You call before you come, 'cause I don't always remember when visitors are coming. I try to keep things on my calendar, writing it down so I don't forget. I'm making a note right now you'll be here tomorrow." She lifted a rumpled, coffee-stained calendar from the middle of the table before her and scrabbled around to find a pen. "Oh dear, you'll have to tell me your name again."

Claire looked on, both troubled and pleased; the calendar was a good idea for a forgetful person, but the suggestion of memory deficiencies increased her unease.

"I use the calendar to help my brain." Tidy raised a finger to her forehead. "I ain't wrapped too tight no more, you see."

Claire smiled at the expression and was about to comment

on it when the doorbell rang. Tidy started at the sound and clutched at the calendar, crushing the corner. The pen fell to the floor unnoticed. Abruptly, she yelled, "Come on in; door's open."

"Would you like me to see who's at the door?" Claire asked. Then, without waiting for permission, she went to the front hall and opened the inner door.

The shape on the other side of the gate announced, "I'm Bernie, from up the street. I heard of a problem with Ivan this morning, and I'm calling to see if I can help."

Looking back into the living room, Claire called out, "Tidy, it's Bernie."

"Oh, here's Bernie," Tidy cried. "Come on in, Bernie," she shouted.

Claire unlatched the outer door and faced a short, stout woman—Irish, she guessed, from the sound of her brogue. The woman looked about sixty, her graying hair showing remnants of a burnished red. Her pale face gathered the freckles of her youth into brown spots. An old-fashioned tan tweed jacket, a wee bit small across her broad chest, topped her gray slacks, faded blue sweater, and sensible (if rather worn) athletic shoes.

Claire stepped aside. "Hello, Bernie. I'm Claire, a friend of Tidy's. Please come in."

Tidy beamed at the sight of Bernie marching briskly past Claire. "This here's Bernie. Oh, I've forgotten your name again."

"We've met, Tidy. I told her I'm your friend Claire."

"Yes, my friend Claire," Tidy echoed.

Bernie moved with practiced ease to the ottoman Claire had abandoned. "How are you, dearie? We've been hearing things have gone bad again for Ivan. Would you like someone to be with you tonight?"

Claire listened with dismay. News of troubles traveled fast in this neighborhood. And who was Bernie, where had she come from, and could she be trusted? Claire berated herself for what might be an unfair skepticism.

"It'd be nice if you'd stay the night, just till I know I'll be all right." Tidy whispered, "Could you?"

Bernie appeared to survey the living room. Her eyes met those of Claire once, bounced to the kitchen door, and came around to Tidy's face again.

Nervous, Claire thought. *How curious.*

"Of course, love. I'll run home and pick up a few things and be right back." Too fast on her feet, Bernie stumbled slightly as she moved to the door.

In and out. Quick, scurrying. Claire frowned. "A visit from Bernie must be nice for you, Tidy. Has she stayed with you before?"

"She comes round now and then and, when Ivan's gone, helps me out."

Perhaps Bernie was the solution to her concern about leaving Tidy alone. *I ought to give this unexpected favor its due*, Claire advised herself.

Within minutes Bernie returned toting a canvas sack, which she placed inside the front door. "I'm going to have a little tea, dearie. Could I make you some coffee?" she sang out as she hastened to the kitchen with peculiar determination.

"Coffee'd be good, Bernie. Thank you," Tidy called from the living room, smiling, content.

Claire observed the situation around her. Tidy's problems of the morning seemed to have floated away. Bernie was like a comfortable nursemaid—warm, cozy, and smartly efficient. Claire reconsidered: perhaps Bernie was not nervous but efficient, taking care of things. Claire nodded to Bernie in appreciation, but Bernie wasn't paying attention. She was filling the teakettle, splashing water over her front and the counter next to the sink. She clanged the teakettle onto the stove and lit the burner. *Maybe efficient but also sloppy and noisy,* Claire thought. Claire wavered between worry and weary. She suppressed the worry and rationalized that perhaps nothing more could be done. It was already afternoon, and she needed to get back to her scheduled visits.

She waved to Tidy and promised again to call the next day. As Claire pulled open the inner door, she glanced down; her eyes narrowed as they landed on Bernie's canvas bag. She paused, grappling with what she was seeing—something with a lid. She pushed open the outer door, turning as she stepped outside to look again at the bag and the golden screw-top lid, about an inch across, on a glass neck. Just as Claire closed the two doors, her brain grasped the sight of a bottle of Gordon's gin. It was unmistakable because a similar bottle of her late husband's still resided in her own liquor cabinet.

———

The gin bottle in Bernie's bag niggled in Claire's mind all afternoon. Although hardly Grey Goose, Gordon's wasn't a no-name plastic bottle either. Nor did Bernie's appearance suggest she could afford Gordon's. Claire's antennae had shot up but only briefly. She carried on to an appointment with Mrs. Baron, who needed a listening ear about her newly diagnosed renal failure and the prospect of dialysis.

By the time Claire reached the tiny bungalow she now called home, she wasn't sure if the bottle in Bernie's bag or the bottle in her own liquor cabinet bothered her more. It had been exactly the emergence of this kind of brooding thought that had driven her to sell the house of her and her late husband's married life, despite advice to the contrary of so many well-meaning friends. In her new abode, her retreat from the rest of the world, she could enjoy the memories of her and her husband's times together whenever she wanted and not have to confront them by default every day, in every room of the old house.

Inside, she dropped her bag of files by her computer and rummaged in the liquor cabinet for the open bottle of merlot. She poured half a glass—her daily allowance. The Gordon's gin on the upper shelf taunted her. Why she had kept it now mystified her. She picked out the bottle and dumped it in the trash. She didn't drink gin; there was no point in keeping it. *There, the bother banished.* Would that all her husband's ghosts could be so easily disposed.

Wine in hand, she paced through her quarters. *Not much larger than Tidy's,* she mused. She liked the minimalist nature of her new digs. Small rooms, diminutive garden, tiny kitchen—perfect for her nominal cooking needs. The pocket-size home felt like a cocoon; the walls enveloped her, keeping her safe inside.

Claire constructed walls and fences and drew lines around her life expertly. She supposed she succeeded as a social worker because of this ability. Boundaries, the social workers called these dividers. Real; imagined; carefully thought out; thrown up hastily, impetuously, recklessly—anything to keep from getting too close. Too close to what? was the question—a question social workers rarely tried to answer. They found other ways, like humor, to deal with the inevitable sorrow, misery, and grief that their work engendered. They tried to find something ridiculous in the cases they rambled through in a day: the hat lined with tinfoil (to keep the alien vibrations from driving the client nuts); the huge collection of toilet paper in the garage (leaving no room for a car); the cross-eyed cat who burped after eating. They then shared these stories with someone who understood why they found them funny. Claire frowned; her someone had died on her.

In her new surroundings, with her new avocation, she was now reinventing herself. Reinventing: the modern paradigm for retirees—or widows. Make a new life to replace the old. She'd begun by divesting herself of tiresome possessions. The old kitchen leftovers of his first marriage and the furniture of his parents' home had gone to thrift stores. The stuff she and her husband had purchased together in their early years (which she'd secretly disliked but accepted because she was in love and wanted to please), she'd donated to a charity garage sale.

Wandering with the still-untouched glass of wine in hand, she came to the window overlooking her postage-stamp garden. Under the sill she had placed a small table of her mother's, dressed with a piece of Guatemalan weaving and a single framed photograph of their daughter. She stared at the photo, the grin, a suggestion of mischief. Her husband had taken the photo, which was her favorite image of her only child. When she'd moved from the house the three had shared, other photographs had been relegated to one scrapbook, which now lay hidden on the shelf under the coffee table, buried by old *New Yorkers*, *New York Times Book Reviews*, and crossword puzzles.

Her thoughts drifted to Tidy and the photograph of Mr. Browning. Odd that Tidy called him that: Mr. Browning.

Chapter 2

Tidy

Tidy's eyes popped open with the sun. The set of blinds on the windows had long ago fallen in disarray, one hanging by a single screw and the slats of the other gaping where some large object had bent them. After a year of their progressive disassembly, she'd told Ivan to rip them off completely. Now the light from the easterly view streamed into her bedroom, early and unobstructed.

In truth she had been awake for over an hour, lying still with her eyes closed, hoping to bring on more sleep. Instead her thoughts had roamed among the events of the day before. It had been like one of those TV shows, the way the cops had taken Ivan out of the house, his hands cuffed behind him. Now she was alone again. But that's right; she wasn't alone. Bernie was asleep nearby.

With the early light infiltrating the room, she grew restless and threw the covers aside, exposing a small cache of items hidden in the bed: tissues, new and used; her black wallet; an envelope of old photographs; a mail advertisement for life insurance; a gray knitted skullcap; her dentures. She swung her bony legs over the side of the mattress, reached behind her for the skullcap, and placed it on her head, working it to the left and right to get it on straight. Her feet found the pink fluffy slippers close by on the floor, and she pushed herself gently into an upright position.

She started for the kitchen to make her morning coffee but turned back to find her robe. It was supposed to be on the bed but wasn't. She muttered, "I know I put it here. Got to be."

The commotion, and Tidy's grousing, wakened Bernie, who had been asleep on the couch in the living room. "What is it, Tidy?" Bernie asked, yawning, propping her head on a bended arm.

"Can't find my robe," she grumped.

"The day's early, dearie. Don't you want to sleep some more?"

"No, I want my coffee, but I need my robe first."

Bernie yielded to Tidy's bustle and rose to help her. "Might as well move on with the day," she muttered, yanking on her own robe and slippers.

"Supposed to be on my bed," Tidy whined.

Joining the hunt, Bernie began at the bed, neatening the covers, pulling them up over the vacated space—and uncovering the robe. "Here we go, dearie."

"Thank you, Bernie. You're so good to me. I appreciate you helping me."

"I'm glad to help. Did I see your dentures under the blankets? You want them now?"

"My, yes, that's a right good idea. Put them on before I lose them again." Tidy laughed. "I got a way of losing things, don't I?"

Bernie winked at her and chuckled. "We have a good game of hide-and-seek at times, we do." She turned toward the kitchen. "Shall I make the coffee for you, Tidy?"

"Thank you, Bernie. I need my coffee in the morning."

Tidy continued to putter around in her bedroom, rearranging the vials of pills on the bedside table, searching for articles of clothing in the closet, forgetting what she was looking for. She took out her dentures and deposited them on the bureau top. Why she did this, who could say, least of all Tidy.

She came across a lavender nightgown lumped on the dresser, picked it up, and, shaking it out in front of her, compared it to the one she was wearing. She had on her favorite—the pink one with the violets all over. *Wish they was iris*, she thought. *Love them flowers the most.*

She discarded the purple gown onto a mound of clothing heaped in the chair nearby. Back to the dresser top, she reordered the brushes and papers, old bottles of makeup, and a few pieces of junk jewelry she hadn't worn in years. She tried on a brooch of green glass. These occasional finds pleased her and made the searching purposeful to her.

A pair of plaid pants was another discovery, and she pulled them on under her nightgown. The skullcap and her pink flannel nightie with violets over the purple-yellow-and-blue pants, the green brooch, and the fluffy pink slippers might have appeared absurd to some, but to Tidy the outfit was appealing.

The smell of hot coffee drew her to the kitchen.

Bernie poured the coffee, pulled a cinnamon bagel from the toaster, and, knowing Tidy's tastes, slathered it with butter. "Here, dearie, why don't we put your breakfast on a tray, and I'll take it out to your place in the living room where you'll be comfy."

"Nice of you, Bernie. Thank you."

"I'll get the newspaper so you can be reading. I need to get dressed and get over to the church to help with the brown-bag food distribution. I promised I'd come and lend a hand. You'll be all right while I'm gone, dearie?"

"Bernie, you are too good to me. I thank you for your help. I'll be just fine."

Bernie retrieved the newspaper from the porch, opened it on the coffee table, and disappeared into the bathroom.

Tidy pulled the paper closer and searched for the date just under the big type. She smiled when she found it. "Wednesday, November 13," she whispered.

From the mound of papers on the table, she withdrew the coffee-stained calendar and located Wednesday, November 13, continuing to smile at her cunning. The day was before her.

Unfortunately, on the calendar, November 13 was a big, blank square. In fact, most of the squares were blank. Well, not November 1, on which was written "bank." Of course the first said "bank." She went with Ivan to deposit his check on the first of every month. Sunday, November 3, said "church," although she couldn't remember whether she had actually gone.

On the seventh she had noted "Estate man called," and on the twelfth, "Estate man, 9 a.m." She squinted her eyes in thought. He was the one with the horrible tie; yes, the one Ivan had punched. The images of this incident, none of them good, tumbled through her head. She banished them by putting her eye on November 15. "Clare" was written in the square. She puzzled over the notation for a moment, but its meaning didn't come to mind, and she put the calendar back on the paper pile.

Bernie returned and gathered her belongings, stuffing them in the canvas bag. Something about the wad of nightclothes in

Bernie's hand reminded Tidy of the night before. She squinted in the effort to remember.

"Anything on your calendar for today, dearie?"

"Nothing today," Tidy said, quickly distracted. "Unless I forgot to write it down. I often forget to mark the calendar. I tell folks, but I don't think they know I'm not good at remembering."

Bernie said she thought most people understood Tidy's problem, but Tidy knew the locals had her down as the crazy old lady. They called her names: batty was one description, wacky another moniker. But she often administered revenge with her sharp tongue. She chewed out the guy who waited on her at the corner store, lashing into him for some supposed slight or oversight. She loved telling the bums down the street her appraisal of them ("not worth two dead flies") or giving Mr. Lloyd her opinion of his dog ("damn yappy mutt") or telling Nate what she thought of his manners ("rude son of a bitch").

Bernie had had her share of Tidy's tongue too, and in this moment Tidy sensed another dose coming on. As Bernie finished her cup of tea and began to clear away the dishes, Tidy harked back to the bundle of clothes, Bernie's bag, and Bernie leaving.

"What makes you think you can just waltz in here and help yourself to my coffee?" was Tidy's opening salvo. She wasn't quite sure she was onto her concerns of the night before, but it felt good to bawl out Bernie for something.

"Tidy, dearie, I drink tea, only tea."

"Look at them crumbs. You ate my muffin this morning, didn't you? Finished off the cake last night too, ate the whole thing." Tidy's voice grew louder as her irritation took hold. "I was saving the cake for today. You help yourself to anything you want. You're no better than those bums down the street, begging for something to eat."

"I'm not going to argue with you, my dear. You're in one of your moods now, and I'm on my way. I know you don't mean what you're saying."

"I mean every word. You just take, take, take. I'm sick 'n' tired of people taking from me all the time."

And then it came to her: "I seen you tipping the bottle, keeping it secret in your clothes. Sipping away all night, you were. You say it's water, but I know better. You're just like Ivan, drinking, hiding the booze. And now I'm doing what I do to Ivan—throwing you out. Get out of my house."

"I am, Tidy. Don't worry; I am." She grabbed the bag of her belongings and moved rapidly for the door. "Cheerio, love."

Tidy made no effort to respond—other than to herself. "Bitch," she hissed.

———

So now the house belonged to Tidy again. She'd settle into her routine for the day. *Got things to do,* she thought. The calendar loomed on top of the table before her. Blank. Surely Ivan would … She looked up from her station on the couch, alarmed. *Where is Ivan?* She opened her mouth to holler at him and remembered. In jail again. *Merde!*

She turned on the TV. The picture was snowy, as usual. Squinting at the screen, she tried to determine the program. The sound was up—loud, but not too loud. Tidy was not especially hard of hearing, but the sound of the TV kept her company, and it had to be loud enough for her to hear in the kitchen and bathroom. She needed the voices and music to fill the empty spaces of the house. She didn't, as a matter of fact, watch TV much, because she didn't really understand what the shows were all about. People clapping, people crying, reporters jabbing microphones at people clapping or crying. Bombs going off, fires and smoke, more sobbing people. Contests of some sort with questions that didn't make sense to her, questions being the answers to the ... "Dumber than dirt!" she'd yell at the TV.

She was annoyed, however, that the picture—even if she didn't watch it—was all snowy. The cable TV man had come at least three times she recalled, and the snow still fell. This was not just annoying; it made her mad.

Rummaging among the piles of pulp on the coffee table, she eventually uncovered a piece of paper with the cable TV logo. A phone number appeared at the top. She jerked the phone receiver to her ear and dialed.

"... America's number one cable TV provider. How may I help you?"

"You ain't number one with anything, and you can help me by fixing my TV picher."

The two went through the usual exchange of questions from customer service and acerbic answers from Tidy, until a final determination: the repairmen would not come any more because she hadn't paid the bill.

"I pay all my bills on time, always have," she yelled at the customer service voice. "How do you know if I pay my bill or not?"

"I have your record on my computer screen right now, Mrs. Bourbon."

"Computer! Your computer don't know nothing about my TV, and you are dead wrong about my bill. I got my checkbook here to prove I pay my bills."

Her voice reached a screech that could pierce one's eardrum, but Tidy didn't care. In all likelihood the cable-TV customer service woman had unhooked her earpiece to hold it slightly off her ear.

"Mrs. Bourbon—"

"You listen to me, young woman, I'm sick and tired of people telling me what I'm doing and not doing. I'll call your pres-ee-dent and tell him what you're saying to his customers." She slammed the receiver down so hard the body of the phone, perched at the edge of the tiny table at the end of the couch, fell to the floor. She ignored the crash and rose, muttering, "I'll call your boss. You don't know nothing about how to treat customers. I'll teach you a thing or two. Customer's always right."

Crossing the living room, she heard a beeping sound, like some kind of alarm or the emergency noise the radio broadcast every week. She went to the front door, where the beeping disappeared, but opened the door anyway. No one stood on the porch. Back in the living room the beeping resumed. She began to worry, not knowing what the sound could mean. In the kitchen she checked the microwave and the clock alarm on the stove. That sometimes went off, for reasons she didn't understand either. But none of these obvious and usual places was producing the noise.

"Got to be in here somewhere." Tidy shuffled back to the couch; the beeping had stopped. As she sat, she kicked the phone receiver, which was half-hidden under the skirt of the couch's fabric cover. "Who the hell did that?"

She slid to her knees. Looking like a skulking dog, she laughed out loud. She retrieved the phone and banged it back in place on the table. "Nuisance," she grumbled as she pulled herself up on the couch and sat. She was tired already, and the day had barely begun.

She looked again at the blank square of Wednesday, November 13. A long nothing day stretching out in front of her. *No, no, let's use the brains. The greens in the kitchen, they need cooking. Start them cooking right now.* She had a lot to think about without Ivan.

In the kitchen Tidy found a pan, splashed in an inch or so of water, set it on the stove, and flipped the burner knob to HI. Where were the greens? She scoured the counter and the table and checked the refrigerator. The greens were missing.

"Bitch, she took them. She took them with her. Take, take, take. Bitch," she crabbed. "Need those greens for my lunch. What do I do now?"

She put away the butter Bernie had left on the counter and slammed the canister of coffee into the corner.

"I just drink tea, dearie," she mimicked aloud. "Who does she think she is?"

Tidy plodded to the living room, paused, and then continued to her bedroom, where she made an effort to straighten the bed again, not approving of Bernie's attempt. She pulled the sheet and blanket back over her cache of special items and plumped the pillows. She wandered around the room, realigning the pill bottles on the nightstand, moving her black purse to the closet, bringing out the red one, finding her wallet under the bedclothes and depositing it in the purse. She had in mind going to the grocery to replace those greens. *Time for a shower first,* she decided and made her way toward the bathroom.

Although some of her senses might be dimmed, Tidy's sense of smell was still quite keen. Something was burning. In the kitchen she followed the odor to the stove and found a pan, empty of anything, over a high flame. She turned off the burner and stood rigid, shuddering. *What have I done?*

She reeled around, tramped to the middle of her small, cluttered dwelling, and shouted, "Goddamn you, Ivan, where the hell are you?" Her shoulders slumped, and she lowered her head, staring at the purple carpet. Her voice hoarse, she whispered, "I need you."

Ivan

The afternoon of Ivan's scuffle with the real estate man, the sheriff's department brought him to the county lockup in the basement of the Martinsville courthouse. He was close to sober when they booked him and escorted him to a holding cell. One of the guards recognized him. "Not again, Russkie. You might as well make this your permanent home."

Ivan sustained his silence. Originally from Odessa in the Ukraine and therefore technically not Russian, he'd long ago given up trying to get geographically ignorant Americans to understand the difference. He sounded Russian, so what else would anyone, including prison guards, think he was?

He sat hunched on the hard mattress in his cell, his drunken stupor evolving into deep depression. The individual moments of the encounter in Tidy's living room that morning remained a bit of a blur, but Ivan was pretty sure he had stepped over some line this time. Although his alcoholic binges recurred frequently enough these days, it was rare for him to be so drunk he couldn't recall the incident that landed him in the tank. He massaged his right hand and rolled his weighty head slowly, in an effort to stop the foghorn booming through his brain.

The path leading to his county lockup visits had begun ten

years previously with a beating at the hands of some thugs. Nobody said it was the Odessa mafia; nobody said it wasn't. The injuries he'd sustained had resulted in disabilities, which had meant unemployment, and the idleness of unemployment had led him to the local bar. Before long the cops had hauled him in for drunk and disorderly and then public nuisance, trespassing, and oh so many other misdemeanors.

But now he perceived a difference. The ache in his hand, for instance. A shock when he ... what? *Oh God, oh God. I hit the man. I hit him ... bang—with the rings. Blood.* Ivan looked at his hand, and the fact that the rings no longer encircled the middle fingers of his right hand penetrated the alcoholic cloud.

When he'd left the Ukraine—at least twenty years ago now—his uncles had given him the two heavy rings, set with several carats of rough-cut, antique Alexandrite. The uncles had sold family heirlooms to buy the rings, urging him to take the rings out of the country and sell the stones later, to help start his new life.

Ivan had never sold the rings. He called them his insurance, hanging on to them, just in case. The green-encrusted bands were all he had left of his homeland, and now they were gone. He closed his eyes against a memory of pain. The cops had used wire cutters to cut the rings from his swollen fingers and had dropped them in a plastic bag. "Evidence," one cop had said. *Evidence of what?* Ivan now wondered with a heavy headache.

The little misdemeanors of his previous arrests had resulted in fines, community service, court-ordered AA meetings, and, more recently, a few weeks in the prison down the road. But "evidence" had never been involved before. His meaty hands worried the tops of his knees while his thoughts worried the significance of evidence.

———

"Mr. Demidovsky, it's time for you to go upstairs and find out what's what." Two deputies from the county sheriff's department unlocked the cell, cuffed Ivan's wrists and ankles, and walked him to an elevator. The three remained silent on the ride to the third floor.

Ivan felt grubby, now some days without a bath. They had given him soap and a towel to use at the cell's washbasin and clean prisoner's garb for the court appearance: a ruby-red T-shirt and thin yellow cotton pants, both surprisingly large on Ivan's stocky frame. Still, he could detect his rank body odor. The slipper socks on his feet were too warm, but he knew better than to try to fiddle with them. His sense of dread deepened the higher the elevator rose.

On the third floor, the doors slid back to reveal an empty corridor leading to a chamber for the in-custody defendants. "Have a seat," one of the deputies said, waving him into the narrow room. Three of the four ceiling light fixtures were out, making the space gloomy, matching Ivan's mood. The bench along the wall was hard oak, but at least there was the wall to lean against. "We'll call you when it's your turn, but I guess you know that."

Ivan had seen Deputy Michaels here before and remembered him as polite and unusually retiring for a deputy. Michaels unshackled Ivan's wrists and looked on him almost as if he cared. "One of these days, Ivan old man, you're going to end up either dead or sober. You should figure out which one and get on with it." Ivan wasn't listening. He squinted through the wired glass wall between the custody chamber and the courtroom, hoping to recognize someone familiar.

Tidy had come once and posted his bail. Just once. She'd said afterward she was sorry she'd done it and would never do it again. Her tirade later about putting up her own money for his release, only to watch him end up back in jail, hovered in his memory. Even as he heard her harangue in his head, he still hoped she might appear today and spare him the discomforts of imprisonment.

But there was no sign of her. And how could there be? She wouldn't know about the hearing, he acknowledged, and without him to drive her there, she had no way to get to Martinsville.

The court came to order at 9:15 a.m., and the proceedings began. The clerk called two cases before his—a continuance and a reassignment—and then rattled off another long string of numbers. Deputy Michaels pointed at Ivan. He rose and scuffed his way to the open window in the glass wall through which he could communicate with the court. His stare pierced a crack in the oak wood floor in front of the bailiff. Thus he hoped to avoid the quagmire of uncertainty ahead.

"Mr. Demidovsky, do you understand me?"

Ivan started; his eyes flashed to the judge's bench and immediately came back to the courtroom floor. The judge … a woman! But she hadn't said anything. Ivan wasn't sure what he was supposed to understand.

"Mr. Demidovsky, do you understand English?"

Oh, that. "*Da*, yez."

"You don't need an interpreter?"

"No." He hadn't been asked these things in previous appearances, but when he dared take a longer glimpse of the judge, he understood. Judging by her face, together with her voice, she must be a new judge, younger than most. Ivan hadn't stood before her yet; thus she didn't know the deadbeat repeat offender cowering in the window. Ivan didn't know if this would be good or bad.

"Mr. Demidovsky, you are being held for assault and battery regarding the incident involving Mr. Reed Johnson, on November 12, at 642 Main Street, Oakmont." Judge Chang looked up from her file and over at Ivan, as if appraising him for this crime.

"Mr. Demidovsky, can you afford an attorney?"

Ivan was confused. Why didn't she ask if he *had* an attorney? That was what she was supposed to ask.

The judge kept her eyes on his face, passive, waiting.

It didn't matter. The answer was always the same. "*Nyet*, I sorry, no."

"I refer you to the public defender. Bail is set at sixty thousand dollars. This case is continued to Monday, November 18, Department Four. Thank you." Ivan was done.

He stepped back and reclaimed his spot on the wretched bench. He counted two more no-goods who hadn't had a turn yet. At least he wouldn't have to wait much longer. Soon he was shuffling back to his cell, his ankle shackles clinking dully around the hot socks.

———————

In the evening, after the meal that passed for supper, Ivan requested permission to use the jail phones. In the phone booth he leaned against the wall in a crestfallen posture and asked the operator to place a call to the only phone number he remembered.

"Hello."

"We have a collect call from Ivan Demi-something. Will you accept the charges?"

"Oh Lord, I suppose so. Ivan? You there? What's happening?"

"Tidy, I sorry. I stupid this time. I so sorry."

"You dumb Russkie," she said, but quietly, not angrily. "What are they going to do with you?"

"I dunno. I afraid they deport me, back to Ukraine, iz so bad."

"What's your lawyer say? I thought you're supposed to go to detox classes or something."

"No lawyer yet. I stand before judge. Judge said I get lawyer, but no one comes. I sit in cell all day. I'm afraid, Tidy. Hitting real estate man very bad."

"You know that. Bad as okra dipped in shit and rolled in corn flour."

Ivan never understood Tidy's southernisms—even after all these years. In this case, however, the "dipped in shit" was enough for him to know he *had* crossed the line.

Chapter 3

Claire

Tiny, precise writing filled the boxes of Claire's calendar: appointments to keep track of, phone calls to make. Wednesday, November 13, was chock-full, but she needed to find a spot for Tidy. Midmorning, as the trail of clients led her north to south, Claire called Tidy on the phone to confirm an appointment.

"You come any time," Tidy said in her cheerful I-love-visitors voice. "Come on in when you get here. The door's open."

Claire hoped she didn't mean that literally. Oakmont was a small town, but as part of a large metropolis, it sustained all the urban crime one might expect. And in this, the twenty-first century, *no one* left their front door "open." Even with Ivan or Bernie for company, Tidy leaving her front door unlocked seemed imprudent.

On the peppermint porch that afternoon, she rang the doorbell. The outer door *was* unlocked, and on opening it, she found the inner door ajar. Tidy's hollering to "come on in" was audible, but even so, Claire called out as the door swung open with her rapping. "Don't go making all that racket. I told you to come in," Tidy yelled.

"I'm sorry, Tidy. I didn't want to walk in unannounced and startle you."

Claire was encouraged to find Tidy up and dressed, if a little on the bizarre side. A lilac-colored blouse topped purple-yellow-and-blue plaid pants. *When is the last time I met someone in plaid pants?* Claire reflected. If she couldn't honestly compliment Tidy's outfit, she at least easily found another conversational launch. "Purple must be your favorite color," she said, with a glance at the carpet.

"Yes. Come spring purple iris are all over my garden too. Mighty pretty then."

"I have no doubt it's lovely."

Tidy hesitated in the middle of the room and turned to stare at Claire still standing by the hall entrance. "Who'd you say you were?" The grandmother clock on the far wall ticked five times before Claire responded.

"I'm from the county Senior Outreach Services. We met yesterday. Do you recall?"

Tidy remained rooted, stuck. Was she trying to remember? Claire waited in silence, not wanting to interrupt the process.

In time Tidy focused again on Claire's face and grinned. "Let me get my teeth. I think I look better with my teeth."

Several responses came to Claire, but she decided instead on a smile as Tidy toddled off to her bedroom.

Claire's visit the previous day had been unexpected; she hadn't the time to pay attention to some of the first-visit basics, such as assessing the home interior—to gauge its appropriateness and safety for her elderly client and to learn what she could from its contents. While she waited now, Claire made mental notes.

The rug hadn't been vacuumed in some time. An enormous accumulation of paper blanketed the coffee table. Mounds overflowed onto the floor. Framed photos, old magazines, church bulletins, and address books dotted the surfaces of other furniture pieces—a desk, a breakfront. On a small dining table, a lovely pair of antique silver candlesticks and a small milk glass candy dish (empty) resided without ceremony. The breakfront contained a set of china and numerous knickknack statues of angels, Bambis, and birds; crystal dessert plates lined the top shelf. At the edge of her mind, Claire registered something missing.

"Tidy," she called out, "is Bernie still here?"

"Goodness no," Tidy replied as she returned to the room, indeed looking a little less mouse-like with her dentures in place. "She can't stand me very long. Just comes to eat my food, drink my coffee."

"But she had tea … oh, never mind. Why don't we sit and talk." Claire scowled at the uncomfortable ottoman, wishing for some alternative, but to suggest any change in routine at such an early stage of their relationship might be upsetting. It was one of the things she'd learned early on working with elders: don't mess with their habits.

Tidy took care of matters in any case, sliding into her established place and saying, "You sit on the ottoman so I can see your eyes. I know a person by their eyes."

Now face-to-face with Tidy, Claire blinked with uncertainty and wondered where to begin. New clients were like jigsaw puzzles to Claire, a challenge to put together, particularly as she discovered the nature of the various pieces. With the time to delve more deeply, she acknowledged that many issues presented in Tidy: living alone, being frail and absentminded at the very least, leaving her front door open … And now with her tenant cum in-home care person gone … such a strange arrangement.

"You told me yesterday that Ivan's been living with you for a long time."

"Yes, someone beat him up one night, while he's driving his taxi. A bad blow on the head, then limping and not seeing too well. He couldn't work. He needs a place he can afford on disability, so I rent him the back room. Always been a good tenant: pays his rent on time, keeps things clean, cooks for me. How I miss his cooking."

Claire, now more patient, noted Tidy's repetition was to be expected. "When he's not helping you, what does he do?"

"Round the corner with his cronies in the bar or going to AA meetings up at the church. Court tells him he's supposed to go every day. I think he goes one day to the church, one day to the bar—evens out." She chuckled. "But he's helping around here too. Does the yard, vacuums, cooks for me. I love that noodle dish with sour cream."

"Yes, yes, it sounds like something Russian, and I bet it's delicious." Claire's impatience was creeping back. Hoping to tamp it down, she asked, "What do you do for meals while he's, um, away?"

A small silence ensued; the conversational flow had been interrupted. Tidy turned restless, her hands on her upper arms, her fingers tapping, her eyes searching the back of the house, and her feet shuffling in place. Claire wondered what this behavior meant.

"They tore down the Oakmont Grocery, so I go to the corner store. Nothing much, but they have what I need."

"The store down the street to the left? You mean Nelson's?" Claire pointed in the store's direction.

"I do." Tidy's restless movement stopped, and she appeared close to anger, glaring at Claire.

She is so transparent. Claire frowned. *I only wish I understood her body language.*

"Isn't Nelson's a convenience market? Do they stock the food you need for all your meals?" Claire waited for a response, but the subject had evidently run its course with Tidy, and she didn't reply. "How would you rate your health, Tidy? Any problems?"

"Healthy as a hog."

"Do you take any medications?" Claire's agenda for an initial visit also covered an assessment of the client's well-being, including a survey of medications.

"Them pills?"

"Yes, is there a list some place, or may I look at the prescription bottles?"

"You'll find a list on the wall in my bedroom and the pills beside the bed. Help yourself." Tidy picked up the newspaper and made a show of reading it.

The chaos of Tidy's bedroom overwhelmed Claire. The bedclothes were rumpled, and the dresser top was covered in underwear, brushes, cosmetics Tidy clearly didn't use, purses, keys—huge rings of more keys than Tidy could possibly have locks for—photographs, more papers, and envelopes. A wastebasket by the bed overflowed with used tissues. Four tubes of Bengay were parked in various places in the room.

Claire located the list of prescriptions on the wall by the closet. Many medications had been added or crossed out, so Claire had to question its accuracy. Still, she removed the paper for closer examination. *Curious there's a list at all,* she thought, *and someone attempts to keep it up to date.* Claire couldn't imagine Tidy making this effort.

Looking for the prescription bottles at the bedside table, she almost gagged. Disgusting—and that was saying something for Claire, who in her recent work had become nearly immune to the filth of some clients' homes. At least a dozen vials (many empty), along with several other bottles of vitamins and over-the-counter pills, lotions, and salves, stood on the table like a ragtag army. A few quarter-size puddles of cough syrup dotted the surface. Individual pills, taken out of the bottles but never consumed, stippled the tabletop, some disintegrating in the cough syrup. Tucked in among the pill bottles, two plastic dosage cups from cough syrups crouched, one with a mixture of pills, the other stuffed with a cotton ball. A dirty glass of water sat precariously near the table's edge. The cloth shade of the bedside lamp was yellow with age and blackened in a spot where the bulb must have rested too long. Instinctively, Claire wanted to sweep the table clean into a trash bag, scrub the sticky stains, and start over. But no, she simply picked up those pill bottles rattling with some contents and returned to the living room.

"Tidy, when do you usually take your medicines?" she asked as she dumped her pharmaceutical bounty on the desktop.

"Some in the morning, some at night. Ivan puts them in this pillbox for me. Here, beside me." On the end table by the couch was, indeed, a large plastic container with a separate section for each day and for each day a separate place for morning, noon, and bedtime—a week's worth of pills. Claire shook the container; pills rattled inside some of the compartments.

"Do you remember which pills you are supposed to take in the morning?"

"No. Ivan knows, puts the right pills in the right box for me."

Claire went over the list from the wall with care and paired the names of medications not crossed out to the bottles from the bedside table to the pills in the pillbox. Remarkably the bottles, the list, and the pills in the pillboxes all matched. Ivan had done a good job.

Claire's final analysis identified six medications: one for cholesterol, another for an overactive thyroid, a beige monster (*How on earth does she swallow it?* she asked herself) for osteoarthritis, a muscle relaxant for bedtime, one she didn't recognize and would have to look up later, and a small, round pale-yellow one. Claire paused to decide what she wanted to say about this pill.

"You take Aricept ..."

"Very important," Tidy said earnestly. "It's for my Al's Imers. Those pills help me remember things. I don't ever forget that one."

Claire suppressed a laugh at the unintentional pun; Tidy was serious, and the reason for taking the drug wasn't in the least funny. "Your doctor said you have this condition?"

"Yes, about a year ago. Did a whole mess of tests and then told me I have the sickness. Don't feel sick; I'm not sure the doctor knows what he's saying."

With her mind churning on the implications of this latest discovery, Claire sat staring at Tidy. As if on purpose, in order to compound Claire's concerns, Tidy went off on Ivan not being around to help—once again. "So many things to remember," she complained. "Like locking doors at night. The sun's still shining when I go to bed, and I'm not thinking about locking the doors. Ivan goes round every night, on his way to bed, making sure we're safe and secure."

"Perhaps if you kept the door locked all the time, you wouldn't have to worry." She wondered if Tidy caught the sarcasm.

"I can't be doing that." Tidy shook her head. "Every time someone comes to visit, I'm having to go open the door. Too much trouble."

As Claire rose to return everything to the bedroom, she spied another telltale brown plastic vial lying on its side behind the lamp on the end table. "Looks like I missed one. What's this?" She brought the vial closer to read the small print.

"My pain pills," Tidy said. "I get bad pains in my neck and back, especially at night. Arth-a-ritus, the doc says. He gives me those for the pain."

"Vicodin." Claire shook the bottle—full. One hundred tablets, the label indicated, 5 mg hydrocodone / 500 mg acetaminophen, "as needed for pain." They had been dispensed a week before—one hundred of them. "Do you take the Vicodin often, Tidy?"

Tidy's face went blank.

"Do you have the pain often?" Claire asked. One hundred pills for "as needed" felt to Claire like the medication was overprescribed, and this wasn't a medication an elder should just have lying around.

"I don't remember. I think I must. I'm going to the pharmacy plenty of times to get more."

Claire watched her client for a moment, silently. The more she learned about Tidy, the more she believed Tidy belonged in an assisted-living facility. Such a facility would solve all Tidy's problems: meals provided, medications dispensed correctly, social contact and entertainment available, full-time staff to oversee her welfare. And her apartment would be cleaned regularly! After quickly filling the empty spots in the pillbox,

Claire took the pill bottles to the bedroom and returned the list to the wall.

Back in the living room, Tidy shuffled her way to the kitchen, mumbling to herself. She started at Claire appearing from the bedroom but recovered in an instant. "I'm making me a cup of coffee. Could I put on some water for you too? I don't know where my manners been. I should have offered you coffee when you arrived," she said.

"Thank you, Tidy, but I need to be on my way. Could I visit again in a day or two? Perhaps we could have coffee together then."

"That would be just fine. I like having visitors. You come along any time. Door's always open."

Tidy

Tidy sat in the silence following Claire's departure. *Pleasant to have visitors; wish they'd stay longer.* She went back and forth whether she wanted to like Claire or not. Claire unsettled her, coming so soon after the business that had delivered Ivan to jail. Tidy puzzled over the possibility that Claire had been sent to investigate her.

Another social worker had come way back when Ivan had been arrested. This social worker had made sure that Ivan's disability check was assigned to Tidy, so he couldn't cash it and use all the money on booze. This ensured she'd receive her rent—a good thing.

The new woman, Claire, didn't seem to be doing good things, in Tidy's judgment. Mostly she asked all those questions about Ivan living with her. Plain nosy, almost accusing Tidy of something. The questions about how she got her groceries, for instance, rankled Tidy. What business was it of Claire's where she went shopping? Tidy considered the question for a moment.

Without Ivan, getting her supplies over at Oscar's in Ridley took more effort. Usually Ivan drove her to Oscar's, and they enjoyed an hour meandering up and down the aisles, talking about the meals he would prepare with the food they picked from the shelves. Without Ivan, shopping for groceries was no fun. She'd go for the junk from Nelson's, or she'd have to ... *My, we can't be thinking about driving ... No, we can't be thinking about that at all.*

Tidy looked toward the doorway. And the front door. Why had that Claire made such a fuss over her leaving it open? She hated having to get up from the couch every time the doorbell rang. Much easier to holler out for the visitor to come on in.

The top of all nosiness? Getting into her medications. *Meddlesome!*

Tidy's irritation rose with all these thoughts, and she grew restless. She wandered to her front window for a peek out onto the street, to check for happenings of interest. To the left, at the street corner, Blackie, her pal, slouched against a fire hydrant. *Well, well, let's go on down and have a little chat with Blackie. Take my mind off my troubles. Always got troubles. Ivan in jail for one.*

She devoted several minutes to locating her black slip-on shoes and denim jacket. If it was November, and she believed it was, the temperature outdoors would be cool. The jacket eluded her for a while, until she thought to check in the hallway. The denim, hooked on the wall, partially covered a long, slick navy coat.

Outside on the stoop she paused upon seeing the activity at the corner. Rap had joined Blackie. Talk about nosy people; Rap was the worst. He often stopped by when Ivan was away to ask if she needed any help, except he didn't help—unlike Blackie, who brought her bags up from Nelson's and took out the trash on collection days. Even though she didn't invite him in, Rap would come along with Blackie, to collect the trash for the cans, he said. But Blackie did the collecting; Rap just prowled around poking into her things. *Nothing but a pest.*

A car pulled alongside the men at the corner. An old Cadillac, red, with fins and lots of chrome. Two men sat in the front seat; the passenger cranked down the window and spoke to Rap. Blackie stood a few paces back and watched, as did Tidy. The passenger handed over a wad of cash—a thick wad. From his hind pocket, Rap plucked a plastic bag, held it up momentarily for the passenger to see, and then passed it into the car. The window closed, and the Caddy pulled away. Tidy turned toward her door, showing her back to the men in the car. She knew a drug deal when she saw one, and she certainly didn't want them to know she had seen their goings-on. All the sport of having a chat with Blackie evaporated. She went back indoors.

What a rathole she lived in. She should move, but where to? Everything she understood (even if that was drug deals) and cared about (like her home) existed right there on Main Street. Mr. Browning had said it: their life was on Main Street.

Chapter 4

Claire

Friday morning Claire glanced at her list of appointments, laid out for her driving convenience. Tidy was number two, after Mrs. Schultz, who was in the hospital.

Claire had called on Thursday to determine if Tidy would mind a morning visit. "Land sakes, no," Tidy had said. "You come along as early as you want. I'm up with the sun." Being November, the sun wasn't rising all that promptly in Claire's opinion, but she delighted in a client who had *early* in her vocabulary—without a *not* in front of it. Her other clients complained how everything in their lives took twice as long as it used to. If they finished breakfast by eleven, they were lucky … and then bathing, such a slow process with the arthritis, etc., etc. Claire had learned patience, although in practice she often found it difficult to restrain herself.

"I'll see you at ten," Claire had said.

"I'll be here," Tidy had chirped.

Friday turned out to be sunny and unseasonably mild. Claire drove her sensible Honda Civic north on the shoreline road, a pleasant ride with Saint-Saëns's Piano Concerto No. 2, Ashkenazy at the piano, for accompaniment in her CD player. She hummed along.

At ten, Claire found Tidy not only up and dressed—in navy bell-bottom pants and a fuchsia blouse—but with a suggestion she was about to depart, as she'd donned a black faux leather jacket. "Are you going out?" Claire tried to hide her surprise.

"I thought I'd go get some groceries. Without Ivan, I got to do something about food, and I'm not doing that Meals on Wheels business. I bet you were going to tell me I should do Meals on Wheels. Everyone thinks us old folks should be eating Meals on Wheels. Stuff tastes like cardboard, and I'm not fond of cardboard."

Claire grinned at Tidy's assumption. Meals on Wheels had been her thought when Tidy mentioned groceries. Most of her clients enjoyed the service and preferred the simplicity of the food to the trouble of cooking, even if they could cook. But there were a few like Tidy, who complained to conceal this loss of independence.

"You're taking a walk down to the corner store?"

"That dump. They don't have food worth eating. I need my greens and sweet taters, catfish, and maybe some ready-made ribs. Pretty good at Oscar's."

Oscar's? In Ridley? How does she get to Oscar's? And how on earth does she eat ribs with her dentures? But Claire didn't voice any of this and simply asked, "Since I'm here, could we talk for a minute or two?"

"Goodness me, of course. I'll sit in my place, and you sit on the ottoman so I can see your eyes. I know a person by their eyes."

They resumed their positions, Claire again yearning for a

more comfortable perch. Low and without a back, the ottoman forced her to sit straight, a tiring thing to do for any length of time. Her eyes roamed the room looking for an alternative. The desk chair, too far away, wouldn't allow for good eye contact. Trading the two seats was a possibility, but Tidy seemed set in her ways, and moving furniture around might upset her. Claire gave up the idea and straightened her spine—again. Her client's gustatory ventures were more pressing.

"So you were going out to do a little shopping at Oscar's?"

"Only place in these parts you can get grits, and the deli serves up ready-to-go fried chicken with biscuits and gravy. I used to make the best biscuits. Oscar's are good, but mine were the best. Made them for my restaurant back when. People came from all over for my biscuits."

"You had a restaurant?"

"After the war. Married to Billy then. He earned good money in the shipyards, and we got ourselves into business. A restaurant, a bar, and in a while a grocery store too. I managed the restaurant and the store."

"You did the cooking for the restaurant?"

"No, Bertha. She was my cook, but I liked to do some—the biscuits, corn bread, corn puddin' too."

Claire loved the way Tidy's southern drawl became accentuated when she talked about the past. She didn't love the idea that Tidy went to Ridley for her groceries. "Tidy, may I ask how you get to Oscar's? Ridley's quite a distance from here."

"No business of yours." Her gaze slipped to her lap.

"I know, Tidy; I'm just wondering if we might help with your transportation so you don't have to drive." It was a wild guess or a cheap shot, Claire realized, but she had seen a large white Pontiac sticking out from behind the house.

"I been driving all my life, since I was sixteen. Never an accident. No tickets, not even a parking ticket."

Curious response, Claire thought. *A quarrelsome issue with some history?*

"I'm sure you're a good driver," Claire said, although she could imagine how this elderly woman drove: ten miles an hour, taking forever to turn a corner, idling at a changed traffic light until the pileup behind her was blasting horns, trying to get her to move on. "But I worry about what might happen if you are in an accident."

"Haven't you been listening? I don't have accidents. I'm a good driver."

Claire was familiar with the argument. It had been the last straw with her parents fifteen years ago; after that final loss of independence she'd had to move them to a facility. That event was one of the reasons she'd turned to the Senior Outreach program to occupy her time. Payback, for all the mistakes she'd made in that year while learning about but not wanting to know about losing things to old age. She had thought dying of cancer (as her husband had) was horrific, but dying of old age was trying, tedious, and torpid, as you were gradually stripped of dignity, self-determination, health, sense and senses, strength, and stability. And the most profound privation was losing one's independence. Her father had sworn at her when she'd snatched the car keys from him for the last time. Never in all his fatherly days had he ever used a swear word in her presence.

"*You* may be a good driver, Tidy, but not everyone else is. What will happen if someone hits you?"

"You mean when all those crazy drivers are out there, smashing into others? I hear it on the radio. Seems like there's an accident every two minutes. But I don't go driving same time as the crazies. I wait until they're all at work. *Then* I head out."

Of course. Claire sighed. *Who said this woman is demented?* "Accidents happen everywhere, though, Tidy. In a parking lot, for instance, someone might back into you. Then what happens?" The scenario played in her mind: Tidy squaring off with the other driver; the other driver asking for her driver's license and insurance papers. At ninety-two, Tidy couldn't possibly have a valid driver's license, could she?

"I've got the insurance—that's what's required. Insurance pays for the damages."

Taking a bit of a risk, Claire asked, "What if someone finds out you don't have a driver's license and they call the police?"

"I'd pay them off," Tidy said, with an air of bravado.

"Pay off who, the cops or the other driver?"

"Both. Done it before," Tidy said, beaming at her cleverness.

Although amused *and* horrified, Claire sensed a dead end. She would have to come back to the driving issue; it couldn't be ignored. For now, she veered to another idea. "Let's look at this from a different angle. You're making payments on the car, am I right?" Tidy refused to respond. "The car payments and your insurance premiums must be quite a chunk of money each month. I would estimate that the same amount of money would be enough for you to use taxis to take you anywhere you wanted to go." As she spoke the words, Claire acknowledged to herself that Tidy wouldn't understand the premise. Even so, she was not prepared for the vehemence of Tidy's response.

"Here's what I'm telling you about what you're saying. You take a taxi, you have to wait, sometimes in the rain. I had to wait a half hour for that cab to come, take me to the hospital. A half hour I was in pain, waiting. When I'm ready to come home, I wait some more. Outside the hospital, I got no place to sit down, waiting for that damn cab to show up. I go back inside and tell them to call again. 'He's coming,' they say. I could hardly stand I was so tired and sick and in pain. Finally he comes, takes me home, and demands his tip. He don't deserve no tip. He don't deserve nothing, making me wait and wait.

"In my car I come and go as I please. I'm warm and dry as I please, and I'm not waiting and waiting for someone to help me. In my car I help myself. You've got to be blind if you can't see that."

All reason had been punched out of Claire's arguments. Her spine curved in defeat as she watched Tidy sink back into the cushions of the couch. The skirmish disappointed them both. *Checkmate*, Claire thought as they sat, mute.

After a few moments to allow the ruffled air to disperse, Claire asked gently if Tidy had heard from the police about Ivan.

"No one tells me nothing."

"Would you like me to call the sheriff's department and ask?"

"What they got to do with me?"

"Do you remember the police who came after Ivan tangled with the real estate agent?"

Tidy snorted. "Tangled ... Ivan bopped him good. He deserved it, that man, trying to get me to sell my house. What right had he?" She leaned forward for emphasis as her voice became more strident.

Claire shook her head at Tidy's recall of Monday's incident but refrained from comment. "Would you like me to call about Ivan's status? I'd be glad to."

"Yes, please do. I need him back."

Claire pulled out her cell phone and found Jane Rios's number quickly.

"Newfangled phone," Tidy mumbled. "Silly looking; can't hear nothing on them."

Jane answered on the second ring.

"Jane, it's Claire. I'm with Tidy Bourbon, and we were wondering if there's any news of Ivan Demidovsky?"

"Thank you for calling and for checking on our friend. Last I heard Ivan has a court date early next week for what's called a counsel-and-plea hearing. That should tell us if the charges have held up so far, and then the grind of justice will carry on. He's charged with assault and battery; use of a weapon is mentioned, and I believe 'great bodily harm' is also in the indictment. Somehow I don't think paying a fine or doing community service will get him off this time. He'll end up going to trial or taking a plea bargain, would be my guess."

The severe language of the charges stunned Claire. She suppressed an urge to blurt out her alarm in front of Tidy. "That's a, ah, heavy charge," she said as evenly as possible.

"It does seem a little disproportionate to the event. The assistant district attorney may have a strategy in mind to effect a specific outcome."

Claire lowered her voice. "A release isn't likely anytime soon then."

"I'm guessing the DA's office wants to put Ivan away for a while. Can't say I entirely disagree, although I expect your job will be more difficult as a result."

"You know it. I think we're going to be a bit disappointed here." Claire looked sideways at her client. Appearing oblivious, Tidy sat motionless, peering into the space in front of her.

Claire rang off and explained to Tidy, in the plainest terms possible, Jane's disclosure.

"I know that," Tidy said.

"Know what?"

"About being in the court. He's going to be on his best behavior. I told him."

"You've spoken to him?"

"Of course, he always calls me from jail. We talk, and I tell him how to behave so they let him out faster."

"He calls you from jail." Claire repeated to help herself believe.

"'Course he does." Tidy's face eased into a smile. "He's got no one else. Who's going to tell him what to do? He isn't smart enough to know."

"Does he call ... how often do you talk to him?" *She can't be making it up, can she?*

"Phones when he can. Has to call collect, so I have to pay. Isn't that something? Can't even make calls on his own dime."

Claire stared at her client. This case was nuts.

At the end of the day, wrapped in fatigue, Claire returned to her nest in the southern reaches of the county. She poured her half glass of wine, sat down at her computer, and began to type up her notes from the day's visits.

She came to Tidy and leaned back to think. She laughed aloud. *An alcoholic Irishwoman, a drunken Russian, and a senile old lady—a houseful of clichés. No, not clichés, are they? They're human beings, with needs, wants, and all the desires of earthly mortals. And what am I? Pushy social worker? No, no, social*

*workers aren't pushy. Maybe me, but not all. So I'm not a cliché—
or am I and don't recognize it?*

Her musing faded as her focus reverted to Tidy. The case
screamed *assisted living*. Just the management of medications
would be worth it. Claire snatched a pen and Post-it to write a
note to herself to bring a second pillbox next time so Tidy would
have two weeks of pills. Without Ivan around, someone needed
to keep her pillboxes current—an obligation Claire would face,
until she found another solution.

And why not the Royal Manor for that solution? The Royal
Manor in Nortonville would offer the perfect environment
for Tidy, Claire reasoned. She'd be safe, looked after, with
other people around her. Tidy was such a social person; the
companionship by itself would brighten her days.

Claire rose and wandered to the window overlooking the
yard. *Tidy wouldn't be living like me if she were in the assisted-
living facility,* she thought, staring blankly at the winter-bare
garden. *Alone, no one to share thoughts with, to cook for, to
annoy, to watch old movies with, to love.* She turned abruptly,
marched to the music system, and flipped on a Bartok violin
concerto. Her late husband hadn't cared for Bartok.

Claire had never in her life lived alone. She appreciated
the change, she told herself. No one to argue with her, no
compromises to make, no acquiescing to avoid confrontation.
So much easier. Except it wasn't, and Tidy reminded her of why.

Claire and her husband had argued once about where
to go on vacation one year. They'd finally decided on Italy,
even though Morocco had been her more exotic choice. She
had wanted to go in October when it would be cooler, but he'd
said the altitude in Italy gave them an advantage in September,
and anyway he'd had important meetings in October. They'd

rented an apartment above Lake Como, walked the old trails in the hills over Menaggio, ferried across the lake to the earth-toned buildings of Bellagio, and eaten succulent mussels in the trattoria along the shore as sailboats darted in the unpredictable winds. They'd embraced in their September love. He'd been right about the altitude; it hadn't been too hot.

Living, interrupted by dying.

The phone ringing broke into her reverie. Jane. Ivan's plea hearing was set for Monday at 9:00 a.m. Would Claire attend?

"You think I should?" Claire asked.

Jane said she planned to go and added, "You might learn something more about Ivan and whether he's likely to be a factor in your work with Tidy."

Claire took her point. They arranged to meet Monday, just before nine, by the court's parking lot entrance.

Chapter 5

The Courtroom

The courthouse bustled as usual with lawyers, court personnel, family, and "court chasers" milling around in the corridors.

"Department Four," Jane told Claire as they walked through the security area of the foyer. "Judge Letty." Although not tall, Jane had the compact physique of someone who worked out in the gym every day. She unvaryingly dressed in a tailored navy pantsuit with an unremarkable white blouse, her badge easy to find on the lapel of her jacket. Her trappings were plain, but there was no mistaking her presence. She strode to the stairway and the upper level, Claire quickstepping to keep up.

The two found seats in the back corner of the small courtroom, joining friends and family members involved in other cases appearing before the judge that morning.

The brisk walk of Judge Byron Letty, through the door from his chambers and up the steps to his bench, suggested a more youthful vigor than his actual age. A kindly but deeply creased face spoke of too much sun in his youth; his bald pate was liberally spotted brown. He wore half-glasses and thus had a Dickensian semblance, especially as he studied the court participants from the height of his perch.

The clerk called out the first case, reciting a long string of numbers and the names of the relevant parties. Claire turned a glance of disappointment on Jane. Not their case; they might have to wait awhile.

The courtroom was similar to the one of Ivan's first appearance. A separate room—bulletproof, glassed in, and iron grated—held the defendants still in custody. Ivan sat in the far corner, slouching down in his seat as if trying to minimize his presence. The hard bench seemed unfair to Claire. Even if they were criminals, some decency might be afforded them for their long wait.

As the court clerk rattled off the second case number, Ivan's public defender rose and moved to the podium next to the defendant's window through which he had contact with his client. The sheriff's deputy jerked his thumb at Ivan. In an attitude of complete dejection, Ivan pushed himself off the bench and shuffled to the gap in the glass.

Judge Letty examined each of the case participants; satisfied, he nodded to the assistant district attorney (ADA). "Let's hear what you have, Mr. Worthington."

ADA Benjamin Worthington made his argument for a charge of assault and battery against Ivan. For background, he citied a long sheet of drunk and disorderlies, trespassing while under the influence, and threats of assault. But this time Mr. Demidovsky had gone too far, Worthington emphasized; he had made contact with the victim. "There is evidence the defendant used weapons likely to produce great bodily harm." Worthington threw back his broad shoulders to emphasize his confidence in this charge. Benji (a nickname he despised but had learned to accept) looked like a high school wrestler, short and wide. His face, while boyish—soft skin, nary a fuzzy hair visible on his chin—had the intense look of a snake about to strike.

A comical presentation, Claire mused. She took an instant dislike to the ADA, believing he was a presumptuous, juvenile jerk. Despite her recollection of Patrolman Rickerts's banter about "lethal rocks," the idea that Ivan's little scuffle had actually included a weapon seemed absurd.

"Are we trying to make a case for felony assault then?" the judge asked.

"Yes, Your Honor."

"And the weapon—*weapons?*" The judge stared at the file to be positive of the plural. "How many weapons does it take to dent someone's cheekbone? What are we talking about here?"

"Mr. Demidovsky was wearing two heavy rings with large, rough-cut gems set in them. The rings were in effect not unlike brass knuckles. They caused serious damage to Mr. Johnson that would not have otherwise been inflicted by Mr. Demidovsky's right jab."

Judge Letty peered out at the ADA.

Claire tensed. Perhaps she was wrong about the rings being weapons. She knew that when weapons were attached to assault, the charge was much more serious.

Judge Letty had heard enough from the ADA and swung his gaze to Ivan's attorney. "Mr. Randall, is there a defense in this matter?"

Public defender Derek Randall—young and eager, Claire sensed—stood to address the court.

"Your Honor, the rings in question were pieces of jewelry, not weapons. Mr. Demidovsky always wore the rings—for twenty years, in fact. He did not don them specifically to injure Mr. Johnson."

"Your Honor," ADA Worthington interjected, "the case law—"

"Mr. Worthington, hold your horses. Mr. Randall?"

"Secondly, the swing Mr. Demidovsky executed was not premeditated. He was upset with Mr. Johnson and lost control. He was admittedly intoxicated; the bodily contact was accidental—unforeseen, if you will."

"All right. Now, Mr. Worthington?"

"The case law demonstrates that a fist can constitute a weapon, and an adornment to a fist can constitute an enhanced weapon. In addition, Mr. Johnson's statement makes it clear he was not in any way threatening Mr. Demidovsky at the time of the attack."

"Attack," Judge Letty repeated.

The ADA fiddled with papers on the table before him.

The judge looked at Ivan. Ivan shifted on his feet, avoiding eye contact with the judge. He lowered his eyes instead to the court reporter's machine: inanimate and nonjudgmental.

Finally, Judge Letty spoke. "There appears to be a legal argument here. We will proceed. Mr. Demidovsky, you are charged with assault and battery in the matter of Mr. Reed Johnson, at 642 Main Street, Oakmont, on the twelfth of November. Do you understand the charges brought against you?" Judge Letty appeared neutral, maybe even bored.

Ivan lifted his head, took one speedy peek at the judge through his own heavy glasses, and, as quickly, lowered his shaggy head. It looked like a nod.

"Mr. Demidovsky, you need to say the answer out loud."

Ivan swallowed before opening his mouth. "Yez."

"How do you plead?"

Ivan turned to his public defender. Although Randall whispered through the window to Ivan, his voice carried to the far corners. "You want to say 'not guilty,' like we discussed." The room was not constructed for secrets.

Ivan looked from the public defender to the judge. His eyes on the judge's chin, he said, "I not sure."

Randall's eyes went to the ceiling. "May I have a moment, Your Honor?"

"Pleez, Mr. Judge, he say I say 'not guilty.' I don' understand. I guilty. I hit real estate man, but I was drunk. I try to help my friend. It is her house—"

"Mr. Demidovsky." The judge leaned into his microphone to be certain his voice overrode Ivan's. "It's not the time to tell me what happened. I simply need you to tell me if you wish to enter a plea of guilty or not guilty. Do you understand *me?*"

"Yez."

"Your Honor," Randall tried again, "may I have that moment, sir?"

Judge Letty nodded.

"Listen." Randall positioned himself in the defendant's window to get his face in Ivan's space. "You need to plead not guilty in order for me to properly prepare your case. I need time to get you a deal, if I can. And you *need* a deal, Mr. D." Ivan bowed his head, and Randall pulled back to look at the judge.

"Ready to try again?" the judge asked. "Mr. Demidovsky, how do you plead?"

Ivan's head came up once more. This time he and the judge stared at one another through and over their eyeglasses. Ivan acquiesced. "Not guilty."

Claire was concentrating on poor Ivan when Jane poked her

arm and pointed with her eyes to the central aisle at their right. Shuffling down the aisle, clonking her cane, came Tidy. She was dressed for her appearance in court: black pantsuit, white blouse—a bow at the neck, lopsided—and a black Cossack-looking hat.

Tidy reached the gate separating the case participants and the audience. With a poke of her cane, she propped open the swinging gate and proceeded to the judge's bench. Not a single person tried to stop her. The bailiff stared in disbelief but remained like a rock at his post. The court reporter's hands hung above her machine, as if arrested in flight. The ADA and public defender were as stunned as Claire and Jane, not just by Tidy's appearance but also by her determination.

The expressions on Ivan's face changed with the seconds: surprise, pleasure, sadness, fright. His whole body slumped as he anticipated the berating he was sure she had in mind.

The judge, his head down, making notes, hadn't responded to the noise of Tidy's arrival. An incessant stream of people came and went in his courtroom throughout the session; he was too busy to bother noticing. But now he sensed a stirring of the air in the room and looked up. Tidy stood before him. A Christmas-red shopping bag with crossed candy canes hung from her wrist. Those attending in the courtroom might have pondered its contents, and if they'd asked, Tidy would have described the contents as the essentials for this trip: her wallet, tissues, an empty prescription bottle, her last trash-collection bill, and a three-year-old birthday card from Ivan.

"I want to make a statement," she said with unusual dispassion.

The judge shifted his gaze from Tidy to the assistant district attorney to the public defender to his bailiff. "Are we having witnesses at this hearing?" he asked without a trace of sarcasm.

Since none of the principal players but Ivan knew this person (and Ivan was numb with fear), no one knew what to say—except Tidy.

"My name is Tidy Bourbon, and I want to tell you about Ivan. He is a good man."

The judge stared at her. His hand came up to summon the bailiff, but he paused.

"He lives in my home, and he helps me. I am very old now, and because I'd live alone otherwise, he is important to my welfare. I need him to cook and clean for me, drive me to the hospital when I have appointments. Ivan is the only one who knows how to care for me. I've come to ask you not to put him in jail."

Tidy's speech astounded Claire: the articulation, the correct grammar, the absence of southern twang. In her whole presentation, Tidy was a different person: standing straight, her hands still, her eyes focused on the judge.

Indeed everyone's eyes were on Judge Letty. Although he was close to retirement, with many years of varied experiences, and apparently a quiet and unflappable man, there were many in the courtroom who wondered how often ninety-two-year-old women approached his bench without summons.

"I appreciate your concern, Ms.—ah—Bourbon, is it?"

"Yes. Tidy Bourbon."

Judge Letty regarded the audience and tapped with his gavel to still the tittering noises. The act seemed to help the judge keep his own composure.

"Well, Ms. Bourbon, you say Mr. Demidovsky lives with you?"

"Yes."

"And how long has he lived in your home."

"Maybe fifteen years, I forget."

"I see, and has he done this sort of thing before—assaulted people?"

"No. Never."

"Ah."

The judge eyed the ADA. "Is there evidence of *other* wrongdoing here?" His implication was clear to nearly everyone who was privy to the case at hand but not to Tidy, who wasn't aware physical abuse of her person would be of concern, and certainly not to Ivan, who was still paralyzed by Tidy's appearance.

The ADA shuffled the papers before him. "No, Your Honor. The sheriff's department checked it out. To the best of our knowledge Mr. Demidovsky has not taken advantage of his situation in Ms. Bourbon's home."

Judge Letty returned his gaze to Tidy. "Ms. Bourbon …" He hesitated as if the name continued to baffle him. "Mr. Demidovsky has been drunk before—you know this?"

"Yes, I do."

"And you want him to continue living with you, ah, after he is released from custody?"

"Yes, I do. Right now. Please. I need him to help me." Tidy was unwavering and remarkably polite.

Judge Letty sat back in his oversize chair, keeping his sight on Tidy. After a long moment of reflection, he said, "You came all the way from"—he tilted forward to search his papers for an address—"Oakmont to tell me this?"

"Yes, I did."

He paused again, his face impassive, but in his eyes anyone

could see his mind working. The courtroom was silent and expectant.

"Is the victim pressing charges?" Judge Letty sighed in the direction of the ADA.

"No, Your Honor. Despite the injury, Mr. Johnson said he does not particularly care what happens as long as Mr. Demidovsky pays in some way. The DA's office, however, can't ignore the violence underlying this incident and the need to protect our public."

Jane turned to Claire. "Oh, please," Jane sniffed.

Judge Letty nodded, appearing to take the information into account.

Claire could understand the difficulty the DA's office faced with Ivan. He didn't have the money to pay fines, he was already doing more community service than he could be sentenced, and keeping him in jail for a week or two apparently had no consequence whatsoever. Claire could believe that the DA's office hoped with this case to bring cause to put Ivan away for a while. A more lengthy imprisonment might save the county time, money, and personnel and possibly dry out Ivan sufficiently that he might be retrained for some employment.

Claire knew Judge Letty to be a thorough, careful, and fair judge. Her mind swam with what was possibly the judge's own conflict: Give the DA his wish for prison, or heed the plea of the ninety-two-year-old woman standing before him.

At length Judge Letty raised his eyes to the courtroom, examined the entire gathering, and made a slow sweep of the table below him. "I find the testimony of this witness credible. Madame Recorder, have we taken her testimony?"

The court recorder, after recovering from Tidy's surprising

appearance, had indeed brought her hands back to her keyboard. "Yes," she responded.

"Either of you," the judge asked, gesturing left and right to the ADA and public defender in turn, "wish to cross?"

Although ADA Worthington's mouth was open, it wasn't to emit words. His jaw was locked with incredulity.

Randall wasn't going to say anything. Tidy's appearance was in his favor. He shook his head in the direction of the bench.

Judge Letty returned his attention to Tidy. "Ms. Bourbon, I appreciate your appearance here, and I'm sure Mr. Demidovsky does too. I believe your testimony will be taken into account at the appropriate time."

There was no doubting everyone involved in this case held a different perspective, but Judge Letty held an independent opinion.

"I must tell you, Ms. Bourbon, that Mr. Demidovsky needs to get some control over his apparent alcoholism. He has been ordered by the court once or twice before to sober up, and he hasn't. You are aware of this?"

"Yes, I am. He tells me everything."

Judge Letty picked up his pen, twisting it in his fingers. Up to this point he had not broken eye contact with Tidy. But now he closed his eyes briefly. He might have been saying a prayer. Claire and Jane were on the edge of their seats. And so was everyone else.

His gray eyes once again fully open and directed at Tidy, the judge resumed in a thoughtful tone, "Ms. Bourbon, you seem to have a good relationship with Mr. Demidovsky, and I understand it is important to you what happens to him." He paused, apparently still working out in his mind a resolution.

Claire noted that Tidy was uncharacteristically quiet, as if holding her breath, as she well might have been.

The judge put down his pen with resolve. "Mr. Worthington, Mr. Randall, sidebar, please."

The ADA and public defender approached the bench, as requested. The court sat in attention. Microphones were turned off. The three-headed huddle would not let the room-of-no-secrets hear a thing.

It was a good five minutes before the group broke up. The ADA glowered and the public defender shrugged as they retreated. Claire watched with a curious eye; Jane with an experienced eye; Tidy, about to collapse, with an exhausted one.

The judge, to put the court on notice, said, "There will be a short recess." Randall proceeded to the defendant's window and inserted his head into the opening to speak to Ivan.

In a fine act of charity, the bailiff pulled a chair around behind Tidy and gently guided her to sit. Tidy plonked her cane to dispel any weakness with the sitting. Another three minutes went by.

Randall came back to his podium and nodded to the judge. Those in court who understood breathed a sigh of relief. A plea bargain.

The judge placed his hands flat on his desktop, leaned forward, and spoke with assurance, his gaze sweeping the entire cast before him. "I understand you wish to change your plea, Mr. Demidovsky. Is that correct?" Silence. "Mr. Demidovsky?"

"Da."

"That's a yes?"

"Yez."

"How do you plead?"

Silence. Ivan remained numb—and mute. He looked at his

attorney. Randall mouthed the words, and Ivan, staring at him, said, "No contest."

The judge ran through the usual stuff for a change of plea, including the business about a "no contest" being the same as "guilty." Ivan said "yez" at the appropriate places.

"I read the file of this matter carefully, and I am aware of the case law regarding fists and weapons." He waved one hand at the ADA but kept his gaze on Tidy. "I am taking into account Mr. Demidovsky's long list of misdemeanors and your concerns, Mr. Worthington, about his repeated appearances in this court. But with further thought I do not believe there was any malicious intent to his right jab, as you call it."

Not a single word was whispered in the expectant courtroom.

"With the agreement of the DA and a no-contest plea from the defendant, I am charging Ivan Demidovsky with one count felony assault—with *no* enhancements," he emphasized, looking squarely at the ADA. "I'm sentencing him to the Blackman County rehab residency program for a maximum of one year. I am also ordering a psychological evaluation to determine if he needs any further counseling. If after six months he is still at Blackman and appears to have control over his emotions and whatever else is driving him to drink, I will deliberate the possibility of reducing the charge to a misdemeanor and suspending his sentence with probation. In the meantime, you, Ms. Bourbon, might want to consider other options for any assistance you need in your home."

Judge Letty surveyed the remaining participants in the case. "Is this clear to everyone?" Everyone nodded. "Then I think we are finished." He rose and exited to his chambers to prevent any further comment—from anyone.

ADA Worthington slumped in dejection while Randall

struggled to keep a smirk from his lips. Ivan dared to glance at Tidy, his eyes watering.

Claire and Jane made silent signs with their hands in their laps. Jane did two thumbs-up; Claire tapped her fingers against her thumbs in applause. The courtroom murmured various opinions of this conclusion.

Tidy stood, looking confused. Judge Letty's last statement to her seemed cruel. *What "options" do you mean?* she wanted to shout at him. Without Ivan, there were none to be "considered." Her eyes turned to Ivan, who was already shuffling out of the custody room. Although her eyes were dry, the sadness they registered was unmistakable.

———

As the court began to move for various exits, Claire jumped up and hustled to Tidy's side.

Tidy's face showed alarm at Claire's sudden appearance. "What are you doing here?" she snapped, sharp and accusing. The politeness of tone for the judge had abruptly disappeared.

"I came to find out about Ivan, so we would know what happened," Claire gently improvised.

"Ivan tells me everything. No need to stick your nose in."

"I'm sorry, Tidy. I realize you talk to Ivan frequently, but I thought I should understand his legal case, in case there were any implications for you."

Tidy peered again at the custody room, now empty.

Claire glanced over at Jane but found her talking to the ADA. She was sure Jane would forgive her departure without a good-bye; she wanted to take advantage of this moment. "Tidy, how did you manage to get here? Oakmont to Martinsville is a good fifteen miles and a twenty-minute drive—on the freeway."

"I took the bus," Tidy said, her eyes challenging Claire.

Claire expelled a breath to gain patience. "I wonder if you would like a ride home?"

Tidy's face relaxed, and she smiled. "That would be mighty nice."

Ivan

Back in his cell Ivan sat with the realization that he had failed once again, although he couldn't make out in what way. He knew Tidy had tried to save him, and he'd still come to grief. But he didn't know how. Hadn't his fist been right? The real estate man he'd hit—that man hadn't looked honest. That man had been too smart (and Ivan wasn't talking about intelligence), trying to talk Tidy out of her house. He deserved the smash, taking advantage of an old lady.

Not right; Ivan admitted he *had* let down Tidy again. But it was the vodka, he concluded. Ivan's twisted thoughts caused his head to pound, and he closed his eyes.

In the earlier years of Ivan's tenancy with Tidy, his little drunken episodes hadn't mattered much. But with time the incidents had escalated, not only in number but in noise and intensity too. Tidy's neighbors had begun to complain and call the cops more often. After his fourth arrest, the City of Oakmont, county of Sobrante, needed to find a way to keep this man from taking up space in their jails and using up city and county resources: police, public attorneys, various county processors, jail attendants—all those people who spent portions of the workday on Ivan. "A *waste* of time, salaries, and benefit costs," the district attorney's office bellowed. "Get him out of our system!"

A social worker had been sent to counsel Ivan and had talked him into joining Alcoholics Anonymous. At first he'd adjusted well to the program. He'd become downright cheerful and had busied himself with cleaning and fixing around the house; gardening; and cooking an abundance of kissel and kasha, pelmeni and piroshki. "I never ate so good," Tidy had said to anyone who would listen. "Ivan behaves and keeps himself busy with useful doings."

———

On the first of the month after his court hearing, Ivan called from the Martinsville lockup. "Tidy, my check come?"

"'Course. What you expecting?"

"I'm in jail. They don' always send it."

"The money's here all right."

"You cash the check, Tidy. You need it all now I not there."

"I surely do. I'm having so much trouble with the bank and expenses. You're saying I can use all the money?"

"Pleez, Tidy, pleez."

"Thank you, Ivan."

"What you do about food, Tidy? I not take you to grocery, like always."

"Ivan, you know I take care of that myself."

"No, Tidy, you not drive. This not good. If cop stops you, you in big trouble." He had seen her behind the wheel once— like some Halloween creature, gaunt, wide-eyed, wispy gray hair spiked, leaning over the wheel, squinting through the windshield, tiny in her bulky sedan.

"Iz Blackie helping, Tidy?" If Blackie offered to carry her purchases from the corner store, she might not need to drive to Oscar's.

"He's here, doing good, since your ass is back in jail."

Ivan cringed. "I know, Tidy. I should be up north at the rehab place, not still here in jail. No one tells me anything."

"You should be yelling at them. Tell them to do what they's supposed to."

"I'm afraid if I make too much noise, I get deported."

Ivan's mind buzzed with all his imagined horrors. In desperation, he changed the subject back to Tidy. "Iz Rap coming too?" Ivan worried about the bums down the street. In his opinion these men were the real no-goods, exploiting her circumstances—stealing her cash, for instance, because they believed Tidy had lots of money.

"What business is that of yours?" Which meant the boys were snooping.

"You keep your wallet in your purse and put the purse in closet, Tidy. Those bums come in and snatch when you not looking."

"Tired of you telling me that. I take care of myself."

Ivan was confident Rap and others visited regularly while he was gone—yes, in jail—and did snatch-and-runs at any opportunity. Comments in the bar had convinced him this happened, and not infrequently. To avoid more quarreling, Ivan made a hasty escape. "Be careful, Tidy, bye-bye."

———

Back in his cell, Ivan sat on a platform that passed as a bed, ruminating over his situation, sinking slowly into a tired stupor.

Tidy's command over his income kept her from complaining too much, but still he knew she found it hard to tolerate his drunkenness. Many times he'd blunder his way to his room to sleep off his hangover without incident. But all too often at the end of his drinking bouts he'd crawl to the front door, find himself locked out, and launch into a loud tirade, mostly in Russian, which pissed Tidy off.

She'd open the door an inch and bawl, "If you're going to have a hissy fit, do it in English. Otherwise, I can't understand a word you're saying. Therefore, I'm not listening." And she'd slam the door in his face.

———

Ivan woke with a jerk, the door in his dream smashing his nose. His right fist pounded the mattress, and his torso twisted in his half-conscious distress. His eyes wide open now, his physical thrashing ceased, but the mental battering continued unabated.

Why *was* he still in jail? Tidy's well-being was in jeopardy. Maybe she was right and he was a bum. But what could he do now to change his circumstances? He stiffened with the image of being loaded on a plane bound for Moscow or, worse, Odessa. Which would be worse, he didn't know anymore. He did know that if he was deported, Tidy would fall prey to the Oakmont vultures. He must get out of jail to protect Tidy. The castigation raged on.

Ivan sat up as the clanking noises of breakfast trays being distributed moved toward him. Runny eggs, charred toast, watery orange juice, weak coffee. He groaned. That tray alone should motivate him to start screaming for help. But how to do that, scream for help?

Over the years Tidy had kept his life in order. She threw him out; she took him back. He went to jail; she allowed him to return on his release. It was a mystery to Ivan why this happened. The concept of companionship was not part of his life's vocabulary.

His years had been devoid of friendship, in fact. As a boy, he'd kept to himself on his parents' advice. Political factions had made them uneasy, and you never knew with whom your neighbor sided. As a merchant seaman, he'd harbored thoughts of escape and hadn't been about to share these with anyone. Once on the shores of America, he'd maintained his silence for fear of being discovered and shipped home. Driving a cab had provided the ultimate solitude. No single fare had lasted more than a few minutes—an hour to the airport at most. The majority of these busy people had preferred to keep to themselves too.

It wasn't until he'd moved in with Tidy that he'd known what it was like to live with another adult; to greet this person every day; to share thoughts, observations, dreams. Well, no, he didn't really lay bare personal matters—feelings or emotions or nightmares—with Tidy. She didn't allow him the space in her life to open up in that way. Still, she was a companion of sorts.

And he missed her.

Chapter 6

Claire

On the Tuesday following Thanksgiving Claire called Tidy to make another appointment. As she dialed the phone number, she wondered if Tidy would remember her. She had made a few visits between Tidy's court appearance and the holiday, continuing to assess Tidy's ability to live alone. Claire's suggestions of a move to more appropriate housing had been met with indignation, even hostility. Although she didn't discuss with Tidy her cognitive decline as the relevant issue, Tidy's recent-memory hiccups were troubling for Claire. Claire had some experience in this regard. Her own recent memory had moments of decline too, much to her disgust.

The phone rang seven times, and Claire was about to hang up when the burring stopped, the receiver apparently lifted. Heavy breathing came across the line, then a bang, sounding like the receiver had been dropped. From a distance, "Shit." Claire waited. Finally, Tidy's scratchy voice sputtered in her ear, "Hello."

"Tidy, this is Claire Richards, the social worker who's been visiting recently. Do you remember?"

"Why yes, of course I do," Tidy replied in a stronger, brighter voice. "When're you coming again? I thought you'd be back before now."

"It's been only a few … never mind. I'm in your neighborhood today. May I stop by?"

"You can visit anytime. I'm here."

"I'll be there in about twenty minutes."

"The door's open; you come on in."

Claire sighed.

Twenty minutes later, as promised, Claire rang the doorbell and waited. Despite Tidy's usual invitation to "come on in," Claire kept to appropriate routines. No sound came from within. She put her thumb to the bell again. Nothing. She tried the outer gate: unlocked. And then the inner door: locked—for once.

Ringing the bell a third time, she added the beat of her fist to the door. Claire assumed Tidy's yelling at the buzz of the doorbell was her habitual way of greeting visitors, but maybe it wasn't. Still, less than thirty minutes had passed since Claire's call. She rang and rapped the door again. Silence. She took her cell phone from her jacket pocket and dialed Tidy's number. She could hear the loud ringing inside the house—twelve times. No answer.

Claire didn't know Tidy well enough yet to wonder if she should be alarmed. What could happen in twenty, twenty-five minutes? A stroke, a heart attack, but Tidy's medications hadn't suggested significant heart problems. Claire clicked off the possibilities: Tidy might have fallen, broken a bone, hit her head. Unless she was unconscious, Tidy could still yell.

Claire went around to the back of the house. The Pontiac

squatted in the yard, a huge car for such a frail person to drive. How in the world *did* she maneuver that monster? *Later, later,* Claire chided herself. *Find out if Tidy's alive first.*

She pounded the back door and put her ear to the door to listen. Nothing. She returned to the front walk, flipping over in her mind what to do: call the cops, call Jane, or wait.

"Hello, there you are," Tidy's throaty voice came from a few doors down the street. A thin pink housedress, worn and faded with age, and a blue denim jacket two sizes too big hung on her bony figure. She wore white slip-on shoes—also ill fitting—and was scuffing along as if trying to keep them on, plonking her cane with one hand, and holding a paper cup of steaming liquid in the other.

"You said you were coming later, so I went out to get me some decent coffee," Tidy said. "Now you're here, let's go in so we'll be warm."

Claire was dressed for the brisk winter day in fleece and wool pants, and she had a layer of tissue—okay, fat—on her frame. Tidy's skin hung on her bones like gauze—thin, leathery, blue with veins and poor circulation. Tidy's denim jacket was unbuttoned, and her feet in the floppy shoes were bare. Claire shivered involuntarily at the sight.

Tidy labored up the four steps of the front stoop, managed to get the outer gate open, and placed her cane to hold it while she struggled to push the inner door with her shoulder. She turned to Claire with alarm. "It's locked. I never lock it. Who locked my door?"

"You went out for coffee—maybe you locked it then?"

"No, it's too hard for me to pull all the way shut."

Claire opened her mouth to start her lecture, but Tidy's apparent alarm stopped her. "It's a sticky door; let me try. You've got your hands full." Claire grasped the handle, pushed down on the latch, and shoved with some force, as she had moments before. "Yes, it appears to be locked."

"I haven't got my key," Tidy muttered, her voice flat. She stood, awkward, between the gate and door, one hand holding the cane, the other the coffee.

"How about your pocket? Here, I'll hold the coffee; you check your pockets."

Tidy's pockets were empty.

The two remained on the stoop puzzling over their problem. Then Tidy's face brightened, and she laughed. "Come on, we'll go round to the back. I think I went out that door, 'cause you told me to keep the front one locked—even during the day, ain't that right?"

Indeed the back entry was unlocked. "Always open," Tidy mumbled as she pushed the door. "Don't care what you say."

Tidy wandered into the house, leaving Claire, uncertain, in the doorway.

"May I come in?" Claire called out.

Tidy flinched at the sound of Claire's voice but made her usual speedy recovery. "Why sure, we'll just sit down and have our little chat."

Claire hesitated at the entrance to the living room as Tidy plodded to the yellow-gray couch and slumped into the gray cushions. She studied Tidy for a moment: her gray hair looking as if she had been in front of a fan going full blast, her graying pink housedress under the faded jacket, the awkward white sandals—no, they were gray too—that had fallen off her feet as she'd sat.

Claire glared at the ottoman. Her back ached just looking at it. *No more*, she proclaimed silently.

"Come on, sit here where I can see your eyes," Tidy said, launching into her routine.

"Tidy, would you mind if I brought the desk chair over to sit on?"

"Land sakes, no. Make yourself comfy however you like."

Why didn't I do this days ago? "Thank you, Tidy." *My back thanks you too.*

Claire was poised to launch into the purpose of her visit when Tidy leaned forward. "You know what went on last week?" She gestured conspiratorially toward Claire with the coffee cup. Brown liquid sloshed out, spraying a lump of papers on the table. She ignored the mess, her eyes bright and eager. "Thursday. Calendar said Thursday was Thanksgiving. You know what happened?"

"I couldn't guess, Tidy. Tell me."

"That no-good Blackie. He goes down to the Methodist church for the holiday meal they're having. Serving turkey and all the trimmings, he told me. He ate his dinner and asked them to pack up one to take to his friend. Big bag it was. Turkey, sweet taters, *two* huge slices of pie—pumpkin and apple." She paused a moment in reflection. "Stuffing was plain, a little dry. Not like the stuffing I used to make." She looked at Claire and giggled. "I'm not complaining. That Blackie is the nicest no-good there is."

Claire grinned too, pleased. Not only had Tidy enjoyed a Thanksgiving dinner, but she remembered it.

With such good humor in place, Claire turned to one of the reasons for her visit. Before she'd left for the holidays, Claire had brought the extra weeklong pillbox and filled the two boxes with a full two weeks worth of pills. "Are you remembering to take your medicines, Tidy?"

"I do. Look, these here boxes are open." She reached forward to pluck the two oversize pillboxes from the table in front of her.

Claire gently took the boxes. "But not all of them. Last Wednesday morning is open but not Wednesday evening. All the boxes for Friday and Sunday, closed ..."

"That's just the trouble without Ivan. He always made sure I took my pills."

Claire sat fingering the pillboxes, lost in her own thoughts.

Tidy rambled on, "The house is dirty, I have to take myself to the doctor, and I finally had to order up that cardboard from Meals on Wheels. So many troubles when he's not here."

Claire jerked back to the present, not quite believing her ears. "You called Meals on Wheels? Yourself?"

"Rude. How else would I call them?"

"Yes, I'm sorry; I wasn't implying ..."

"Canceled it after the first meal. Food's too bland."

Okay, Ms. Social Worker, take the bull by the horns, Claire thought. She put the pillbox down. "Tidy, I think we need to talk about the problems of managing here by yourself."

"What do you mean? You're going to tell me what to do? I've been doing for myself all my life. Nobody tells me what to do."

"Tidy, I only want to be sure you are safe, with enough food to eat and transportation for whatever you need." Claire knew this would be the battlefield.

"This isn't the first time Ivan's been in jail. I can take care of myself."

Against her own better judgment, Claire plunged on. "What if you run out of toilet paper—what would you do?"

Tidy didn't answer immediately. Her eyes shifted to her lap. *Here we go,* Claire thought crossly. *She's going to tell me a lie.*

"Nelson's, down at the corner, like I told you. I get what I need at Nelson's. Old Blackie that's hanging around—dealing drugs—he carries my things up to the house, if I ask. I give him a dollar or two, and he's happy."

"Didn't you say you went over to Oscar's?"

"I never said so." Suspicion snapped into Tidy's voice.

"You told me last week."

"Couldn't find the time. Too busy."

Claire did not believe her and frowned. "Do you go out otherwise, to church maybe?"

"To church, of course. The Baptist one at the top of the hill."

"How do you get up the hill? It must be too far to walk."

Tidy sat mute.

"The car in the back, it's been moved." The second she'd said it, Claire regretted the words, but since half the accusation had been uttered, she might as well finish. "Have you been driving?"

"Only to church. Could you check my medicines and be sure I've enough for the week? I'd be much obliged."

Claire paused, hoping Tidy might read in her silence that she both noticed Tidy's attempt to manipulate the conversation and disapproved. Then she asked, "May I get the pills from your bedroom?"

"You know you can. Why you asking?" Tidy's hands crawled along her bony arms in irritation.

Claire collected the pill vials and filled the empty boxes, noting how many of them had not been opened. She ran over in her mind what the meds were for and what the implications of sporadic consumption could be. She had no idea, other than it couldn't be good. She'd ask her pharmacist friend. As she returned the vials to the bedside table, she remembered the Vicodin.

"Tidy, have you had much pain recently? From the arthritis you told me about?"

"Every night I go to bed. Neck, shoulder, back, knees. Arth-a-ritus in them all."

"You're taking the pain medication?"

"What medicine? I have no medicine for pain."

"The Vicodin. Last week we decided the bottle should be on your nightstand. I wrote 'for pain' on the bottle, to clearly identify the medicine."

"I don't take any pain medicine. What're you talking about?"

Patience, patience. Claire took a deep breath. "I'm not finding the Vicodin with your other medications, and I wondered if you had taken one of the pills and put the bottle someplace else?"

"Why would I do that?"

Claire contemplated dropping the line of questioning but made one more stab. "Okay if I look around for the medication, Tidy? You might need those pills tonight if the pain comes back."

"Do what you want," Tidy answered wearily.

Claire searched every logical location in the bedroom, the kitchen, and the living and dining rooms. She returned to the living room to find Tidy mopping up the coffee spill with some tissues. "Place is a pigpen. I can't keep up all the cleaning, now Ivan's not here. Don't much like being alone at night either. Without Ivan, I'm by myself."

"It must be hard, Tidy." Another bull—and here, the horns: "Have you ever thought of moving to a place where everything—"

"Don't you be talking about moving!" Tidy shouted. "Don't you be telling me I should sell this house. I'm not selling. I'm going to live here until I die."

She had heard the argument before, but Tidy's ardor still surprised Claire. So much for assisted living—today. Claire had in mind wearing Tidy down into submission. Surely one of these days she'd capitulate just to get Claire to stop the nagging.

"Have you seen Bernie? Is she coming around to spend the night with you?"

"No, I tell her to keep her fat self out of my house. She just comes here to eat my food and drink my coffee. She takes stuff too."

Claire came to attention. "What do you mean? What does she take?"

"My kitchen towels. What would she want with my kitchen towels?"

"A mystery. Are you sure that's what happened?"

"Are you calling me a liar?"

Claire shifted her feet and lowered her voice. "No, Tidy, I would never call you a liar. I'm sorry Bernie made you angry. The day Ivan left, she seemed to care you were alone, and staying the night with you was a kind gesture." *The gin notwithstanding,* Claire added silently.

"Not if she's going to eat everything in my refrigerator—*and* take my kitchen towels. She's not welcome here anymore."

Claire recognized a mind-set not likely to give in to reason and knew it was time to go. She sighed, rose from the chair, and started for the door.

"She came last week." It was nearly a whisper. Tidy's head was bowed, and Claire couldn't read her face.

"Who, Tidy? Who came?" Claire's murmur matched Tidy's.

"Bernie." Tidy's eyes searched the space in front of her.

"Thanksgiving. She thought I might be lonely, it being a holiday and all."

"How thoughtful of her."

Tidy looked directly at Claire. "She steals from me, and she visits me on Thanksgiving. How am I blessed?"

"By the good in everyone, Tidy, and by people who do care about you."

Tidy folded her hands as if in prayer. Claire felt a catch in her throat and repeated her personal mantra: *Thank heaven for friends and family who love me and embrace me, no matter how I am. Being alone is a part of life. Being lonely is a condition of life.* But the pain of being alone and the hurt of being lonely seared Claire's heart.

She moved toward the door, believing Tidy calmer and with a little reason trickling through the mist of her mind. Perhaps a synapse or two had fused momentarily and Tidy might understand she could have falsely accused people who were friends.

"Care about me? They just steal from me." Tidy humphed. The calm of the previous moment dissipated. "Come here acting all nice and then *steal* from me."

Claire halted her departure again. Why did Tidy harp on the thievery. "Why would they want to take your things, Tidy? And who are 'they'?"

"Robbing me blind."

Claire reminded herself not to argue and to just be with Tidy in the moment. "What do they steal?"

"My kitchen towels and my medicines."

Ah. "Medicines are disappearing?"

"They're in here all the time, looking around."

"Who is looking around?"

"Blackie, Rap, and that bitch Bernie. It's always take, take, take with that bitch."

Claire worried. Vicodin had become a street drug used to make methamphetamines, so the medication was often snatched from elderly people. "Are they taking your pain medication, the Vicodin?"

"Why'd they want my pills? Nothing wrong with their thyroid."

"No, I'm talking about the pills you have for your pain. I haven't been able to find them, and I wonder if these are the pills you think they've taken."

"Sons of bitches. All of 'em."

As with many Tidy conversations, this one began to spin down a path of no sense. Nevertheless, the idea of street bums ripping off Tidy's Vicodin disturbed Claire. Ugly scenarios swirled. True, Claire had an active imagination, but she had worked in neighborhoods of drug use, making, and dealing— and was all too aware that where drugs were found, so was violence.

As Claire again turned to leave, Tidy snapped, "You put that chair where it belongs. I can't be moving furniture every which way. Put it back where you got it."

"I'm so sorry. I forgot," Claire responded. *She's certainly good at ordering people around. A skill developed during her days as proprietress of the store and restaurant, no doubt.* Claire didn't think she'd like working for Tidy. Too bossy. "Here we go, right back to the desk."

Tidy burst out with a gush of giggles. "I'm telling you, aren't I. The chair belongs by the desk. Thank you."

Claire replaced the chair and ran through her mind what to do about the Vicodin. Stay and try to find out more? No. Since

Tidy's mood had lightened with the chair business, better to leave her in good humor.

"Are you going to be all right for another few days, Tidy? Shall I call on you later in the week?"

Tidy smiled, her face brightening. "You come anytime. I love having visitors."

———

At home that night, Claire wrote up her notes for the day. She came to her visit with Tidy, sat back, and closed her eyes. *This case is insane. Tidy is vulnerable, but without her cooperation, what are the alternatives? Public guardianship? Conservatorship—and who in the world would be a conservator for that woman?* The question amused Claire. *Not me!*

Conservatorship or public guardianship wouldn't work anyway, because they required court appearances and proof of her inability to care for herself. There was already evidence of how well she could present in a courtroom, and if she was able to order up Meals on Wheels on her own, how could anyone say she was incompetent?

Then Claire had another idea.

———

The next day Claire called the Langley Clinic and asked if they had someone who could administer tests to measure Tidy's cognitive competency. The examination might provide something more objective than Claire's observations of Tidy's condition.

The clinic referred her to Brian Moore, who agreed to make

a house call. Claire was pleased. She was sure Tidy would balk at going to the clinic, but she might be amused if the test came to her.

Claire was acquainted with Brian; they had worked together on occasion. A retired and widowed psychiatrist, he volunteered for various county agencies to evaluate the mental and emotional status of clients, to facilitate referrals to appropriate services, clinics, or doctors. Brian was a gentle man with warm and kind brown eyes and a calm, sweet nature elderly women adored. Claire felt sure Tidy would find him agreeable, which should make the evaluation easy to accomplish.

Claire and Brian arrived together at the peppermint porch. Pointing to the stoop, Claire asked, "What does this tell you about our client?"

He smiled. "Colorful?"

Claire laughed. "She is that."

The doorbell brought the now-familiar yelling. Claire thought she heard Tidy squawk, "Door's open." It was. Brian's eyebrows shot up.

"I know; I've been trying to get her to understand the danger," she whispered.

They filed into the living room, finding Tidy, as usual, on the couch. The tiny room felt crowded, especially with Brian's height of over six feet.

"Tidy, I'd like you to meet my friend Brian. He's come to talk with you, ask you some questions. I mentioned him when I phoned about this visit."

"You may have, but I don't remember, and I don't like the looks of him. He thinks he knows everything. Is that so, young man?"

"I'm glad to meet you, Tidy, and no, I don't know everything.

For instance, I don't know why you sound so cross. Are you angry with me?"

"How could I be? I just met you," Tidy said, still in a tone of displeasure.

"True, but I've been looking forward to talking with you about Louisiana. I'm quite fond of the state."

Claire beamed. *Oh, Brian is good. Get her talking—on a favorite subject.*

"I was never so glad to leave a place in my life," Tidy said emphatically. "Hot, damp, stinky, living with a bunch of family no-goods. I packed my bag and skedaddled. Went to Los Angeles with Millie. We cleaned homes in Hollywood, till I met my no-good husband."

Brian frowned. And so did Claire. So much for the agreeable, easy-to-accomplish interview.

"Claire tells me you once owned a restaurant over in Ridley. When was that?" Brian asked.

"Just after the war." Tidy smiled. Claire exhaled with relief. "We had the restaurant and a bar too, up on Fifty-Second. Billy ran the bar, but the restaurant was mine. Mighty fine business back then. We started with cheap eats, but in the fifties when times were right again, I served Louisiana food—chitlins, gumbo, catfish. Bertha Mae was the cook. She cooked up the best fries in the county. People came from all over for her fries. We made good money after the war."

"I love gumbo, and I wish I'd been around to taste those fries." Brian paused, and Claire drew a breath, anxious for him to keep Tidy on track. "Have you lived in this house since then?" he asked. Claire relaxed again, listening to Brian jolly Tidy along, inviting her to tell her stories until they were chatting like old friends.

When Tidy came to Ivan's arrival and hesitated, Brian filled the gap. "Tidy, has anyone given you tests for your memory recently?"

Tidy looked confused.

"Has your doctor or anyone at the hospital played memory games with you?"

"Oh, you mean when I'm supposed to remember words and things."

"Yes, that's the idea."

"Maybe once at the hospital, like you said."

After more back-and-forth on taking tests, Brian brought out his mini mental test—thirty questions to test mental dexterity.

At the Senior Outreach Services meetings, Claire and the other staff often joked about having to practice answering the questions themselves to make sure they were still capable of *giving* the tests.

"What day is it? Year? Season?" one of them would quiz. "Now draw a clock with hands showing three o'clock."

"One of these days the digital generation is going to have a hard time with that one," someone would crack, making the staff giggle.

"Count back from one hundred by sevens."

"Oh, come on," Claire had groaned when she'd first heard this question.

Gales of laughter had erupted from the rest of the staff. They'd begun to chant: "One hundred, ninety-three, eighty-six, seventy-nine, seventy-two ..."

"You've memorized it!" Claire had exclaimed.

"You better too," they'd said with more chuckles and chortles.

Claire listened with interest as Brian now administered the test to Tidy. "What's the date today, Tidy?"

"You don't know? How do you be giving these tests if you have to ask such a question? I know 'cause I read the paper every day. You should too."

"I'll remember next time."

He went through several more language, attention, and recall questions and then placed a blank piece of paper on the table in front of her.

"Could you pick up that paper for me in your left hand?"

"What if I'm right-handed?" Tidy demanded.

"Are you?" Brian asked.

"Of course."

"Then it should be easy to know which hand is your left."

Tidy did as directed but not without a look of disgust and a mumble sounding like "dumb."

"Now, fold the paper in half."

With a breath of resignation, she did so.

"And place it on the floor."

Claire's mouth twitched.

"You're wanting me to mess up my house putting things on the floor that don't belong?"

"I'll pick it up for you, if you like, but you need to show me you can follow my direction."

"Dumb," she said—out loud—dropping the paper in front of her.

"How about reading what I've written here and doing what it says?" He gave her a paper with the instruction "Close your eyes."

"How am I to read with my eyes closed? You're not very smart with this testing."

And so it went. Brian was patient and fortunately possessed a fine sense of humor.

Tidy didn't get far with counting back by sevens, but her score came to twenty-six out of thirty overall.

Claire and Brian congratulated her on the results.

"I still got something upstairs, don't I?"

Brian broke his impassive psychiatrist expression. "Oh yes, Tidy, I do believe you have a full house." He grinned as he rose to depart. "I'm pleased we've met, and thank you for helping me with these tests."

"You come and test me anytime you want, young man. I'll be practicing the counting backwards, and I may surprise you one day."

Brian laughed. "You surprise me now, Tidy. Not many people your age do so well. And thank you for calling me young."

Claire followed Brian outside and walked the half block to his car.

"She's quite a character," Brian said. "I'm glad I got the call to make this visit."

"Thanks for coming, Brian. Good to see you again."

The air between them swished with a breeze. "I was wondering if you had time for lunch," he said. "Paul's Café up the street?"

Claire stepped back as if the breeze had intensified to a gust. She stood rigid, her mind blank. She stared at him, dumb, mute, a pounding in her ears, alarms beeping. A shallow breath escaped from her lungs. She was not prepared for the panic the "breeze" had created.

"Perhaps another day," Brian said softly. "I have a full schedule today too," he added, as if Claire had already issued that excuse. "I've enjoyed the contact, Claire. Good luck with Tidy. She looks like a handful."

His blurry figure climbed into his car as Claire planted a weak smile on her lips and kept her eyes wide so the water would not spill. Brian tooted the horn in salute as he pulled away. A minute, maybe two, passed before Claire regained her senses. She brushed back her hair, stirred by the breeze, and walked resolutely to her car. She jammed the key into the ignition, fired up the engine, and quickly jabbed the CD player "off" button to extinguish its music.

At the stop sign, she flapped the paper in the seat beside her to determine who was next on her list of visits. Ah, Sarah, seventy-six, recent stroke, still struggling with extremity weakness. She ran through the salient points of the case, reminding herself of the issues she'd need to check during the visit, and stepped on the gas excessively.

Chapter 7

Tidy

The calendar hung together by one staple, the pages bent and ragged on the edges. Food stains spotted most months, and pen scratchings appeared in more squares than usual. At times Tidy filled in the days with diary-like recordings just to occupy the space. "Didn't go to church" on some Sundays. "Mr. Browning's birthday, I think" on December 4. "Took a walk to the park" was a frequent placeholder. When the weather provided a warm, dry day, a walk might be a recurrent activity. She didn't make up the calendar entries (most of the time). Her index finger now pointed to December 20, the Friday before Christmas: "Claire was here." She counted out three more days: December 23. What should she write in this block for today? "Alone for the holidays"?

Claire's visit on Friday had been pleasant, she remembered. Claire hadn't hassled her about going to the la-di-da manor, for once, and she'd brought some ginger cookies in the shape of Santa Claus. "A black Santa," Tidy had said, and they'd had a good laugh. Claire had fixed them coffee, Tidy recalled. Claire had poured herself a mug but hadn't drunk much. Tidy had poured the leftovers back in the pot, to warm up later in the day.

They'd talked about Christmases past, family traditions. Tidy couldn't remember any traditions with her kinfolk, so she'd settled for talking about food. Every holiday in Louisiana involved food. Corn bread with sorghum syrup might be served on Christmas morning. She'd told Claire about Ivan's blini with canned peaches, sour cream, and honey—a heavenly dish she relished, especially at Christmastime.

Claire had asked if Tidy planned to go to church. Of course she would go to church on Christmas Day. Everyone did. Claire had given her some nonsense about calling the church to ask for someone to pick her up, so she wouldn't have to walk up the hill. Ha. Tidy thought that was a joke. She wasn't going to walk up no hill. She'd drive herself to church like she always did. She should start hunting for a good outfit to wear—something to do today. She'd look for the black hat with the veil—fancy and festive for the holiday. She scribbled "Look for hat" in the square for the twenty-third.

When she went to her bedroom closet to begin the search, the thought of Claire going away for the holidays came to her mind. How did Claire get to go away? No visits on Christmas? Everyone at home went around visiting, saying "Happy Christmas!" and all, taking little cakes to the neighbors, having a spot of eggnog. But no, Claire had said she wouldn't be making visits. She was going away.

Ivan was already gone. No blini from him.

She found the hat she wanted and put it on. Was this the hat she'd worn for Mr. Browning's funeral? Black, must have been. She frowned. Not exactly festive, but fancy. She wandered to the living room and Mr. B's picture on the desk. Gazing at him through the veil, she berated him missing Christmas again. "Just makes my holidays boring," she murmured at his sepia face. "'Member the time we drove to the mountains? Made snowmen, went ice skating, watched the fools on skis falling down everywhere?" She smiled. *Good times when you were around. Now you're not, and that pisses me off.* She tried to sound angry in her head, but she couldn't be cross with Mr. B. Still, she was disappointed.

The loud jangle of the phone interrupted her reverie. She wondered who'd be calling at the holidays. She sat on the ottoman—why did anyone sit on this horrible thing?—and picked up the phone.

"Is this Mrs. Bourbon? I have a collect call from Ivan Demi. Will you accept the charges?"

"My, yes. What a surprise."

"Tidy, iz Monday. I always call Mondays."

"Monday, yes, I was just noticing on the calendar. Merry Christmas, Ivan."

"Christmas not for two days, but the phones will be too busy for me to call, so I call on my usual day."

"You're not getting out for Christmas? You've never been in jail on Christmas."

And so the conversation went, with Tidy growing more irritated with yet another person who had abandoned her for the holidays.

"I'm sick and tired of waiting on you to come home and start cooking. What will I have for Christmas dinner?"

"The soup kitchen has meals for the holidays," Ivan offered.

"I'm not eating with all them druggies for Christmas. You need to get yourself out of jail and come back here and cook me some blini."

"I try, Tidy. Merry Christmas."

With nothing further to say, she slammed the phone down to punctuate her irritation.

———————

Tidy knew it was more than a week after Christmas because New Year's had passed several days ago and the old calendar had finished. She didn't have a new one, so there was no way to count the days and figure out which one she was having. "Newspaper," she mumbled and made her way to the porch.

It was still dark outside, so it must be early, but not so early the paper hadn't arrived. Surely was cold. In the ambient streetlight, her breath puffed in front of her face.

Inside she flipped open the paper to find the date: January 9. Something about January 9 stirred a memory. *Maybe Claire's coming. Better be getting dressed pretty soon, if so. Claire is always on time.*

She decided to get coffee first. Tidy needed warmth on her insides these chilly winter mornings. Last night had been cold— freezing cold. She had added pink sweatpants to her pink fluffy slippers and had pulled on the red sweater *and* her Christmas sweatshirt—the one with the three elves—over her violet nightie, with her gray knit skullcap topping it all. The clothing had been bulky in bed, but with an extra blanket thrown on top, she had been warm enough.

In the kitchen she set the water on to boil and turned to the weather page in the newspaper. Yes, she was right; they were talking about freezing temperatures this week. Freezing temperatures outside, but why was it so cold inside?

Something about the cold caused her mind to race. She paced

back to the living room to check the thermostat for the heater. The pointer was set at seventy-five, as always. But it didn't feel balmy. It made her angry.

Yesterday. She remembered being on the phone and being angry. Something to do with money. Her brain paced with her back to the kitchen—faster than usual. But while her feet had a known path, her brain zinged and zanged without getting anywhere.

The teapot sat still and cold. She had forgotten to light the burner. She flipped the dial. The tick-ticking of the pilot light had no effect. She remembered it was the same problem she'd had yesterday. She'd called someone to complain. Yes, it was coming back to her. She'd called the gas people because she couldn't turn on her stove.

The phone call to the gas people reminded her of Claire's call and her pending visit. She abandoned the kitchen and its cold stove, plodding to the bedroom. A cloud of breath pulsed from her mouth—just like outside when she'd gone to collect the newspaper.

In her bedroom Tidy picked up and considered some pants but decided the pink sweats were warmer. A pair of athletic socks appeared under the pants, and she sat on the bed to put them on. An improvement. The red-and-black baseball cap hung from a hook by the mirror. She put the cap over the gray knit skullcap, and her head felt better too.

She dragged the top blanket from the bed to the couch for good measure. She'd be sitting snug now. The phone rang, and all her lonely anger of the day before came rushing back. She had called and called. And Claire was supposed to come and help, Tidy thought. Why hadn't she?

Tidy grabbed the receiver and yelled, "When are you coming to help me?"

Claire

The tone of Tidy's voice in answer to Claire's ring was disconcerting.

"Tidy, this is Claire Richards. Are you all right?"

"Oh, honey, I've had better days, but the good Lord be willing, I'll make it through."

Claire balked at the "honey" (even her husband knew not to call her *honey*), but at this juncture in her work with elders, she understood enough to leave it alone. "You sounded a little upset. I said I'd be back to you yesterday, but I—"

"You could have; I wouldn't know."

"You're not angry with me?"

"No, goodness no. Why'd I be angry with you?"

"I'm going to be in your neighborhood later this morning. May I come by?"

"You know you can. Anytime. Door's open."

Of course. "How about eleven?"

———

A game of chance, Claire thought as she packed her bag with files, notepad, pens, and cell phone. Would Tidy remember the appointment in three hours' time? Although Claire's other clients were all elderly and many also lived alone, Tidy was an enigma among her caseload. She not only lived alone but by herself in this world: no relatives to watch over her, nor friends to be concerned. Tidy had long since pushed Bernie away, and without Ivan, no one cared, period. Okay, Blackie, but his caring seemed to be limited to the trash and holiday meals.

Claire chewed on these thoughts as she backed out of her driveway. No one—except possibly Ivan—minded if Tidy lived or died. Claire paused as she looked for traffic in the street. *What happens when she dies? Is there a will? She must own her property outright, and at its present value, she could live like a queen the rest of her life—if she sold the house.* Claire smiled to herself. She wouldn't even utter the word *sell* in Tidy's presence.

With better luck than usual, Claire slid into a parking spot directly in front of Tidy's house. *Even with the house's shabby condition, the location itself should bring big bucks ... as long as the green stoop can be ignored,* she mused. The door was cracked open; Claire rang the bell and stepped inside.

Tidy stood in the middle of the living room in an unusual morning costume. She wore oversize white athletic socks with her signature pink slippers. Pink sweatpants were pulled up underneath the lilac nightie. Her top half ballooned with several layers. The familiar gray crocheted cap was topped by the baseball hat. All with good reason: the house was freezing.

"Tidy, is the heat on? It's a little chilly in here."

Tidy reached her throne more quickly than usual, sat, and drew a blanket over her legs. "Not chilly. Freezing. I've called and called, and they don't do anything."

"Called who?"

"'Lectric people. They're saying my electricity's been stopped. Why would they stop electricity to an old woman?" Her voice was whining, but then she shook her fist in the air. "This is an outrage!" she shouted.

Claire mused that a TV news camera to capture this outrage right now would be a treat but quickly berated herself for the joke. The lack of heat was a serious matter. "Who did you call, Tidy? Can you show me the number?"

"Here somewhere." She floated her hands over the coffee table. Scraps of paper with scratchings on them poked from magazines. More phone numbers appeared on the calendar and in the margins of the newspaper tossed on top.

"Do you remember which of these numbers you called?" What was she thinking! A foolish question to ask Tidy.

"Doesn't matter. No point to calling. All you get is some robot telling you to press one for this, four for that, and by the time they say five, I can't remember what one is. Why do they do this to old folks?"

"I agree, Tidy; it's not fair." In the center of the living room, Claire spun a full circle, looking at every surface for a phone book. "Where's your phone book?" *Really ... who even has a phone book now?* "I'll call." Remembering protocol, she added, "I mean ... if you would like me to help?"

When she wasn't busy, Claire could appreciate the rationale for making sure the client wanted assistance. But in this case, she didn't see what difference it made. *On the other hand,* she argued with herself, *I need to be careful with Tidy. She's been clear she doesn't like people "messing" in her affairs.*

"You do what you want." Tidy was rearranging the papers on the table.

"Were you able to talk to a *person* about the electricity, Tidy? I mean did you have a conversation with, um, a real person?"

"Didn't. Called the operator, asked her."

"The operator?" Claire stared. Operators no longer existed. Well, they did, but getting one to talk to you wasn't easy.

"You dialed 411?"

"What's that?"

"Do you *have* a phone book, Tidy?" Claire reminded herself not to be exasperated.

"In the kitchen, I guess." Tidy pulled the blanket up around her waist.

Claire went into the kitchen and found chaos—dirty dishes everywhere; open jars of jam, not just one, three!; a box of cereal on its side, some of its contents sprayed to the edge of the counter. *Glory, we've got to get someone in here to help.* She shook her head in dismay. Under the toaster oven, she found a phone book, only four years old. *Dumb,* she berated herself and dug into her pants pocket for her cell phone. Miraculously the number for the gas-and-electric company in Tidy's phone book matched the number Claire's cell coughed up.

Five menus and two minutes later with a real person, Claire discovered Tidy hadn't paid her bill for the last three months. The customer service guy said they hadn't received any communication at all from Tidy, despite repeated warning notices. "Her account shows we gave her the usual warnings, including a call I made myself yesterday. She called me 'cat shit.' We had no choice but to cut her off."

"She's ninety-two and not well," Claire said, trying to hold her voice steady. She wasn't sure whether to laugh or call this guy on his insensitivity. "It is really cold today, as you must know."

"Yes, ma'am."

"So what can we do here? If we guarantee some kind of payment, would that help? Or let me put it another way: What needs to be done at this very moment to get her electricity back on and heat in her home?"

"She can't go somewhere else for a day?"

"No, she can't." Where in the world could Claire find a

safe place for Tidy? There was the shelter on Third ... wasn't that a picture: Tidy, Blackie, and Rap!—all bunked down in the Third Street church basement. "No, it is not possible to move her!"

The man on the other end went away, to speak to a supervisor. Claire truly hoped the supervisor would be sympathetic and didn't blame Tidy for calling the guy cat shit. She smiled at Tidy.

The man came back and said, "If a credit card number is available, we could charge the card the past due and get Ms. Bourbon back on within the hour."

Three minutes later Claire located Tidy's Bank of America card. Tidy grumbled about charging something that should be paid by check. Claire said it was the only way and read the number to customer service. Tidy stopped complaining and pulled the blanket up under her armpits.

Claire decided to sit this one out with Tidy. She confirmed with Cat Shit the gas and electricity would come back on within the hour, and yes, he did give her his real name and extension in case he was mistaken. She withdrew from Tidy's house for a few minutes to call and postpone the next two visits while collecting an extra sweater from her car. Normally her elderly clients kept their homes too warm for her, so she usually left the sweater in the car. Today she was glad the added warmth was at hand.

While they waited for electricity and heat, Claire turned to the source of the problem. "Tidy, do you pay all your bills yourself, ah, every month?"

"Of course." The response was quick and emphatic, a diverting ruse of Tidy's Claire had come to understand.

Claire changed tactics. "I live alone too, and I need to mark my calendar with a note to pay the bills. Once I forgot to pay the phone bill, and the phone company cut me off." An absolute lie, but Claire hoped it sounded empathetic and Tidy would respond.

Tidy whispered, "Phone, water, newspaper a couple of times. I'm throwing the bills out with newspapers or something."

She's embarrassed, Claire realized. In an effort not to disturb the air of intimacy, Claire quietly said, "I can arrange for someone to come and assist you, Tidy, so those things don't happen, and you wouldn't have to worry about remembering everything. How would that be?"

Tidy didn't answer. She stared into the void just above the calendar. Claire waited. Sometimes silence helped settle a matter more than words. After a minute, however, she had to try again: "Tidy, I have some friends who would like to visit and help you pay the bills, write the checks, and make sure the electricity stays on."

Still subdued, Tidy said, "Last winter, I had no hot water. Did you know you need 'lectricity to get hot water?" Her bearing slumped, a knowing defeat.

Claire closed her eyes. So the electricity had been turned off before. She wondered how many times. Her eyes returned to Tidy's face. "I'm sorry you've had such a hard time. I'd like to make this easier for you, if I may." Claire tried to mix her sympathy with coaxing toward a sensible solution. "I bet you'd enjoy a visitor once a month to help keep the bill paying straight."

With surprising calm and composure, Tidy repeated a familiar statement. "I don't want anyone messing in my life. I can do these things. I just can't remember them sometimes."

"The visitor would come to work with you, Tidy, to help you remember," Claire responded.

A pause for a breath, and then Tidy cried, "My money is my private business."

Claire winced. "Is your checking account with Bank of America?" Tidy's credit card was, Claire's brain reminded her, and it was the closest bank to Tidy's house.

"It is." Tidy smiled. "The manager, Emily, she's just the sweetest one to me. She's always telling me how glad she is to see me." Tidy perked up, as if the memory of this agreeable woman was a tonic.

Claire rejoiced. She had struck gold: Emily was a friend and fellow volunteer for the Senior Outreach program.

———

That evening Claire called Emily to ask if she had any ideas about how to help Tidy.

Emily replied swiftly, "I think I'll ask Julian."

"Your husband?"

"He's the accountant. He could fix Tidy's finances with his eyes closed." With an MBA, early experience at an accounting firm, and now ten years in his own thriving business as a tax accountant, Julian was indeed an expert. "He needs something to broaden his outlook on life."

Claire decided not to inquire what that might mean but applauded the idea of Julian's help. "You'll ask him?"

"Tonight."

Chapter 8

Julian

A nd so on Monday, January 13, Julian stood on the peppermint porch.

Weird, he thought, *right here in the center of Oakmont.* He had approached the tiny house from across the street, observing the overshadowing buildings on either side. The house's facade appeared woebegone in its surroundings, in desperate need of refurbishing. To Julian, the structure spoke of aging, decrepitude, and decay. And it was depressing. Julian, with his relative youth; lean, trim physique; and impeccable clothing—freshly pressed khakis; light-blue oxford shirt with nary a wrinkle; carefully knotted, conservative dark-blue tie; and navy jacket without a speck of lint—belonged in a well-ordered business office, not on the green porch of a rundown house.

He stood on the stoop, wondering if any accountant in the world ever made house calls. Turning, he surveyed the street to determine if anyone was watching and then rang the bell. He heard the yelling Claire had told him to expect.

The inner door opened with a yank and a grunt, and a

disembodied voice came at him through the screen. "You're late." Julian stepped back at the accusation. "You think I can wait around all day for you to come just anytime?"

"Um, may I come in?"

"You better come in before I lose my patience, you being late."

"Ah, I believe it's eleven o'clock, the time of our appointment." Always prompt for appointments, Julian thought it rude when his clients were not punctual.

"I been up for hours, waiting on you. You coming in or not?"

His eyes darted to the street again before he pulled the outer screen open and stepped inside. Her back to him, Tidy retreated slowly, stooped, banging a cane. She had a chaos of gray hair and was wearing baggy black pants; a sweater, once white; and pink fluffy slippers, the kind he'd seen girls in college wearing in those moments he'd accidentally caught them in their nighties. Julian cringed briefly.

He closed both doors, noting the inner one, swollen with the winter rains, latched with difficulty. He stood in the tiny entryway, pinned in by his new client, who was now stationary at the edge of her living room.

"What are you here for? Did you say?"

"To help you with your bills, writing your checks."

She thumped her cane. "You are not writing my checks. I do that. Been doing it all my life."

Julian's whole being sank. Great beginning, and why didn't she keep going? The hall was so stuffed and stuffy. His left sleeve brushed against a lightweight wool overcoat on a hanger hooked on a nail in the wall. A flimsy, old-fashioned housecoat dangled in a similar manner. They made the hall all the more crowded, as if the clothing hung on people.

"Perhaps we should sit down and talk about, ah, why I am here."

"I got to go slow so I keep my balance. Harder these days." She started forward, aiming for the couch, poking her cane at an ottoman as she rounded the coffee table. "You sit there, up close, so I can see your eyes. I know a man by the look of his eyes."

"Uh, thank you."

She settled into the lumpy cushions, her cane banging against the coffee table. Julian sat on the ottoman—a low seat for his six-foot stature. His knees came up toward his chin. He tried scooting his feet back along either side of the stool, but the strain on his lower spine caused considerable discomfort. He brought his feet to the front again and placed his long-fingered hands on top of his knees.

"What's the matter with you? You looking nervous as a long-tailed cat in a room full of rocking chairs."

Julian stared at her surprisingly smooth face. *What on earth is she talking about?* He caught the sparkle in her eyes.

Tidy giggled. "You never heard this one afore, I'm thinking."

"Well, no," Julian confessed, flustered.

"Bless yo' pea-picking li'l heart."

He tried not to squirm, perplexed about what to say.

"And listen here, you need to come earlier. I'm not so good in the afternoon. In the morning, I know what's going on. I get the newspaper on the porch and check the date. Then I know which day we're having. The only way, 'cause I'm two bricks shy of a full load. They tell me I have that Al's Imers disease," she said. "Hard for me to believe; I don't feel sick."

Julian arrested the slump of his spine. Along with the physical discomfort of his seat, the woman herself made him increasingly uneasy. By far his eldest client—ever—her manner was alien. No other client required home visits, for one thing—straightaway an anomaly. And Julian rarely dealt with anomalies. His business was based on code, law, regulations— easy for him to understand, easy for him to apply.

And now this talk of Alzheimer's. Why hadn't Emily told him about Tidy's infirmities? He studied her face. The dark eyes had turned soft and strayed into a void between their seats that wasn't between them but some deeper space Julian couldn't fathom. She looked lost. Julian was well acquainted with being lost. Most of his life he had wandered through a cold, gloomy forest, never finding a familiar, comfortable place. No familiar, comfortable people either, like a mother, who had died early in his third year.

"Tidy," he said softly, worried, unsure, "may I call you Tidy?"

Her eyes flipped to his face, as if he'd disturbed her from a daydream. "You call me anything you want," she replied testily. Then she chuckled, a light, playful laugh. "My real name's Teresa Bourbon," she said, pronouncing *Bourbon* through her nose. "But I'm called Tidy since growing up." And she launched into the well-practiced tale of her childhood in Picouville.

Her story flooded a hollow in his psyche, but Julian struggled to regain some equilibrium as he wondered when he was going to get to do his job here. As she prattled on, he recognized something Emily had described to him. Tidy must be lonely, and this was what lonely people did—talk. Julian would rather bury his loneliness—in work, for instance. It was one thing his clients liked about him.

At the moment, however, he felt confused. The old woman bewildered him. Already he sensed this job was too personal, too intimate, and intimacy frightened Julian. Even after years of marriage, he sank in agony when Emily wanted to share her private thoughts, in hopes that he would do likewise.

He'd chosen his profession for its lack of ambiguity. Accountancy involved numbers, facts, tables, forms—nothing deep, sensitive, or emotional. In his office, with a desk between him and his client, he conducted business seriously, within carefully constructed parameters, with as little personal interaction as possible. Sitting on a low stool almost toe-to-toe with the client perched on a sofa caused his hands to turn clammy.

To dismiss the moths fluttering inside, Julian concentrated instead on an inspection of Tidy's home as he half-listened to her life story. It was small and not exactly clean. Crumbs, dust balls, and white bits of something (he didn't want to think what) flecked the purple carpet. At the end of the hall, laundry machines. Convenient, if a little odd, he thought. He cringed at the mass of paper on the coffee table. A side table by the couch held a lamp shining down on the remains of her breakfast—a bowl of cornflakes melted in too much milk. Disgusting.

Tidy came to a breathing place in the story, and Julian took the advantage. "Tell me again your last name?" He pulled a small notepad from his back pocket, flipped it open, and stared at the empty page as if it contained critical information. "I'm not sure I have the right one."

"My daddy's Cajun; last name's *Bour-bon*, like the French. Now I say *Bourbon*, like the drink.'"

He thought Tidy Bourbon a strange name, but in only ten minutes, the eccentricity seemed apt. She presented like an elderly aunt who came from some foreign place, still speaking with an accent and reminiscing about the old country and not especially concerned with her appearance anymore. His eyes glided to the pink sweatband pushing her hair to the top of her head, a bunch of wavy strands sticking straight up. *Not eccentric,* Julian amended, *bizarre.*

"Now I want to know your name. I didn't catch it when you came in."

"Julian McBain, that's Scottish."

"Anybody'd see it. Look at your red hair, pasty-white face, blue eyes, freckled hands. Oh, I remember now. You're the man who's supposed to help me write my checks."

"Right, that's me—the check writer—I mean *assistant* check writer."

"Lordy, I'm glad you showed up. Where's my calendar?" Tidy scrabbled around on the low table in front of her, extracted the stained calendar, and handed it to Julian. "Look at this, thirteenth of the month today, and none of my bills are paid."

"Yes, the days are getting on," Julian said, relieved her attitude about him might have changed.

January was spread out on a large calendar from Bank of America. The upper pages displayed photos of the older bank buildings in the area. He knew the calendar; he had five: two at home and three in his office. His were clean, pristine, and devoid of personal adornment. Tidy's was decorated with names, phone numbers, indecipherable notes, and scribblings, mostly in the margins. The squares for each day, where Julian's precise printing announced appointments on his own calendars, were predominantly empty on Tidy's calendar. But not the square for January 10. He squinted at the scrawl. "Check man" crowded the block.

"Don't worry; it's not too late. We'll attend to everything here together," he said.

Claire had emphasized that Julian should not make noises

about taking over her finances. Tidy should still appear to be in charge. His problem at the beginning, he realized, was that he'd said he was the check writer. *She* was the check writer. He, apparently, was the "check man."

And the check man needs to get a move on if he is to accomplish anything this morning, Julian thought.

"Is this where you keep your mail?" Julian waved his hand over the coffee table, with an inward groan at the heaps of paper.

"All there. I'm not throwing anything away 'case it's important."

"May I ... ah ... okay if we go through these papers together and sort them out? You could tell me which ones are the bills we need to pay." This wasn't going to be easy for Julian. An overachieving accountant with a business attitude, he told his clients what they needed and then did it, quickly and efficiently. He despised wasting time diddling around.

The two spent a half hour attempting to order the confusion on the table, putting things in piles, the sense of which Julian felt sure Tidy couldn't possibly comprehend. The exercise gave him a chance to make note of items needing attention and to guess what might be missing. For instance, did she own the house outright? He asked her about this.

"You mean do I still pay money for this shack?"

"Yes, do you have a mortgage?"

"I made repairs to the foundation a few years back. Got a loan then."

"Do you use payment coupons?"

"The booklet, you mean?"

"Yes. Any idea where the coupons are?"

"We didn't find them on the table here?"

"No, no coupons."

"You're sure now?"

"Quite." Julian fidgeted. "Could they be in another place?"

"I sometimes keep important things under the couch, hidden. We could look there."

Tidy rose from the sofa and moved aside. Julian stiffened with the sure knowledge she expected him to search under the couch for her. He scanned the floor: scattered cornflakes, a tissue, a pill, and stains of spilled coffee dotted the carpet. He examined his clean slacks with a crisp crease down the front. He glanced at Tidy. She caught his eye and smiled.

On his hands and knees, Julian swept his hand under the couch, wondering if the area had been cleaned anytime in fifty years. He touched some papers and pulled them out: old church bulletins, her checkbook (at last), a travel magazine, a postcard reminder of a doctor's appointment, a Christmas card.

"Those are my important things," she said.

"I'm glad to have found the checkbook, but the payment booklet for the line of credit isn't here."

"What are you talking about?"

"I didn't find the coupons."

"No, I mean that line thing. You're using words I don't understand."

"You're not familiar with your line of credit?"

"You know it. You're saying things I've never heard."

Julian peered at her. Was she provoking him? "Perhaps I used the wrong term. We're discussing the payments on your house, and we still need to find the coupon book." Julian spoke with care, trying to hide his annoyance.

"Oh lordy, what do you suppose ..." She turned unsteadily and lurched toward her bedroom, mumbling. Without her cane she appeared to be leaning into a strong wind.

Julian, still on his knees, tensed with the fear she might pitch forward to the floor. Nothing in his life as an accountant had given him a clue how to effect anything for a client who was so loopy, old, and decrepit; nothing suggested how he was to apply his financial principles in this case.

As his eyes followed Tidy hobbling away, they passed over a photo on the bookcase by the bedroom door. He got to his feet to investigate. The picture frame held a portrait of Tidy in her forties, he guessed, her face full and round, her hair dark abundant and wavy, her eyes dancing. Vitality radiated from behind the glass. He recognized in the photo the client he should be serving.

After several long minutes, Tidy returned to the living room, with a small start when she caught sight of Julian. She stood stationary for a moment searching his face. Julian stiffened with her uncertainty, until she said in a surprisingly offhand manner, "What was I looking for?"

He sagged. What had she been doing in the bedroom all this time? Their eyes locked, and he repeated in slow, painstaking tones, "The coupon book for … The coupon book."

She remained immobile.

"Your house payments," he tried again.

"Oh, that's in my purse with my wallet. I forget where I put things sometimes." She retreated to the bedroom.

"Oh God," Julian moaned quietly.

In a comparative flash, Tidy returned waving a pad of paper, jubilant.

"Wonderful," he enthused with only a thread of sarcasm.

Tidy handed the coupons to him and shuffled off toward the kitchen. "I'm going to get me some coffee. You want a cup?"

Julian glanced at his watch. He had been with her for over an hour and had achieved so little. And now she had wandered off to make coffee. He peered at the portrait of the younger Tidy. The face of a sensitive and intelligent woman gazed back.

"Tidy, how old were you in this photo?"

She returned from the kitchen and joined him at the bookcase and giggled. "Long time ago that was. In the sixties, I believe. Sure look different, don't I?"

"I like the photo. Your eyes … those are your eyes." He could think of nothing else to say, since he hardly recognized her otherwise. "Why don't you have a seat, Tidy?" She made him nervous as she stood, swaying. The fear of her toppling over arose again.

She tottered to the sofa and plopped herself down, evidently forgetting the coffee. As loathsome as he knew the ottoman to be, he resumed his position. "I'd like to ask a few questions about your finances, if you don't mind."

"Ask away." She smiled.

He peeked at her. *How vacant can a life be when you smile at an accountant asking questions?* he mused.

"Where does your income come from?"

"There's Social Security, and I get a pension from the city. After I closed the restaurant, I worked in the public-safety department for fifteen, twenty years." Her eyes shifted to the photo they had been inspecting. "Must be more than twenty. Working for them when that pitcher's taken. I'm in my office suit. I dressed professional then."

"Yes, you look very … businesslike."

He glanced at his watch again. This appointment should have been an in and out: gather the information, note the numbers, document the activity, back to his office to set up the accounts. Swift, straightforward. The forced slowdown, the useless prattle he had to listen to, the chaos of the information—he was peeved. More than that, a fury of frustration grew in him. *Why am I even tolerating this irritating client?*

Then he remembered. Because Emily had asked him to help, and he wanted to please Emily, the first person in the world he'd discovered he *could* please, unlike the aunts who had taken charge after his mother had died. Tidy reminded him of those aunts. He perceived he would never satisfy Tidy ... and that was a problem for him. Even as a small child he'd sensed his aunts hadn't wanted the burden of his upbringing, but he'd kept trying to please them, hoping one of them would hug him, tell him she loved him, keep him for more than one school year.

He turned his attention to the slight gray figure on the couch. She grinned. Julian ground his teeth. He wondered why, even for Emily, he should want to please this woman.

"Tidy, I need to get back to my office. I wonder, may I return at the same time tomorrow to finish up?"

"You come on over anytime you want. I'll make you some coffee, and we can chat some more."

Chat. He examined the creature before him—unpredictable, exasperating, baffling. She smiled again, and he expelled a long breath. He inscribed his business card with the appointment information and planted it on the corner of the coffee table.

"I'll see you tomorrow morning at eleven."

"Buh-bye," she crooned.

Julian stuffed the notepad back in his pocket and exited in three long strides. He turned to pull the inner door closed with a hard yank and just missed Tidy leaning over the coffee table to reorganize the piles of papers.

Tidy

Tidy considered the papers on the table, moved some from one pile to another, made two more groupings, and stacked a pile or two more compactly by tapping them on the edges. She smiled. Time for some coffee.

Hadn't she made a mug of coffee before the man interrupted her? She tottered to the kitchen, but no mug sat on the counter, and the coffeemaker was cold. Funny, hadn't she asked the man if he wanted some too? He might've refused. Rude, if so.

She went about heating water and dumping three heaping spoonfuls of instant into the mug—she liked her coffee strong— before splashing a generous portion of cream on top.

Back on the couch, she sat sipping, reflecting on the freckled man's visit. He'd been polite, maybe too proper, and nervous, fidgeting all the time. She supposed he knew his business, but at times he'd acted as if he didn't understand a word she said, like she spoke some strange language. *He* was the one talking peculiar, with his fancy words, "lines" of this and that. And nosy! Why'd he get on about the coupon book? And where she kept her important things? That was definitely nosy, going under the couch, searching for her important things.

She gathered the Christmas card from Ivan, the travel magazine (she loved looking at the pictures of foreign places and imagining herself in the pictures), the church bulletins (1992), the doctor's appointment reminder (she squinted at it, a June date, and this was January, for sure), and shoved them back under the couch where they couldn't be found.

He'd talked on about so many different things, and with all his walking around, stirring up a hubbub, and demanding the coupons, he'd worn her out. She was relieved that he'd finally left, and that was saying something for Tidy—to be glad for a visitor's departure.

She found his card on the table's edge and remembered that he would be coming again. Yes, he'd written down "Tuesday, January 14th, 11 a.m." She found her calendar and jotted "check man" in the square for Thursday, the sixteenth. Three days away. She'd have to keep up, so she didn't let the appointment get past her.

Agreeable of him to come to her house, not like the doctor who insisted she go to his office. How she wished for the olden times when you got sick and the doctor came calling at your house. Made more sense, especially if you were old and had a hard time getting around.

Speaking of doctors: Ivan had better be out of jail by June so he could drive her to the appointment; otherwise she might miss it—unless she drove herself. She quivered at the notion and scowled at the thoughts of Ivan being derelict in his duty again. She'd burned the bottoms of three pans trying to cook things. She had to rely on Blackie to take out the trash, and he sometimes forgot, so the baskets in the house overflowed. The yard was overgrown too. What was there to do about that?

She crossed the room to examine her photograph—the one the pasty-faced man had seemed to appreciate. She'd been heavier then; Mr. Browning had once said he liked her curves. *Curves, my foot, more like fat,* she thought.

She smiled, gazing at the other photo. Mr. Browning had been kind to her. In their childless disappointment, he had tried to fill the void with generosity and compassion. He'd surprised her with small gifts and taken her out to dinner often (the source of the "curves"). They'd enjoyed road trips, and once they'd flown to Hawaii (what a luxurious vacation) for their tenth anniversary.

A week later his cancer had been diagnosed.

Tidy sighed and retreated to the couch to close her eyes on the memories that followed.

Chapter 9

Julian

Julian arrived for his second appointment to find Tidy in a nightie and bathrobe, along with the pink fluffy slippers.

Claire had warned him this might happen. "Tidy's days are not necessarily distinguished by errands, appointments, jobs, the way ours are," she had explained. "She doesn't always perceive a need to get dressed."

"Surely she'll put on regular clothes for my appointment," Julian had protested.

Claire had shrugged. "She might not remember you're coming."

"I'll call her before I go, as you suggested."

Claire had smiled. "Good idea, but it doesn't mean she'll remember after she hangs up or that she will be appropriately dressed by the time you arrive."

Old ladies and nightgowns—just the image upset him, let alone *dealing* with the business of old ladies in nightgowns. The old aunties popped up again. Over the years he had turned their images into crones, witchlike, ugly (well, they were ugly). They too had worn bathrobes and slippers a lot—or so it had seemed to the young boy who kept yearning for his mother.

He had called Tidy at ten thirty to say he'd be there in a half hour. She had argued that he didn't have an appointment. She had marked her calendar for Thursday, not Tuesday—and today was Tuesday. She knew because she had seen it in the newspaper.

Julian was momentarily stumped, until she yelled in his ear, "You coming today or not?"

After being tempted not to go, he agreed to come. Now, a half hour later, she wasn't dressed for his visit. He hadn't counted on bathrobe and slippers.

Move on, Julian reasoned. *Easiest way around the problem.* Resigned, he took up his position on the ottoman and stared at the jumble of papers on the coffee table.

"I'm going to get my coffee. You want some?"

"What have you done ... No, no coffee, thank you. What's happened here?"

Tidy continued her amble to the kitchen. In a fury, Julian seized the papers on the table and, with the efficiency of an accountant, rearranged them again. It had taken an hour the day before; today, three minutes. He assembled only two piles this time: bills and junk.

Tidy returned and settled on the couch, sipping her coffee. Julian grabbed the pile of bills. He began flipping the papers, a small effort at hiding his irritation at Tidy for reorganizing his piles.

"Your payment on the line of credit is not much ... Let's see, what else? Gas and electricity, phone ... Ah, you have cable TV, and here's a payment on a cemetery plot."

"Very important," Tidy interjected.

"And you're making payments on a car. A car," he repeated. "You still drive a car, Tidy?"

"That's no business of yours. You're here to pay my bills, not tell me what to do."

"I wasn't … yes, right." He took his eyes back to the papers, pausing a moment to let the air clear. *Surely she doesn't still drive,* he thought. He'd have to ask Claire about the car. "Insurance premiums for the car too," Julian said. With a glance at Tidy, he put down the bill and carried on. "Here's your medical insurance—monthly again."

"Biggest rip-off," Tidy interrupted loudly. "They're taking money left and right. I pay three hundred eighteen dollars a month for services, and every time I have an appointment with the doctor, they send me to a nurse. What good's a nurse? I demand to see the doctor. Then they charge me twenty dollars just to sit in his office. What's the three hundred eighteen dollars for? I'm asking."

With her strident complaining, Julian wondered about her blood pressure. "It's hard to figure how these things work sometimes," he said, trying to comprehend how she remembered the exact amount of her medical insurance but not where she kept her line-of-credit coupon book.

"Let's talk about the regular monthly expenses," he said, rattling the fistful of papers. "The bank will pay some of these bills automatically for you—the utilities, for instance. We'll have the bills sent to the bank, and the bank will pay them out of your checking account. I'll set that up—I mean, would you like me to call the bank and set that up for you?"

Tidy brightened at once. "You call that Emily woman at the bank. You know her? She's the nicest person. Always greets me like I'm somebody. She'll take care of this for me."

"Ah, good, I'll phone Emily and handle the matter." But then Julian remembered one of Claire's instructions: don't do anything behind her back. "I have a better idea. Let's both of us call Emily now. You could tell her … ask her to have me … let her know she … We could have the payments taken care of for you." Instinctively, Julian didn't reveal his relationship to Emily. Why not, he couldn't have said.

Tidy became downright cheery with the idea of calling Emily. "Here's the phone; you go ahead."

"Maybe you should talk to her first."

"You dial the number; I'll talk when she answers."

Julian picked up the clunky old phone receiver to dial the number he knew by heart. The spiral cord attached to the receiver was so tangled and foreshortened that as he lifted the receiver, the whole apparatus fell off the table with a loud clank. He regarded the phone in disbelief. Who had antiques like this anymore? *Surprised it isn't a dial*, he carped to himself.

For several aggravating minutes he dangled the receiver to untwist the cord, and finally, with the phone back on the table, he started again to dial Emily's number. Wait, he shouldn't have this information—although was Tidy paying attention? He peeked at the couch. Her eyes were inspecting his every move. "Ah, what's the number for Emily?"

"How am I to remember such a thing?" she asked with mock annoyance.

Bank statements would have appropriate phone numbers—and he started, realizing no statements had surfaced in the paper-sorting exercise. *Jeez, this is like home repairs,* he thought. *Every problem you fix, you uncover two more.*

He was about to ask for a phone book when she said, "All my important numbers are written in this notebook." She reached over to the side table and picked up a miniature spiral pad. She opened it and turned several pages, squinting at each, finally finding the one she wanted. "One of these," she said, handing the pad to Julian.

Five scribbled numbers covered the page. Only one was identified: "Church." Julian recognized another for Emily's branch of Bank of America. Not labeled, but so what? He was tired of this game. "Here we go," he said and proceeded to dial Emily's direct line. He didn't have enough patience left to deal with the irritating menus on the main number.

With the first ring, he passed the phone to Tidy. As he did, he discovered she had the volume on her phone at the highest setting. The sound emitting from the receiver blasted so loud he'd be able to hear everything said on the other end of the line.

Emily answered on the third ring, as usual. "Bank of America. This is Emily McBain." Oh Lord, the same last name! Julian waited for some sign of recognition, but Tidy proceeded without hesitation.

"Emily, this here's Tidy Bourbon. How're you?"

"Why, Tidy, I'm fine. It's good to hear your voice."

"Mighty fine to hear yours too. Now listen, there's a young man here I want you to talk to. I want you to do what he says."

Add demanding *to unpredictable, exasperating, and baffling,* Julian noted.

"Of course, Tidy. If he's there now, would you like me to speak to him?"

Without another word, Tidy handed Julian the receiver.

"Mrs. ... ah, Emily." He felt foolish.

"You didn't tell her we're married, did you?" Emily asked.

Julian wished she'd speak more quietly, but how could she know about the loud volume on Tidy's phone? He flicked a peek at Tidy, but she appeared oblivious. Even so, he stood and moved as far away as the phone cord would allow. Emily's voice burst into his ear; he wanted to hold the receiver some distance from his head but dared not. "That's correct," he said louder than necessary, hoping Emily would catch on to the problem. "I'm here to help Tidy, um, Mrs. Bourbon with her accounts— ah, her checking account." He glanced again at Tidy. She sat on the couch staring into space with a slight smile, contented, like a sated cat.

"You may be right, not telling her," Emily said. "We'll talk about it later."

Julian reviewed with Emily his proposal for some of Tidy's bills, and Emily said she'd bring the forms home that evening.

"Everything okay?" she asked.

"Very fine," Julian said. "I'll pick up the forms later."

Emily giggled. "See you at dinner."

Julian winced. He must tell her to whisper next time.

He hung up the receiver, flipping the long coiling cord into a pile. Tidy watched with a quizzical expression. To still any further words about the phone call, he grasped at another accounting problem. "Tidy, do you use credit cards?"

"Of course I do. What kind of question is that?"

"Which ones, and where are they?"

"Right here in my wallet." She brought a fuchsia-red vinyl tote bag from the other side of the couch into her lap and started rummaging around. She pulled out a comb, a medicine bottle, a few envelopes.

Julian leaned forward to see the envelopes but fell back as Tidy unearthed a small black folding wallet with Velcro closures. On the outside, in a plastic window, he spied her driver's license. How could that be? She was ninety-two years old! He'd have to check the DMV regulations, and he privately hoped he never found himself in a car on the same street with her.

She ripped the outer Velcro closure and unfolded the wallet. Slip pockets for five credit cards were empty. She yanked open another Velcro flap, dug around, and came up with one card, which she handed him.

"This is your medical insurance card," he said, fingering the plastic.

"I'm supposed to be finding credit cards," she confirmed, worried.

"Yes, you thought we'd find them in your wallet."

She passed the billfold to him and sat slumped, staring straight ahead.

Julian turned the wallet over, glancing at the card in the plastic window: not a driver's license but a state-issued identification—very similar, almost identical, in fact, to a driver's license. So what was the deal with her car? His mind whizzed around the matter for a moment before he forced himself to continue hunting for the credit cards. He scrutinized every pocket, flap, and slip of the little black item, but nothing else turned up.

He turned his attention to Tidy. Her expression was full of distress … oh, imminent tears, he was sure. Julian shifted his feet. Weeping females unsettled him. Emily wept on occasion—usually around that time of the month. Hormones, she said.

His knowledge of female matters was mostly textbook, and anyway, the primer didn't elaborate on weeping. Occasionally he made Emily's tears abate by giving her a hug, but he couldn't imagine giving Tidy a hug—that would be inappropriate at the very least. Worse, his memory of hugging old ladies (the crones) was distasteful, even nauseating. He focused on the sheaf of bills. If he didn't look at her, maybe she would contain the crying on her own.

He considered a change of subject to get them beyond the sticky moment, but her financial picture was deficient without details of her credit. "Do you use one credit card or more? Do you know?"

"Know? You mean do I remember?" Her hands started wandering up and down her arms, massaging her neck, scratching her scalp. The reiterative motion irritated him, but at least she had retreated from the hint of tears. "Why are you asking me things I can't remember? I'm always in trouble remembering."

Julian debated what to do about her memory problems—acknowledge them or ignore them?

They both sat quietly for a moment, gathering their thoughts—at least that was what Julian was doing. "Tidy, I'm sorry. I didn't mean to insinuate anything about your memory. I'm trying to help you in the best way I can."

"Best way? ... Humph ... Is sloppy, I'm thinking."

The criticism stung deeper than it should have. He heard voices from the past, never satisfied, forever picking at him for minute misdeeds. "I'm just trying to understand your financial position. Getting all the numbers right can be confusing."

"You confused? I'm not believing it. Using your big words." Her face squared off with his. "Saying things I don't understand. You were sure of yourself the minute you walked in here." In almost the same breath, she said, "I use one credit card. Visa from Bank of America."

The grandmother clock on the opposite wall ticked. The steady pulse of the clock brought his heartbeat into rhythm before he continued. "Can we think together where the credit card might be?" His words were as measured as the clock.

Tidy answered stolidly, "Should be in my wallet."

"But it's not; where else could we look?"

Her face went blank. Was she thinking? After a minute of silence, he asked again, softly, gently, "Any idea where the credit card could be?" He was trying. She was a statue. "Perhaps we can remember where you used it last?" One of the aunts who'd raised Julian had applied this technique whenever he'd lost his toy dump truck or baseball mitt. "Did you go shopping yesterday? Groceries? Gas for your car?" Julian tried not to wince. Here was the driving thing *again*. "An appointment?"

She staggered up from the couch, teetering so severely Julian jumped up and put his hand under her arm to steady her. "I went to the hospital yesterday," she said, jerking her arm out of his hand but waiting while she regained her balance.

"The hospital! What was wrong?"

"Nothing." She trudged to the middle of the room. "I need some pills, so I go and hassle them doctors to give me the prescriptions. They give me a prescription for the pain pills, and I get them at the pharmacy." She stood at the door to the kitchen. "You want some coffee?"

"Wait, Tidy. Did you use the credit card for those pills?"

"How else was I going to pay for them?"

Julian closed his eyes a moment. "What were you wearing yesterday, when you went to the hospital?"

"Wearing? My clothes … Oh, I see. Maybe my credit card is in a pocket or something."

Julian nearly shouted hallelujah. "Perhaps if we checked the clothes you wore. Do you remember which ones?"

"Let me think: the brown pants, the green blouse. Oh! I

know! I took the black bag. That red one didn't match, so I took the black one!"

"And where is it?"

"Oh, well, now. Must be in the closet." With surprising agility, she bustled into the bedroom.

Here we go again, Julian griped. He followed her as far as the doorway, perplexed. Her shuffling one minute and quickened pace the next puzzled him. The vagueness and then the relative sharpness of her mind baffled him. How had her medical card ended up in the red bag and the credit card in a black one? *Focus,* he told himself.

"Must be here," she said, her voice muffled in the closet as she searched the jumble of clothes hanging on a drooping pole. She surveyed the garments, mumbling, fingering a jacket hooked on the door, brushing a speck of lint from a long skirt.

"The black purse, Tidy, what does it look like?" he asked.

"Black. On a hook in here someplace." She moved lingerie and nightclothes and sweaters to finally expose a lump of synthetic leather. "Aren't we lucky?" she said as she turned toward him with a bright face and the ugliest black purse he had ever seen. "Right here all along." She waved the bag, which was so worn the ersatz material was cracked and the imitation-gold ornaments hung by threads.

"Is the credit card in it?"

"What credit card?"

Julian sucked air through his clenched teeth.

"Are we looking for … Oh, yes, I used it at the pharmacy to get my pills. Here, in the front pocket." She plucked the piece of plastic from an outside pouch.

Chapter 10

Julian

"Is there new mail?" Julian asked without preamble. It was his third appointment, January 15, and still the bills remained unpaid. His patience was dwindling.

"Right here, if there're any." She smiled and sat back.

His eyes dispiritedly roamed the mounds of paper on the top of the coffee table, stopping when they reached a book on the far edge—a Bible. It was a well-used copy, the page edges brown and the spine broken. Several thick bookmarks jutted from the top. Julian reached down and plucked the book from the table. He flipped open to one of the marked places. The bookmarks were credit cards.

"What's with these credit cards?" His voice had an incredulous edge.

"What you talking about?"

"Here, in your Bible. You have *three* credit cards stuck in the pages. The other day you told me you only had one."

"I only *use* one. They're always telling me to leave the cards I don't need at home, so they don't get lost or stolen. Ole Macy's don't like you returning things anymore; Penney's is too far away. What's the other one?"

"MasterCard."

"Never understood why I have that one. Never use it."

"Not carrying unnecessary cards is good advice, although it might be better to put them away someplace—not leave them out here, exposed." Without thinking, he pushed the cards down flush with the edge of the pages so they didn't look so conspicuous.

He returned the Bible to the table, pawed through the papers, and found a two-month-old bank statement for the checking account. He frowned. *Why wasn't the statement in this mess two days ago?*

Examining the statement, he noted with satisfaction her pension and Social Security checks were direct deposits, but he seethed at two checks returned for insufficient funds. More rummaging into the chaos on the coffee table turned up a savings account statement, listing a deposit of $500 and a transfer of $300 from the savings to the checking account.

He vacillated between the satisfaction at finding the statements and the absurdity of their absence only two days earlier. He concluded he might deal with both better if he moved his base of operations to a secretary at the end of the room. The accompanying diminutive chair with a holey cane seat provided a slight increase in comfort over the ottoman. Tidy seemed content to remain silent on her couch while he worked out in his mind all the ramifications of her financial shortcomings.

The $500 deposit in the savings account reminded him of a conversation he had had with Claire the day before. "Ivan normally pays Tidy rent from his disability check. I'm unsure of the amount, but this could be a problem for you. The Social

Security Administration isn't going to pay Ivan to live in the community if he's in prison and the county is paying his expenses," Claire had said.

"Yeah." Julian had smiled at the thought. "That's like double-dipping."

Claire had rolled her eyes. "The point is, Tidy's income will be down by his rent, and I'm guessing this money is an important component of balancing her budget."

"Cripes."

Julian glanced sideways at the figure on the couch. She held up the newspaper, allegedly reading the front page, flipped it over, harrumphed, and flopped the section back to the headlines. "Tidy," he said loudly to interrupt her concentration, although she couldn't possibly be reading the paper. "Is this five-hundred-dollar deposit in your savings account from Ivan?"

"His rent. Pays on time every month."

"Yes, the deposit was made on the first." He paused, certain his next remark would embark on a prickly subject. "Tidy, I'm concerned you may be living beyond your means."

"No idea what you're saying." She flapped the paper to straighten the fold, as if the conversation didn't interest her.

Julian expelled the air from his lungs and, following a count of five, said, "You're spending more than your income."

Her face showed no comprehension.

"You don't have enough money in the bank." That resulted in the impression he hoped for, although not the response he wanted.

"I do too. Always have."

"Tidy, do you realize you will not be receiving Ivan's rent now that he's in prison?"

"What do you mean? His disability check comes to me. It doesn't matter he's in jail."

"I don't understand."

"I'm his payee. His check comes to me!"

Julian frowned.

"The social worker says he's boozing his money away, so she gets the disability check sent direct to me."

After a pause to think this through, he supposed it might be true. "Even so, Tidy, the disability money is *his*, and if he's in prison, the Social Security Administration isn't going to send him—or you—the money. That would be double-dipping … Never mind; let's concentrate on the fact that his disability check won't be coming while he's in prison."

He had lost her a few moments back, even before the "double-dipping." She had slipped into her inner self, staring at the space in front of her. Julian scanned her face, wishing he knew what she was thinking—or if she was in fact thinking.

After a moment she focused on the wall across the room and said, "Happened before, but he's never in jail long; didn't matter much. The judge says this time he's going to be away many months."

Julian puzzled over Tidy's thought processes—the way she fought his questions, went into that peculiar inner place, and then, without explanation, returned to the present, quite often with the answer he needed. He lacked the patience to try to sort out how this happened. He had been sent to solve her financial problems, not her brain problems.

She stared at her lap, her hands patting one another. Julian shrugged and turned back to her statements.

Emily had suggested he examine both her checking and savings accounts for a better way to manage the income and outflow. "Obvious," he muttered: combine the accounts. Her savings wasn't a huge amount, so the interest, at the present rate, was relatively small. The penalties for returned checks to the checking account outstripped the interest.

"I have it, Tidy." He spoke fervently, rousing her attention.

"Have what?"

"I'll combine your two bank accounts into one—"

"You'll do no such thing!" she shouted. "You don't touch my accounts."

Blast, he'd forgotten the rules. "I'm sorry, Tidy. I didn't mean I would *do* anything. I think—"

"*I* think you want to take over my business. I'll call my friend Emily at the bank and make sure you don't get into my money."

"Okay, but you see—"

"No, *you* see. This is my business, not yours."

Julian wondered if he could ever learn how to manage this client. "Right, yes, I hear you. I understand, Tidy. Yes, I do." He turned back to the desk, agitated. Rustling the papers, he tried to decide what to do next. *Go on to something else,* he counseled himself.

He returned to the ottoman, wishing his knees didn't ache so much. "I brought the forms we need for the bank to pay some of your bills. They're all filled out. Your signature's all that's necessary."

"What do you mean the bank will pay my bills? They're not that dumb. I'm not signing anything. *You're* supposed to be writing checks to pay the bills."

Julian tensed. *I should quit now. I don't need this battle,* he argued with himself. He wanted to get up and hurl himself out the door! But he'd been brought up to be polite and respectful.

Being rude was unacceptable, and notwithstanding his feelings about the situation, he knew walking out on her now would be rude.

"The other day," he said, trying to remain calm, despite the rage inside, "we talked to Emily at Bank of America about having your bills sent to the bank for payment from your checking account."

"You mean Emily's going to take care of this for me?"

"If you sign these forms."

"Hand them over. I trust her."

He offered the form for the utilities and handed her a pen. She grabbed the paper and pen and paused. She appeared to be reading the form, the pen poised but still. Julian steamed. *Why can't she just do what she's told?*

"Says here the company name should be written in this blank." She passed the paper back to him.

Julian took the form slowly, watching her face before glancing down, and yes, one blank in the middle had not been filled in. He leaned over to the coffee table and penned the utility's name. Her eyes drew his gaze like two magnets.

She sparkled. "Caught that mistake for you."

He frowned. "Yes, you did."

His stomach roiled. He wasn't supposed to make mistakes. He'd spent his life making sure he behaved, doing things right, everything in order. Otherwise one cantankerous auntie would pass him on to another meanie. "Too much trouble," they would inevitably say, and they would call a sister to complain, announcing it was her turn.

Tidy scrutinized each form he handed her before applying her signature. When she had signed all in her bold, slowly penned autograph, he folded and stuffed the lot into an envelope, telling her he would mail them on his way home. Not exactly a lie. He looked forward to playing postman and placing the forms directly into the hands of his love—although he might have to rail at Emily about how exasperating it had been to get them signed.

Julian had intended to pay the current bills during this visit, but he didn't think he could endure another minute in Tidy's presence. "Looks like I've run out of time. I'll come by tomorrow to write the checks."

Of course he would. He never left a job undone.

"You slow or something? Takes me a couple minutes to write my checks. Taking you *days.*"

Tidy

Tidy did enjoy the check man's visits. She got a kick out of teasing him a little. Couldn't tease Ivan. Mr. Browning, now, he'd been a good tease himself. But Freckles? Gloomy as a graveyard, no fun. *Problem when you're old is everyone you used to laugh with is dead,* she thought. It was lonely when there was no one around to talk to. Freckles only wanted to talk about money. Dull as a beetle. At least Ivan took her for drives, although only to the bank and grocery store—that wasn't what she'd call fun either.

She and Mr. Browning would go driving up the coast, stopping at the vista points and imagining what lay beyond the wide ocean they faced. On the way back, lunch at the Seaside Café in Mendocino would provide another diversion.

They used to walk in the park too, the one covering over two blocks, a square of green with jungle gyms for the kiddies. They'd sit on the bench and watch the children run and play. They'd taken pleasure in watching the innocence, the abandon, the joy of a good long slide ride, even the tears of a fall off the swing.

One day a little girl—maybe four years old, curly black hair, round face, pretty—had come over and asked if they had a little girl she could play with. She'd stared at them when they'd said no, not in disappointment but in bewilderment.

Tidy supposed that had been the last time they'd gone to the park.

If the little dark-haired girl had been ours, how old would she be now? Tidy frowned in the concentration of the math problem. Maybe she'd be like Emily. How splendid to have a daughter like Emily—pleasant, calm, fetching, friendly.

Her daughter would visit often, take her shopping, invite her over for Sunday dinner. Tidy went on daydreaming, having little conversations in her head with her daughter. She had always said they'd have a son, a fine, upstanding man like Mr. Browning. But now that she was old, she thought a daughter sounded better—Emily being better than Freckles, for instance. If she had had a son, would he have been like Freckles?

Chapter 11

Julian

Julian took an early lunch break and walked the two miles from his Ridley office to Tidy's Oakmont home. He'd decided that his patience with Tidy lasted about a half hour and that it might be best to take her in small doses. In fact, this had been Emily's idea. She seemed to understand how Tidy's irksome behavior irritated Julian, and with the deftness of a lover, she'd gotten him to see how to get around the problem.

Thus for the fourth time he stood on the green stoop. He rang the doorbell but didn't bother to wait for her hollering and the long minutes it took her to come to the door. When he had phoned to tell her he was coming, she had said, "Come on in; door's open." So he did as instructed. He closed the door, turned to the living room, and halted, petrified. The couch was empty. *Oh God, what if she's still in bed or dressing or bathing or ...*

"Tidy?" he shouted.

"I'm here; you don't have to go yelling." She appeared from the bedroom, dressed, if a little bizarrely. "What's happening today? We going to get those bills paid, or are you going to keep fussing about other stuff?"

Here she goes again, he thought. "Yes, ma'am, we will write the checks today." Without fail.

He crossed the room to his station of operation. As he passed the coffee table, he recoiled at the sight. His careful work from the previous visit, left on the desk, now lay strewn the length of the low table. A bread crust, junk mail, and pervasive tissues were interspersed among the envelopes, which were stamped here and there with the brown circles of overflowing coffee cups.

Although Julian would bristle if you called him a neat freak, his office desktop was always devoid of papers by the time he left for the day; his closet at home had shirts at one end, suits at the other, pants in the middle; and his socks drawer went from black on the left to brown on the right. Tidy's house brought his obsessive-compulsive tendency to the surface, but having been instructed by his "supervisors" (Claire and Emily) to tread lightly about the clutter in Tidy's house, Julian often found himself biting his nails and, when he couldn't help himself, making paper piles. The idea of important documents buried under coffee-stained church bulletins set his mind buzzing.

"Tidy, do you have a box we could use for your mail?"

"A box?"

"Like a shoebox. We need an old shoebox in which to stack your bills and statements."

"I throw out old shoeboxes, don't you? Extra in the closet makes a mess."

"Of course, a mess in the closet." Julian sighed. "I'll see if I can find a shoebox by our next visit. There's probably one in *my* closet."

Tidy gazed on him as if he were some exotic animal—which *kept* shoeboxes.

He picked through the chaos on the table, transferring what he needed to the desk, and withdrew the checkbook from the desk drawer. He stared at the papers and the checkbook. It was time to prepare the checks for her signature and to prepare himself for reviewing the whole affair with her, as he had been instructed to do. "She must feel she is still in control," Claire had emphasized.

Julian had called Claire the day before to complain. Emily had suggested the call, hoping Claire might relieve his irritation. "It would be much easier if we got a power of attorney and I managed everything from my office," he'd grumbled. "Then Tidy and I wouldn't have to meet and torment each other."

"I'm sympathetic," Claire had said, "but we need to help her preserve what dignity and independence we can. When *you're* old and people start getting into your affairs, you'll understand."

"Never," he'd said under his breath.

He lined up the bills to be paid, wrote the checks, and made the entries in her checkbook ledger. Tidy, settled on the couch, sipped from a paper cup she'd retrieved from the end table. *Probably yesterday's coffee, with scum on top,* Julian thought callously as he stood.

Emily had coached him to explain every detail to Tidy before sealing the payment envelopes, and now he wondered how this activity could physically be accomplished. Should he ask her to sit at the desk? No, the desk was too tiny. He would need to lean over to show her … No, not good. He didn't want to lean over her, looking down … no. Draw up another chair? No, two chairs would crowd the small space. He concluded, no matter how awkward, he would have to sit on the couch beside her. Side by side they would share the paperwork. His chest was tight.

"Tidy, may I sit with you to show you the bills for this month and have you sign the checks?" She gaped at him, silent. "I'd like to review these bills and payments with you. May I sit on the couch beside you?"

Her expression of confusion broke into a broad smile "You want to sit on this lumpy couch with me?" Tidy laughed. "Why, boo, I reckon you might could." She patted the cushion next to her in invitation.

Julian twitched. What was she talking about? *Boo?*

"Come on, sit down. You look like you been struck dumb."

Julian cleared a space on the coffee table and placed the papers and envelopes in front of her. He edged around the table to sit and hesitated. A bowl of congealed oatmeal, a number of used tissues, her red vinyl bag, the day's newspaper, and a vial of pills occupied the couch beside her. Julian didn't think of himself as a prig, but he did have trouble picking up used tissues, and the oatmeal was gagging.

"What's the matter now?" she demanded.

"The seat beside you ... some things on the cushion where I should sit."

"Set them anywhere you want. I don't mind."

He grabbed the newspaper and the bowl and took them, out of sight, into the kitchen. Tidy discarded the tissues into the wastebasket beside her, alleviating that anxiety. The pills had rolled into the gap between the cushions. She held the red tote bag in her lap and brushed the seat next to her as a gesture of removing any further debris. Julian's gaze lingered on the dust-gray cushion. *Just sit down,* he told himself, *and get on with things.*

He showed her the income and expense listings and pointed out every bill and payment in turn, discussing the amount and whether it was more or less than the previous month or if it was one of the amounts that didn't fluctuate. He babbled on, placing each check on her red vinyl bag—not such a bad lap table, it turned out—for her signature.

Tidy seemed to find the exercise strangely calming. Julian, on the other hand, was on edge, wondering when her next outburst would occur and what nonsense he would have to deal with.

"You'll find the stamps in the top drawer," she said quietly, pointing to the desk.

Julian moved to the desk with deliberate, unhurried steps. Her unusual composure felt like the air before a tornado strikes: gray green, unnaturally still, and moist. From his boyhood days in southern Indiana he knew the presentiment: Would the twister fall out of the sky or not? It was almost better when she was ornery. Then, at least, her disposition was unambiguous.

He tested the breeze with a moistened finger. "Do you want to mail these envelopes, Tidy, or shall I?"

"Do you trust me?" she asked.

"Would you trust me?" he countered.

She cackled unexpectedly. "I don't know you well enough to trust you, but it's too cold out to walk to the post office. I'll let you mail them."

Oh, she'll let me. He smiled. *She's giving me permission.*

This gust of confidence caused him inexplicably to prolong his visit by reviewing again which of the bills they had set up for automatic payment. Back on the ottoman, he explained every detail with near enthusiasm. "The best part, Tidy? No more stress about the electric bill."

"I'm never worried about that business."

"I would be. If I didn't pay the electric bill, they'd turn off my lights."

"I'd sit in the dark."

"Yes, so I heard."

———

With the January bills paid, Julian asked his supervisors if he could take a break from this wacky client.

"Don't stay away too long," counseled Claire, "or she might forget who you are."

Julian scoffed, "I don't think so."

But in his office a few days later he worried. Would she forget? Without pausing to wonder why, he called her for another appointment.

He enjoyed the brisk walk to her home, the cool air spurring him on. His spirited stride quickly drew him to Oakmont, his usual long-arm swing hampered by a box for black loafer-style shoes, size 12, double-wide—empty and lidless.

Tidy appeared cheerful and expectant. "What's that under your arm, looking like a shoebox?"

"It is—a shoebox. I brought it to help us organize your papers." He passed the box over the coffee table, like a priest blessing an altar. "I'm going to leave the box on the desk. I want you to put all your mail in the box. Then when I visit, I'll sort— that is, I'll help *you* sort the mail to determine what's important and what's not."

"Why would we do that?"

"Tidy," he pleaded, "work with me here, please?"

She giggled. "Frustrated, aren't you?"

Julian stood before her, the shoebox held at his chest in both hands. From his height he considered her to be like a cat that had just deposited a hairball on his new shoes. He refused to react but barely masked his irritation.

She peered up at him through the tops of her eyes, coquettishly, her face wrinkled in pleasure.

Should he shout and stomp out? Or join her fun? He smiled and reached over with the shoebox to bop Tidy ever so gently on the top of her head. She burst into guffaws. Julian bopped the top of his own head. Peals of laughter rang about the tiny house.

With a broad sweep of one hand, Julian pushed the papers from the coffee table onto the floor and placed the shoebox on the now-bare table. The altar was redressed.

For the next half hour, the two chatted about the papers as Julian sifted through them and extracted the important pieces to be deposited in the shoebox.

"How often do you go to Pizza Hut, Tidy?"

"Who're they?"

"Trash!" Julian exclaimed and jubilantly flicked the Pizza Hut broadside into the wastebasket.

He was sitting on the damn ottoman, but for once, he didn't seem to mind.

"My goodness," he said, "here's the third appeal from Security Banking to get another credit card."

"Triple trash," Tidy bubbled.

"Okay, now, Tidy, this one *is* important," he said as he pulled out another envelope.

"I hear a lecture coming."

Julian bridled momentarily but quickly returned to the game. "Bank statement."

"From our friend Emily."

"Yes, our friend." He smiled. The warmth of Emily filled him and spilled over into the room, embracing Tidy as well as Julian. Emily had found the shoebox for him and had suggested that in time he might come to like Tidy. *Possibly,* Julian now conceded.

The mound of paper sorted, Julian took the shoebox to the desk and placed it on the shelf above the writing surface. "Perfect place," he effused.

"Looks like a misplaced shoebox."

"Tidy ..." he pleaded.

"Okay, I'm going to remember. Put my mail in the box, every day."

"Thank you. Thank you very much. I'll be back in a week to check. I don't want anything on this table." What was he doing? He sounded like a mother entreating a child. "That is, I know you'll be sure to put everything in the box, so this table will ... have more room for your coffee."

"You can be all the bossy you want, boo, but I only do things I have a mind to."

Julian missed the jibe. Here was this "boo" business again.

———

A week later, Julian stood before Tidy on the opposite side of the coffee table. "Have you been putting your mail in the box on the desk as we agreed?" He was acting like the reproving mother again—something he'd missed in life: a mother, let alone a reproving one. He made an exaggerated glance over to the desk and smiled with satisfaction at the envelopes stacked in the box.

"Of course." She sounded put out.

Then he looked at the coffee table. The paper strewn across its length and tumbling to the floor had not diminished. Three windowed envelopes roosted in open view. "What about these?" He leaned down to pick them up.

"What about them?"

"Looks to me like mail, which means they should be in the box, right?"

"Just came today."

From the postmarks, he doubted it. He had been dreading this visit for the squabble he anticipated, but the periodic insufficient-funds issue had to be addressed. In Julian's considered opinion, the problem was the car. The loan payment, the insurance, maintenance, gas—altogether they came to over 10 percent of her total expenses. And she had no license to drive the vehicle!

In his usual businesslike attitude, Julian would not equivocate. "Do you still drive your car, Tidy?"

"What if I do?"

"I was wondering. I mean, I'm not sure, but, well, I don't think you have a driver's license."

"I do too!"

"Where is it?" he challenged.

"Here in my wallet." She yanked the little black billfold out of the red tote bag by her side and shoved the displayed card at Julian. He leaned back at the aggressive move.

"Tidy, that's not a driver's license. It's an ID card. Look at this." He took out his wallet with a similar plastic window displaying his license. "They're almost identical, but mine says 'driver license' at the top, and yours says 'identification.'"

She stared at the two, squinting. *Irrefutable evidence,* he nearly gloated.

"I been driving all these years with this license; can't be nothing the matter with it."

You just haven't been caught! Julian wanted to shout. "Okay, okay. My point here, Tidy, has to do with your finances: with the car payments and the insurance, you don't always have sufficient funds to pay for everything else."

"I do too!"

He shuffled papers aimlessly, borrowing time. She glared at the coffee table and picked at her bathrobe.

"Tidy, when I pay your bills … sorry, when *we* write your checks next month, the balance in your checking account will not be adequate to cover your expenses. On your last bank statement, here," he said, jabbing the relevant line with his finger, "is a returned check because of 'insufficient funds'—that means not enough money in the account. Every time a check is returned for insufficient funds, the bank charges you a fee: thirty-five dollars, every time, which makes matters worse. And we need to remember, Ivan's rent is no longer available."

She sat up straight and fixed Julian with a hot glare. "Emily tells me I have enough money for everything. I called her the other day, and she said I have plenty of money. Why'd she tell me that, if it's not true? She's not a liar."

"No, I'm sure she's not." *Why didn't Emily tell me about this phone call?* His neck turned warm with displeasure. "I don't know why she would say your checking account has adequate funds, because it doesn't."

"I've enough money all these years. Nothing's changed!"

"Remember, Ivan's rent—"

"Emily tells me I have enough money." She slammed the newspaper on the table.

Julian let the verbal feathers she'd blasted into the air float back down as he rearranged papers and fiddled with his pen. Was the delight of his last visit an illusion? "Why don't we call your friend Emily at the bank and make an appointment. Perhaps she'll help us get to the bottom of this problem."

"Going to see Emily'd be good. She is the nicest person to me. *She* makes me feel important."

Julian barely heard Tidy's jibes by this time. In any case he was already having a conversation with Emily in his head. *How could you not tell me …?*

———————

Over dinner, Emily calmed Julian with her assurance that Tidy had not called her recently. "She's remembering something from the past. We've discussed her accounts for years now, Julian, and with Ivan's rent going into her savings account, she *has* been able to manage her bills, with the occasional transfer of funds to the checking account." Emily rose to fetch a dish of her apple cobbler, Julian's favorite. "You were clever to suggest a visit with me."

"It wasn't clever. I want someone else to take it on the chin with this woman." Emily laughed and ran her fingers through his hair and down the line of his jaw. He kissed her hand. Nothing could change his love for her.

Chapter 12

Tidy

Julian poking at her car ownership annoyed Tidy. More than annoyed, she was tired of everyone saying she shouldn't be driving. That Claire woman was the same, talking about having accidents. Anyone could see she was a good driver. *No tickets, no tangles with the po-leece, never a dent in my fender.* What right had they to tell her she shouldn't own a car? *A car I have a license to drive, no matter what Freckles says.* And it did not cost much! She never went far; the car consumed hardly any gas. She took the Pontiac up to Arnie's for an oil change occasionally. Arnie sent her a postcard reminder. Other things were attended to when Arnie suggested they were necessary. She didn't know about maintaining cars, so she always said, "Fine, just keep her running smooth-like." She paid for these repairs no problem; Arnie took credit cards.

In her bedroom, muttering, picking through the piles of clothes, she pulled out a pair of brown pants. "Now where's that green blouse?" she asked the bedside table. In the closet, of course. "You got those hose I was wearing yesterday?" she asked the top left bureau drawer. By the time she had sufficient clothes on to appear in public, every piece of furniture had been addressed.

"I'll show him," she exploded at the mirror while brushing her gray wisps forward to curl around her cheeks. On a nail to the left of the mirror hung several rings of keys. Ivan had hammered in the nail. He'd spent too many hours hunting for keys, he said, often finding them in the door lock or outside the trunk of the car, for instance. He had gently chided her at first but in the end had decided a nail on the wall would be easier for her to locate and remember.

She grabbed all the keys now, sorting them as she turned each one over: front door, back door, basement ... *What's this one? Ha! Here's the car.* She dropped the others on the bureau but retrieved them immediately and placed them back on the wall. Ivan's plaintive cries rang in her ear. "Pleez, Tidy, put back on nail. I put nail especially for you. Keys always on nail." Easier, not necessarily easy.

She squeezed the car keys in her fist. "I can so drive *my* car," she blasted at the back door on the way out.

The front seat was adjusted for her short legs. The first time she used the car after Ivan went to jail was always a trial, getting the front seat just right, back and forth, back and forth. But now her feet reached the pedals perfectly. Never mind that the steering wheel nearly creased her abdomen.

She jammed the key into the ignition and turned it. The engine coughed only once before she stepped on the accelerator, pumping the pedal. She knew how to get *her* car started.

She switched the gearshift to reverse, watching the shift indicator to be positive the arrow pointed to the *R*. One time she'd moved the handle too far and gone forward instead. The paint on the fence at the corner still showed where she had collided. The fence behind her had two broken slats. Well, four had been broken. Ivan had mended the first two, but he hadn't had a chance to fix the others before the cops had hauled him off again. Ivan was inconsiderate in that way, not fixing things promptly. "Damn Russkie."

She couldn't turn her head sufficiently to look behind the car. Sometimes she remembered to check the rearview mirror, but mostly she stepped on the accelerator, and when she thought she'd gone far enough, she stomped on the brake. She repeated the motions until she had successfully navigated the three-point turn necessary to head in the right direction up the driveway.

At the end of the drive, she made a quick survey of Main Street, left and right. Fortunately, traffic was light that morning, and she pulled out, turning left, without a single screeching brake or blasting horn.

Freckles should see me now! Driving down Main Street, in the middle of Oakmont. Everyone on the sidewalk stopped and watched how well she drove.

Three blocks south she turned left again, continuing on Westside Drive, heading for Ridley. Halfway down the block, her eye caught a flash of red—a young woman's blouse—and her foot jerked from the accelerator. She hadn't brought her red bag with her, her red bag with her black wallet, which contained her license. She knew the rules: the license should be in the car with her, in case the cops stopped her.

At the next corner, her foot went down abruptly—on the accelerator. She turned right with a little too much speed on, and a tiny bit of rubber greased the curve. A car entering the intersection from the left swerved to miss her. The honking horn unsettled her further. "Hold your horses. I got to go back; don't be making all that noise at me."

Turning right again, she faced a ramp, and with a glance to her left, she discovered it was a one-way street; the only option was to proceed up the ramp. At the top, she came to the freeway, the cars whizzing by in terrifying haste. She slid to a standstill, trying to think through what to do. A car rolled up behind her and honked with annoyance. She had no choice but to go forward.

As she pulled onto the freeway, her uncertainty changed to anxiety, which soon spun into fright. She drove at speeds she hadn't experienced in a decade—even with Ivan chauffeuring, because they never went far afield. She gripped the wheel in fright and concentration to keep the car from wandering out of the right lane.

"Just need to get off at the next exit," she murmured. Two exits had already passed by the time she came to this thought, however. Her eyes zipped to the signs. They confused her. How could she be going to San Francisco? Oakmont wasn't anywhere near San Francisco. You had to cross the bridge to get to San Francisco, and in that moment, she realized she was on the bridge approach with no way to turn back.

I'll stop at the tollgate, she reasoned. *The lady there can help me.* She figured to follow the car before her—that would keep her in the right lane. The line of cars slowed as they approached the tollbooths. With disbelief, she watched the car in front of her drive through the booth without stopping. "Cheat," she murmured. "Where are the cops when they should be catching the cheats?"

It was her turn at the booth. She crawled to a stop. Car horns began to blare. "Hold your horns. I'm no cheat; I got to pay."

Oh, her heart pounded her ribs: without her wallet, she hadn't any money. She lowered the window to explain her predicament to the toll collector, but no person occupied the booth. The horns blasted louder and with more insistence.

Tidy's breathing turned shallow, her mouth dry, all cottony. Something was awfully wrong here. There didn't seem to be any way to get around the problem except to drive on through like the guy ahead of her. A dampness spread across her forehead. She crept onto the bridge.

Her hands clutched the steering wheel, her bony knuckles pronounced by her grasp. She leaned forward into the wheel, peering through the windshield, hoping for some miracle to show her the way back.

The traffic at this time—midmorning—moved at the speed limit, and room opened up for those behind her to maneuver around her. The honking horns ceased as she crept over the broad span. She eased across three lanes to position herself for the first exit, and at last the lane swerved to an exit ramp. The horns started up again as she took the curve at a crawl.

At the end of the ramp she made an immediate right and parked at the curb. Only then did she become aware of her quickened breath and the tremble in her hands as she released the wheel. "Lord, help me."

Knuckles rapped at her ear. She flinched. The Lord wasn't usually that prompt. A slight black man peered through the window. "What you want?" she snapped, anger masking her fright. The man's lips moved, but some kind of muffler deadened the words. "What you saying? I can't hear anything."

The man flapped his hand up and down.

She rolled down the window. "What are you saying?"

"I was wondering if you needed help," he said.

"What makes you think I need help?"

"You looked scared about something."

Tidy's gaze went to her private place while she revisited the horrifying drive across the bridge.

"I want to get back to my home." The statement sounded sad and yearning.

"Where's that—home?"

"Oakmont."

"Long way from here."

Tidy's shoulders dropped with the weight of this knowledge. She knew it was true but wished it wasn't. "You get in and show me back to Oakmont; I'll pay you." She understood the power of money.

The man said his name was Isaac and got in the passenger seat. Clipped close, his kinky hair, mostly gray, suggested a senior status. He lived in the Tenderloin but back in the day had lived on the east side too, he told her. His cheap, dusty black pants and black T-shirt reflected his past working in the shipyards and warehouses along the waterfront. He'd "retired" a few years back when he'd busted his leg. It hadn't healed well, and no one wanted a stevedore with a gimpy leg. He mostly wandered the streets now, yakking with the homeless, steering the newbies to the best shelters and food kitchens.

With surprising gentleness, Isaac guided her back onto the bridge, giving her careful instructions, with long lead times before turns, reminding her to use the turn signal. He never once gasped with her erratic steering or groaned with her slow speed.

Tidy sighed with relief as they crested the hill by the Oakmont Baptist Church.

"Nice place," Isaac commented as she pulled into her driveway.

"Been my home for fifty years. You come on in for some coffee, and I'll get you your money."

Chapter 13

Julian

Julian picked up Tidy the next day for their bank expedition. He had called her a half hour before, pleading with her to be ready, and held his breath while waiting for her to come to the door. She was dressed. Black pants, with a flare at the end of the legs, bunched at her ankles, and a lavender top, of some shiny synthetic material, bagged at her waist. Her white shoes were scuffed and miles too big. Julian couldn't figure out how she kept them on her feet. The whole outfit looked as if she'd raided a free-clothing-in-the-park place.

Inside the bank, they approached the customer service desk, prominently placed in the lobby to the right. Emily was expecting them, and she smiled—her only-for-Julian, warm, I-love-you smile. Julian froze. In this instant he recognized that he and Emily hadn't talked enough about how they should behave during this appointment. He had convinced her they shouldn't admit to Tidy they were married. She was opposed to this idea and worried about not telling the truth.

"We don't tell her anything; we won't be lying," Julian had reasoned.

"Still, we'll be deceiving her."

"How?" Julian had asked, trying not to sound irritated by what he thought a trivial matter.

Emily had acquiesced, looking down at her hands in her lap.

He'd reached over and taken her left hand, fingering her wedding ring. "With care we will not say any untruths."

"If Tidy had any idea we lived together, she'd be suspicious. She'd think we talk about her over supper."

"And we don't. Emily, please."

"All right," Emily had yielded.

Now, in the bank, with Tidy, Emily beamed at him like a new lover.

"Hello, Emily," he said in his best businesslike voice. "Tidy and I are visiting today because we are concerned about having adequate funds in her checking account to pay her bills."

"I have enough money," Tidy interrupted. "Miss Emily here has told me, many times."

Emily smiled and invited them to take the client chairs in front of her desk. She leaned toward Tidy. "I believe what you say is true, Tidy, but let's hear what Mr. McBain has in mind."

Julian squirmed. *Emily, please, please don't use my last name.* He glanced at Emily's desk. Her nameplate—the slab of black plastic in the tinny gold frame, announcing she was *Emily McBain*—was missing. *Oh, you darling,* he thought with great relief.

"The issue is clear." Julian launched his argument. "Ms. Bourbon has, on average, more expenses than income in any given month." Buoyed by Emily's perceptive initiative with the nameplate, Julian spoke with confidence, leaning forward to tap a finger on Emily's desk as if punctuating his delivery. "We don't seem to be able to pay everything from her checking account, and when we come to paying irregular bills, like taxes and car insurance, we definitely need to transfer more money—"

"Yes," Emily said crisply, interrupting Julian's efficient recital. "Tidy," Emily said, turning to their client, "do you understand what Mr. McBain means?"

Tidy harrumphed but remained silent.

Emily pulled a piece of paper from the corner of her desk, turning it for Tidy to read. "I wrote this down for you. On the first line is the income deposited every month."

"My Social Security and my pension. Always been enough for me."

"Some of the time that's true," Emily said. "Here is a list of the checks for your bill payments last month: electricity, TV, phone, your cemetery plot—"

"Very important," Tidy interrupted.

"Your medical insurance—"

"Cheats," Tidy muttered.

"And your car payment and the car insurance," Emily finished.

Julian stuck out his chin and opened his mouth. Emily silenced him with her eyes. "Occasionally your pension and Social Security are not quite enough."

Because, Julian wanted to shout, *she is paying for a car she doesn't have a license to drive but drives anyway!* He started to bite his nails. Emily's hand came up and moved marginally in his direction but stopped before descending. Julian spotted the gesture, glared at her, and flattened his hand on the desk.

"Remember, Tidy, you have two accounts here in the bank—a checking account *and* a savings account. In the past we had Ivan's rent going into the savings account ..." She paused to discover if Tidy followed her explanation. Tidy's eyes fell to her lap.

At last, Julian crowed.

"So if you didn't have enough to pay your bills, we transferred money from your savings account to your checking account. You and I would make the transfer here together."

"You keep telling me I have enough money to pay for everything. Why are you changing your mind now?"

"If we put all your money *together,* there is sufficient money to take care of the bills."

Emily had such patience, Julian noted.

"But some months the balance in the checking account is a little low, and we move money from *savings* to cover the extra expenses."

"That's another thing we've been discussing," Julian interrupted.

"Who's 'we'?" Tidy barked.

Emily stifled a smile.

"You and I, the other day," Julian said. "I spoke about combining your two bank accounts ..."

"And I told you you'd do no such thing."

"But without the rent money—"

"He won't be in jail long," Tidy countered.

Julian glared at Emily. She lowered her eyes to her desk blotter and, following a short silence, said quietly, "I think Tidy has depended on her savings account since the war and would like to keep it intact, ready to use when she needs extra money. There is a sufficient balance in that account to cover the irregular expenses without Ivan's rent."

Tidy beamed. "You see, I told you. Emily here understands

my money business. She knows exactly what I need." Tidy turned to Julian and scowled. "Not like you."

"Perhaps," Emily continued, "we could have an arrangement to transfer money when it's necessary."

"I don't want this man to mess with my money. He doesn't know about these things. I want you doing the money moving."

"I can't, Tidy, without your permission and signature. The bank wants to protect your money."

"Good, because I don't trust this man."

"But Juli is …" Emily began.

Julian blanched. Emily had used her endearment, her nickname for him. *Bad idea, oh, this meeting was a bad idea.*

Emily's eyes went wide in horror. "Mr. McBain," she said, in a lower voice.

Julian watched, terrified, as Tidy looked up sharply, her quick eyes flicking from one to the other. "Juli?" She smiled and then cackled. "Juli! That's a girl's name."

"I misspoke," Emily tried.

"No, no, Juli is a wonderful name for this man. A short name for Julian. I like it."

Julian smiled weakly. "Julie *is* a girl's name, Tidy, and I am, I do believe, a man."

Her eyes slanted toward his face, but she said nothing.

Julian jumped back into the savings account business, hoping a change of subject would get them beyond this perilous moment. If they started arguing again, surely the incident would be buried in some abyss of Tidy's faulty memory. Julian spoke furtively. They needed to move quickly. Emily played along.

"What if each month Mr. McBain tells you how much money needs to be transferred and writes the information on a slip of paper? You come for a visit and bring the paper with you.

You'll sign the paperwork, and we'll transfer the money from one account to the other."

Tidy smiled. "I'll look forward to visiting you."

Julian grunted. "Sounds like it might work."

Emily stood, taking Tidy's hand in farewell. "I'm happy with this arrangement, Tidy. It will be a pleasure seeing you more frequently."

Tidy's eyes bounced from Emily to Julian. "I'll enjoy those visits more than this man's. Oh, I know he's supposed to help me, but he's no fun, all business. You're so much nicer."

"I think Mr. McBain will be good for you, Tidy, and you may be surprised. You may warm up to him after a while."

"Humph" was the end of that conversation. Tidy shuffled out of the bank, banging her cane in exaggerated annoyance. Julian followed, dutiful.

Tidy

Tidy was restless after the bank visit. She felt on the edge of something and couldn't quite pull it out of the fog swirling around her. Drawn to sit at the desk, she toyed with the shoebox, taking out the papers and putting them back.

She understood the reasoning behind the money transfers. She did remember that Ivan's rent was supposed to disappear when he went to prison. Yes, there was plenty of money to cover her expenses—*including* the car—if she made the transfers. Her eyes gleamed with amusement at her feigning ignorance over these matters. She thought it was great sport watching Freckles get twitchy.

Yet something else about the bank meeting distressed her. Maybe the business of not enough money and everyone changing their story. Well, not Freckles. He was adamant on that topic: not enough. Emily understood everything—the transfers, Tidy's deposits and bills. Why didn't Emily do the check writing, instead of Freckles? But Emily had a job at the bank and had to sit at her desk and take care of people coming in ...

Something about when they'd walked into the bank came to Tidy. Emily had stood at her desk, welcoming them—gracious, friendly. She'd had a warm smile.

Tidy traced the course of the visit in her mind, examining each action for an offense. She watched the scene like a movie; the camera moved from left to right—Emily to Julian to Emily again.

Emily was such a sweetheart. Like a child, Tidy mused, young, innocent. Young enough to be her own child or grandchild maybe. And *Emily* was a good name, but she'd wanted a boy. She would have named him Andre. Andre Browning sounded distinguished.

She rose from the desk and wandered to the back bedroom and stood in the doorway. She had planned to put the cradle in the corner and a rocking chair by the window; she'd wanted to paint the room a sunny yellow.

The boy would wear knickers, argyle socks, a cap—blue, the cap would be blue. He'd grow up to become a doctor, not a taxi driver. He'd have more brains and ambition than a taxi driver. He'd marry—someone sweet, like Emily. They'd have youngsters. Two'd be right, one boy, one girl. They'd come visit on Sunday, for dinner. Laughter would play through the house. The little ones would scamper about and run outside to their daddy's swing hanging from the corner tree. She'd join them in ring-around-the-rosy and hide-and-seek.

Her eyes swept the drab bedroom. Empty.

Chapter 14

Julian

"I put an ad in the paper this week," Tidy said.

"An ad for what?" Julian asked absently as he wandered the living room hunting for pieces of mail. It was a week after the bank visit, and although plenty of paper had been stuffed in the shoebox, Tidy's diligence in this exercise hadn't lived up to his expectations—those expectations being higher than most. The automatic payments by the bank wouldn't start until March, so he needed to locate the February bills. Hopefully he wouldn't find any surprises.

"An ad for Ivan's room. I'm not keeping that room waiting for him forever, and you telling me I need the money. So I advertise in the newspaper. Lots of people been calling."

"You're kidding." She had his attention now. "Have any of them come to take a look?"

"Two already. I told one—a lady—she could move in right away. She's bringing me the rent later today. And I won't be alone tonight."

"What does this lady do?"

"What you mean?"

"Does she have a job? How does she earn the money she's going to pay you?"

"No business of mine, as long as she has the money."

"I see."

"She's a fine woman, says she been living on the other side of town but likes my room better."

"I see." Julian was at a loss for something more intelligent to say. He didn't like the idea of Tidy renting the room to some unknown. Her financial troubles weren't desperate, in truth. *Lonely? Okay, so she's lonely,* he thought. *But you don't solve loneliness by renting rooms.* As with many of Tidy's dilemmas, Julian's limited ability to untangle them spurred him to return to the problem of hers he did understand.

"You don't need more money, Tidy," he said, gathering envelopes from the coffee table. "You need to *spend less,*" he lectured. "If you got rid of your car, you wouldn't have a care in the world." He strode to the desk. "No account transfers either." *End of argument!*

"Without Ivan, I'm afraid sometimes, 'specially at night." She was talking into her lap, her dispirited voice almost a whisper. "Alone, I get the willies, all jittery like."

Julian stilled his hands of the paper shuffling. "Have you considered moving to a senior place, where they provide your meals and the staff takes care of your needs?" Emily had told him about these homes—not nursing homes, he couldn't remember what she called them.

"I like my life the way it is. I'm too old to move, and I want to die here. I'll be fine when Ivan's back, but meantime I need someone else living in my house, so I'm safe."

Julian sank into the desk chair to make notes about the mail he had found. He had no idea how to respond to "so I'm safe." He would continue to do what he had been sent to do. He began to chuck the junk without bothering to review it with her—too much trouble. He brooded over the pile of envelopes: nothing but bills, charity pleas, and financing deals.

He was staring at a take-out menu for the local Chinese restaurant when she roused him with "You got chill'un?"

"Children? No, not … well, not now."

"Married and no young'uns, that's a shame."

"How do you know I'm married?" Julian started to panic.

"You're wearing a ring. I'm no dummy. You're married."

"Oh, yes," he breathed out.

"I've no chill'un either … sad. You and your wife should get busy and get you some youngsters before it's too late. They'd be a light in your life. Couple of little ones would've made me happy as a hog in a mud puddle. Now life's a big bayou, and I'm stuck wading along, getting nowhere."

A melancholic blanket shrouded the room. As Tidy grieved her lack of offspring, Julian ruminated on the depressing scenes with Emily about having a family. He and Emily had done everything gynecologically they could manage themselves but remained childless. The options left seemed to be adoption or in vitro, and they'd argued long and hard about which it should be. Emily wanted to adopt ("There's so many needy children"). Julian wanted to try in vitro ("The baby would be ours"). After a few months, they'd both grown tired of the arguing and had agreed to give it a rest.

Tidy's words echoed in his mind: "a light in your life." Yes. Although he loved his wife with all his heart, he realized Tidy was probably right. A family, a child, might fill the void he felt. He straightened the papers on the desk again. He should be returning to his office, although he supposed what he really needed was the brightness of the day, a solitary walk in the woods, or a long swim in the ocean.

But no, instead, to his surprise, he continued the conversation with Tidy, prolonging his time with this cranky client. "Why did you leave Louisiana?"

Tidy seemed surprised by the question too, her sharp eyes studying him for a moment. "Nothing much in Picouville. After my mama and pappy passed, I live with this auntie and that. None of them wanted me, so when Millie says she's going to Los Angeles, I begged her to take me too."

"You were an orphan, like me." Julian smiled, despite the gloominess of the earlier moment.

"You, an orphan?" She stared at him, her mouth slightly open with disbelief.

"Which auntie did you live with most?" Julian asked.

"Aunt Bessie, the old hag. Dumber than a bag of hammers and pitchin' conniptions all the time 'bout how bad I been."

Julian laughed. "Aunt Matilda was my nemesis. I called her Silly Tilly behind her back, until one day she heard me chanting the name to my friend Fred and I got a spanking to end all spankings."

Tidy joined Julian's laughter, and the two sat for another half hour trading stories of their orphaned lives. Finally, he remembered the work at his office. He rose to go.

"I've enjoyed our talking," Tidy said. "I knew you were a good man right from the beginning. Now I know why."

Julian grinned. "I guess I'll have to come back on Monday to finish up, write the checks."

"You say the bank's going to write the checks. Why'd I sign all those forms?"

"You're right; the bank will pay some of the bills, but not until March."

"Come March I won't see you then?"

"No, I'll still be visiting. Some bills the bank won't pay, and we'll need to be on the lookout for the irregular expenses—taxes and car insurance, for instance."

"That's good, boo, 'cause I'd miss our little chats."

Julian was thrown off by "boo" again, but the thought of Tidy missing him was truly unsettling. What could he say? That he'd miss her too?

"I'll be back Monday ..."

"I'm always here."

Tidy

Julian's departure left Tidy in conflict. Their conversation had pleased her. Wasn't it a hoot they were both orphans? Julian reminded her of Mr. Browning. Why was that?

She and Mr. Browning used to talk on all sorts of happenings too—about their past, about affairs in the community. He'd been the Oakmont city manager for a time, although his real job had been with the cannery out on the Point. He'd said he managed the "back office," a position she'd never quite understood, but he'd made a good salary, and they'd lived well.

She went to his portrait on the bookcase. He hadn't been a handsome man. It had been the glasses; the frames had always been too large on his thin face. It hadn't mattered, because he had been a kind man.

Every Friday he'd brought her a bouquet of flowers, a note tucked in with the blossoms. "For the love of my life." "These are as bright as your eyes." "I love your smile." He'd honored her birthdays and their anniversaries with lovely gifts of silver or pearls and had whisked her to showy restaurants in the city for extravagant dinners, replete with candlelight and champagne.

They'd gone to church Sunday mornings and spent those afternoons in some companionable way. In the spring they would walk the hills among the wildflowers; in summer they would take picnic lunches out east or go to the shore and stroll the beach, looking for driftwood.

When they'd purchased the house on Main Street, they had been aglow with their cozy little nest. "The second bedroom in the back is perfect for a nursery," he had said. That was, she recalled, the only time he'd ever said anything about children. Month after month had gone by, and nothing had happened. Why hadn't he said anything? Why hadn't she said anything? Then he'd died. She sighed. *Too late. No chill'un.*

They'd had only seven years together—pleasant, agreeable years. She'd been thirty-eight when he'd died—too old to do anything about youngsters. And even though, in the succeeding years, a man or two had shown some interest (possibly dancing once or twice—she wasn't sure now), she hadn't really cared, because she'd supposed it was too late for little ones.

She turned toward the kitchen. A mug of coffee might be something else to think about.

Chapter 15

Julian

Midmorning Monday Julian reached for the office phone to call Tidy and tell her he was on his way. The cell phone on his belt interrupted with a buzz. Tidy. In one horrifying second he conceded the mistake of placing his business card on her coffee table.

"That woman renting my room, you know what she is?"

Not "This is Tidy" or "Hi, how are you?" or "Is this Julian speaking?"

"Nothing but a low-down prostitute. I get up this morning, and what do you suppose? A man is in my kitchen. I ask him what he thinks he's doing in my house, and he tells me his *lady* friend had him over. In my house!"

"Tidy," Julian tried to interrupt.

"I kick them out, and then I pick up her things and throw them out on the stoop. She's not coming back in here. I locked the doors on those filthy people."

"Tidy ..."

"I'm a good Christian woman. I'm not having no prostitute in my home."

"Tidy, Tidy, I was about to call to ask if I could visit this morning. May I?"

"You come over anytime," Tidy chirped.

The sudden change to her usual bright, cheerful voice puzzled Julian.

"Door's open ... Oh, no, I remember now; it's locked. You'll have to knock and ring the bell. I'll come let you in."

"I'll be by in a half hour."

Julian walked out of his office building shaking his head. *How do you protect someone like Tidy from themselves?* he brooded as he strode briskly toward Oakmont's Main Street.

He spied the stack of boxes and plastic trash bags on the front stoop as he rounded the corner below Tidy's house. He wondered idly what Tidy proposed to do about the money the woman had paid her. He decided he wouldn't ask; she'd tell him it was none of his business anyway.

He knocked and fell back with the immediate screaming through the door. "Who's there?"

"Julian."

"Thank you, Jesus." The lock thonked heavily, and Tidy grunted with her effort to open the sticky door. As he reached out to help with a gentle push, the door popped with such force it crashed against the wall and would have bounced back and hit her but for her well-placed cane. "Glad you're not that low-down lady. Look at her junk on my porch. She's gone and left a mess, making my house like a pile of rubbish."

"Didn't you tell me you put her things out here?"

"May have, but it's *her* mess, and she better clear it away soon, or every bit's in the trash."

"Did you tell her you intended to throw her out, Tidy?" Julian asked as he entered the house.

"Yes, I did. I told her and that garbage man she brought in here they were to leave pronto and not come back."

"She may be surprised to find her belongings on the front porch."

"I don't care. I'm not having her in my house again."

Tidy was wearing a quilted vest stained with spilt coffee over her nightgown. The fuzzy, Cossack-looking black hat sat squarely on her head. Julian stared at her bare feet as she lowered herself onto the couch. The house was freezing, which accounted for the hat and the vest; her feet must be ice cold.

"What's going to happen about renting the room now?" Julian asked.

"I'm calling the feller who came by before, the other one who wanted to rent. I told that woman she could move in because I thought she was a lady. Wrong kind of lady, I know now."

"Have you any idea where this man works, where he lived before?"

"Said he had a job driving a cab. He likes this room because it's close to the cab stand. He can walk to work."

Julian puzzled over this information. He was reasonably certain Oakmont didn't have a taxi stand. The town had none of the usual places where such a thing might exist. "Which cab stand did he mean, Tidy?"

"Why're you asking all these questions? What business is it of yours?"

"I'm just not sure about you renting to some guy off the street." *Where's Claire when she's needed?* he thought.

"He's got a job; he's got the money to rent the room. That's enough for me."

"Tidy, do you remember calling me a while ago? The woman who had rented the room upset you."

"What do you mean I called you? You called me, saying you were coming for a visit. And I'm telling you what happened here."

Julian quickly considered the best course of action. "Maybe we should call Claire. Have you told her about these renters?"

"Why would I go yakking to everyone in town about what I do? You county people are as nosy as you can be. I'm taking care of my business all my life. I'm not stopping now."

"Tidy, I'm not with the county ... Please, let's call Claire."

Tidy sat up straight on the couch, and Julian expected further argument. Instead she grabbed at the phone receiver. The tangled cord, as usual, put the receiver on too short a leash for Tidy to bring it to her ear. The receiver slipped from her hand and went crashing into the coffee table. "Shit." She sat back, all huffy. "What's that buzzing noise?"

"The dial tone on the phone, Tidy. Let me get this untangled so you can call Claire."

"Why should I be calling her?"

"To talk to her about the difficulty of renting your room to someone trustworthy," Julian said while letting the dangling receiver unwind itself. From the corner of his eye he caught the changing emotions on Tidy's face: anger, doubt, sadness. His own emotions moved with hers: angry he was the one left to untwist her life, just like the phone cord; doubting, after the cord was untangled, he could make a difference; then sad he was so ineffectual.

"If you'd like to make a call, please hang up and try again." The loud voice disrupted the gloomy room.

Julian pressed the phone disconnect and handed the receiver, with a new dial tone, to Tidy. She hesitated. He waited for her to ask what she should be doing. Instead she said, "I don't know the number." Julian, being good with numbers in general, recited it from memory. He hovered close in order to hear both sides of the conversation.

"Hello."

"This here's Tidy."

"Tidy. What a pleasant surprise."

"No surprise to me. And it isn't pleasant neither."

"What's bothering you?"

"The check man is here, and he's causing trouble."

"Trouble?"

"Yes, he's saying I shouldn't be renting my room."

Julian's neck turned red. "I didn't—"

In a louder voice, Tidy continued, "One day he's saying I don't have enough money; the next he's saying I do and I don't need to rent the room. Then he's saying I'm renting to bad people ... but I already know that bitch was bad. The new man is fine. Drives a cab, and he's got money to rent the room. And it isn't any business of the check man."

Claire interrupted the harangue. "Tidy, I was thinking about coming for a visit today or tomorrow. Perhaps you and I could talk about all this then. May I stop by in the morning?"

"You coming to visit, you mean?"

"Yes. How would tomorrow be?"

"Mighty fine."

Claire said, "Why don't you tell Julian I'll be visiting soon? He'll feel better if you tell him I'll be calling on you."

"I'll look forward to your visit," Tidy said cheerfully. She thumped the receiver into the phone console and looked at Julian triumphantly. "She told me to tell you to bug off."

Julian started to bristle but surprised himself when he instead laughed. He quickly coughed and brought his hand up to cover his jaw to disguise the laughter. Too late. A peek at Tidy, and he laughed harder. Tidy giggled, chortled, and finally cackled.

"I guess I'll be bugging off," Julian said. "I'll come back tomorrow to finish the February bills. See you." He let himself out the door, stepping around the mess on the stoop.

When Julian reached the street, he felt unaccountably despondent. He walked the long way back to his office, shunning the busy boulevard connecting Oakmont and Ridley for the quieter residential streets and the small park they surrounded. His thoughts went to Emily and the evening she had introduced Tidy's plight to him.

The arguments about their infertility had made the evenings chilly and conversations over dinner strained. On this particular evening, however, Emily had cooked her coq au vin, one of his favorites. If he'd been a little more attuned to her wiles, he might have recognized a plot. She'd asked if he ever felt lonely.

"Not with you around. How could I be?"

"I meant before, while you were growing up."

"You know I did." In his mind he stood at the edge of a soccer field, knobby kneed, never invited to join the neighborhood game. He'd moved too often to make friends, or so his aunties had told him. In truth, he was sure everyone had thought him a dweeb—too smart for the other kids; not smart enough according to the aunties.

"The Senior Outreach group is trying to assist an elderly woman over in Oakmont. She needs help paying her bills, writing checks, keeping track of her expenses ..." The hook planted, Emily had reeled him in.

"She's lonely too," Emily had said.

As hard as he tried, Julian couldn't shake that thought. And his reaction to the baggage on the stoop penetrated his soul deeper than he would want to admit. *What an inglorious affair for Tidy's long life: renting a room to a prostitute because she thinks she needs the money to survive.* So sad.

But Julian knew it couldn't be just the money that led Tidy to do these things. He wondered, was she so desperate for company she'd welcome anyone off the street? Even a prostitute?

———

After getting the February checks into the mail, Julian considered taking a two-week break. After only a week, though, he realized the bank statements would be in, and he decided he should check for problems. His desk was cleared by midafternoon, and he called Tidy for an appointment. He drove by on his way home. Miraculously he found a parking place directly in front of the green porch. He sprang up the steps of the stoop and jabbed the doorbell. Not waiting for Tidy to holler, he swung open the outer gate to charge inside, but his entry was blocked.

A young man, short, Hispanic-looking, in brown pants and a white T-shirt, his feet bare, stood squarely in the doorway. He had a dark complexion, dark eyes, and shiny black hair—a handsome dude. Julian startled himself with that expression. Handsome or not, what was he doing in Tidy's house?

"I'm Pedro. Tidy's here; come in."

Julian's bewildered face amused Tidy. "Surprised you! This here's Pedro. He's my new tenant. The bitch didn't work out, so Pedro's here. Paid me a whole month's rent. Cash. I got plenty of money now. You don't need to worry about paying those bills anymore." She beamed at Julian. "I'm fixing the money problem myself."

Julian had forgotten about the new renter. "My name's Julian. I look after Ms. Bourbon's financial matters. I visit every week or two." He glared into Pedro's eyes, making sure Pedro understood how seriously he took the "look after" part. He didn't care for the fact that Pedro was a man. It didn't sit right.

Pedro returned Julian's scowl. "Lucky for her she has so many people taking care of her."

"I'm trying to remember if Tidy told me about your job. You work ...?"

"I got a job."

"Driving a cab."

Pedro shook his head. "Ms. Bourbon's confusing me with someone else."

"So what do you do, exactly?"

Pedro's short, compact body quivered as every muscle reacted. "I work for a janitorial service." The words lined up like stones.

"Regular hours?"

"You think I'm some kind of day laborer?"

Pedro's strong accent did suggest he hadn't been in the States long, but his English wasn't bad, Julian grudgingly admitted. "I'm wondering if you have a green card."

"You insulting me?"

Julian ignored the challenge. "Who do you work for?"

If Julian had been a little more streetwise, he would have seen the possible danger. Pedro's whole being was like a clenched fist. "Nate's Nighttime Cleaning."

"You work at night."

"Aren't you the smart one."

"Your hours are what?"

"What business is it of yours? You her bodyguard? You look too puny to me."

Julian seethed. The suggestion that his six-foot-two-inch frame was inferior to Pedro's five-foot-five … stocky or not … He was incensed. But Pedro had the build of a weight lifter. Julian was a runner. They were in tight quarters—weight lifter's advantage.

Julian took a step back. "Look, I'm sorry. I want to be satisfied that my friend is okay—financially. It would help if we knew your employment is secure."

Pedro hesitated, and Julian sensed a minute release of tension. "You want to know if I can pay the rent? I can."

"Did you live around here previously?"

Pedro audibly sucked a breath in. "You can't let it go, can you?"

"Most rentals ask for references."

"Sorry, you're right." A long exhale. "My wife threw me out last week. I've been sleeping in my car since then. With the deposits, I haven't been able to find anything I can afford. Ms. Bourbon is a lifesaver."

Tidy took her cue. "He understands my rules. I'm not having any fooling going on here. No one else in his room. He keeps things clean. He behaves. He can stay as long as he's proper."

Julian huffed, and Pedro smiled. "I've promised."

Turning to Tidy, Pedro said, "I got to go collect some of my things before my wife gets home from work. Need to get a move on. See you later." He grabbed a plaid shirt hanging on the desk chair and put it on as he hurried to his room. In a moment he left by the back door, hauling a black denim jacket over his shoulder.

Julian glanced at Tidy, who was flush with her cleverness.

"Glad you like Pedro." She smiled. "He's right nice. Been helping me around the house too, vacuuming and all."

Julian surveyed the rug and grudgingly acknowledged the lint and hair and bits of food normally strewn about had vanished. Even an old coffee stain near the kitchen had disappeared. *So he can vacuum*, he thought derisively. "Is he paying you a good rent?" Not a well-formed question, but Julian's curiosity rushed the words from his mouth.

"Paying me six hundred a month."

Julian was aghast at the thought of paying $600 to live with Tidy. He blurted, "He paid you with a check?"

"No, he had a big pile of bills in his pocket. Counted out six hundred while I watched."

"And you put the money in the bank?"

"Heavens no. I'm keeping it here for my groceries and things."

"Keeping it where, Tidy?"

"In my bag, where else?" Tidy rummaged around in the red vinyl bag at her side and withdrew her black Velcro wallet. She opened it to display a wad of bills.

"Tidy, six hundred's a lot of money. Wouldn't it be safer to make a bank deposit?"

"You're not very bright sometimes. Why would I put the money in the bank and then just take it out again 'cause I need to buy something?"

Julian smiled wanly. "Okay, but if you're going to keep the money here—which I would not advise—then I have to be confident you made the transfer we discussed to cover the February bills. Did you?"

"I did not. You're slower than a herd of turtles. I don't need a transfer now. I got all this money from the rent." She glared at him. Julian's shoulders slumped, and he gave up the argument, moving to the desk to check the shoebox.

It was missing. "Tidy, where's our mailbox?"

"What're you talking about?"

"The box where you're supposed ... Ah, you need—that is, we *agreed* you would stack your mail ... you know, all the envelopes."

"The big ole shoebox?"

"Yes, the shoebox."

Tidy smiled. "I decided to hide my jewelry, so that Mexican can't steal it. I put my good things in the box and hid it."

Julian sighed. "Where did you put the mail then?"

Her smile faded. Julian watched her begin to concentrate, her eyes darting left and right and then landing at her lap. Her face emptied of expression. "I'm thinking," she said softly.

Julian addressed the love of his life, in absentia: *I'm dying here, Emmy. Dying. How can I possibly do this job when this ... this grandmother keeps changing the rules?*

"In the bottom drawer," Tidy interrupted Julian's silent conversation. "I been putting all the envelopes in the bottom drawer of my dresser."

"In your bedroom."

"Yes." Tidy brightened, having brought this troublesome question to a satisfactory answer. "You go take a look."

Julian entered the bedroom and faced the dresser. He had to squat to reach the bottom drawer. His nose came to the level of the dresser top and an open jar of Bengay. The sharp medicinal smell distracted him. Auntie Meg, the eldest, had used the stuff, always complaining of aches and pains and holding Julian responsible for them.

He shook his head and pulled out the drawer. He stared. *Oh*

God. Thoughts of Auntie Meg vanished. A pile of envelopes, advertisements, grocery ads, and flyers for credit cards cluttered the left side. The rest of the drawer contained lingerie ... bras, panties, stuff that shone like silk but probably wasn't, and a boned garment looking like a corset—not that Julian had ever seen a corset before. As his eyes passed over this mass of lace and nylon and hooks and hems, they came to a piece of metal, half covered by a bra cup. There was no mistaking the appearance of a gun barrel.

"You finding the mail?" Tidy called from the living room.

"Yes, yes, I found ... I found the mail," he yelled back. With a single fingertip, Julian raised the bra cup. It was a small gun. Julian had no knowledge of guns, had never even had one in his hand, ever, having avoided any military service, thank goodness. But, in any case, his mind went numb. *Why is this weapon in Tidy's underwear drawer?*

"What's keeping you then?"

Julian came out of his shock, quickly scooped up the mail, stood, closed the drawer with his foot, and returned to the living room. He sat at the desk and began to sort the papers, his brain whirling with his discovery. With his head down, he spoke into his hands. "Tidy, did you tell me once you were afraid? Being here alone, I mean."

"Afraid? Why should I be afraid?"

"You told me you were uncomfortable staying in the house alone."

"I'm not alone anymore. Pedro's living here with me now ... like Ivan. He's taking care of me. I don't need to worry about a thing."

Julian picked up the next piece of paper—notice of a check returned because of insufficient funds, the car insurance. He turned his full attention to the issue. This was what he was here for: fixing her finances—not discovering guns or helping her with her loneliness or safety. That was Claire's job.

"Tidy, we have a problem." He rose from the desk and moved to the ottoman. He hated the wretched stool, but he would avoid sitting on the couch unless absolutely necessary.

"What kind of problem?"

Julian spelled out the whole explanation of income and outgo, once again, and how sometimes the checking account came up short. Tidy returned with the usual ranting about how "that Emily" said she had enough money to pay for everything. He explained the transfer process once more. It was a tennis volley, back and forth, back and forth.

Her backhand lob: she had enough money now, because of the money from Pedro's rent.

"But you've got that money in your wallet." Overhand smash of her lob. "We can't write checks on your wallet."

"That's a good'un." Tidy grinned and slapped the side of her thigh. "You're funny when you want to be." The tennis ball bounced to the edge of the court and stopped, waiting.

Her face turned sober.

What now? Julian fidgeted.

"You take this money and put it in the bank, so we don't have this kind of trouble again."

The corners of Julian's mouth twitched. "I shouldn't make a cash deposit for you, Tidy, but we could go to the bank *together.* Why don't we drive down to the bank and get Emily to deposit the rent money for you?"

"What fun." Tidy smiled.

Julian didn't think any of this was fun.

At the bank, the manager informed them Emily was with

another customer. Tidy was disgruntled; Julian was relieved. They stood in line to make the deposit at a teller's window. Tidy rapped her cane impatiently while Julian alternately shuffled his feet to avoid the cane and glanced furtively around the bank lobby, hoping no one noticed him with the ornery old lady.

After delivering Tidy home, he sat in his car for a good fifteen minutes thinking about the pistol in Tidy's drawer. Questions swirled in his mind: Should he tell someone? Claire? She should know, for her own protection. Maybe she already knew. But if she did, why hadn't she told him—for *his* safety? Did Tidy have a license for the thing? Was he abetting a criminal? Tidy, a criminal? Had she ever shot the gun?

So many questions he wished he didn't have to ask, so many questions he really didn't want to know the answers to.

Chapter 16

Claire

On Friday Claire got a call from Tony Powell, an Adult Protective Services caseworker. He'd recently taken a report regarding a Tidy Bourbon, and a routine check with the sheriff's elder-abuse department had indicated Claire was involved. Tony said the caller had given an account of Ms. Bourbon ("Is that pronunciation correct?") driving erratically and some distance from her home.

"How far from home?" Claire asked.

"She lives in Oakmont, right? Our caller said he met her in San Francisco."

Claire was stunned. "What makes you believe the caller was not telling a tall tale?" she asked, although she judged the story too outlandish to be made up.

Tony said the report had sounded genuine to him. The caller had given details of his encounter with Ms. Bourbon at the bottom of the Fremont Street ramp on the San Francisco side of the bridge. Ms. Bourbon had been lost, frightened, the caller had said; he'd offered to show her the way back. "He admitted that the incident happened some time ago, said he was sorry he didn't call earlier. He's been helping over at the Mission shelter, and it slipped his mind."

"Seriously, he said that?"

"Yup. May have been something else that caused him to forget. 'Helping' at the shelter may mean he's homeless and had other things to attend to first."

"Did this caller have a name?"

"He asked to remain anonymous, although at the beginning of the call he identified himself as Isaac. Said he's from San Francisco, but he knows 'the system.' That's why he called us; he knew Ms. Bourbon's county agency was the one to contact. He felt sure Ms. Bourbon could use some help."

Claire bristled slightly with that statement. It implied she wasn't doing her job. No, no, she knew better.

"Sergeant Rios said you were on top of the case and your report would be reliable."

That was better.

"Is there anything you think we could do to help?" Tony asked. "I don't mean to make it sound like we're dumping this back on you, but I'm not sure what we could do that you're not already doing."

"Thanks for your confidence, Tony. I'd say we're pretty tuned in to her needs and the problems she's having. We've put a money manager in place, and I hope to get her to accept some in-home services, if not move to an assisted-living facility."

"Would it be okay to say good luck? From what Sergeant Rios told me, you've got your hands full."

Claire laughed. "I'll be calling you if we need more assistance. Thanks for the report from this Isaac fellow."

After hanging up with Tony, Claire brooded about the

driving business. She knew Julian wanted the car to vanish, along with its costs. If Tidy'd move to a facility, she wouldn't need to find her own transportation.

Since it was Friday, it was too late, she concluded, to do anything productive about the problem. She only hoped Tidy had been frightened enough that she'd stick close to home for a while. She made a note to call Julian on Monday afternoon.

Julian

Tax season was pinching Julian's free time, but midday on Monday he blocked out an hour to check Tidy's mail. He approached her house with some trepidation. Would he have to look in the underwear drawer again? The idea forced him to reconsider the gun in the dresser. What should he do about it?

Tidy looked at ease, almost content. Julian considered that Pedro's presence might be having a positive effect after all, but he didn't have time to take this line of thinking any further as he came upon a staggering sight. The coffee table was covered with envelopes and flyers, but they were, curiously, stacked in piles. The stacks seemed to have something to do with size or category—department store sales announcements in one group; postcard advertisements in another; letters from banks, windowed envelopes, and political solicitations in their own piles. All the mail was organized, orderly, cornered, evenly spaced across the table, in an almost obsessive way. As he might have organized them, Julian mused.

"Tidy, what's this on the table?"

"Nice and neat, ain't it?"

"Is this all the mail?"

"Yep, I've been working on this arranging every day."

"You didn't put anything in the bureau drawer?"

"No."

"Nothing?"

"Why you want to get into my drawers?"

Julian's prior feeling of contentment evaporated as Tidy glared at him.

"Quit your snooping around."

Julian grabbed the stack of window envelopes, figuring these would be the most interesting to him and stalked to the desk. A quick inspection turned up an envelope with FasTrak as the return address. Curious. Inside he found notice of a fine for driving through the Bay Bridge FasTrak lane without a payment device. *Must be some mistake,* Julian thought. In the upper right corner a small photograph of the offending vehicle's license plate was displayed. *Has to be a mistake.* While Tidy puttered in the kitchen, making coffee, he snuck out the back door for a quick peek at the license plate on her tank. It matched.

"Tidy." He stood at the kitchen door. "Did you and Pedro go someplace in the car together?"

"Pedro drive me someplace? Well, if that don't put pepper in the gumbo. Why would he do such?"

The gumbo bit washed right over him he was so bent on the FasTrak photo. "I'm not sure, but here, we have a bill for your car going across the Bay Bridge and not paying the toll." He flapped the envelope noisily.

"What're you talking about? I never drive so far."

"Did Pedro borrow your car?"

"He says he won't drive my car for nothing. Says it's out of date."

As he tried to think what "out of date" might mean, Julian eyed the FasTrak photograph again. Without hiding his actions this time, he whipped open the back door and peered at Tidy's car. The registration tags on the rear license were two years old.

He banged the back door shut, strode into the living room, and flopped onto the desk chair. *Her account is overdrawn, so she accepts boarders to make ends meet,* Julian ranted silently. *Not only is this car sucking money out of her account, money she needs to live on, she is actually driving it. Driving! With no license*—and *expired tags!* His mind was in a rage.

Tidy passed him on the way to her throne, a cup of coffee in hand. He wrestled with the papers on the desk for a while but couldn't concentrate. This car business was dangerous. She could kill someone. So much noise was jangling inside his head he almost missed her quiet voice from the couch.

"I got lost, made a wrong turn. Somehow I'm on the highway. Cars speeding so fast, I was scared. They're honking and honking. I couldn't look at the signs to figure what to do. I just keep going, hoping to find a place to ask. At the tollbooths, I wanted ask the toll person, but no person's in the booth. Thought I was in a closed one, but cars behind me kept honking and honking. So I go ahead. I was confused."

Julian detected the possibility of tears again. He stood, hesitated, and, without thinking why, moved to sit by her on the couch. He interrupted her tale, in hopes of changing the emotional direction. "How did you get home?"

"On t'other side of the bridge, I pulled over and asked a man for directions. He's telling me I'm a long way from home. I tell him I'll pay him, if he'd get in the car and show me how to get home."

Julian's jaw didn't actually drop, but his silent reaction was otherwise similar. "Did he tell you his name?"

"He might have. I don't remember."

"But you paid him."

"Two hundred dollars."

"*Two*—" Julian started to explode; Tidy's expression stopped him. "Two hundred," he said more gently.

"Had to take a taxi back, he said. Cost him, he said."

Julian sank into the couch. To stop the bizarre images of Tidy's bridge crossing coursing through his brain, he summoned himself to task: call Claire. She *had* to deal with this business now because it was insane not to.

He told Tidy that he had to get back to the office and that he'd come again at noon the next day. When she didn't respond to the prospect of a visit, he thought, *She must be seriously upset.*

He walked only as far as the corner and pulled out his cell phone. He related the story to Claire, getting all worked up again. "Two hundred dollars to some bum off the street, who's now well informed of where the money bag lives. What was she thinking?"

"Julian, I know—"

"What do you mean, you know? How can you know? How could you—"

"Julian!" she yelled against his rant. "Adult Protective Services called me on Friday to describe the incident. Her savior made a report to them. She was desperate, Julian, and it sounds to me like this bum, as you call him, was a Good Samaritan. We shouldn't judge."

Julian spun on his heels in frustration and then slumped against a sidewalk tree. "Thanks for the *we* when you meant *me.* But listen, Claire. The business of her driving is more serious. She could kill someone." He jabbed the tree with his fist.

"Let's do this …"

He lowered his head with relief. Claire wouldn't argue this time.

"Disable the car. Dismantling the battery should be good enough. Put a note under the hood, near the battery, saying something like 'Please do not repair this car. The owner should not be driving.' Then if Tidy can't start the car and calls a mechanic, they won't put her back on the road—hopefully."

"What if she sees me messing with her car? She'll have my neck!"

"Visit her tomorrow, and call me when you've left her. I'll phone her then and keep her busy for a few minutes while you go around to the back and fix the car."

———

The next day, Julian walked briskly to Tidy's house. For once, he wasn't concerned about her finances; the car business had to be dealt with. Would Tidy remember he was supposed to come by today? He couldn't remember if she'd said it was okay or not. He smiled at the notion the two of them could be equally dotty.

He rounded onto Main Street, striding briskly. A waist-high picket fence—painted white, thank heaven—began at the corner of Tidy's property and extended the length of her yard along the sidewalk, with a break for her front walk. At the edge of the yard, he stopped, puzzled by the scene before him.

A ragged-looking fellow was bouncing around, throwing handfuls of grass in the air, and yelling. "I worked all morning. How can you say I haven't done anything?"

On the sidewalk, Julian cocked his head. Tidy screeched inside from an open window, "I'm not giving you one damn dime."

The guy in the yard looked to be in his thirties. He was tall and slim and was wearing jeans, a white T-shirt streaked with grass stains, and a denim jacket smeared with mud. *Probably one of the locals from the bar around the corner,* Julian judged. The man's brown hair, uncut in a while, curled below his ears. He hadn't shaved in at least three days.

"I've done everything you asked me: clipped the shrubs, pulled the weeds from the flower beds, cut the grass better than you, you old bat head. You're just like they said, loony."

"Don't you be calling me names. You got no respect. And the lawn looks like shit, all those weeds."

"I can't help it if there's more weeds than grass. Pull up all those weeds, nothing'd be left."

"And so I'm not paying you. They're still weeds. The neighbor's dog'd do a better job than you."

"So call the neighbor's dog and get him over here, but you got to pay me for the work I've done. You owe me for three hours."

"I don't owe you a dime, not one stinking dime."

Julian listened dumbstruck, but after a moment, he sensed a need to act. He marched to Tidy's front door, rang the bell, and knocked, as usual. Tidy bellowed, but the words went out the window to the yardman, not to Julian. The door stood half-open, so Julian let himself in.

He paused in the doorway to the living room, viewing Tidy's backside at the window. With a fury of slamming doors, clomping shoes, and loud verbiage, the yardman ripped through the back door and shouted, "You old hag, you do this to everyone. I'm never working for you again." He saw Julian and lowered his voice but continued to rail at Tidy for not paying what she owed him.

Tidy turned from the window, almost losing her balance as she moved too quickly, her eyes blazing hot coals, her face taut with her anger. She flailed her arms at the man. "Get out of here, you bastard. You no-good good-for-nothing. Get out!"

Julian, still speechless, looked on. He had little experience with people high on something, but the wildness of the nameless yardman's eyes, his exaggerated movements, and his raucous voice suggested he was not entirely sober. Then again, Julian's knowledge of this form of life didn't extend far. The guy might be strung out on speed, and Julian would have no notion. In fact, Tidy didn't sound all that different from the yard guy—strident, out of control, abusive—and Julian was *certain*, relatively certain, Tidy didn't drink or do drugs. It was a ludicrous idea, but Julian thought it was also rather funny: a ninety-two-year-old woman on speed.

The amusement slithered away as the yard guy marched across the living room, brushing past Julian. He whipped open the inner door and slammed the outer gate so hard two hinge screws already loose fell to the stoop. He resumed his yelling outside, getting into his car. "I'm telling everyone in town—including the dogs—not to work for you. You are a cheat." He started his battered Chevy and peeled out of the parking space, leaving a modicum of rubber on the street.

In her best voice Tidy screamed, "You're a goddamn crook."

Julian stood still against the living room wall, not sure how to follow up on this scene.

Tidy, lurching toward the couch, was immediately transformed by his presence. "Juli, you're here. I'm glad." Cheerful.

Julian watched her emotions change as if someone had flipped a switch. Angry ... cheerful. It confounded him.

"Who was that?"

"Friend of the bums down the street. Said he'd trim up my yard for me, make it neat. You look yonder and tell me if he did anything," she said.

Julian poked his head out the window and examined the yard work from another perspective. Piles of grass clippings and trimmings from the bushes spotted the tiny yard. He remembered the yard being seriously overgrown, but now pockets of air appeared among the blackberry brambles along the back fence; the oleanders at the side property line had been trimmed into a uniform hedge; the flower beds close to the house were winter bare and muddy with the recent rains. The yardman had been right about the weed-choked lawn. "Appears he did something; maybe he hasn't finished," Julian said, trying to be equivocal.

"Man ain't worth two dead flies," she ranted, but catching Julian's eye, she laughed.

Julian couldn't help smiling too. "Another southern expression?"

"May be, but it sure is that SOB. Don't deserve a dime. Calls me a cheat, but he's crooked as a dog's hind leg." She chuckled.

The tyrant of the previous minutes morphed into the softer southern lady. *What's next?* he mused. He shook his head, not believing the word *lady* could come to mind in conjunction with Tidy. He wandered about the living room looking for pieces of mail. As his gazed reached the coffee table, he sighed. It had been swept clean. Only a few window envelopes lay on the desk.

"I trashed all those piles from yesterday. They're just a few I wasn't sure about, so I put them on the desk for you. You know better what's important."

Julian kept his eyes on her without comment for a moment.

He tried to imagine what had happened in the last twenty-four hours.

"Are you thinking me out of my mind?"

He didn't, and that was the problem for him. This Tidy seemed sound, balanced, and ... what? Normal? It was as if he were dealing with a whole new Tidy.

The envelopes were solicitations, clever in their appearance: "free medical equipment" was written on the outside of one; "your last chance" on another; "lower your property tax for only $98" on yet another. One was a deal for a reverse mortgage: "more income for your golden years." *How do the crooks get away with this kind of solicitation? Preying on the vulnerable senior population,* Julian fumed. *It's obscene.*

"These are nothing we need to worry about, Tidy, but thank you for saving them for me." Without any other reason to continue the visit, he made his exit to call Claire and get the car business done. "I'll be back soon," he told Tidy as he left.

He went around the corner, sat on the bus stop bench, and tried to pull together all his thoughts about the "old bat head." It had been pretty ill mannered of the yardman to call her that. The scene had been funny in its way but not fair to Tidy. He thought back to his earlier visits when he'd come close to calling her something similar to a bat head himself. Now having experienced a broader range of her activity, he was becoming afraid for her.

The image of the gun crashed across his conscience and merged with the different personalities he'd seen Tidy exhibit. *Whatever does she use the gun for? Why does she even have a gun?*

He yanked his cell phone from his belt and called Claire.

Chapter 17

Claire

Claire was relieved by Julian's attentions to Tidy's financial matters, and he provided some oversight with his more frequent visits. His supervision in fact had proved commendable when he'd reported Tidy's rental activity. Claire had visited to check out the situation. Despite Julian's objections, she'd found Pedro rather charming, sincere, and hardworking.

On the ottoman the next day she struggled to guide her and Tidy's chatter around to transportation, but to no avail. Thus she was not able to judge whether Tidy had been affected by her trip to San Francisco.

Julian "fixing" Tidy's car gave her some relief. News stories of seniors plowing onto sidewalks and injuring—or worse, killing—people were scary. Statistics were especially onerous for drivers over eighty. She didn't recall seeing anything about drivers over ninety.

These problems didn't surface if you died early, she brooded. *See what you missed?* she silently addressed her late husband.

When her mother had died at eighty-six, Claire had made

that age her own benchmark. She needed to be gone by then, she'd vowed—but not too much earlier. Before she checked out, she wanted time to watch her daughter's life develop, perhaps have the pleasure of a grandchild. How to manage the time left was her dilemma. Whenever she visited a client in a skilled nursing facility, she pledged to drive over a cliff before allowing herself to end up in such circumstance. But if she could no longer drive, no longer had a car to drive, how would this be accomplished?

Julian

A few days after he unhooked Tidy's car battery, Julian called her with a flimsy excuse to ask for a visit. So, okay, he was curious. He wondered if she had discovered his vandalism and if her sense of order regarding the paperwork would last. And in spite of himself, he wondered if anything else was going on in the "fun" house.

She said, of course, he could visit anytime. *Door's open,* he mimicked to himself as she herself said it. But he grinned at the familiar phrase. He took pleasure in the fact that it was familiar.

He set out along the boulevard, enjoying the sunny sidewalk, passing tables outside the coffee bar and the produce in bins against the windows of Joe's Fruits and Vegetables. Fiona's Floral Shoppe came next; her buckets of budding narcissi and yellow bursts of forsythia and pots of early tulips and daisies were stacked in tiers. The flashes of color caused Julian to stop. He surveyed the display, wondering which would be finest. A small pot of violets hid at one end—tiny deep-purple blossoms with yellow streaks in the center. She might like them, he mused, or would she scoff at them, call them puny or the wrong shade of purple? He stood with indecision, looked at his watch, at the violets, and finally resumed his hike to Oakmont—empty-handed.

At the corner of Tidy's property, Julian paused and examined the yard. Tiny, like everything else about her real estate, it had, nevertheless, a certain charm. The winter rains had turned plants green again, and a few bright-red azaleas poked through the brambles, trimmed by the yardman. Pure-white calla lilies grew hardily against the warmth of the house. A singular purple hyacinth braved an otherwise vacant plot in the center of the garden.

His gaze moved around the yard to the house and slammed to a halt at the front stoop. Tidy sat on the steps, watching him.

"Waiting for you. Taking your time."

"It takes me thirty minutes to walk … doesn't matter. I'm surprised to find you out on the stoop."

"Beautiful day. I thought I'd enjoy the sunshine." Her eyes never left Julian's. Disconcerted, he shifted his eyes back to the garden but then returned his attention to her face. Her eyes continued their calm regard of him.

"Shall we go inside?" he asked, hoping to break the spell.

"No, I want to show you something."

She led him around the house to the back corner where a half stairway descended to a basement door. Using her cane for support, Tidy struggled down the stairs, bringing both feet to one step before moving to the next. Julian watched her for a moment before realizing he should be helping her. Embarrassed and defensive at once, he rationalized that she hadn't asked him for assistance.

With a key she extracted from a sweater pocket, she unlocked the door and flipped the switch for a bare lightbulb in the center of a single unfinished room. The floor was roughly planked; the bottom edge of high windows at the far end sat at ground level. The space covered about half of the house's footprint. Unpainted wallboard had been tacked onto supporting studs to form crude walls. There was no ceiling, just the beams for the floor above.

A few cartons and two broken chairs—all covered with an inch of dust—lay scattered over the floor. An old steamer trunk occupied a central position. Tidy made straight for the trunk and knocked on the top, as if she wished to enter. Instead she demanded of Julian, "Open this. You have to undo the catch."

Julian approached slowly, leery of the unusual activity. The damp air in the basement smelled of mushrooms growing in the corners. But it was too cold for mushrooms. The dankness sent a shiver down his back.

The hasp on the trunk flapped open; he pulled up the tongue and lifted the top. A small, beautifully carved cedar box lay inside the otherwise empty space.

"Mr. Browning," she said. "His ashes. Been here all these years, and I want him buried with me. He was a good man."

Julian froze. Ashes … ashes of her dead husband?

"No one knows."

Why did he have to?

"I'm asking you—be sure he's buried with me." She turned and plodded out of the basement into the sunshine.

He lowered the lid of the trunk and followed her, brushing the sleeves of his shirt as if to rid himself of the basement's dank and death. Tidy was already at the back door, letting herself inside. Julian closed the basement door and started to call after her for the key, but she had disappeared. He retreated slowly, trying to process what had just happened. In his accountancy work he had often been asked to construct financial documents for his clients' later life and witness some end-of-life papers, but becoming the warden of someone's ashes was sobering and, for Julian, disturbing. He considered making a speech to her about this task being beyond the purview of his work. *And anyway, she isn't dying*, he thought. *Why show me the cedar box now?*

He came through the back door and regarded his client moving toward her throne. A bewildering ache formed behind his eyes. Julian had no experience with death as yet. An orphan, yes, but he had been barely three when his parents had died in a car crash; he had no memory of the time. Passed from relative to relative, he'd never experienced real family intimacy. He had never been close to anyone, until he'd met Emily. And if asked, he would say he was too young to have to think about death.

He threw back his shoulders to banish the emotion and strode into the living room to begin searching for papers and mail. He'd meant to bring a new shoebox, but the evening before, just as he'd headed for the closet to search for one, Emily had diverted his attention.

Looking down at a new mess on Tidy's coffee table, he recalled this diversion and was buoyed by the pleasure of the memory. He sifted through the mound on the table and uncovered Tidy's calendar. He idly looked over the last few weeks. Every one of his visits was noted, and noted accurately on the days he'd come to visit her. "Check man here today." A smile tugged at the corners of his mouth. Jottings of other visitors spotted other days: Claire, Bernie, and Blackie. In the box for the previous Sunday she had written "Tidy alone today."

Another shroud of depression descended. In the years after his parents had died, Julian had been alone too—in spirit, if not actually. The mantle of loneliness had finally faded when he'd met Emily. Her sunny disposition and enthusiasm for life filled him with unexpected joy. Tidy might be ninety-two, eccentric, and often loony, but looking at her sitting on the couch, he beheld his boyhood self: sad and desolate in the loneliness.

He was drawn to the ottoman as if it might provide comfort instead of physical distress. A cascade of questions tumbled through his brain. How had she met Mr. Browning? How long had they been married? When had he died? She must have cared deeply for him; she had saved his ashes. For how long?

After a minute of undisturbed silence, Julian couldn't manage to articulate anything more than "I'll be back later in the week." He rose to take his leave. The mound on the coffee table could wait.

In her soft southern voice, she replied, "Thank you. You've been mighty kind."

———

On Monday, Julian sat in his office considering the manila file on the desk before him. The name Tidy Bourbon was neatly printed on the tab. Her address and phone number were written on the outside cover. Inside, the folder was empty. So unlike Julian. He normally kept fastidious notes: the client's financial goals, accounts to remember. After a client meeting, he would write a summary of the matters discussed, conclusions made, actions agreed upon. He typically logged every client phone call, and every time he opened a client file, he noted the day and time and work completed.

He had taken Tidy as a client two months ago; visited her, often several times a week; called her for appointments; and gone to the bank with her. But the file before him was devoid of even a Post-it. He had no idea what to say about what he had been doing all this time. Making notes about her financial affairs seemed irrelevant somehow.

———

On his next visit to Tidy, he found her sitting, complacent on her throne, sipping coffee, the snowy TV blaring, the newspaper in her lap.

"How're things today, Tidy?" he hollered. She couldn't have heard him, so, somewhat rudely, he grabbed the TV remote and muted the sound.

"What do you think you're doing?"

"I thought we could communicate better if we could hear each other."

"I heard you all right. Things are fine. About time you showed up. That new shoebox you brought is overflowing."

Julian went to the desk to sit and pulled down the box for his new running shoes. Nothing but junk, until he uncovered one envelope from the tax assessor's office—the property tax he had been expecting. He opened the bill, and the anticipated bad news doubled: she owed *both* installments. The first installment, due in November, had never been paid. "Now we've got trouble," he mumbled.

"What kind of trouble?"

Julian glowered. She had excellent hearing, he fumed, despite the volume on the phone and the loud TV. "Property taxes," he said, grinding his teeth.

"Never pays them."

"Evidently, but you'll be in trouble if you don't."

"Thought you said we was already in trouble."

Not unlike Tidy's hearing, his sense of humor was selective. He took a second or two to decide on his choice for this moment: funny or not. He smiled. "This house is fraught with trouble, Tidy." Before she cut up again, he said, "The bill for your property taxes is here, and 'we' owe some big bucks. That's our trouble today."

"First trouble of the week, can't be all that bad. We just transfer more money, don't we?"

Julian sat in amazement. Was it possible this matter might be negotiated with so little argument? "Yes, easy as pie. I'll write out the transfer on this paper; you take it on down to Emily at the bank. Meantime, I'll make out a check here, and you can sign it now. I'll hold the check a day or two while the money is being transferred, and then I'll pop the payment in the mail."

She signed the check, and he pocketed it along with the bill.

Julian continued to sit at "his" desk, reluctant to leave but not knowing why. The longer they sat—Tidy quietly on the couch, peering out into the space of her living room, Julian twiddling his pen, lost in his pensiveness—the more he sensed an unease. Daring to look directly at her, he found her staring at him.

"What? What's on your mind?" he asked.

"You know everything, don't you?" Tidy often made this sort of accusation, only this time it didn't sound like an accusation.

"Not everything, no; I don't think so, Tidy," he said carefully.

"You know things I don't, and I'm thinking you know what I need to know." She sat composed, solemn, and intent.

"What do you need to know?" he asked, wary of her unusual mien.

"I want you to look in the closet—the one in the hallway."

Julian stood and moved nervously toward the front door,

the pistol in her underwear drawer and the chest of ashes in the basement not far from his mind. "I wasn't aware of a closet here," he said.

"It's hidden."

Another secret stash! he thought. *What will it be this time?*

"Directly opposite the door, where my coats hang on those hooks. Take the coats away, and you'll find a door."

Apprehensive now—but admittedly curious too—Julian lifted the coats. He had never noticed the door, so well hidden by the coats, but then he'd never lingered in the cramped space.

It wasn't a closet, in fact, but a hidey-hole, two to three feet square and raised off the floor. One coat covered a tiny knob; the other obscured the hinges and edges of the door.

Tidy regarded him closely. "Go on; open it." He pulled the small knob cautiously. Inside the wall space a single cardboard file box rested. "All my important papers. Bring them here," she commanded, but not in her usual loud, commanding voice.

He extracted the box. Written in the "contents" space on the side of the carton was "house deed, car deed, loan papers, will, correspondence, etc." Clearing a spot on the coffee table, he set the box before her. She lifted the top and brought out several manila envelopes, putting all back but one. "This is my last will and testament. I want you to read it."

Julian hesitated before taking the proffered envelope. "Are you sure, Tidy? A will and testament is very private stuff."

"I'm asking you to read this," she said more assertively. He opened the envelope and took out a single sheet.

"What does it say?" she asked.

"This is a simple will, leaving all your property and possessions to Mrs. Abigail Torrey."

"She's dead."

"Oh."

"What happens to my belongings if I die with this will, being Abbie's dead?"

"Your estate would go to your nearest living relative."

"There's none." A pause ensued while they each weighed the import of this fact. "What happens then?"

"Your estate goes to the State of California."

"That can't be."

"You should get a lawyer and write a new will."

"Can't trust no lawyers."

"It would be better if you did."

"I made that will myself before; you can help me make a new one."

Julian returned the will to the envelope and looked up at Tidy. Their eyes met, perhaps in agreement.

Chapter 18

Claire

On Friday, Claire found Tidy on her feet, pacing. Claire stood just inside the living room, watching as Tidy continued on to the kitchen.

"Coffee?" Tidy called back.

"No, Tidy, you know I don't drink coffee. What's the matter?"

"Why do you think something's the matter?"

"You seem ... upset, like something's wrong."

"That man."

"What man?"

"The one in Ivan's room. He's stealing from me."

"Pedro? Stealing? What exactly is he stealing?"

"Things."

"Come on, Tidy, what's going on here? What are you talking about?"

"Food. Medicine. Letter opener."

"Letter opener? Why do you think he's stealing these things?"

"They aren't here, are they?"

"Well, I'm not sure. Here's a letter opener on the coffee table where it usually is. Do you have another one?"

"It's gone, the opener."

"Tidy, your letter opener is on the coffee table. Has something else happened?"

"He's taken things from me, and I want him *out* of here."

"You don't want him renting the room? You want him to leave?"

"That's right. He's not going to live here anymore."

Claire waited. She knew well enough that elders with Tidy's cognitive issues could take any number of turns in their thinking. She could only wonder what would come next.

"He's a thief. He's stealing from me all the time. I won't have a thief in this house."

"Tidy, please sit down, so we can figure out what to do." Tidy on her feet in a fit of agitation, especially without her cane, was risky.

Tidy ignored the suggestion. "I'm tired of the stealing. They're always taking advantage."

"Tidy, please, sit down. I can't think why you're carrying on like this."

Tidy stared at Claire a moment, as if she were perplexed by the request. Then she sat, silent, her body stopping all movement. The fireworks ended, and the night sky went blank.

"Tidy?"

"Everyone steals from me," she whispered.

"Who is stealing from you?"

"All the men, take things of mine."

"What things?"

"Everything. Dish towels. Pills. Food. Letter opener. It's silver."

Claire's focus narrowed. "Silver?"

"Belonged to Mr. Browning. It's worth something, he told me. It was a wedding gift."

"You're positive it's missing?"

"Of course," she said, her strident tone returning.

"Why do you think Pedro stole these things?"

"He's living here, ain't he? He's nothing but a low-down, no-good, lazy son of a bitch who should be up, making my coffee." She pounded the sofa cushion with a fist. "He's out drinking all night, comes back to sleep off his boozing."

"Tidy, he works at night. He told you; he works for a nighttime janitorial service."

"He's supposed to be here when I get up."

"You mean he wasn't here when you got up this morning?"

"Yes, he always is."

"When you get up in the morning, Pedro is here. Where? In the kitchen?"

"He makes my coffee, just like Ivan."

The confusion did not disturb Claire. She was familiar with these inane conversations, but she had to be on the lookout for hidden concerns.

"The door to Pedro's room is closed. Is he in his room?"

"How would I know?"

"It's ten o'clock in the morning. He's most likely asleep?"

How could he still be asleep with all this yelling going on? Claire wondered.

"He should be awake, making my coffee."

"He works at night. Remember? And sleeps in the morning."

"He's supposed to be up, making my coffee. We need to go

get the noodles, sour cream, the beet-soup things, onions. He's a lazy bastard, sleeping off the drink."

"Tidy, you're talking about Ivan."

"'Course I'm talking about Ivan," she said loudly. "The no-good drunk," she spit out.

"Tidy, Ivan is in prison. A few months now. Pedro lives with you now, and he's probably asleep."

Claire moved closer to Tidy in an attempt to calm her and to change the focus of their conversation. Her shift instead spurred Tidy from the sofa. She grabbed her cane and tottered toward the back of the house. "He is not asleep; he's a no-good drunk."

She came to Pedro's room and whacked her cane against the door with surprising force. The door swung open. Claire stood behind her, ready for the battle that must be coming. The room was empty, the bed made with military precision. In fact, the whole room was immaculate, almost sterile. "Must be round at the bar, that no-good." But her invective collapsed. She appeared as surprised as Claire by the vacant and orderly room.

Tidy returned to the couch, subdued, defeated. Claire sat on the wretched ottoman. The air settled in an effort to cleanse itself of the unjustified and unnecessary vitriol.

Claire considered Tidy's opening topic—the stealing. Something had provoked her rant. She wondered what. She glanced at the dining table where the candlesticks had resided. They were missing. She must have moved them and forgotten. Claire decided to wait for Tidy to bring it up again.

"He has a new job," Tidy said softly.

"Pedro?"

"The man renting my room. He gave me his rent, first of the month, and told me he's working days now. Good for me, 'cause he's here at night. I'm better, not alone at night."

"He said he has a new job…"

"I don't remember. Just wish he knew how to cook those noodles."

Claire smiled; the harangue was over. "Speaking of noodles, have you heard from Ivan?" she asked.

"A few days ago. He's real depressed. Says he thinks they're going to keep him in jail forever this time. He misses the noodles and sour cream too. We talked about the food he's going to cook when he comes back. A rare steak, that's what he wants: a good juicy steak." Tidy chuckled, a quiet, despondent laugh. "He's still got the teeth to eat steak. With my dentures I'm glad for the noodles."

Claire watched Tidy's face. The intimacy of that exchange between Tidy and Ivan surprised and strangely disheartened her. It spoke of companionship and caring. These had been pleasures of her marriage—a solid relationship, deepening with their years together. The resemblance to Tidy's liaison with Ivan shocked her. But as a result, she recognized all too well Tidy's loss and the consequence. Lonely. The word squeezed her heart. *No, not lonely,* Claire resolved. *Isolated.*

Isolated was easier, less emotion. Tidy lived on a street with no residential traffic, no appropriate shopping, none of the services she needed, no green space in which to enjoy fresh air. Claire cataloged the reasons for assisted living. It didn't have to be about loneliness.

Of course, the consequences of isolation were … With a snap of her head, Claire banished the tugging toward emotion and attended to her client. "You must be lonely without Ivan," she said softly.

"It's mighty quiet around here without him. Pedro's always sleeping or working. He's no fun."

"Tidy, I realize you're not in favor of moving to a senior facility, but—"

"I'm not doing that, and you know it." Her voice rose, heading for strident again.

"You're a sociable person, friendly. You like to be with other people. You'd really enjoy—"

"I won't sit around and do that knit-and-crochet shit. Bunch of snobs."

"The places I'm thinking of—one right over in Nortonville—have lots of different activities. They organize bus trips to the mountains—"

"Who wants to get on a bus full of old fogies who can't even remember your name?"

"We should go visit the Royal Manor together, take a tour, have lunch, talk to some people who live there. It's a beautiful place, like a fancy hotel, linen on the tables in the dining room."

"Not interested. I have a home I take tours of every day. Don't have to pay for lunch neither."

"The lunch would be free."

"Awful food, I'm sure of it. I like my greens and fries. Bet they don't serve greens and fries at your la-di-da old-folks manor."

"They help with transportation too, take you shopping, to doctors' appointments ..."

Tidy's face snapped to Claire's. Claire remained impassive, waiting. Tidy broke the deadlock, lowering her eyes to her lap, mute on the subject.

Claire conceded defeat for the moment. Plenty of her clients had resisted moving to assisted-living facilities, with many of the same misgivings as Tidy. When they'd finally made the move, nearly all had been pleased and remarked that they wished they'd moved sooner. She had to admit it was unlikely Tidy would be one of those.

She was sure she wouldn't be one either. She herself hated bingo.

Chapter 19

Julian

At the beginning of the week, Julian had called Tidy to say he was coming to check the mail. The utilities should be sending statements of direct bank payments, instead of bills. Tidy had answered his call in a breezy voice suggesting she was in reasonable spirits.

For the moment anyway, Julian had thought. *Her life is like a roller coaster. No, that implies too much fun. Her life is like a revolving door. Each time she spins to the other side of the wall, I have no idea what craziness will turn up.*

Now, as he stood in her living room, he wondered what cuckoo deal would be in the pile of paper from the coffee table. He settled down at the desk to examine the gathered mass. He found the bank statements first. Damn. "Tidy, you made two large cash withdrawals in the past two weeks. What are they about?"

"None of your business. I need money to buy things."

So it would be the irascible Tidy today. At least Julian was on safer ground with this Tidy.

"Altogether it was five hundred dollars, and as a consequence your checking account was overdrawn when a couple of checks arrived for payment." Taking her to task about her finances was easier than talking about her long-dead husband. "You should warn me when you need that kind of cash. We'll have to transfer more money from your savings." He realized too late that he sounded reproving again.

"I already transferred the money for the checks. I went to the bank like you told me and gave my friend Emily the paper."

"That was the transfer we made when we wrote the checks. *Then* you made these withdrawals."

"I did. Miss Emily told me I could."

Savvy enough now, Julian didn't even speculate if Emily had told her this recently or if it was a memory from times past. He'd ask Emily, but in the meantime more money needed to be moved to the checking account. How on earth would he get Tidy to make this transaction? He delayed making the effort with another concern.

"Where is the money now, the cash you withdrew?"

"In my wallet." Tidy grabbed her red bag and scrounged around, but no wallet appeared. She withdrew, piece by piece, the contents of the bag—the inevitable tissues, a couple of mail advertisements, an empty vitamin jar, a red-and-black plaid scarf, and an envelope.

Julian leaned in. The water bill. He slumped on the ottoman. He had forgotten. The bimonthly bill was due this month. He hadn't realized it was missing. *No, not missing,* he corrected himself, *in Tidy's bag.* In her distraction looking for the wallet, she didn't notice Julian lift the bill from the growing detritus on the couch.

The bag empty and still no wallet, Tidy began to search the

area around her, turning over all the newspapers and flyers on the table. She rose from the couch and hobbled to her bedroom, mumbling. With a pen, Julian picked through the refuse on the couch but soon gave up. The wallet should be visible among the—*Oh gag*—used tissues.

Leaving her to hunt for the wallet—or whatever she was doing in her bedroom—he took the time to go back over the mail and ran the monthly numbers again. Given the water bill discovery *and* the extra cash withdrawals, she was, he grumbled silently, seriously overdrawn.

Minutes later Tidy returned to the middle of the living room, agitated, alarmed. "Gone. Stolen. So much money." Her eyes searched the corners of the room. "It's Bernie. She's always stealing from me."

"Who's Bernie?" He remembered seeing the name on her calendar.

"She comes over to help me now and then. She came here when Ivan went to jail. She took my wallet."

"Tidy, Ivan left weeks, months ago."

"Bernie came after, sleeping on the couch. She always taking stuff, but this is the worst. Bitch."

"Should we check with her? Maybe she'll remember where the wallet is?" Julian was alarmed. Five hundred dollars was a lot of money for Tidy to lose. "When was she here last?"

"Just here."

"Does she live nearby?"

"She's up the street but always snooping around, looking for something to steal. Eats all my food, drinks my coffee. Thieving bitch."

Although stolen money could be construed as a financial

matter, a "thieving bitch" was definitely *not* within the scope of Julian's charge. He pulled out his cell phone to call Claire.

Tidy saw the phone and went into a rage. "Don't you call that bitch. I won't have her in my house."

"Tidy, I'm calling Claire to see if she can help us. May I do that? Please."

Tidy nodded.

Lucky for Julian, Claire was only ten minutes from Oakmont and had time to spare before her next appointment.

"Hurry," Julian said just as Tidy let loose with another "bitch." "She's not talking about you," Julian added and ended the call.

"Claire will be here in a few minutes. What about under the couch, Tidy? You told me once you keep important things under the couch. Did you look there?"

"The bitch took my wallet. Why would it be under the couch?"

With a muffled moan, Julian got down on his knees. "I'll take a look." He not only didn't find the wallet; he found nothing. "Ah, I'm not finding anything under the couch."

"What do you mean? I keep all my important things there."

"Well, I'm not finding anything now," he said. Not a very bright comment for the situation, he supposed; in fact, it was a stupid remark.

With surprising agility, Tidy went down on her knees, groping under the couch. "The bitch took it all!" she screamed. "She cleaned me out."

At Claire's knock, Julian opened the door and stood aside to allow her to enter the living room first. Tidy continued her feverish hunt under the couch, grunting with the effort. Without hesitation, Claire crossed the room and reached down to help

Tidy back onto her feet. "Come on, Tidy, let's sit down for a minute. Tell me what's happened."

"The bitch took everything." Her eyes darted like a hummingbird, and her hands moved in some kind of sign language.

"Who are we talking about?" Claire asked.

"Bernie, the bitch," Julian said. He bent his head toward Claire to quietly describe what Tidy had told him.

The corners of Claire's mouth twitched upward, but she managed to hide her smile as she turned to focus on Tidy's face. Claire took the moment. "Tidy, unless I'm missing something, Bernie hasn't been in your house for two or three months, since she stayed the one night and stole your kitchen towels. I mean, she *hasn't* been back, has she?"

"I wouldn't let that bitch in here for anything."

Julian's mind reeled with all the accusations. *Who steals kitchen towels?* "According to Tidy's calendar, Bernie has been here this past month." He picked the calendar from the table and handed it to Claire.

"Bernie was last here a week ago," Claire pointed out. "You noted the visit on your calendar."

"Then she couldn't have stolen your wallet, Tidy," Julian broke in, "because you went to the bank yesterday to make the, um, second withdrawal."

Claire met Julian's eyes. He rolled his; she took hers without expression back to Tidy's face. "You always keep your cash in your wallet, so Bernie can't have stolen your money," she said with all her social worker bland calmness. "I'll help you and Julian look some more. You and I will start with the bedroom, and Julian can search the desk drawers and check anyplace where it might have disappeared with the newspapers."

Of course, Julian thought. *You're brilliant, Claire.* Lodged in a bunch of newspapers, the wallet might have been thrown out with the trash.

But his heart started to pound as Claire headed for the bedroom. Searching that room meant she would look through the drawers of the dresser. The image of the handgun, peeking from under the bra, frightened him. Why hadn't he told Claire about the gun?

Claire sensed his unease and tilted her head in question. "Julian?"

"Ah, nothing. I was trying to remember if I had already checked her dresser drawers."

"You searched earlier?"

"Just in the dresser drawers."

"You did no such thing," Tidy said.

"You may not have seen me. I took a peek, since we know you sometimes stash some of your important things in the bottom drawer." He stared meaningfully at Claire, but by her expression, she was clearly puzzled. So she wasn't aware of the gun. How could he keep her from finding it by surprise? *Not my problem. Claire is the expert ... Oh, be careful, Claire.*

"I'll check the trash cans." Julian quickly exited to the back landing.

On the way out he passed the door to Pedro's room. Pedro. The screwball activity of the last hour slammed to a halt. He stood on the landing, his thoughts careening around this new possibility. He decided he wouldn't introduce the idea and launch another attack. After his initial irritation with the man, Julian had relented and allowed that the guy was what he said he was—a hardworking bloke whose marriage was in a bad patch. The wallet had to be misplaced, plain and simple.

Julian turned to the trash cans. He wasn't happy pawing through Tidy's garbage, but he didn't complain out loud. He was too busy listening for exclamations from Claire.

A good half hour passed while the threesome investigated all possible corners, cans, and crannies. Tidy, frustrated at first with the elusive wallet, turned jubilant at finding long-lost items—a photo of Aunt Bessie, a glass candy dish, a prayer booklet from the church up the street. But in the end the wallet remained lost.

"Nothing in her dresser drawers?" Julian asked Claire.

"No." Claire frowned at him.

"The left bottom drawer? Tidy's told me she keeps important things in that particular drawer sometimes."

"No!" Claire threw an exasperated glare at Julian.

"Still think the bitch took it," Tidy mumbled.

"She couldn't have, Tidy." Claire abandoned her annoyance with Julian to attend to Tidy.

"Do you remember the last time you had the wallet?" Julian again tried his auntie's tactic. "Did you go shopping yesterday? Did you pay for anything after you went to the bank?" He avoided Claire's pointed stare.

"Came right home. Too tired."

The atmosphere hung heavy with defeat. They were at an impasse. Claire said she had to leave, and Julian made excuses for departing as well. He couldn't face Tidy's anger and loony behavior any longer and certainly not alone.

"Keep looking, Tidy," Julian said. "Walk through yesterday in your mind. Maybe you'll discover a place you went where you used some of the money." Julian fleetingly berated himself for yet another idiotic remark to Tidy. Telling her to walk through her mind ... *really*!

"I told you I came right home."

"Yes, okay. You call me if you think of anything, and keep looking," Julian finished.

Outside on the sidewalk with Claire, he started to fume. "What's with her? Five hundred dollars and she loses her wallet!"

"Julian, calm down. First of all, we can't stand here in front of her house and continue to talk. If she sees us, she'll think we're conspiring about her."

"Well, aren't we?"

Claire laughed. "Let's drive our cars around the corner. Then *you* are going to tell me what the business with her dresser drawers is all about."

Two blocks off Main Street toward the water, on a quiet residential street where mothers pushed strollers and retired men walked their dogs, Julian turned on Claire and began a rant. "We should get a conservator assigned—for her own good."

Claire put up her hand to stop him, unsuccessfully.

"How can you say she's competent!"

"I had her tested recently for mental capacity," Claire said. "She got a twenty-six out of thirty."

"You're joking. The other four must be the part when you can't remember what's happened to a very large wad of cash."

"The test is a screening device, and the results don't always jibe with our observations in the field. It doesn't measure judgment, which is what I think you're complaining about. We can't declare her incompetent, but we do need to keep a careful eye on her environment, to watch for signs of deterioration."

"What you're proposing sounds like damage control."

"A good description. We want to reduce the possibility of abuse."

"The possibilities are already rampant! Drug dealers down the street—"

"You know about that?"

"She lets just anybody live with her, with money and valuables lying around. Unless we install a guardian, how can we protect her? If we can't change her ways and we can't protect her, what good are we?"

"As long as she insists on living on her own and she doesn't exhibit any behavior that says she is a danger to herself or society, we're vigilant from the sidelines."

"That's preposterous. All this time and energy spent on an irascible, ornery woman who simply wants to live in her own home when she really can't."

"What would you have us do, Julian? Leave her to the wolves?"

"Why not put her in a home where she is safe?"

"I've tried; she won't agree."

Julian wrung his hands in frustration. "If we let her life fail in some way, couldn't we get a court order to put her in a home?"

"How would you have her fail, Julian? Stop paying her bills? Allow the community riffraff to rip her off? We need to do what we can to keep her life stable. That's why we are so pleased you are helping her. And now," Claire said with a smile, "you are going to tell me about the dresser drawers."

"I wanted to be certain you searched them thoroughly." Julian's rage subsided to nervousness with the introduction of this subject. "She does stash papers and ... other things in the drawers. Odd, I thought."

"Elders often create caches in various places of their homes and yards too."

Oh, Julian knew about concealment and hiding places.

"For some reason, some seniors—especially those without an adequate support system—don't trust their environment and consequently do things like keep money under the mattress."

Julian smiled. "Did you look there?"

Claire laughed. "Yes, as a matter of fact, I did.

"Come on, Julian, you're not being honest with me about the bottom bureau drawer."

Julian drew a breath and related his encounter with the gun.

Claire was contemplative, not perturbed, as Julian thought she ought to be. "Well, she's moved it to another hiding place," she said, revealing she had searched the drawer carefully. "You didn't happen to notice if it was loaded?" she asked casually.

Julian gasped. "You expect I'd pull it out and examine it?"

Claire smiled. "No, I wouldn't have touched it either. We needn't worry at the moment. We've thoroughly searched the house, and neither the gun nor the wallet turned up."

"How do you do this, Claire, work with people like Tidy who live on the fringes of our society?"

"She's not on the fringe, Julian. She worked for the city for fifteen years, ran her own businesses, kept—keeps—her own property. She has been, and still is, a solid citizen of our community. Did you know she was once president of the Oakmont Chamber of Commerce?"

"A month ago I'd have said you're kidding." Julian stuffed his hands in his pockets, searching the sidewalk for insight. "I guess I'm not saying she's in the margin but that she is so alone—no family, no friends, except people whom she alienates with her cutting criticism." Julian went on to tell Claire about the note on the calendar: "Tidy alone today."

"She needs more socialization, and when things are calmer—"

Julian scoffed. "I don't think she'll ever settle down. She's not happy unless her life is in a whirl."

"Good point." Claire looked at Julian with new respect and opened the door to her car.

"Claire," Julian said to stop her departure. "Has Tidy ever called you 'boo'?"

Claire laughed. "More of her southern talk. It's an expression of affection, Julian. She likes you!"

———————

Midafternoon Julian's cell phone rang. Tidy was calling to say she had found her wallet.

"Where?"

"In the oven."

"In the oven," he repeated, wondering how to respond to *this* lunacy.

"I put it there so no one could steal it. Who would think to look in the oven for a wallet?"

He laughed. "*We* certainly didn't! How did you remember the hiding place?"

"I turned on the oven so I can cook my potpie. Things began to smell peculiar."

"I bet." He tensed with the memory of that other item, missing from the dresser drawer. "Was anything damaged?"

"No, just a lot of smoke and smell. Cooking money stinks, did you know?"

"You didn't find anything else in your new hiding place?" He braced for the answer.

"Only stinky money."

Julian choked on a deep breath.

———

Julian considered the mid-March date and the fact that he hadn't accomplished any financial oversight while looking through Tidy's trash earlier in the week. The bank statements were due, and he needed to check that all the automatic bill payments had been made. He sighed. These visits were proliferating like rabbits. Not only aged and eccentric, Tidy was becoming one of his most time-consuming clients. And all this nonaccounting stuff, disabling cars and writing wills, was eating up more time.

On top of these irksome matters, a winter storm had swept down from the northwest and had been delivering several hours of needed rain with no sign of stopping. Julian didn't relish going out in the deluge. Perhaps he'd ignore the appointment or call and say he had other urgent business. But if anything, Julian was principled; if he'd said he'd see Tidy, he would. He picked up the phone to call and confirm.

She answered more promptly than usual.

"Tidy, this is Julian."

"You'd better get over here quick." Nuts, she had remembered the appointment. "I don't care if it's my day or not, just get over here."

"What's wrong?"

"That man stole from me."

Julian groaned. "I was coming to see you anyway. Give me fifteen minutes."

"If we're going to catch him, you better come now."

"I am, Tidy. I am."

Twenty minutes elapsed before he closed the computer file he had been working on, dragged his London Fog from the closet, retrieved his still-dripping umbrella from the back entryway, and drove the two miles to Main Street. He spent ten minutes searching for a decently nearby parking space. Oakmont's business didn't yet warrant a parking lot, and with the rain, everyone wanted to find a close-in spot on Main Street.

Looking and feeling like a drowned cat, Julian was truly peevish by the time he jabbed Tidy's doorbell. He pushed his way through the door, which was not latched, let alone locked. He should be concerned, but today he didn't care.

Tidy was standing at the entrance-hall doorway, leaning on her cane. "You're looking like something the dog's been keeping under the porch."

"Should I be insulted?" With the belt of his coat hanging loose, the cuffs of his pants soaked, and his hair askew from the wind, he *was* slightly disheveled. "Listen, Tidy, you brought me out in this storm because you said something terrible happened. What's going on?"

"Pedro, that thief. Left this morning with all my silver. Packed up his belongings and left, with my silver wrapped in the clothes."

"Where was he going?" He couldn't get excited about this crisis, which probably wasn't a crisis.

"I told him to get out of my house. He is the worst thief I've ever had. Taking the silver, and my jewelry too. I want you to call the po-leece."

"The police!"

"They need to track him down and get my silver back. He took all my money, hundreds of dollars. Everything in my wallet."

"Where's your wallet now?" How could they be going through this ridiculousness again? He started toward the kitchen to look in the oven.

"Right here," she said, arresting his stride. From the red bag she withdrew the black wallet, flat. She ripped all the Velcro closures to display the emptiness.

His stomach went sour. He wanted desperately to call Emily and wail, but he couldn't in front of Tidy. He could, however, call Claire.

Claire's phone flipped immediately to voice mail. He left a frantic message.

"You don't need to be calling no social worker. We need the po-leece before he escapes." She had lifted her cane and now whacked it on the coffee table.

"I'm not sure …"

"I'm telling you to call the po-leece." She raised the cane in the air—defiant. Or was it a threat? The gesture confused Julian because he felt threatened. He tried Claire again, but as Tidy continued her invective, he dialed the police department to report the theft.

———

Officer Rickerts responded within minutes. Tall and bulky, probably from all the gear on his waist under his raincoat, Rickerts appeared to be about Julian's own age. Oakmont was his beat, Rickerts told Julian, and even on a sunny day, bagging a few tickets at the four-way stop at Main and Newton Streets was his only diversion. A call to Ms. Bourbon's home was always more entertaining. "That is," he said, to correct this slightly unprofessional comment, "I've made calls here before; I'm familiar with the, ah, situation." Water dripped from his coat, adding to the runoff of Julian's umbrella by the door.

Tidy told her story with remarkable clarity and, Julian

judged, with schoolbook grammar. If Julian had been privy to her courtroom appearance, he would have recognized the same polite and correct response to authority.

Dave Rickerts was impressed with her story, especially as it didn't appear to involve any drunken Russians. "Do you have a list of the items this Pedro stole, Ms. Bourbon?"

"My silver and my money."

"What kind of silver?"

"Candlesticks and my letter opener."

"The letter opener ..." Julian began but couldn't go on. Rickerts lifted his pen and glanced at Julian. Julian shrugged.

"You mentioned money. How much?"

"Five hundred."

Julian got up and paced to the end of the room, where he turned and opened his mouth to speak. What should he say? *If you sniff around, Officer, you might smell the money?*

Rickerts looked on patiently, but when Julian spun toward the window, mute, the officer continued with Tidy. "Candlesticks. Two?"

Tidy nodded.

"So silver—a letter opener and candlesticks—and five hundred dollars. That's it?"

"No, something else. What, Juli? What else did he take?"

"You mentioned your jewelry," Julian answered, talking to the window.

"The jewelry's in the shoebox. I told you."

Julian glanced meaningfully at Rickerts and hoped he was getting the picture. He huffed as he began to wonder if *any* of the stuff had been stolen, although he had to admit the candlesticks, once on the dining table, were missing.

"He just left," Tidy continued to Rickerts. "If you hurry,

you'll probably find him at the bar around the corner—him and those no-goods from down the way."

"Ms. Bourbon, did this Pedro ever hit you, push you, anything of that nature?"

Tidy picked up her cane and whacked the coffee table. "That's what he'd get if he did."

The stalwart Rickerts flinched a tiny bit as the tip of the cane landed less than a foot from his shin. His face remained impassive, however, as he folded his notebook and tucked it into his jacket pocket.

"Stealing from an elderly person is a serious offense, Ms. Bourbon. Worse than stealing from me or Mr. McBain here. I'll turn the case over to the detective who works these crimes. I'll also file a report with our elder-abuse-prevention department. I mention this because you might get calls from them."

After a brief exchange into his shoulder microphone, Officer Rickerts thanked Tidy for her information and gave her a card with his phone number and the case number relayed by the radio. "If you think of anything else ..." He handed a duplicate card to Julian.

The card inspired Julian to pull out one of his own. On the back he wrote Claire's name and number and "Senior Outreach Services." "She might be able to shed some light," he murmured with an exaggerated glance at Tidy. Rickerts shrugged and pocketed the card.

With the officer's departure, Julian also waded through the puddle in the entrance hall to the door. He wasn't in the mood to be concerned about her financial status. He stomped out into the rain.

Winter storms in Northern California rarely lingered, and the next day was sparkling. At noon Julian walked to Tidy's, his disposition less than sparkling.

He had talked with Claire the previous evening. She'd commiserated and made suggestions for his next visit. "Follow her lead. If she brings up the events of today, just listen and remain neutral—if you can."

Julian missed her pointed comment. "I didn't like the guy all that much, but I can't imagine Pedro would steal from her, just as you suggested the other day. I think she ran him off with her carping, complaining, and meanness."

"Quite possibly, but we can't ignore the possibility something did happen."

"Claire, the letter opener disappeared weeks ago, and who'd steal a smoldering wad of bills? The jewelry was part of the loot—and then not. The only thing not accounted for are the candlesticks, and I bet they're buried in her dishwasher."

"She doesn't have one, Julian."

"I say she's a nuisance, eating up time and resources." *His* time and resources, specifically.

Yet here he was, back the next day, flipping through all the paper in the living room until he finally found the bank statement. Everything was in order. *How unusual for anything to be in order in this house,* Julian thought, glowering.

With his tasks complete, he was ready to depart, but he dawdled a minute, wondering if any memories of the day before lingered for Tidy. "Have you had any calls from the police today?" he asked her. Not exactly what Claire intended, but he couldn't think how to get to the subject otherwise.

"Police? Why'd they be calling me?"

"About Pedro?"

"Pedro moved out over the weekend, went back to his wife. Says they patched things up. He's grinning like a possum eatin' a sweet tater. Unless being happy is against the law, the po-leece have nothing on Pedro."

"But ..." *This is not my job,* Julian reminded himself. He decided to simply call Rickerts and explain the Pedro-stealing stuff was just a mix-up.

Tidy

Tidy's home was empty again. Quiet again. A little too quiet. Although Pedro had worked all day and kept to his room most of the night, around dinnertime he usually spent some time in the kitchen, cooking his spicy, greasy food. She'd sampled a taco, a burrito, and some bean dish, but the prevalence of tomato and cheese hadn't interested her palate. She pined for Ivan's creamy sauces and roasted meats.

She hadn't enjoyed Pedro's cooking, but she had enjoyed their nice little chats as they ate. She was fond of his family stories, especially about his two children, Juanita and Pepe. The boy's real name, what was it? José maybe. She thought Pepe ought to be Pedro's nickname. *He's peppy, like Pepe,* she chuckled. None of it mattered now. Pedro was gone.

The house was hollow, all echoey, same as when Ivan had first gone to jail. With her "man" in the house, she could go to the back room, bang on the door, and Ivan would appear, to give her some sense of company, at times even companionship. Keep the blues at bay. She worried about becoming so sad she couldn't get up in the morning.

Mr. Browning's dying had made her depressed. She missed their Sunday afternoons in the hills to the east, watching the hawks laze in the sky, picking up fruit from the orchards, taking long walks in the dry grass along the pasture fences, talking to the cows.

She giggled at the memory—talking to the cows. They'd made up conversations between Bessie (voiced by Tidy) and Bud (Mr. Browning)—nonsensical cow conversations, the kind of fun that made a marriage glow with warmth. They'd held hands as they walked.

Loneliness was not having anyone with whom to hold hands.

When Billy had gotten killed, there had been nothing, no feeling. She frowned.

She'd met Billy in Los Angeles while cleaning homes of the rich and famous with Millie. Billy had swept her away to San Francisco, where he'd said he'd make good money working in the shipyards. After the war and their quickie wedding, they'd had enough money to open up the restaurant, then the bar, and later the grocery store too. Billy had managed the bar—and some other "business" that must have made trouble for him. One clear October morning, the cops had come to her door to tell her they'd found Billy's body down near the dump. She remembered remarking to herself that the day was too beautiful to end up in a dump.

Nevertheless, his departure had infuriated her. He'd left a pile of debts, owing everyone in town. What right had he to spend so much money—most of it her money? Her businesses had made more than his. He'd been cheating on her—and not that kind of cheating.

She stabbed her cane at the ottoman in remembered irritation. "I was so mad I'd've killed him, if'n he weren't already dead." She used that line in any retelling of the story; she liked it for the picture of her fury.

The flock of no-goods banging on her door, demanding their money back, had fueled her fury. "Money back from what?" she had blasted back. Those debts had been Billy's business, not hers, and she wouldn't have them demanding anything from her.

At a game-and-fish shop over by the pier, she'd purchased the small handgun. The store owner had led her to a shooting range out back and shown her how to use the weapon. After an hour of practice, she'd spotted the target with every shot, once within an inch of the bull's-eye.

Billy's pals had soon left her alone. Her reputation as fearless, even cocky to the point of being scary, had made Billy's debts seem uninteresting. Tidy had settled down to running her restaurant and grocery with remarkable efficiency and success.

When she'd married Mr. Browning, she'd given up the businesses. He'd wanted her with him for days in the country, taking the train to Seattle to visit friends, entertaining in their own home. She'd been a good cook, and Mr. Browning had loved showing her off.

They hadn't been rich, no, but they'd never lacked for money either. She'd been stingy with herself most of the time—she'd had difficulty shopping for clothes, for instance. Mr. Browning, although not extravagant, had enjoyed the good life. Her financial situation when he'd died had been comfortable but not easy.

Tidy's weakness—if it could be called that—was her generosity. She liked helping others; for instance, loaning out to Mary when her baby took sick. The fact that Mary had never paid Tidy back didn't bother her. Over time, her friends may have found her an easy mark, but she hadn't noticed. She was not suspicious by nature (despite recent developments) and believed her obligation to the community to help others overrode any personal need. Her work at the Baptist church at the top of the hill was legendary. She'd taken in the homeless on occasion, helped them get back on their feet. If that meant giving them some money, so be it.

So at age ninety-two her savings had dwindled, and she existed on a precarious financial ledge. She came to that edge as she contemplated Pedro's departure. His rent went with him.

Tidy looked out the window. Julian would soon be haggling about how much money she'd need to pay bills, and she'd be making those transfers again. He would get all mad when she'd protest. The image made her almost smile. She thought that transfer business was a nuisance and unnecessary. If Emily at the bank said she had enough money, she had enough money. But no, Julian had to have his way; he'd insist she trudge down to the bank every month and give Emily his note. Why he had to write it all down was a mystery to Tidy; she could remember the number between the house and the bank. He made such a display of writing the note and emphasized her diligence in its delivery.

It was as if he were writing Emily some secret message. She puzzled on this idea. What kind of secrets could they have?

Chapter 20

Julian

Julian arrived exactly at 9:00 a.m. and found Tidy still dressed in her nightgown, robe, and slippers. She paced small circles in the middle of the living room, head lowered to watch her feet. Incredibly, a week had passed with no Tidy catastrophes. Her demeanor this morning suggested the hiatus had ended.

"Are you all right, Tidy?" Julian surveyed the living room for any sign of trouble.

"Didn't sleep well. I don't sleep well when I'm alone."

"I'm sorry. May I check around for any mail?"

"No need. It's all in the box, like you keep telling me."

"I'm pleased to see the shoebox full again, but, oh, here's something on the table."

"Came today."

"How about in your bag?"

"My stuff, nothing for you."

He took a deep breath. It was going to be one of those days

with Tidy. "I'll get started. Why don't you make some coffee for yourself while I sort these papers?"

But Tidy continued her mincing circles. Julian shrugged and began his tasks at the desk. He picked through the mail, howling at the sight of two envelopes from Bank of America. Notices of insufficient funds; he could tell without opening them.

"Tidy, did you transfer the funds we talked about two weeks ago?"

"You're always making me move my money." Her circles had brought her closer to the couch, and she fell back into the cushions, distracted, staring into space.

A pang of concern and guilt overcame Julian. She appeared so fragile and sad; he wanted her to be well and happy. With surprising solicitude, he sat beside her on the couch. "Are you sure you're okay, Tidy? You seem unwell."

Tidy twisted to face him. "I'm not sick. I'm fine." She glared at him.

"Okay then, here's the situation: if we didn't make the last transfer, your property taxes drained the checking account, and there isn't enough money for the rest of your monthly bills. You need to go visit Emily and make another transfer."

Why hadn't she visited Emily? Julian frowned at the thought. She loved those visits.

"I'm writing it down on this paper for Emily," Julian continued. "Take it to the bank, and she'll help you make the transfer."

"You're always telling me there's a problem. Before you started coming, I never had troubles. I'd call Emily, and she tells me I have enough money. You come along, and all a sudden I don't have enough. She tells me someone transfers my money.

I think you're that someone. I saw you put my check in your pocket. That's why the money's gone."

Julian was stunned. "Tidy, I think we're a little confused. I didn't steal your money."

"You have me transferring money, and that Emily, your wife, is taking it. That's why I never have enough money in my checking account." Tidy's voice became loud and shrill. "Everybody is stealing from me. I'm not having it anymore."

Julian stood in shock.

"You're a no-good, stealing thief. Trash, both of you. Robbing my money, my silver, all my important things. You get out of here, and don't ever come back."

"Tidy, I don't think you understand ..."

"I don't want to hear any more of your filthy lies. You're the one making me sick. Taking money from my wallet. Finding my things under the couch. I've seen you on the floor, looking." She pounded her knees with her fists, rocking back and forth. "Get out of my house. Right now!" she screeched, her eyes crazed. Every muscle in her body was taut to the point of collapse.

Julian turned to move away, reaching for the envelopes on the table. Tidy sliced her bony hand to his wrist. "I want you gone. Son of a bitch." Her voice was now low and menacing. "Don't touch another thing of mine. Get out!"

He retired slowly from the couch, wary, but as Tidy continued to batter him with growling threats, he moved more quickly to the front door.

"Trash, both of you," she shrieked.

He stood on the sidewalk outside, clenching his fists, looking wildly up and down the street. Never in his life had anyone screamed at him. His disgruntled clients never shouted. Even his aunties had never screamed at him. Tidy had howled, sworn at him. Worse still, she'd accused him of stealing from her!

He couldn't imagine how Tidy could know about Emily being his wife. In his car he whipped out his cell phone, realizing with annoyance he had turned it off when he'd arrived at the office that morning and forgotten to reactivate it when he'd left for Tidy's appointment. There was a message from Emily. He ignored it and phoned her direct line.

"Julian?"

Without preamble he wailed into the phone, "Tidy knows we're married."

"I've been trying to reach you. Your phone was turned off. She called a few minutes before your appointment and asked if I was Scottish. I said no. She said, 'But your name's McBain, like Juli, and he's Scottish.' I was so flustered I didn't know what to say. Then she said, 'He's not your brother; he's your husband.' She started ranting about stealing and no wonder she didn't have enough money and how I lied to her and you were a no-good, and then she hung up on me. I tried calling back, but she wouldn't answer. I'm so sorry, Juli."

"I'm sorry too, Emily. I don't understand how all of this has become twisted in her mind."

"What are you going to do?"

Julian considered for a moment. He had worked with Tidy long enough to know a little about how her mind worked. Like with the yardman, once it was in her brain that he hadn't done the job, she didn't owe him anything—that was it. No reasoning would change her mind. Her capacity for a different view vanished.

"There's nothing to do. I've been fired."

Chapter 21

Ivan

Ivan called Tidy on Mondays, since the prison phones were not as busy the day after the weekend. He didn't dare call every Monday, as much as he wanted to. The calls had to be placed collect, and knowing Tidy to be cost conscious, he worried she might refuse to accept the charges if he called too often.

On the last Monday in March, over four months since his appearance before Judge Letty, Ivan was restless. He needed to talk to someone, and Tidy was the only person he dared call.

"Hello?"

Ivan was close to tears at the sound of her scratchy voice.

"I have a collect call from Ivan D. Will you accept the charges?" The prison operator couldn't be bothered with his last name.

"Hell yes, put him on."

"Tidy …"

"Ivan, that you?"

"Tidy, I don' know what's going on."

"What do you mean?"

"I just in cell and never see anyone."

"You're in jail. What do you expect?"

"I'm supposed to go to the place to help me with my drinking."

"Must not be your turn. How's the food?"

"Awful. Always awful. I want to be making stroganoff, grechka, kotleta po-kievsky."

"You're causing my mouth to water. When are you getting out so you can be cooking here again?"

"I don' know. It's what I try to tell you. No one says anything."

"Can't you call the woman who helped you before?"

"The social worker? I don' remember her name, and if I did, I don' know how to phone her."

"What do you mean?" Her irritation was clearly escalating. "You're dumb as a bucket of rocks. You phone me, don't you?"

"Tidy, please don' get mad at me. I so sad here."

"You're sad! What do you think I am? I'm tired of trying to keep things going, and you not here helping."

"I sorry, Tidy. I want to help you."

"You help me by getting your butt out of that place. I got no one to carry my groceries. I have to drive myself to the doctor, and I hate driving. You being in jail is nothing but trouble."

"Okay, okay, I try to get out. Bye, Tidy."

"Try to get out" was his usual exit line. It placated her for the week. He put the receiver down slowly, thinking. If he couldn't help her, he'd find someone else to do the job. He'd call Miki, his old buddy at the cab company, and get him to go by and visit Tidy. Miki could at least take her shopping. That would take the pressure off.

But for every solution there was another problem: he didn't know Miki's phone number. He sat in the phone booth brooding until the brute next in line started banging his fist on the window.

The following afternoon, morose and forlorn, he plodded to the phone room again and waited his turn to call. He recited to the operator the only number besides Tidy's he might hope to remember.

"Misha's Cabs," Tasha answered on the first ring. Ivan swallowed a sob. Tasha's charming, heavily accented voice brought on a rush of homesickness.

The operator did her thing, feeling obliged to botch his full name to this unusual beneficiary of communication from Ivan. "I have a collect call from Ivan Deemee-dove-sky. Will you accept the charges?"

"Oh, I don' know. Hi, Ivan. Mr. Feduleyev not here. Can I take collect call with no asking?"

"Ma'am, are you going to accept the charges or not?"

"I'm not sure; boss is away," Tasha prattled on.

"I'll take that as a no. Sorry to have bothered you." And the mean operator broke the connection. "That's it, Mr. D. Wanna make another call?"

"Nyet." Ivan slammed the receiver down and stalked away. Why was everyone against him? Why wouldn't anyone help him, so he could help Tidy?

As he exited the phone room, his eye caught a row of phone books lined up on the table along the far wall. Why hadn't he seen them before? Maybe, just maybe, he could find something in a phone book to improve this situation. His friend Mikhail, Miki—as opposed to the boss Mikhail, of Misha's Cabs—his last name was Nabokov. Ivan brightened with his cleverness.

His gaze passed over the phone book titles: El Centro, Wayland, San Jacinto, Oakmont, Ridley, Nortonville. His brilliance dimmed rapidly as he realized he had no idea where Miki lived. Not Oakmont, he was sure of that. Most of the Muscovites resided in Wayland. The Ukrainians inhabited the town next door, Nortonville—close but not too close. In fact, ex-Soviets were sprinkled throughout the Bay Area. He swiftly realized how little he knew about Miki, but he would not be deterred from the only flicker of ingenuity he had had in weeks.

He opened the Wayland volume, and his spirit sank with the number of Nabokovs in the one book: five, including one Mikhail Nabokov and two M. Nabokovs that might be Mikhail Nabokov.

He ripped the back page from Oakmont and, in the margins, copied the numbers with a pencil stub he discovered behind the Nortonville phone book. Locating the pencil relieved him of asking the guard or, worse, one of the other inmates in the room for a writing implement. He tried not to have any interaction with these people. They all hated him, or so he thought. He was sure they viewed him as disgusting and would happily refuse, along with everyone else in the world, to help him.

He moved on to the other phone books and flashed on the possibility that Miki might live with relatives, meaning his phone number would be in someone else's name. Opening the third book, he gave in to despondency: Nabokovs populated nearly every town in the Bay Area.

The following evening he resolved to start by calling one Nabokov each night. In this way the odds of disappointment were minimized. The hope he'd find his comrade sooner rather than later preceded his nightly visit to the phone room.

He started with the Mikhail Nabokov living in Wayland, who would not accept the charges. Nabokov number two hung up without responding to the operator's question. Number three swore in Russian and slammed the receiver down. The fourth Nabokov's phone had been disconnected. Why? He must have moved. Ivan fell into a new funk. Maybe his pal Miki had split for New York. Ivan tried to remember when he had last spoken to Miki—since he'd last been released from jail, before he'd been thrown back in? Or earlier? Time was often compressed for Ivan, as his life didn't have many marks of distinction— events or occasions—by which to solve these puzzles. Confusion overcame him.

On the fifth try, he got lucky.

To the operator's question came a low growl: "Why should I pay for his phone call?"

In desperation Ivan blurted, "Miki, it's me; I'm in jail again. Pleez, Miki, help me; talk to me."

"*Govno, da*, I take call from this *alkash balvan*."

Chapter 22

Claire

Claire's Tuesdays now began with Tidy, and ringing the doorbell had become perfunctory. Today the gate hung open, and the inner door was ajar. Still, with care to her protocol, Claire knocked and, in doing so, pushed the inner door further into the hallway.

"Get in here," Tidy bellowed. She stood at the end of the coffee table, with the receiver of her telephone to her ear. The cord was coiled and shortened as usual by several twisted knots, and Tidy listed to one side to keep the phone on the table. "Hurry up. I don't know what this man wants."

She was wearing the pink nightgown but no robe. Her hair sprung up in a gray, thinning rendering of Medusa. She stamped her bare feet, jabbing the phone receiver toward Claire. Her other arm was heavily wrapped in what looked like an elastic bandage from her hand halfway to her elbow. A sling hung limp and unused around her neck.

What happened here? Claire gasped. She took a deep breath

and swept the sight into her brain for temporary storage. Without so much as a frown, she took the receiver from Tidy.

"You talk to him," Tidy said. "I can't understand a thing he's saying."

Claire sat on the ottoman to deal with the foreshortened cord. "Hello, my name is Claire. I'm a friend of Tidy's. May I be of assistance?"

"This is the Bank of America fraud department. We have seen some unusual activity on Mrs. Bourbon's credit card, and we're phoning to verify the expenditures."

"He took my car. He took my credit cards. They've been calling all night," Tidy yelled, her eyes bulging with the effort. "He said he would help me, and he stole my car." She flung her bandaged arm slightly and cringed in pain.

"Who stole your car, Tidy? ... Oh, excuse me," Claire said into the phone. "Please hold on a moment."

"That man who came to help me. Took me to the doctor because of my arm. He stole my car." She stamped her feet again, tottering slightly.

"Tidy, sit down. We'll sort this out. Sit down for a minute while I talk to the man on the phone."

Tidy collapsed onto the lumpy sofa, continuing a staccato mutter.

Claire turned her attention to the caller. "I'm sorry, sir. Please tell me again about this call. I'd like to help, if I can."

"We believe someone has been using Mrs. Bourbon's Visa card, and we are trying to determine if she made any of the purchases recorded in the last twenty-four hours. I need some information from her."

"May I help with the information?"

"It's the matter of privacy; I must talk directly to Mrs. Bourbon."

"Of course. I wonder if I could have your name and number and call you back in a few minutes after I talk with Ms. Bourbon. I just arrived, and I'm not sure I understand what's happened and how it affects your call. May I have the number?"

"Certainly. My name is John Brower. This is the Bank of America fraud department. Here's my direct phone number."

Claire plucked a Post-it cube and a dull pencil from Tidy's table. By then, having missed the first few digits, Claire said to the patient man, "I am sorry, could you repeat—"

Tidy screeched, "He stole my car!"

"Tidy, let me finish, and then we can figure out what to do." Trying to maintain her composure, Claire recorded the phone number as Mr. Brower repeated it and then said into the phone receiver, "I need to talk to my friend here. I'll call you back in a few minutes." She hung up while Tidy continued to shriek about the car. Claire's mind whirled with questions: What did fraudulent expenditures on Tidy's credit card have to do with a stolen car? How could the car have been stolen if Julian had disabled it? And why had Tidy not mentioned *anything* about this trouble an hour ago when Claire had called to confirm the appointment?

Claire tried to untangle the knotted phone receiver line, gave up immediately, and slapped the receiver back on the phone. She folded the Post-it with Mr. Brower's number in half so it wouldn't stick to her clothes and stuffed it into her pants pocket. Drawing the ottoman closer to the couch, she sat almost knee to knee with Tidy.

"Tell me what's happened."

Tidy retreated into her inner space, mute.

"Let's start with your arm."

"I fell and hurt my arm." Though not exactly hushed, her voice was lower and less strident. "This man came and said he would help me, take me to the hospital."

"When did you fall?"

"Yesterday, no, two days ago."

"Today is Tuesday. You fell Monday or Sunday?"

"I don't remember." She slumped back into the couch, her arms dropping to her sides, the one with a thick bandage landing with a muffled thump. The sling hung like an empty feed bag down her chest.

"It doesn't matter." Claire leaned forward. "Who was the man who took you to the hospital?"

"He's been here before. Told me he'd help me anytime."

The locals on the street corner rose swiftly to mind. "Someone from the neighborhood?"

"I don't remember."

"Did you go outside to the street and find him?"

Tidy continued without listening to Claire, "He's coming to take me shopping, he says, and wrote his name in my book." She swept away some newspapers with her bandaged arm, wincing again and muttering, "Goddamn," and then produced her address book.

"You're acquainted with him."

"He's been here before. Wrote his name and phone number and told me to call anytime I need help."

The repetition irked Claire; she wasn't sure why. She had visited only last Tuesday, and Tidy hadn't mentioned anything of this nature.

"Do you think you can find his name in your book?" Claire asked gently, trying with a calm voice to ease Tidy's agitation.

Tidy looked at the purple spiral-bound pad in her lap as if she had never seen it before. "I don't know." She opened it and turned the pages slowly but didn't appear to be paying attention to the entries.

Claire leaned over and gently extracted the book from Tidy's hands. "Never mind; we'll look at it later. Tell me what happened when the man came. You had fallen ..."

Then an awful thought intruded: What if this mystery man had *caused* the injury? Several horrific scenarios collided across Claire's mind. Physical abuse was a definite possibility, and the trauma of such an event could be contributing to Tidy's memory loss.

"Tidy, how did you fall? Tell me again how it happened."

"I was doing my laundry. There's a step in the back where the washing machine is. I have to be careful, or I miss the step. Done it before." Her energy, focused on telling the story, seemed to settle her. "This time I fell, but I pick myself up and go on about my business. Later my arm started to hurt real bad."

"This was yesterday? Or Sunday?"

Tidy's face went blank; her eyes slipped to her lap. Claire watched her turn inward again in an apparent effort to find the memory she wanted. "I can't remember," she murmured. A mantra, and in its repetition Claire heard the anguish and frustration.

Claire continued softly, "When you hurt your arm, did you phone the man to come help you?"

"No, the next day. I went to bed, but my arm was hurting so bad I couldn't sleep."

"The next day he came and took you to the hospital?"

"I asked him to take me. He drove."

"He had a car?"

"No, in my car, like Ivan."

"Like Ivan," Claire repeated, trying not to sound doubtful or irritated. Whoever he was, he must have discovered the disconnected battery and fixed it.

Tidy became defensive. "Ivan's always driving me to the hospital, driving me everywhere. He took care of me. These things wouldn't happen if Ivan was here."

She had to say it, Claire groaned silently. "I'm sorry, Tidy; I got us off track. The man took you to the hospital in your car. What happened then?"

"They said my wrist's sprained real bad. They put this bandage on. Told me to keep the wrist in the sling and not use my arm." She flapped the loose sling with her good hand. "Impossible." She used her injured arm to gesticulate in her usual manner and flinched. "Still hurts."

Claire lifted the bandaged arm and gently inserted it into the sling. "So they put on the bandage ... Did you go home then?"

"The man drove me home. I was grateful." Her voice turned soft and forgiving. "He stayed with me in the hospital while they did x-rays and the bandage, waiting for me. I thanked him for staying with me."

Claire waited, not interrupting the story. She longed for something in this retelling that would jar loose the name or some identifying image of the mysterious man.

Tidy sat silently for a moment, perhaps also longing for that essential item. Nothing.

"Tell me what happened when you returned from the hospital. He brought you home ..."

"I was tired, hurting, been hurting so long. The hospital gave me a prescription for the pain."

"A prescription for pain?" Claire repeated.

"Like I said. I ask the man to get the pills at the pharmacy. Gave him some money to pay for them."

"You gave him some cash? How much?"

"I gave him my wallet, like I do Ivan."

Claire marshaled her patience to hold eye contact and keep her face impassive. She didn't want to get into the Ivan thing again, and she feared Tidy would recognize what she had just said: she might have done this to herself.

Claire repeated slowly, quietly, kindly, "He took the prescription and went to the pharmacy … in your car?"

In Tidy's lap, the fingers of her left hand gently tapped the bandage. Her eyes vacant, her voice a whisper, she said, "He hasn't come back."

Claire let some space into the conversation to ease the tension.

Tidy reclined further into the cushions, and her eyelids fell. "Oh Lord, what's happening to me?"

Claire felt her emotional hurt. She let Tidy rest a few moments and then asked, "Who was he, Tidy?"

"He said he came to help me."

"You knew him?"

"No. He's a friend."

"Someone from the street? Blackie or Rap?"

"No, no."

"Are you sure it was a man? Could it have been Bernie?"

Tidy opened her eyes like a startled deer, and Claire's attention sharpened. She watched Tidy searching.

"No, a man." Tidy slumped again with resignation. "Just like Ivan."

Claire stood to shake off her annoyance.

"He wrote his name in my book," Tidy insisted.

Claire snatched the purple notebook and flipped the pages.

She was familiar with most of the names, or they were women. Claire believed Tidy's memory was correct about the perpetrator being a man. Women didn't usually steal cars, for one thing. She went back and forth through the pages. Only one name stood out: Scott MacIntosh. She had never heard of him. "This man, Tidy, Scott MacIntosh?" she asked, pointing to the entry.

Tidy squinted, leaning forward. "That's the one." The relief in her voice was palpable. "He wrote his name and number and said to call anytime I needed help."

At last, Claire thought, reaching for the Post-it cube and dull pencil to jot the information. But nothing about the entry looked or sounded right; the ink was smudged and water stained; it must have been written some time ago. Still, she wrote the name and number on a Post-it. She again folded the note in half and stuffed it in her pocket.

"Tidy, tell me one more time about the fall. Tell me how you fell. Where did you fall?" Claire wanted to go over the material again, hoping some new detail would pop out and the mystery would be solved.

With her eyes closed Tidy told her story again without protest. Claire recognized the fatigue and loss Tidy was experiencing. "I was changing the laundry, from the washer to the dryer, you know. I missed the step ... I wasn't ... I just fell."

"The man wasn't here at that time?"

"No, I wouldn't have fell if he was here. He'd be changing the laundry."

Since Tidy's eyes were still closed, Claire allowed herself a twitch of a smile. She pictured a man doing Tidy's laundry, pulling bras and panties out of the washer and putting them into the dryer. What man would do such a task?

She wondered again if this person was a woman. Who (other

than Ivan) would take Tidy to the hospital and stay with her, in what sounded like a kindly manner?

Who were Tidy's friends, other than street people? Claire hadn't thought through the idea of street people. She wondered about Blackie. He had shown unusual kindness at Thanksgiving. He helped with her groceries on occasion, and it made sense that he would have driven her car, as he didn't have a car himself.

"What did you do after you fell?"

"I went to bed."

"You went to bed after changing the laundry?"

"I hurt so bad."

Tidy's expression suggested she might shed tears at any moment. That was rare for her, Claire noted. The memory of the pain must be ... Claire started. Not a memory. "Tidy, does your wrist hurt now?"

"Yes."

"How badly?"

"A lot."

Scott, or whomever, hadn't returned with her pills. In fact, there was no longer a prescription to get the pills anymore, and Tidy had been suffering—how many hours?—from the sprain.

"Oh, Tidy, I'm so sorry." She went into the bedroom and picked through the chaos of medicine bottles on the nightstand. The Vicodin bottle was still missing, and Claire scolded herself for not having pursued this matter. She'd never been able to put her finger on the real nature of that problem, so it had been forgotten in the mass of other Tidy troubles. Methodically she checked the bottles on the table as her thoughts about the Vicodin moved around.

She picked up the last bottle on the table: Tylenol with codeine. The prescription had been filled over a year ago.

Why had she not seen it before? *Move on,* Claire told herself. Although the prescription had been written over a year earlier, the use-by date was still valid. With relief Claire grasped the vial and moved quickly to the kitchen for some water.

She handed the water and one of the Tylenol to Tidy. "Here, take this. It should help."

Without so much as a look at Claire, Tidy took the pill and drank the water, exhaled deeply, and closed her eyes. Claire sat with Tidy's silence and oncoming comfort while continuing to think about the question at hand.

In the quiet Claire's mind stirred: she should be getting help. "Tidy, I think we need to call the police."

Tidy's head came up with a jerk. "No, not the po-leece."

"Why not?"

"They don't like me."

"Tidy, a crime has been committed here, and we need to tell the cops."

"No, they think I'm crazy."

Ah, that's it, Claire thought. The cops probably did consider her wacky. Tidy had called them frequently when Ivan acted up, and after the Pedro incident, her credibility with the police must be poor. But something *had* happened this time. The credit card business was financial abuse certainly, and quite possibly physical abuse had occurred too. Cops, no question.

"Tidy, I'll do the talking with the police, okay? They're not acquainted with me, and as far as I know, they don't think I'm crazy ..."

Surprisingly, the remark caused Tidy to slide her eyes to Claire and smile. "No, you're not crazy."

"Then may I call the police?"

"Yes, but you'll have to do the talking. They'd never believe me."

Claire dug in her bag for her cell phone. She kept the nonemergency numbers for the police departments of the towns where she had clients. She rarely used them, but they were useful when she needed them ... like now.

———

The doorbell rang only a few minutes later. Tidy started her usual shouting. She got out, "Come on in," but then her voice faltered. She turned to Claire, her face pinched. "The door's open" was barely audible.

Claire was already moving to open the door for the young man in uniform. *Too young, young enough to be my grandson,* she thought. He wore no hat, and his dark-brown hair was longer than Claire imagined the police force allowed. His blue eyes were a surprising feature to his otherwise Native American face—high cheekbones, clear light-brown skin. His uniform was new, crisp. "Officer Jordan," he said. "I took the call."

"Please come in," she replied. "I'm Claire Richards, social worker for the county Senior Outreach Services. Mrs. Bourbon is in the living room." Claire offered Jordan a chair, but he ignored it and remained standing. *Bad form,* Claire chided, *maintaining his authority through dominance.* "This is Mrs. Bourbon." Towering over a ninety-two-year-old woman just wasn't right. Claire scowled, glaring at the standing officer.

Looking down at Tidy, Jordan placed his hands on top of the bulky equipment hanging off his belt. Claire thought the pose ridiculous and inappropriate and huffed—as if he'd notice and change his stance. She shifted her own posture by sitting on the ottoman where *she* at least could lend a sense of compassion.

"Would you like me to tell Officer Jordan about the thefts, Tidy?"

Jordan shuffled on his feet and opened his mouth to speak. Tidy cut him off. "You understand what happened better than me."

Claire glowered at the officer. *Okay, Officer Jordan, go ahead and tell me you have to have the story directly from the victim.* But he remained silent, his own gaze intent on Tidy.

"But, Tidy," Claire said, "you must interrupt me if I get anything wrong." Jordan seemed to have decided to humor her, so Claire would return the favor.

"Okay, okay," Tidy replied tiredly.

Claire related the incident, as simply and factually as she was able. Tidy was quiet and still, staring at the space between her knees and the coffee table. Claire finished, and Jordan came alive to take command. "Mrs. Bourbon, how old was this man?"

That was a good question, and Claire wondered why it hadn't occurred to her to ask it. Would she have to give Officer Jordan points?

Tidy looked up at the patrolman's face and said in her most mordant voice, "Older than you."

Claire jumped in before Jordan reacted. "How about me, Tidy? Was he more my age?"

"Maybe."

"Mrs. Bourbon, you gave the man your car keys?"

"Yes, and he stole my car."

To Claire, Jordan said, "That's a problem."

"I understand. But we are pretty sure this guy also took her

wallet with some cash and has used her credit cards fraudulently."
Claire described the call from Bank of America.

"We'd be better off if we had the evidence of unauthorized
expenditures. Without something concrete to go on, we can't
even work the case." He glanced at Claire; she nodded.

"Mrs. Bourbon, do you remember the man's name?"

Tidy's eyes flared in concentration. "I can't; I just can't."

In the long pause that followed, Claire scrutinized the
officer's face, trying to determine his thought process. Then
with surprising gentleness, Jordan said, "This man didn't cause
you to fall, Mrs. Bourbon?"

Claire tilted her head in consideration. He might make the
grade eventually.

"Like, did he push you?"

"No, nothing like that," Tidy said.

Jordan glanced at Claire. She shrugged. "To the extent I've
been able to determine, the fall happened as she's described,"
she said in a muted tone.

Jordan made a notation in his notebook. "How about the car,
Mrs. Bourbon? Can you describe it to me?"

"Big ole white Pontiac. Three years old, no, maybe thirteen.
Let's see, I bought that car when the other one gave out. At
Arnie's, where I buy all my cars. Yes, three years ago, maybe
thirteen."

Jordan remained composed. "The license plate number?"

"Written on the tag of the key chain for my car keys. I'll
go get ..." She leaned forward to rise from the couch but then
realized the problem. She looked at Claire.

More attentive than Claire had given him credit for, Officer
Jordan stepped in. "The DMV will help, Mrs. Bourbon. We
can search for the information under your name. Don't worry."

Mindful of Julian's earlier report on the registration problem, Claire remarked as coolly as possible, "You might want to note that her tags are two years old."

Jordan looked at her impassively for a moment. Without further comment, he made a quiet call on the radio clipped to his shoulder. Several numbers came back from the dispatch operator, including one Claire recognized as a case number.

With relief Claire thanked Jordan and added, "Will you report this to Jane Rios? These events might interest her."

"Lieutenant Rios?" Jordan's eyebrows rose; his brow creased. He straightened his stance slightly, as if Lieutenant Rios had just entered the room. The hardware hanging from his uniform gave off a muffled rustling. "I'll phone her as soon as we finish. Meantime—my card." All business, he pulled out two cards, one for Tidy, one for Claire, and wrote the case number on each. "If you remember anything else, please call and reference this number. It will help us monitor your case."

"What do you want to keep track of me for?" Tidy had been listening. "See what I been saying?" She glared at Claire. "These cops don't like me. They ..." She halted, her face shocked. "Ivan," she blurted.

"What about Ivan?" Claire's voice flagged. How could this be another "just like Ivan"?

"He said he's a friend of Ivan's. Ivan told him to look after me, take care of me."

"The man who took you to the hospital was a friend of Ivan's?"

"Said Ivan called him. Ivan's worried about me and wanted the man to come by and help me."

Officer Jordan stood immobile, watching, listening—not interrupting, Claire was glad to acknowledge.

"Did he say how he knew Ivan?" Claire asked.

"He's another Russkie. Talks just like Ivan."

"Russian ..." Claire said, looking toward Jordan.

"Cabdriver, just like Ivan. He came all last week. Fixed the car. Took me shopping. Took out the trash. Vacuumed everything. Just like Ivan did for me."

Claire nodded. All the "just like Ivans" now made sense. "Do you recall his name, Tidy?"

She scrunched her eyes in thought. "Some Russian name: Dovsky, Misha, Boris, Blini. I can't remember."

Jordan let out a muted huff of frustration.

Turning to him, Claire said, "It's possible if you contact Ivan, you'll discover who the guy is."

"And where would we find this Ivan?" Jordan asked.

Claire smiled weakly. "Somewhere in the prison system, I believe."

———

As Jordan left, he suggested Claire call as soon as she had more information about the credit card fraud. "We can't go after this guy until we have hard evidence of wrongdoing."

Claire said she'd get back to Bank of America straightaway. She pulled out the pieces of Post-it to locate the phone number.

At John Brower's prompt answer, Claire clarified more fully her role with Tidy. She hoped Brower would believe her about being a social worker. She gave him the number of the Senior Outreach Services, in case he wanted to check up on her.

He thanked her for helping him but said he still needed to ask Mrs. Bourbon's permission to talk with her. Would Claire put her on the phone? "Just procedure," he apologized.

"I understand, and I appreciate your patience." Turning to Tidy, Claire explained about the credit cards and asked if Tidy wanted her to follow through. She should get Tidy to sign a release, but more explanations would likely squirrel the whole matter. In Tidy's brittle mood, her tolerance might give way.

"You do what you want. I don't understand what's happening, and I'm not going to try and figure it out."

"The man on the phone needs your permission to talk to me."

Tidy took the receiver and without preamble said, "You talk to her all you want. I can't understand anything," and handed the phone back to Claire.

In a bored but not unkind voice, Brower said he guessed that would do. The last two purchases on Tidy's card had occurred at the Raley's supermarket in Wayland ($125.67) and Kragen Auto Parts in Pine Hill ($256.49).

So he wouldn't bother to verify Claire's credentials. *I guess there's nothing in the procedure manual about social workers.* Her laugh lines crinkled briefly.

"Does Mrs. Bourbon shop at either of these places?"

"She doesn't *usually* venture so far from home," Claire replied, mindful of the unimaginable story Julian and the APS caseworker had related to her of Tidy crossing the Bay Bridge. "And certainly purchases at an auto parts store would not be in any way usual."

"When was the card discovered as missing?" Brower asked.

"I'm not sure, but I believe yesterday about midday. Does that coincide with this surprising activity?"

"Exactly," Brower answered. "I'm going to cancel the card immediately, and please tell Mrs. Bourbon"—he paused a moment as if he too was struggling with the name but didn't want to ask—"she will not be responsible for these charges. We'll issue a new card and send it to her tomorrow. There is a fifty-dollar processing charge, that's all. If, ah, she has any questions, you have my number. You will be sure she understands?"

Claire caught the subtext of Brower's words: *please keep me from having to interact with this loony lady again.*

Claire assured Brower she would handle the situation and then found Officer Jordan's card and called him. She didn't bother with the dumb protocol. Tidy was too tired to care, and Claire was too irritated with the inefficiencies.

She described her conversation with Brower to Jordan. Unauthorized use of Mrs. Bourbon's credit card, Jordan said—especially given her age and condition—qualified as elder abuse, a felony. "Be sure and get copies of the card statement as soon as possible," he added. "The car business is still a little iffy, with the key and all, but if the car isn't returned within a few days, we may tack on another charge."

Claire thanked him for the explanations and said she'd call if anything else came up.

Tidy sat listlessly, gray smudges under her eyes, her head tilted to one side, her whole demeanor sagging.

"Why don't you crawl into bed, Tidy, and get some sleep?" Claire suggested.

Without a word, Tidy pulled herself out of the couch and shuffled off. The painkiller took effect, and she was soon snoring softly.

Here we are again, Claire thought, *a vulnerable elder, taken advantage of … If she was in an assisted-living facility …* Claire sighed.

Glancing at her watch, she noted she had missed two appointments and would soon be late for a third. Tidy's physical and emotional state, however, worried her; the idea of leaving her alone didn't sit well.

The phone rang. The computers for Safeway supermarkets had flagged two credit cards in Mrs. Bourbon's name for unprecedented activity in the last twenty-four hours. "Several large purchases at three different stores," the accounts manager reported. Claire explained the predicament and told the manager a police report would be sent as soon as possible.

With that call, Claire had an inspiration. In her cell phone, she found the number she needed and placed the call. "Julian, I'm at Tidy's. There's a problem here, and we need your help. Any chance you could come over?"

"You've got to be kidding. That woman wouldn't let me in the house."

"She's asleep now, and anyway she'll have forgotten she fired you as soon as she realizes she needs you to help her out of this mess."

Claire bit her lip. Would Julian be naive enough to believe her? Apparently he was. He agreed to come, telling her he would reschedule his only remaining appointment for the day.

When he arrived, he told Claire he knew of four credit cards.

"Good, you can work on canceling the other three," she said. "I'm off to see the rest of my clients." She slipped out the door quickly. Julian was right behind her.

Even out of Tidy's hearing, he spoke in a forced whisper. "What are you doing, leaving me alone with her? What if she wakes up and finds me—and not you?"

"Just be solicitous, and call me if she throws you out," Claire said as she escaped into her car.

He started to fume, but Claire drove away with a wave.

Chapter 23

Julian

Inside Tidy's house, a current of nostalgia swept over Julian. He hoped Tidy would indeed forget she hated him. He missed keeping her finances organized and trying to help her understand her financial situation—as exasperating as it could be. He missed ... well, he just missed her. She was becoming a fixture in his life, a piece of his life he was ... deriving satisfaction from.

He wandered around the house, looking for the Bible, finally locating it on the dryer. The credit cards were missing. But with telepathic forethought some months ago, Julian had pulled the cards from the Bible and noted the numbers. In the desk he found his notes.

A sense of urgency to fix the misfortune spurred him into action. Despite the lingering hurt of her accusations and her meanness in making those allegations, he wanted nothing more than to relieve the grief and soothe the pain of this invasion. In the kitchen, where he wouldn't disturb her rest, he began calling the credit card companies.

He called Emily too, told her the story, such as he understood it, and asked her to check Tidy's ATM activity. He assumed that card was also in her wallet, and if somehow the thief had acquired her pin number, he'd probably be siphoning from her bank account too. Emily soon reported the creep had indeed made two withdrawals, one yesterday and one early today, each at the daily limit.

To cover all the bases, Julian used the Post-it Claire had left him to call the Brower guy. Claire had said Brower seemed friendly enough to help. Julian asked Brower if he would mind faxing copies of the Visa card statements to Julian's office— making it easier when other merchants like Safeway called. Brower refused since he didn't have Tidy's authorization. Julian was annoyed, but of course, he had no business asking without her permission; he'd call again after Tidy woke from her nap.

He went to her bedroom door to be certain she was still sleeping. She wasn't. She was staring at the ceiling and started when she saw him. "Jesus, Lord God." She sat up, crying out in pain as her bad arm swung awkwardly.

"Tidy, I'm sorry ..."

"What the hell are you doing here? You steal my car and my money, and you have the balls to come back? Get out."

"Tidy, I didn't steal your car."

"You wiped me out, took everything. My credit cards. Spending my money. They've been calling me about you from all over town. Now you sneak in and rob me blind—while I'm asleep! I want you out of here this minute!" She shook with her anger. Her voice broke twice as she forced the loud pitch.

Julian stepped back out of the doorway. How could Claire think Tidy wouldn't still be mad? *And now she's accusing me of all the most recent crimes too. Here I am trying to help get the*

mess straightened out, and she lambastes me again! he shouted
in his head.

He half-turned into the living room, but a rustling caused
him to glance back. On her feet, Tidy advanced toward him
with purposeful steps, gripping her cane in her good hand.
She wasn't clasping it to walk with; she was carrying it like a
club. The cane wavered as she tried to gain control of the extra
weight. Julian was under no illusion that she held a weapon and
intended to use it.

"I'm leaving now, Tidy; don't worry. And see?" He raised
his hands, open, palms toward her. "I'm taking nothing with
me. I wouldn't steal from you, Tidy. I have too much respect—"

"Get out." Spit spewed from her mouth.

Julian backed to the hall and turned to open the front door.
It was stuck, still swollen from the rains. His firm push to close
it when he'd come in now impeded a smooth exit. He yanked
twice to force it ajar and fumbled with the outside gate.

The cane caught him on the shoulder. The strength behind
the stroke was minimal, but the blow shocked him.

"Get out, you drunken son of a bitch. I don't want you here,
stealing all my things—my money, my car, my wallet. You just
take, take, take."

"Jeez, Tidy." He spun himself out the gate and closed it
behind him. The cane came down again with a clank on the
back of the door.

When he reached the end of the block, he turned to make
certain she wasn't on his tail. That was silly, of course. How
could she be? Her form was hidden by the outer gate, but her
"son of a bitch" from inside was still audible.

He moved around the corner to get relief and called Claire.
"Don't ever ask me to do that again."

"Are you all right?" Claire asked after hearing Julian's tale.

"More bruising to my ego than my shoulder."

Claire laughed. "I wish I had seen her with her cane drawn."

"Claire!"

"I'm sorry. I'm on my way back. I don't imagine you'll be waiting."

"You're right," he said, and he hung up on her.

He hiked the two miles to his office with overlong strides. By the time he flopped into his chair, he had cooled off, and sadness had replaced his anger. It hurt him that she would hurl such hostility, to say nothing of her cane, at him.

Chapter 24

Claire

Claire regretted causing Julian's displeasure. He hadn't deserved her wisecrack. She would phone him later and apologize. Meantime, she wondered if Jane Rios had heard about the thefts and gave her a call.

Jane said yes, she'd received a verbal report and considered a visit to Tidy obligatory. Would Claire be willing to meet her at Tidy's? "I know it's late, but your presence might be useful, if you have the time," she said. "Our friend can be a handful, and in her stressed state, she'll probably not appreciate more police inquiry."

Claire called to warn Tidy that she and Jane were on their way.

"You all come on in; the door's open."

When the three were seated in Tidy's living room, Claire told Jane the first part of the story, about the fall and the man taking her to the hospital and then departing with her car and wallet.

"You gave him the wallet, Tidy?" Jane asked.

"He needed the money to get my prescription."

"What did he look like?"

"Like Ivan. Talk like a Russkie too."

"His hair was black?"

"No, not black. Red, curly."

"How tall was he?"

"Tall. White, pasty face; blue eyes; freckles all over."

"That sounds like Julian," Claire interjected.

"Piece of trash stole my money and my car. Stole the car because he didn't want me to have it. Said I owed too much and I needed to transfer my money. He's getting all angry because I don't do what he says, so he takes my car."

"Tidy, remember how this friend of Ivan's—the one who talks like Ivan—remember how he took you to the hospital after you fell?"

"He's a kind man to wait all morning in the hospital and bring me back home when I was hurting so bad."

"Do you remember giving him your wallet?" Jane tried again.

"I asked him to go get my medicine."

"What did he look like when you gave him the wallet?"

"I told you ..." She sounded irritated. "Like Ivan—black hair but no beard, blue eyes. They seemed so nice, those eyes. He said Ivan wanted him to help me and he's glad to help. Doesn't cook like Ivan, though. I'm mighty disappointed when he says he can't cook."

"What else did he tell you?" Jane interjected, obviously not especially interested in his lack of culinary talent.

"He drives a cab, just like Ivan, and says he drives by here sometimes, and if I need help, all I have to do is call."

Claire interrupted this exchange to tell Jane that she had

explained to Officer Jordan about Ivan's whereabouts and had suggested that asking Ivan for information might help. Claire wondered if Jordan had talked to Ivan. Jane made grumbling noises and said that as far as she knew Jordan was checking but that she hoped to expedite matters with Tidy.

Claire nodded. "Tidy mentioned that Ivan's friend put his name and number in her phone book."

"What phone book, Tidy?" Jane asked. "Can you show me?"

The purple notebook was balanced on top of the coffee table pile of papers, and Tidy pointed to it. Jane leafed through the pages while Claire recounted her own exploration, finding only the one suspicious name. "Scott MacIntosh doesn't sound right for a friend of Ivan's," Claire said. "If, however, he is in fact tall, redheaded, blue eyed, and pasty faced, Scott MacIntosh sounds like a perfect match."

"Let's call him and find out," Jane said.

Scott MacIntosh turned out to be a real estate agent who had visited months ago, hoping to represent Tidy. "I told her if she ever wanted help selling her house to call me."

"Did she take your name and number?"

"Yes, I wrote them for her in an address book."

"Mystery solved," Jane said after thanking him and hanging up. "Not our man."

Claire turned to Tidy again. "Ivan's friend, you remember him writing his name and number?"

"He did! Aren't you listening?"

Maybe the painkiller's doing too good a job, Claire thought. "Maybe he wrote it down on a piece of paper on the table here."

Tidy smiled and harrumphed, then laughed. "I suppose anything's possible."

"Well, let's get busy," Claire said.

They started in on the papers, picking up each one and turning it over and over, looking for any handwriting. Claire and Jane surreptitiously scanned a second time the pieces Tidy examined, just in case.

Under the coffee table Claire found the phone book she had used to call the utility company some time ago. Phone book … She scrutinized the front and back covers and turned to the inside front cover. There it was: Mikhail Nabokov, with a phone number. "Is this the man's name, Tidy?"

"I told you so, right there in my phone book," she said with immense satisfaction.

Jane called in the details and asked the officer on duty to trace the phone number and call her back. "We'll locate him soon, Tidy."

"Just so you find my car. I can't do without my car."

Claire coughed. Jane didn't blink.

"We'll find him *and* your car," Jane said, "thanks to you for getting him to write down his name and number. Smart of you."

Tidy fairly preened with the compliment. "I want to make sure we got a handle on who he is and where he lives. He says his family has a home over in Wayland, living there a long time."

Claire and Jane locked eyes, puzzle pieces snapping into place. "Wayland … that's good information, Tidy," Jane said.

Claire speculated on the number of first-, second-, and third-generation Russians populating Wayland and which one of them would be so generous as to give up this schmuck who'd taken advantage of an old, helpless woman.

A few of her clients lived in the enclave, and with these visits she had learned that Russians revered their elderly. Thus, she hoped, outrage at the temerity of this fellow would prompt the community to give him up, happily.

Jane's cell rang. "Ah, here we go." The duty officer reported no such number listed anywhere in the 223 area code—or any of the other Bay Area codes. "He's a little too clever for us," Jane said. The trio deflated with the news.

Not just clever, this guy has a lot of gall and patience. Claire was agitated. He'd written down a bogus phone number hours, maybe even days, before he'd committed the crime. He'd waited and watched for his opportunity, careful to leave no footprints in the meantime.

In Claire's, albeit limited, experience, it was family or care providers who committed premeditated elder abuse. Mr. Nabokov was neither. Nor was he a petty thief grabbing a chance to steal or commit fraud. If Tidy was remembering correctly (*And don't we wonder about that,* Claire thought), this guy had hung around for over a week, with plenty of occasions to grab, nab, or steal, but hadn't done the job until Tidy had been at her most vulnerable and had actually *given* him the goods, so to speak. Claire's eyes met Jane's, and she read similar thoughts in Jane's pensiveness.

We still don't know who he is, Claire realized, *and if the phone number is false, most likely the name is too.*

Miki

What had possessed Miki to write his real name but make up a phone number, he didn't comprehend. As he'd written in Tidy's phone book, he hadn't been thinking about ripping her off. He wasn't that kind of guy. In fact, he'd fixed her car, even though the note said he shouldn't, and he'd driven her to the grocery store *and* the hospital. Hey, he was a *nice* guy.

And let's remember, she had *given* him the keys to the car.

Why have a first-class car sitting in her yard with the battery disconnected because she shouldn't drive it? Why not *he* drive it?

Then she'd handed him the wallet, and he'd slipped from being a good guy in Tidy's world to a Russian *moshennik* with more shameless audacity than he'd known he possessed.

Getting her Pontiac *and* his cab out of Oakmont and back to Wayland had inconvenienced him—annoyed him, in fact. He'd delivered the tank to a side street behind a small park to hide it for an hour while he dashed to get his cab out of the area. He hoped no one had noticed the taxi sitting across from Tidy's house for so long.

By late afternoon, the tide had turned on the hideous day he'd spent with the old lady in the hospital. Tooling around town in "his" grand sedan, he bought up stuff as if he'd just won the lottery. All the goodies he'd dreamed of lately—but hadn't the money to purchase—he loaded into the trunk: flat-screen TV, thin laptop with an extra-wide monitor, and iPods for his nieces and nephews (wouldn't they love him now?).

The next day he called in sick and continued his shopping spree: a set of patio furniture for his *tetya* and *dyadya*, new tires for his cousin Sergei, an electric barbeque for his grandfather, and groceries for everyone in his extended family—lobster, crab, steak, caviar, sour cream, and a case of Stolichnaya vodka. Hey, he was a good guy!

For him? A gold watch, a satchel of new clothes, shoes, and a real leather jacket. *Krasivyi*, he looked magnificent. He'd be turning heads at the dance hall. Katarina would be all over him. With the ATM card he managed to pocket $800 before the account shut down. The old bag had the pin number written plain as day in the wallet—even said "pin number" on the shred of paper tucked behind her ID. How could anyone be so dumb?

There were four credit cards in all, three of them previously used for bookmarks in her Bible, along with her Social Security card. She had *given* him the wallet containing the fourth credit card and her state-issued ID. Before rational thoughts had surfaced, he had grabbed the Bible and snatched the other credit cards. He'd left the book on the dryer as he'd exited the back door—stealing a Bible was not worthy of him. He wasn't sure about the Social Security card. He'd have to ask around. Maybe he could sell it with the ID to a harebrained old lady needing a new identity. He snickered with this humor.

He spread the credit expenditures, going fast and furious on one card, hoping the unusual activity wouldn't be discovered before he maxed the account or some overzealous clerk picked up on it. He took care with the stores he selected—always busy, too busy to ask for identification. Two or three times he scouted out which clerks asked and which didn't before approaching the checkout stands. The few times he was asked for ID, he mumbled in a heavy accent that he'd left his ID in the car but remembered the number, and then he recited Tidy's ID number. One clerk, actually noticing the "Tidy Bourbon" on the card, was cheeky enough to look at him and say, "Tidy? That's you?"

"Old Russian name, from my grandfather," he said. "It mean 'titan' in Russian. You know, big guy, like me." He smiled his toothy smile. Beautiful! What a charmer he was. The clerk put the shoes in the bag and handed them over.

And all those stores with self-checkout systems! No ID required, didn't even have to have a pin number. Some didn't require a signature either. The ones that did, who was comparing the signatures, and to what?

He never bought too many things at once in stores with these systems. Too much activity might tip someone off. Oh, and maybe—his mind buzzed with the maybes—cameras watched the machines. He kept his cap pulled low on his forehead and his eyes focused on his goodies as he scanned them. He needn't have worried. Most stores hadn't yet figured out they needed cameras.

After forty-eight hours of more fun than he could remember, he decided to close down his operation. Using the cards any longer would be risky. He cut them into tiny plastic bits and tossed the shards in a neighbor's trash can.

He'd had his spree and made a grand impression on his nearest and dearest, regardless of how near and dear they were to him. Glossing over their frowns, he told the babushkas and *tetyas* he'd been saving up to help everyone—"Lotta big rides, tips you wouldn't believe." His largess was for family, he said. "I got no one but you. I love you all." Not once did he think of Ivan—or his benefactor.

In the matter of Tidy's car, however, Miki was a little careless. He had never owned a car of his own. Although he thought his job as a cabdriver beneath him, it did provide a car to drive. The cab company said no driving his cab except when working, but he bent the rule, as every cabbie did. Now, however, he possessed a car of his own—although not the Porsche of his dreams.

He parked Tidy's tank off the street at night, in the far corner of his apartment's parking lot. He'd have to ask around about getting recycled license plates; he couldn't be sure how long the theft would go unreported. Then there was the matter of those out-of-date tags. Probably safe for a little while, he thought, granted he kept an eye out for any cop who had nothing better to do than nab him for the tags. New plates were the answer.

The old lady didn't know much about him, so why worry?

What information he'd given her, she'd never remember. She'd not point fingers. In her isolation, he couldn't imagine anyone even checking on her for a few days. Heck, he wouldn't be surprised if the cops just laughed at the idea of her car being hijacked. She was too old to drive!

A week later Dmitri told him the word was out for a Russian with a white 1995 Pontiac Cutlass, stolen from an old lady over in Oakmont. He, Dmitri, was sure the gas-guzzler he'd seen Miki driving recently wasn't that car, but he thought Miki ought to be aware of the rumor. *Chyort.* Damn. How'd they get onto him so fast? He'd have to figure out where to unload the tank and how to get back from the dump site without raising any suspicions.

A prickling of anxiety caused his palms to dampen. How many people besides Dmitri might put two and two together— or rather Miki and the old lady's car together? And how did the cops know he was Russian? *Chyort poberi.*

Miki dithered for two days, working hard in his cab as an excuse for not taking action. The third day, on an airport drop, he spotted the perfect place to abandon Tidy's car. The street, with vacant lots and junk cars already littering the area, was a short walk to a BART station. He'd call one of the other hacks at Misha's to pick him up at Wayland. He'd make the dump in the middle of the evening rush hour that very day. Greater numbers of highway patrol lurked in the late afternoon, but they surely were more concerned with cheaters in the carpool lane and not stolen cars, or so Miki's rationale unfolded. During rush hour, however, the traffic would be slow, so the cops had more time to get a good look at the car and the license plate. Maybe early Saturday morning. Yes, much better. Still two more days away, but he figured the wait a wise plan.

He spent Friday busily ferrying people back and forth to BART and downtown Martinsville and was not around midday to observe the plainclothes guy snooping in the apartment parking lot.

At eight o'clock Saturday morning, he drove out of the lot and turned toward the freeway. In his confidence and concentration on the task ahead, he missed the cruiser that pulled in behind him. The cop finally gave a bleat of his siren, jolting Miki out his regretful thoughts of relinquishing "his" car. *Chyort voz'mi.*

He wondered briefly if he could get away with some song and dance about the old lady offering him the car while she recovered from her injury but quickly decided against the idea. If they knew he was Russian and knew where to find him, they knew too much already. Then like an avalanche, the memory of his credit card scam descended. By the time the cop asked him to get out of the car—slowly, keeping his hands in view—he had enough sense to keep his mouth shut and follow instructions.

Chapter 25

Claire

Jane called Claire with the good news a few days after Miki's arrest. "Caught the guy red-handed!" she cried.

Claire's face lit up. "That's wonderful. What a relief!"

"The car's intact too, which should make Tidy happy, although I don't quite get her attachment to it."

"I think she's holding on to the car hoping Ivan will come back and be her chauffeur again."

"If so, she'd better get her tags current."

Claire quickly changed the subject. "Did Officer Jordan talk to Ivan?" she asked.

"I think he's been working a homicide on the south side and had to put this case aside. But we got an anonymous call from someone in Wayland. Heavy accent."

Claire smiled. *Good for them.* "What happens now?"

"I'm not sure. I'll have to get with the DA and explore the territory. Crimes against elders are tricky, and nailing the guy won't be easy. You observed the other day when I asked Tidy who did the deed. She's not what we'd call a reliable witness. Any good lawyer will get him off."

"But he was driving her car!" Claire spluttered.

"But she gave him the keys!" Jane rejoined.

"But she didn't say he could drive it for the next six weeks."

"How do you know she didn't?"

Claire emitted a small laugh. "You win."

———

Curiosity pulled Claire to the courthouse on Tuesday to hear Miki's arraignment. Jane was there too and teased, "You a wannabe lawyer?"

Claire smirked at the jest, although Jane was closer to the mark than she realized. A few years previously Claire had toyed with the idea of going back to school for paralegal training at least and maybe even a JD, if the subject stuck with her. She'd thought the instruction might broaden her background and open up some new career opportunities. Never mind she was in her early sixties. Grandmothers were getting degrees all the time, and she wasn't a grandmother—yet.

Losing her husband had changed her. Alone, one had to think about other things, and with all that thinking, sometimes one's priorities shifted.

Miki was arraigned before Judge Grossman. ADA Benji Worthington asked for time for discovery. The judge said two weeks. Benji's posture hinted at a complaint, but he apparently decided it unwise. *These elder cases require speed,* His Honor would likely remind him; otherwise the victim's memory might falter. Benji should know that by now, Claire ruled.

Since Miki had no criminal record and the ADA had

produced little solid evidence of a felony, Judge Grossman released Miki on his own recognizance. Claire groaned. Benji's face turned red with fury.

A potential felony elder abuse was at stake. Why didn't the ADA speak up? Claire chafed, wishing she was that wannabe now. Miki had taken advantage of an elderly, impaired woman. Okay, Tidy had given him permission to drive the car, but financial abuse was blatant. How could the judge be so dismissive?

With a glance to the left, Claire acknowledged the judge likely had his reasons. The large lawyer bearing down on the defendant's podium might be one. He'd most likely scream the injustice, and the judge's mood, Claire surmised, rejected arguments. Claire probably wasn't lawyer material; she would likely receive contempt rulings for yelling at the judge.

———

Two weeks passed. Claire lost patience and called Jane to find out what was going on. Jane reported that she had phoned Benji once to ask about progress and that Benji's assistant had told her—rather briskly—that the assistant district attorney was too busy with a murder trial.

Claire bridled. After hanging up with Jane, she called Benji and demanded to speak to him. Benji had scooped a guilty verdict the day before, he said, and he would now turn his attention to *all* the cases sitting on his desk, including the elder-abuse case of her concern. He reminded her that guilty convictions in elder-abuse cases were rare. She reminded him that these crimes were getting more attention by the news media. He said he'd love to toss this one for lack of evidence. She said he should at least interview the witness. He said that might be the expedient way to make the case disappear. She said he'd better call Jane Rios and ask her how she felt about throwing the case out.

That afternoon Claire heard from Jane. "Well, you certainly got his dander up. I do believe he hissed at me over the phone."

"You didn't allow him to talk about dismissal, did you?"

"Of course not. He asked if he should interview Tidy, and I said he better had. I told him things would go more smoothly if you were present. I also suggested he videotape the interview. If it turns out well, he could ask the judge to use the video in lieu of Tidy appearing in court."

"Brilliant. Although we recall—don't we ever—that she can be impressive in court. The level of confusion is likely to rise under the stress of being in court, though; better to get the testimony on tape in the familiar surroundings of her home, with fewer people around to muddle things."

"I made those very points to Benji."

"What did he say?"

"He reminded me how articulate and believable her speech to the judge had been at the hearing in November."

"And?"

"He snorted but agreed to taping the interview."

———

The four of them—Tidy, Claire, Jane, and Benji—and the video camera on a tripod crowded Tidy's diminutive living room. Mr. ADA, in his lawyerly, dark, pin-striped three-piece suit, appeared bulky. His curly blond hair and choirboy, cherubic face, however, were the hallmarks of a man far too young to occupy the important position he did. Certainly Tidy thought so.

"When'd they put kindergartners in the DA's office?" she demanded.

An awkward silence hung from the ceiling. Claire, used to Tidy's unmannerly ways, spoke up quickly. "Tidy, Mr. Worthington is a lawyer; he is a law school graduate and has worked in the DA's office for five years now. He's very good at his job." She figured she would give the jerk some credit in hopes of motivating him to nail the abuser.

"Looks like a kindergartner to me."

At least she doesn't recognize him, Claire thought. How would her mood swing if she caught on that Benji had had something to do with Ivan's incarceration?

Claire and Jane remained determinedly placid as Benji stood cautiously and went to the video camera set up in the middle of the room.

"Mrs. Bourbon," he commenced in his kindliest voice.

Claire fidgeted with his unnecessary condescension.

"I'm going to turn on the video camera now, so we can get started."

"You taking a movie of me?"

"Yes." Benji looked at Claire. His eyes held the sneering comment she was sure he wanted to say out loud.

Nevertheless, she focused on the greater good and rescued him again. "Remember, Tidy, we talked about this interview. Mr. Worthington is going to put it on tape so you don't have to make the long trip to the courthouse to appear in person."

"Fine with me," she said as if she didn't care.

Claire was sure, however, that Tidy must be secretly thrilled to see the camera aimed at her. Claire was correct.

"It'll be on the big screen?" Tidy asked. "I've never been in a movie."

Claire grinned. "I don't think you'll be in the theaters, Tidy, but Mr. Worthington might be willing to show it to you on a monitor, when we're done."

Benji frowned. Claire smiled her best "sure you will" smile. Jane coughed.

Benji set the camera to record and spoke the requisite material regarding the case number, the date, place of recording, and those persons present.

"Why're you talking about all them?" Tidy horned in, waving her hand toward Jane and Claire. "This is supposed to be about me."

Benji glowered and ran the tape back to the beginning. "I have to mention your friends because they're in the room. That's required. But you're right. This tape is just about you." He paused—to gather his composure, Claire supposed. "We'll start again, but I must say everyone's name. Okay?"

"Fine with me."

He got through the introduction without complaint. "Mrs. Bourbon, would you state your name and address for me?"

"You just said my name."

"Yes, I did, but could you state your full name for me?"

"Used to be Teresa Madeline Eugenia Bour-bon. Turned out to be too long, so I call myself Tidy Bourbon now."

She gave her address and her age and, without any derisive comment, agreed she was making this tape voluntarily. The room seemed to settle, the air less tight.

Benji reached into his briefcase and extracted a piece of paper with images of six male faces. "Mrs. Bourbon, from this array of photos, can you point to the man who stole your car?"

Tidy took the mug shots and brought them closer to her eyes. Without hesitation she pointed at Miki. "That's the bum."

"Let the record show Mrs. Bourbon has indicated the picture of Mikhail Nabokov."

"Russkie." It was barely audible, but even so, Benji stopped any further comment.

"Mrs. Bourbon, tell me the story of how he stole your car."

She hesitated a moment with an expression of trying to grasp a memory from her pool of swarming images. Then with surprising clarity, Tidy related the entire account, nonstop, without pause or prompting by anyone.

Claire regarded Tidy as she talked. With various scheduling delays, the case was almost a month old now, yet Tidy still had all the detail. She appeared composed, even demure. She held the ADA's eyes for several moments at a time. She hesitated only once when Benji came to the part about the wallet—had she given it to the man, or had he taken it? The break was ever so slight. "He took my wallet."

It wasn't a lie, really, Claire reflected. Tidy had given the wallet to him, yes. And he'd taken it. Claire waited to see if Benji would correct Tidy. He didn't.

Otherwise, it was an Oscar performance. Only a trace of Tidy's southern slang and idioms sprinkled her speech. She refrained from the dropped word endings, and she didn't utter a single cuss.

Claire felt vindicated for her argument with Julian about Tidy appearing before a judge regarding a conservatorship. Tidy had the capacity to hide impairment. How did this happen? Claire wondered. Did Tidy instinctively revert to her career days when "educated" English was important? Or did her intuition assert that she should sound "normal"? Or, calculatedly, did she understand she needed to speak well to be believed?

ADA Worthington leaned against the far wall, scrutinizing

his subject, a semblance of thought reflected in his eyes. As if coming to a conclusion, he pushed away from the wall and stepped forward to turn off the camera. "I think we've got enough to arrest him on a felony charge."

Claire and Jane brightened.

Benji nonchalantly asked Tidy if she would be willing to appear in court to testify. The other two women sat up abruptly, making rustling noises and glaring at the ADA.

Claire's lips were parted to speak.

Tidy cut her off. "Testify? What do you mean?"

"Tell your story the way you did just now, but in court, in front of a judge."

"You want me to come to the courtroom and all."

"Yes. You'd make a good witness in this matter, and I'd like you to tell your story in front of the judge."

Claire couldn't sit still. "You think that's necessary? She's done so well on the tape."

Benji shrugged his shoulders as he packed the video. "If she attests in person, it will have more impact. To bring this Nabokov to trial, her testimony for the judge, and possibly for a jury, will mitigate any difficulty we might encounter about, ah, the way the crime happened. She looks good."

Tidy, following the ADA's words, put a hand to her hair, patting it into better shape. "I can show them my injury," she said as she held up her bandaged arm.

Benji stared at her, appearing uncertain about a response.

Jane interrupted to save any irrelevant comment from Benji. "What about the defense's cross?" she asked. "I'm not sure ... ah ..."

Claire couldn't think of a diplomatic way to come to Jane's

rescue. Neither of them wanted to elucidate in front of Tidy what a disaster a cross-examination of Tidy's testimony would be.

Benji was evidently going to overlook the potential problem. "I think Mrs. Bourbon will do well in court. She's articulate, to the point, and appears to me to be a credible witness."

Tidy beamed at Benji. She smiled widely enough to show all her ill-fitting dentures and then chuckled. "I'm already acquainted with the judge. We'll make a deal with him. Throw that no-good Russkie in jail."

Claire coughed to keep from laughing. Jane turned away to hide her smile. Benji looked at Tidy as if she had just sprouted yellow daffodils in her hair. "We'll assess the situation later and decide what would be best for everyone," he said, his cherubic face recovering from a horrible fright. "All right with you, Mrs. Bourbon?"

Without waiting for a response, he grabbed his camera and escaped like a gazelle followed by a lion. It was not a lion but Jane who accosted him—verbally—at the trunk of his vapid white county car. Claire glanced at them from the living room window. Good. She hoped Jane told the cherubic jerk what a fool he was if he allowed Tidy into the courtroom.

"So you'd like to say hello to the judge again, Tidy?"

Tidy laughed, a full guffaw. "Wouldn't that be fun?"

Claire smiled outwardly but frowned inwardly. If Tidy recognized the judge she wanted to make a deal with was, in fact, the man who had put Ivan in jail, she might not be so amused.

Chapter 26

Ivan

Ivan's daily routine had become a bore. His meals came to his cell, and he kept to one corner of the exercise yard, avoiding contact with the other inmates. He amused himself in the prison library. There was one novel in Russian—Dostoyevsky's *Crime and Punishment*. Ivan thought this a joke—such a title in a library behind bars—but his curiosity was piqued, and he decided to read it, despite the length.

He struggled through the 704 pages—the first time. True, his Russian was rusty, but the injury to his eye (a result of the beating years ago) precluded speedy reading in any case. He read the book now—for the fifth time—more fluidly for the language, if not for the words in print. The nuances of the story might be lost on him, but he grasped some parallels to his own situation (and finally understood the logic of the book's place in the prison library). Raskolnikov's incarceration, and the love he was denied as a result, stirred Ivan's soul. His emotional response surprised him.

When he tired of his struggle, literary and psychological,

he turned to the newspaper for variety. The Raiders were out of the playoffs; the Giants looked good in Florida; the San Jose Sharks were skating their way to oblivion. His eyes took most of the morning to get through the paper. He had never been a fast reader, but his impairment required all the tenacity he could muster to keep focused on the print.

Ralph was the only con who spoke to him, although the conversations had little content:

"Putrid eggs for breakfast."

"I had pancakes."

"You're making that up."

An exchange about their various misdeeds surfaced naturally. Ralph was awaiting his third hearing on felony theft charges and met with his public defender often. Ivan was jealous. Just being able to talk to someone else would be a relief.

Ralph added to Ivan's sense of unease, saying, "You idiot bastard. You should be screaming, 'Injustice.' They've no right to keep you here without some kind of trial."

Eventually, Ralph went uptown for his hearing. He returned midafternoon dashed. "Bastards sunk me for a first-degree burglary. Idiot lawyer didn't do nothing for me." He paced around the exercise yard in his frustration.

By the fence he swerved and in long strides came up alongside Ivan. "Hey, another guy like you showed up this morning. Russian, he said. He knew you. You screwed him, he said."

Ivan's blood froze. Someone "like" him: Russian? Maybe Ukrainian? Or *any* kind of mafia? Any one of those species who might possibly be angry with him sent a cold prickle along his spine and caused his throat to constrict. He had kept away from the Russian-Ukrainian conflict, but there were a few thugs in the Wayland-Nortonville corridor whom he believed knew of his family's business in Odessa, and he was obsessively afraid of them. Thus, the mention of some Russian knowing him and speaking ill of him sent him into a state of near hysteria. He counseled himself to slow his breathing and unclench his fists.

Outwardly he allowed a frown and tried to rationalize this nightmare away. If he had crossed any of the mafia types, surely he wouldn't have gone this long in jail with no incidents, or so he hoped. With extreme trepidation he asked, "He got a name?"

"Mik-something."

"Mikhail Nabokov?"

"Sounds right. Said he drove a cab, same as you."

"*Da*. But Miki no criminal. What'd he do?"

"Ripped off some old lady. Car, money, credit cards. Rinky-dink stuff normally, but DA's trying to paste him with—what's it called? Abusing old people. A felony straight up, if they pin it on him. Stupid bastard."

Ivan pushed away from the wall and brought his fists up in a boxer's stance.

"Whoa." Ralph backed up two paces. "I'm the messenger; don't get those in my face."

Ivan stared blankly at his hands and lowered them. "You in the room when Miki is before judge?"

"Yeah, sure."

"The lady's name, did you hear it?"

Ralph laughed. "Funny name: Bourbon, Tidy Bourbon."

Back in his cell, Ivan paced. What had Miki done? What had he, Ivan, caused by sending Miki to Tidy? She'd be so mad. What if Miki implicated Ivan in these offenses? His mind writhed with imagined horrors. He'd be deported for these crimes—nothing crimes—but if committed against old ladies, apparently abominable crimes, if Ralph had it right.

After dinner, Ivan was first in line at the phones. He waited, shifting from one foot to the other, working out in his mind what he would say to Tidy. He had so many questions: *What he do to you? What happen to car? Did he take you to store, like I asked?*

No, oh no. It was better to not ask her questions. She'd get mad at him for sending Miki, then … In his mind the exchange steamed.

I sorry, Tidy; I so sorry.

You're just a sorry bastard, Ivan. If you'd use your head for something besides a hat rack, you'd see how bad things are for me. You've got to take some responsibility.

She'd said that before. He didn't get the "hat rack" bit, but he knew she wasn't saying anything nice.

A guard opened the phone room, and yellow-suited men swarmed to the phone booths. Ivan was left at the door, his feet cemented to the floor. He couldn't call her. He couldn't bear her rage.

For weeks before, he had been running his daily fantasy like a video. It pictured him walking all the way back to Oakmont to surprise Tidy. She'd be ecstatic to see him, drawing him into her cozy kitchen to set about cooking some blini—perhaps the cherry kind. But now …

She'd throw him out, like always when she was angry. He'd have to go down to the cardboard city under the bridge to spend the night, beg food from the soup kitchen, ask Blackie to find him a bed at the church shelter. All of that was so bad. He'd wander the streets during the day, stop by Tony's—maybe someone would spring for a slug of vodka. There'd be comments in the bar about the old lady throwing him out.

Obviously, none of this would happen now; he was in jail! He had a roof over his head—and iron bars on his windows. A bed, food, all provided, and Tidy couldn't take it away. Could she? Ivan again worried around the idea that he had sent Miki to help Tidy. If Miki was guilty of bad crimes, wasn't he too? The ice water of deportation ran through his veins.

The last time he'd been incarcerated in the Martinsville tank, his parole officer had told him if he got any more arrests, it might be very hard for him to hold on to his green card. Deportation was a distinct possibility. Ivan wasn't sure if this had been an idle threat or not. The best policy, he knew from experience, was to maintain a low profile, stay out of trouble, talk to no one, and keep to himself. Period.

He'd chance nothing. He left the phone room for the library, where he sat slumped at a reading table. The disquiet of the last four and a half months penetrated his confusion. Why had no one come to see him? Why hadn't he been sent north? Why hadn't the judge done something? In his bewilderment he was sure they had him for this old person's abuse thing. There would be another trial. That was why he'd been languishing in the same cell all these weeks. The insight, albeit flawed, sent him into a spiral of despair.

In addition to the library, the prison chapel had become a refuge. Almost daily he asked his warden for a half hour of "prayer." He pleaded that his Russian Orthodox rituals required prayers to be said in a holy place at certain times. The guards had no idea about his religion, he knew, and they didn't seem to care. Ivan was always courteous, so his requests were usually granted. If nothing else, the chapel provided different walls to look at.

He was not a religious man—his early life in the Ukraine had precluded any such training—but he had long recognized the escape a spirituality allowed.

One night when he'd been expelled from Tidy's home, he'd gone to the church on Third Street. Too ashamed to ask for a bed in the basement, he'd snuck into the church proper before they'd locked the doors and curled up in the narthex, next to the lifelike statue of Mary. He'd talked to the Mother above him. She hadn't talked back, levied judgment, or berated him for misdoings. She'd only smiled upon him, comforting him.

He'd spent so much time in the church for AA and the soup kitchen that he'd soon found himself attending and watching the services taking place throughout the day. He'd discovered some measure of peace while sitting in the cool, dark interior.

But he didn't care for the prison chapel much—too stark and cold, with none of the beauty of religious adornment. Still, the idea of a place where no one could harangue you had a calming effect on him. He went almost every day just for something to do. Here was a space to empty his mind of horrible thoughts. He often replaced hideous images with remembrances of the quiet nights he and Tidy had spent together watching TV or listening to the radio or her old recordings of big band music or just sitting. The contrast to their evening rows over his drunken stupors or perceived laziness or lack of ambition was notable.

"What you doing, Tidy?" he might ask.

"I'm thinking of my past, Ivan. Don't you ever put your mind to what's come about in your life?"

"Oh, Tidy, you know what happened to me. I don' need to think this."

Tidy would look at him, smile, and say, "Ivan, you're a good man ... when you're sober."

Ivan sighed with this scene. As he often did at this point in his reminiscence, he made a new resolution to stay away from the bar and the liquor store. Now, if he would just be released, he'd return to Tidy's home and attend to her, keep her safe, look after her, for the rest of her life—he promised this to himself and Tidy and whatever higher power watched over him in that room.

Chapter 27

The Courtroom

Miki had been picked up and arraigned on several felony elder-abuse charges, and maybe, depending on ADA Worthington's diligence with gathering evidence, Miki would be found guilty. Benji had taped the key witness, but he was excited at the prospect of presenting her in person. He felt sure that her testimony would inspire the judge and that the judge would easily move this case to a conviction. Now the scheduled pretrial hearing—Benji's day of reckoning—had arrived.

As Claire took her seat in the courtroom, she was dismayed: the judge *was* the same man who had presided over Ivan's court appearance. If Tidy recognized Judge Letty, they might be in trouble.

Although Judge Letty and ADA Worthington occupied their specific seats again, there was a change of defendants, of course—and this defendant had a private lawyer. The defense lawyer sat in the lawyers' block—a group of chairs cordoned off in the rear left corner, where attorneys could bide their time, awaiting their turn. Four sat in the enclosure. Three chatted like old pals, while Mr. Labinsky—overweight, impeccably dressed, his luxuriant gray hair brushed back from his florid face—remained aloof, scrutinizing a file he'd pulled out of his hand-tooled black briefcase.

Claire wondered about the source of the money for this flamboyant and notorious defender of the Russian community. It couldn't be Miki, who hadn't posted bail at his arraignment. A puzzle: expensive attorney but no bail. Perhaps the Russian quarter didn't want its reputation sullied by this punk, but it was okay if the punk languished in jail for a while?

Parked stiffly at the table on the right side in the front, Benji twiddled with his pen, distracted. His clerk, a paralegal who could have been his mother, leafed through the papers in the files before them, to check on the correct order.

In the long, narrow, glassed-in room to their left, three prisoners in county-orange jumpsuits slouched with various degrees of dejection on the benches lining the wall. Three. Good, Claire thought, the wait wouldn't be too tiresome, even if Miki came up last.

Miki sat at one end of the solid slatted seats, apart from the other two jumpsuits. He held his spine to the partition behind him, head straight ahead. But Claire noticed his eyeballs moving back and forth over the people seated in various places throughout the room.

ADA Worthington had arranged for a secretary in his office to pick up Tidy and transport her to the hearing. Claire had offered to ride with her, but Benji had said Tidy's appearance would be sharper if she wasn't surrounded by social workers. Claire chafed under the characterization and retaliated by labeling Benji a jerk (again). Benji had also denied her access to

Tidy immediately before the hearing. *Schmuck,* Claire thought, an even more satisfying label.

The bailiff called the court to order on the appearance of Judge Letty, and the clerk announced the first case. An attorney from the pool stepped forward to a podium adjacent to a section of the glassed wall open to the dock. One of the orange suits also rose and came to the window—a short Latino, whose face barely showed in the opening, needing a trial date. The business was quickly disposed.

"Line two, one-zero—four-five-two-five—one-zero," the clerk called out.

Miki's attorney stepped to the podium with a confident air and motioned for Miki to come forward.

Assistant District Attorney Benji presented his case against Miki, calling him a miscreant for preying on an elderly woman who had been injured and in pain. Oh, he painted a pitiful picture of Tidy Bourbon's plight and then called Tidy as his first and only witness.

The bailiff escorted her down the court's short aisle to the witness stand. She turned to the left and right, like a queen on parade, smiling when she spotted Claire. She raised her right hand on request and, with remarkable composure, said she'd tell the truth. She sat in the varnished wooden chair of the witness cubicle and turned to eye the judge. She smiled at him, and for one horrible moment Claire feared she'd start talking to him. But no, she recognized her position and instead turned toward the ADA and smiled at him too. Then she looked at Miki—and smiled again.

Neither attorney missed the disclosure. Benji coughed and asked, a little louder than necessary, "Can you hear me, Mrs. Bourbon?"

Tidy stared at his nose.

"Mrs. Bourbon," he said, raising his voice a notch, "we have a hearing device for you to wear, if you are having difficulty. It's important you be able to hear and understand everything said here today."

Tidy's eyes moved from his nose to his eyes. "When I'm listening, I'm hearing just fine. Thank you." The courtroom's audience smiled with her. They wanted her to be a winner and were pleased she appeared sharp and attentive.

She wiggled and straightened her posture in the witness chair, as though she had heard the courtroom's opinion of her. She clasped her hands in her lap, her left wrist compressed now with only an elastic cuff. She turned her full attention to the ADA.

Benji took her through the story in small chunks, being careful to keep the thread clear but not leading her testimony. Claire noted he had prepared well for this confirmation of the crime. Tidy appeared a model witness.

But Miki's lawyer, Labinsky, knew the location of the hole in the dike and started his cross with a strong punch. "You gave Mr. Nabokov the keys to your car, Ms. Bourbon?"

"I already said, he was driving it. Drove me to the hospital, waited for me while they put the cast on my arm, and drove me home."

Labinsky drew a paper from his notebook. "We have an affidavit from the emergency room doctor attending Ms. Bourbon on the day in question and a second from the emergency room admissions clerk. Both of them say Mr. Nabokov did indeed bring Ms. Bourbon to the hospital and that he waited while she was treated and left with her. The admissions clerk adds that he appeared 'solicitous, bracing her as he led her out the door.'"

"I told you all this story, for the other feller. Why are you repeating everything?"

Judge Letty peered at her over his half-glasses but refrained from comment. Everyone in the courtroom knew the ADA's case had taken a turn.

"You say when you reached home you asked Mr. Nabokov to go to the pharmacy and get your prescription pain medication?"

"Are you going to ask all the same questions as that kindergartner over there?"

A ripple of tittering moved through the room. The judge kept his neutral posture, but the humor registered around his eyes.

Miki's lawyer lowered his head and turned his back on Tidy—perhaps to gather his thoughts—and swerved to face her again. "Ms. Bourbon, you may want to listen closely to my questions. They are a little different than Mr. Worthington's. For instance, can you tell me if Mr. Nabokov drove you, in your car, to other places during the week before your fall? Did he take you shopping, for example?"

"Objection. Relevance," barked Benji.

Claire was all too aware that Benji had stuck his neck out by putting Tidy on the stand. He was going to have to work hard to get an indictment.

"I'm trying to establish my client's relationship to Ms. Bourbon." Labinsky kept his eye on the judge.

"Reasonable," the judge declared. "Objection overruled. Please answer the question, Ms. Bourbon."

"What question?"

Labinsky was slow and patient in his repetition.

"Yes, he took me shopping, just like Ivan."

ADA Benji moaned.

"And who is Ivan?"

"Objection, Your Honor. Relevance." In his defeated demeanor, Benji didn't even bother to stand.

Judge Letty frowned. "Mr. Labinsky, are we fishing here?"

"No, Your Honor. The identity of this man is important to establishing usual versus unusual activity and thus whether the state's witness had people drive her in her car often."

"I see. Objection overruled." The judge turned to Tidy. "Ms. Bourbon, you may answer the question."

"I've never been fishing since I left Louisiana, so I can tell you I am not fishing now, and that's the truth, Mr. ..." Tidy leaned forward, twisting to check the judge's nameplate. "Mr. Letty," she concluded politely, if not quite correctly for His Honor.

The judge couldn't help himself this time. His hand went to his lower face. As if that gesture gave them permission, the court observers' titters turned to chuckles.

Claire could have wept. "Poor dear."

Jane sighed. "I think we've lost."

ADA Benji closed the file in front of him. To Claire that seemed to signal his view on any hope of conviction.

"Ms. Bourbon," Labinsky asked, "who is Ivan?"

"Ivan? Oh, Ivan, he's my tenant, pays his rent on time, and helps me around the house."

"What sort of help?"

"Cleans, vacuums, takes out the trash, cooks those delicious noodles with sour cream."

"And does he drive you places in your car?"

"Yes, of course. We ride to the bank and the grocery store; he drives me to the hospital, if I need to go."

"Did he ever go to the pharmacy to get a prescription for you?"

"Well now, let me think … Yes, I'm sure he did. He takes care of my medicines, puts my pills in the boxes to help me remember to take them."

"Why didn't he drive you to the hospital on the day in question, Ms. Bourbon?"

"What do you mean? He did."

"You said a moment ago Mr. Nabokov took you to the hospital when you fell and broke your wrist."

"That's right."

"I am wondering, where was this Ivan? Why didn't he take you?"

Tidy stiffened, almost imperceptibly, but Claire detected it and worried as she watched Tidy's eyes go to the middle space—in order to work out in her mind what had just happened.

You total jerk, Mr. ADA, Claire fumed. *Exactly the travesty we feared, putting her at risk with the court.*

Mr. Labinsky asked again, gently, quietly. He knew how to work this witness. "Where was Ivan when you broke your wrist?"

"Away."

"Away where?"

Silence.

"Ms. Bourbon?" Judge Letty intervened cautiously. "Can you answer the question?"

Tidy kept her eyes down, her arms rigid, her hands as if in prayer in her lap. All breath in the courtroom was suspended, waiting. The clatter of a rapid transit train a half mile away could have been detected if anyone had been listening for it, but they weren't; they were listening for Tidy's voice.

"Ivan's in jail," she whispered, but with the excellent acoustics of the room, the answer reached everyone's ears.

The courtroom was still and silent, waiting. Mr. Labinsky's sonorous voice confirmed her statement. "Ivan's in jail."

Tidy's head snapped up, her eyes ablaze. She flung her hand out, pointing at Miki. "Just where that no-good should be," she yelled. "He stole my car, my credit cards, and all my money. He and Ivan, they're friends. He told me they're friends." She pointed aggressively at Miki. "They both belong in jail."

"Your Honor, I don't know what the ADA's intention is here, but I would like to call the competency of this witness into question."

Benji was on his feet. "The witness is—"

"Not competent," Labinsky boomed.

Benji decided to accelerate the process to deliver himself of this mess. "Approach, Your Honor?"

The judge beckoned the two attorneys to his bench. Tidy turned to watch, but her head buzzed and began to ache. Mr. Labinsky's words echoed in her mind: "Not competent."

Judge Letty agreed with the defense that although Miki had committed a crime (maybe two), evidence of *premeditated* elder abuse—a felony charge—was insufficient. Tidy had given Miki the keys to the car. She had given him the wallet. Her Social Security card and ID card had been found in the glove compartment of the car, and although not an especially smart place to keep such items, who was to say Tidy herself hadn't put them there?

Most of the credit card purchases couldn't be traced to Miki, or the evidence was flimsy or circumstantial. The signatures on the electronic pads were too distorted to identify. None of the store clerks recognized him—even the one who had called him on his name. For two purchases, however—the patio set and the leather jacket—Miki had signed an actual credit card slip. The handwriting expert said it was Miki's signature—98 percent positive. The attorneys agreed to two misdemeanor counts of credit card fraud.

Given this was Miki's first criminal offense—his first offense of anything—a change of plea seemed prudent and would expedite the matter to resolution. The ADA made an offer, and Labinsky encouraged his client to accept it. A change of plea was recorded, and Judge Letty sentenced Miki to a year of probation, restitution of the missing cash, and one hundred hours community service in a nursing home so Miki would understand what it was like to be elderly.

The hearing was adjourned.

———

Claire was outraged; Jane, pragmatic.

"Claire, you know what this is about: elder abuse is our fastest-rising crime *and* the most difficult crime to prosecute. What made you think our case would be an exception? While trying to maintain their independence, this increasing elder population becomes vulnerable to scam artists. These crooks get away with the crimes because the victims are too much like Tidy—confused, forgetful at the very least ..."

Jane sensed she didn't have Claire's full attention. "Is this a lecture I've given you before?" Jane adjusted her voice from a dissertational tone to a more caring one. She added, "I'm sorry; I didn't mean to get carried away. I'm frustrated too at times. It's why I like working with you. You help your clients be more careful, and sometimes you persuade them to rat on the bad guys. *Sometimes* we have a story sufficiently reliable and truthful to get justice done. I'm sorry we were not so successful this time."

Claire turned thoughtful. "It's not so much Tidy's attempt to maintain independence but her resistance to being *dependent* on others. Then when she can't cope and has to seek help, she relies on the wrong people. That's what gets her in trouble."

Claire told Jane her lecture had given her much to think about and a new resolve to keep Tidy, and her other clients, protected from predators. "It's the costumes they come in that confuse seniors like Tidy. The brilliant smiles make it difficult to detect the fangs underneath."

Chapter 28

Claire

The hearing finished and the ADA's earlier ban on Claire's contact with Tidy lifted, Claire drove Tidy home. A grateful Tidy reported that Benji's secretary was not a very good chauffeur. She talked too much, for one thing, jabbering on about her wonderful boss, how overworked he was and all. Tidy had tuned her out, she said, and kept to herself.

Tidy didn't care to talk in Claire's car either. Claire allowed Tidy to have her own thoughts in peace—although Claire suspected they were hardly peaceful. Labinsky had boomed his indictment across the courtroom: "Not competent." Tidy, she was certain, had been pummeled by his words, mortified. *I'd be mortified, if it happened to me,* Claire reflected.

To break the silence, Claire asked, "Do you need anything at the grocery, Tidy? While we're out, I'd be happy to stop."

"No, thank you. I'm worn out. I want to go home and rest."

"Of course." She was so sad for Tidy. Claire rarely—never—let a client's life affect her like this.

Tidy turned to look out the passenger window. In the silence, her pain was palpable.

"You did well, Tidy."

Tidy remained mute, watching the passing landscape.

"What happened today was not your fault."

Rigid and frail, the form sitting next to her was as fragile in mind as in body, having to cope with the hurt, confusion, and rage that must be flooding her being.

Claire pulled up in front of the green porch, and Tidy released a long breath. She sat back into the car seat, facing forward, looking through the windshield.

Claire sat still and waited, hoping for a hint that would give her direction. Nothing. She opened the car door and climbed out. By the time she reached the other side of the car, Tidy had thrown open her door and arranged herself for an exit, sitting crosswise on the seat, her feet dangling out in the air. Claire extended a hand to pull her out. Tidy ignored it and wiggled her rear to the edge of the seat, positioning her feet on the ground. She placed her hands on either side of the doorjamb and pushed until she propelled her body upright. Only a slight grunt suggested there was any residual discomfort in her left wrist.

She grabbed her cane from the car and began a determined, slow-step march to her porch. Claire stood aside as Tidy proceeded to the door unaided, her dignity scarred but not extinguished. Claire rarely felt helpless in the presence of her clients, but she could think of nothing to bring change to this moment.

On the stoop, Tidy faltered. She thrust the cane at Claire, rummaged in the red vinyl bag for several long moments, and then, without a word, seized the cane and started back down the steps. Claire followed in silence. They walked across the front lawn and down the driveway to the rear. At the door Claire reached for the cane while Tidy searched in her bag again.

"Check your pockets, Tidy. The key may be there."

She did, the key surfaced, and with a quivering hand, she struggled to maneuver the key into the lock. Claire rocked on her feet—not with impatience but in restraint of the instinct to pluck the key from Tidy's hand and unlock the door herself. But now was not the time to bring attention to Tidy's inability to cope, with even simple tasks. Tidy did manage to get the door open, and snatching her cane from Claire, she trudged inside. She didn't close the door, and Claire accompanied her as far as the washing machine.

"Tidy, is there anything else I can do for you today?"

Tidy halted, stood fixed, eyes on the floor, and said, "No, you've done enough, and I thank you." She continued her trek to the living room. Claire turned and left, pulling the door firmly closed.

She sat in her car a few minutes before starting the engine. The futility of life at ninety-two. Even with wealth for a cushion, if your quality of life wasn't good, what was the purpose in living so long? Too many things going wrong, too many breakdowns, Claire brooded. Not just physical breakdowns but emotional ones, which at ninety-two were as difficult to recover from as a broken hip. Life had to be worth more than broken bodies and broken spirits. Why, she asked herself, was she thinking these bleak thoughts?

Chapter 29

Tidy

At home again, and alone, Tidy sat on her throne, reflecting on the day. After a few minutes she rose, went to the back entry, and with careful steps continued into the yard.

Against the south wall of the house rested a small, handmade wooden bench. Tidy moved to it and sat, remembering the day Mr. Browning had presented his handiwork to her. It must have been her birthday—the end of May. He'd made the bench for her, he'd said, so she could sit and enjoy her garden in the afternoon sun. And she did that now, shifting her gaze left to right, looking for signs of spring. Her survey of the newspaper that morning had announced a day in mid-April. Time for new growth in the garden.

She swept the yard with her eyes, hoping the season of rebirth would be visible. The late-blooming azalea blossoms were going brown, and the leaves of the paperwhites, intermittent among the azaleas, had collapsed to the ground. Was she too early or too late? No, in the back corner—the sunniest patch of the yard this time of year—some narcissi happily nodded their heads in a slight breeze. One of the wonderful things about living in Northern California, Tidy contemplated in her reverie, was that spring came early and lasted long.

As her gaze worked its way around the yard, the late-afternoon sun played on the new burgundy leaves of the rosebushes against the fence. And, spread among forget-me-nots, tulip blossoms punched through, still tight and closed. "Another day," she murmured to them, "and you'll be bursting."

Her search for signs of spring made a circle around the large flower bed in the middle of the yard. She struggled with its location, so central, important, but a fear of what the plot might—or might not—hold invaded the pleasure of her reverie. Finally, her gaze gathered the circle of earth into her soul.

In this patch, around which the whole garden revolved, dozens of green shoots poked out of the ground, some of them over a foot high. She smiled and clasped her hands before her in praise of these signs of life. Well on their way to a new season of bloom, her beloved iris filled the bed. As she looked on, her sight blurred, and her fingers felt damp. The moisture puzzled her for some moments before she realized tears had fallen. She allowed the drops to descend of their own accord for a while, then brushed them clear of her eyes, and sat straighter. Her hands went to either side of her to feel the bench, and she peered again at the iris, examining each detail.

Of the leaves pushing up to the light, some were narrow—the Dutch iris—others broad and swordlike—the bearded varieties. A clump of native Pacific Coasts and their reedy-looking shoots occupied one corner, with swamp iris from Louisiana crowding in among the natives. Over the years she had collected many different species, but they had one thing in common: purple blossoms, all of them—many shades of purple. Some of the inner segments were yellow, but the falls were purple. Some petals were streaked with white, but purple prevailed in every blossom. Tidy estimated the blooms would be fully developed in about a month. One month.

She wasn't sure how long she had been sitting on Mr. Browning's bench, but the air had cooled and the sun had fallen behind the trees. Time to go inside.

In her living room, she shuffled zigzag across the carpet, fingering chosen objects as she came upon them: the photo of Mr. Browning, her own portrait in her professional outfit, a framed proclamation citing her community service, the milk glass candy dish. She couldn't recall where the dish had come from.

From behind the books beneath Mr. Browning, she retrieved a tiny black lacquer box—Japanese, she seemed to remember—red-orange inside. She opened it and found a pair of pearl earrings, the only jewelry of value she had ever owned. Mr. Browning had given them to her for her thirty-fifth birthday. He had fastened them to her earlobes and stepped back to admire her. She blushed even today with the memory. She positioned the black box on the bookcase between the two photos.

She recovered the silver letter opener from under the middle cushion of the couch and placed it triumphantly on the desk. She loved the opener for the love of the person who had given it to her on their wedding day. No, no, the opener had been an anniversary present. Mr. Browning had presented her with the silver candlesticks on that lovely May day of their marriage.

She thought hard about where the candlesticks had ended up. It had been difficult to find a safe place—from *all* prying eyes and fast fingers—because they were so large. Under the couch didn't work because Juli knew about this place, but under the bed, wrapped in newspaper—ah, there they were, carefully stowed in a shoe box for size 12, double-wide men's loafers. She smiled, thinking how clever she had been to secret away all these precious gifts until this moment.

She placed the candlesticks back on the dining table, and a quiet came over her whole being—no muttering, no words spoken to herself (or anyone else) about the various people she had seen that day (whether or not she had actually seen them). An aura of calmness replaced her usual frenetic activity: searching for her calendar or her address book, checking the mail again. All the currents of air usually swirling around her were stilled. Eventually she went to the bedroom, and without so much as removing her shoes, she lay down and fell asleep.

In the middle of the night, she woke and was disconcerted to find herself lying on top of the blankets still fully dressed. Thinking it must be time for dinner, she wandered into the kitchen. The stove clock told her the truth: two in the morning. The house brooded, silent. Not even the refrigerator motor rumbled. What did it matter, the time? Who cared whether she was awake or asleep?

She went to the broom closet and found a box of black garbage bags. Flapping one open, she stood before the silent refrigerator and yanked open the door to expose the contents. Without hesitating, she removed the half-eaten pieces of chicken, wilted greens, moldy onions, a potato with black spots, a carton of soup, and plastic storage containers, the contents of which smelled bad, and dumped it all unceremoniously into the garbage bag. A slab of butter, a nearly empty jar of jam, and a few stale bagels were all that was allowed to remain.

She dragged the bag across the floor with her good arm and performed the same operation at the pantry shelves—rice she couldn't have prepared if she'd tried, half a bag of flour, a container of brown sugar, a few spices. The strong smell of the cinnamon made her stop for a moment and lift the small bottle to her nose to bring the aroma closer. Visions of gingerbread, molasses cookies, and a sprinkling on applesauce caused her to put the jar back on the shelf. She pushed a bag of Ivan's noodles to the side. Everything else went into the bag. The black plastic balloon was now too heavy to carry. She found the wire tie, closed off the top, and pushed the sack a few inches to a corner by the sink.

With another garbage bag in hand she shifted to her bedroom and swept the top of the bureau—years of debris— into the bag. With a ninety-degree turn, she faced the bedside table and surveyed the chaos of pill vials; cotton balls; puddles of cough syrup; and tubes of Bengay, Vaseline, and hand cream. She hesitated as if making a decision and then picked up an item at a time, plopping each one into the accumulating trash.

Another turn and she faced the commode. Months ago some well-meaning social worker type had ordered it up for her. She shouldn't have to make "the dangerous trek" to the bathroom in the middle of the night to relieve herself, Ms. Well Meaning had said. Tidy had used it because yes, it was more convenient. But without Ivan to empty the pan in the morning, she had been ignoring it. She giggled at what now seemed absurd to her. "Dangerous trek." She laughed out loud.

In the living room with another black bag, she sorted through the piles of paper on the coffee table. All rubbish—had to be. She had separated the bills herself the week before and left them on the desk for Julian. But then she remembered Julian didn't come anymore. "Have to do something about that," she mumbled.

She chucked the old newspapers into the sack, and in an uncharacteristic act of patience, to avoid any mistakes, she sat down to examine each piece of paper, concentrating every molecule of her brain on its content. In a triage-like manner, she tossed the hogwash into the bag, placed the flapdoodle in a "maybe" stack, and put what she believed to be of a serious nature on the desk.

On one of the trips to the desk, she picked up a pen, found an empty envelope to scribble on, and wrote in large letters "Call Juli."

The stacks of tissues on the couch, the contents of the wastebasket, the old church bulletins on the side table, a two-year-old birthday card from Ivan—all the bilgewater went into the bag. (Ivan's card didn't fit the category exactly, but she recognized that sentiment could not be part of her task.) The load this time was not heavy, and she dragged the bag across the purple carpet to place it by the back door.

She proceeded to the bedroom again and stripped the bed, smiling as she found her gray skullcap, checkbook, a singular Christmas card (from Claire), and another tube of Bengay. She stood the card on her now-cleared dresser top, forgetting her rejection of sentiment a moment ago, and took the checkbook to the desk. With the skullcap on her head, she dumped the Bengay in the trash bag and piled the bed linens by the bedroom door.

Standing before the dresser, she was inspired. She fetched another trash bag and swept the clothing from the drawers into the bag, leaving only her favorites in each category: her best panties, her shiny purple blouse, the fuzzy blue sweater, and the only pair of pants small enough to fit anymore.

In the natural order of things, the closet would be next.

Three bags cleared the pole and hooks. In the back corner of the closet, she grabbed the old bathrobe, uncovering a clump of paper concealed in a large envelope. She pulled the envelope to her chest and patted it fondly. *Wouldn't Juli wonder about these papers.* She grinned as she stashed the envelope in the bottom drawer of the dresser—now so empty there was plenty of room.

Three items survived the closet cleansing: a flowery dress for church, a full-length navy coat (old-fashioned but warm), and the hat with a ribbon she liked to wear for Easter. *Well, now, when is Easter?* she asked herself.

She made a trip to the living room to locate the calendar … gone, in the trash bag by the back door. No calendar to rely on … well, she wouldn't have to now, would she? She smiled mysteriously.

To the left of the closet, a laundry basket overflowed with more clothing. She knew she should be doing a washing, but why bother? Instead she scooped the garments into another black plastic bag. As she removed the last blouse from the basket, she gasped. At the bottom lay a small pistol. Mr. Browning's? Or had it belonged to the no-good Billy? No, it hadn't been Billy's. It was *her* gun, purchased right after Billy had gotten himself killed. *My, my, that was a long time ago.* How had the pistol ended up at the bottom of the laundry basket …?

These expeditions into her belongings usually did uncover items of special interest. She would pause to reflect on their history or their use or whatever she managed to remember about them. At times the memory was simply their importance.

She made a total of six critical discoveries during this purge. Together with the pistol and the weighty envelope, she brought the additional four items to the dining table, staring at them as she formulated a plan.

Back in the bedroom she gathered up the sheets and cotton blanket and walked carefully—she didn't have an extra hand for her cane—to the laundry machines. At the step to the laundry area she stopped and tossed her bundle onto the lower floor. She made a slow retreat to her bedroom, retrieved the cane, and, back at that perilous ledge, managed the step down to the machines. *What a lot of work just to wash my sheets,* she thought. "Pain in the behind," she murmured, but not in her wrist, she noted, grinning with her achievement.

With the laundry swishing away and eight bags of trash parked at various locations, she contemplated what should be next. In the kitchen she found a sponge, some old rags, and a small pail. She moved from room to room wiping the surfaces clean of dust, spilled liquids, a little mold in some places, and spiderwebs. As she finished these tasks, she took pleasure in the sunrise. "About time." She beamed at the rays of light streaming into the bedroom. Only a few flecks of dust danced in their way.

Emboldened by the removal of clutter from her house (and in a sense from her mind), she hastened—if her shuffling pace could be called that—to the kitchen to set the coffeepot going. Oh yes, she had saved the can of her favorite brew from her cleansing. "I need my coffee," she said in full voice, even though only the toaster, the table and chairs, the now-empty refrigerator, and the stove (wiped clean) bore witness.

Chapter 30

Claire

Claire stepped closer. Tidy lay in her bed, her eyes closed. In the month since Miki's hearing, Tidy had given every indication of taking the defeat of the court experience in stride. Her complaints of mistreatment, of Ivan's absence, and of everyone's thievery had ceased. Equally astonishing was the appearance of her home—relatively neat, clean, orderly. Outwardly, her conduct heralded a new pleasure with life. Claire tagged the change as acceptance and maybe even relief.

Today, it looked more like defeat. "Tidy, I'm wondering if you should see a doctor. You look ill."

"No doctors. They're no use to me. This is my time, and I'm ready."

Claire stood silent, puzzled.

Tidy opened her eyes, staring directly at Claire. "Stars and bars, you have nothing to say back to me? You're not going to argue?"

At first stunned with this pluck, Claire lost her composure

and laughed. Tidy emitted a dry, hacking cough, but there was no mistaking the mirth it contained.

Claire retreated from the humor. "I'm not sure I believe you are ready to go, Tidy. Only a few weeks ago you carried on about staying in the house until you turned a hundred and two, just like Aunt Marvine."

"Auntie Marvine had better genes than me—the cleaning gene for one. She kept on vacuuming to the day she died. I'm missing that gene, so there's nothing more for me to do here now."

"Tidy, I'm looking around, and your home is immaculate. You told me the other day you did the cleaning yourself."

"One-time deal; 'bout tore me down. I know I can't keep it up."

"There's always the option of bringing in—"

"Don't you say anything about some agency housekeeping nonsense. If I can't do it myself, I shouldn't go on living. I'm a burden for other people if I keep going. No point being more nuisance than I am now."

Shouldn't go on living ... Claire's social worker antennae stiffened. "Tidy, are you eating as usual? Breakfast, lunch ...?"

"What business is that of yours?"

"I'm wondering if your apparent weakness and, well, being in bed at one in the afternoon might be because you're not eating properly."

"I'm taking care of myself the way I want. You don't need to put your nose into these things."

"But ..." Claire began another protest.

"Don't go pitchin' a conniption. You got more sense. If I say I'm ready to go, I'm ready."

Claire backed away, mentally, if not physically. She needed to process this change in her client and decide how to proceed.

Failure to thrive—not eating or hydrating, losing interest in life—it was not so uncommon in the elderly. The usual responses, however—assign in-home assistance, focus more attention on the client, try to lift the depression—none of these approaches could be applied to Tidy. Claire knew Tidy wouldn't stand for it. Stopping normal nutritional intake was one *legal* way to make death happen. Was this indeed Tidy's aim? To end her life?

Claire skipped around in her mind for options. To prolong ... what? To give her time ... time for what? So to end ...

Sometimes there is an advantage to dying swiftly, she ruminated briefly. Although she had been angry when her husband had "abandoned" her so quickly, she was now conflicted, understanding Tidy's wish but not wanting her to die.

If she *was* looking at Tidy's end of life, someone needed to be in her home to look after her basic needs, or she'd require placement in a facility. And Claire couldn't imagine suggesting such a course of action to Tidy.

Placing Tidy in a facility would relieve Claire of her worst fear—following the passage to an end of life. In the past, when a client had needed the care of a facility, Claire had moved on. Family, medical personnel, and facility social workers had taken over, and Claire had not had to be part of the dying process, and for that she was grateful. The slow, painful bone-cancer death of her husband still disturbed her sleep on occasion: his moaning, crying out, her desperate calls for more morphine.

Nonetheless, she couldn't abandon Tidy in a nursing home. It wouldn't be fair. Claire reeled in confusion.

"Just one thing," Tidy's cracked voice intruded.

"Yes?"

"I don't want to be alone these last days. And I don't want no fool from some dumb agency."

Claire's stomach pitched. "What do you intend then?"

"I want Ivan here. I want him to care for me in my last days." Tidy's eyes had closed, but her voice remained clear.

With a deep breath Claire managed the soft message. "Ivan is serving his sentence, Tidy."

"I know, but you can get him out for me."

———

In her car Claire's mind buzzed with conflict. She needed action: keep moving; focus on the problem, not the person for whom she was solving the problem. *Don't dwell on the end of life,* she told herself. She knew she must also keep her distance—establish the parameters of her emotional space—to stay the inevitable hurt, grief, and sorrow from intruding.

Action: Was there any way Claire could get Ivan out of jail, even temporarily? Claire's occasional queries to Tidy about Ivan came roaring back. Tidy had said, "No one's doing nothing … I think they're going to keep him in jail a long time."

Claire's mind snapped to this fact: he shouldn't be in a cell anymore but at Blackman rehab up north.

Distance: Claire had to find someone else to do this for her.

She pulled out her cell phone and began calling. Joan at Senior Outreach Services had a lawyer friend, who knew the clerk at Martinsville courthouse, who could check Ivan's status. That was a start. A few minutes later the clerk reported no record in the system for an Ivan Demidovsky (were they sure of the spelling?).

Back to the Outreach folks, Claire asked if anyone had any

association with the district attorney's office. She needed an insider to get to ADA Worthington. One of Claire's coworkers said she thought her neighbor's daughter had gone to school with one of the assistant district attorneys.

Anita, the neighbor's daughter, called later in the day to ask about timing: When had Ivan been arrested? Had there been a trial? Had he been indicted? Which facility had he been taken to? Other than the proceedings at the hearing before Judge Letty, Claire admitted she didn't know much. "I'll see what I can find out and call you back," she told Anita.

———

That afternoon, Claire checked in on Tidy. She appeared to be sleeping, but was she only sleeping? Claire's heart banged inside her ribs, raising an alarm. "Tidy," she murmured, unable to help the urgent tone.

Tidy's eyes flipped open. "You're back."

"Yes, are you all right?"

"Stupid question, woman."

"Yes, of course, I'm sorry. I need more information about Ivan, Tidy. When did you last hear from him?"

"Two weeks ago, I think; I don't remember so good."

"Have you any idea which facility he's, um, staying at ... in?"

Tidy, her eyes closed again, was smiling. "You haven't found my stash."

"Stash?"

"His letters."

Claire started. "He's been writing you?"

"Of course."

A sadness descended on Claire. Ivan had been corresponding

with Tidy, and she'd never mentioned it. "Did he tell you in these letters if he ever went to Blackman County or, if not, where he is instead?"

"You're not so smart sometimes. There's a return address on the envelopes."

"Would you be willing to tell me where the letters are so I can see the return address? I promise I'll only copy the address, nothing more."

"Promise whatever you want. You can look at them. You can read them. I don't care, as long as he comes back. They're in the bottom drawer of the dresser."

Claire found that the county facility in Martinsville appeared in the upper left corner of all the envelopes. How could he still be in Martinsville?

Chapter 31

The Courtroom

Claire called Anita and relayed the information about Ivan. Anita was as puzzled as Claire, and that evening, she contacted Benji. Anita and Benji had attended the same high school, even dated once or twice. Neither remembered who'd spurned whom, but Benji hoped it had been him. Anita annoyed him—more than that, she persistently plagued him with potent questions, as she was a reporter for the *West County News*.

Benji seethed as Anita asked him about Ivan. He remembered the drunken Russian and expressed surprise that he was writing letters—no, that is, surprise that he was writing them from Martinsville. Why did this have to be his problem? But Anita had him cornered, and he promised to call her after the weekend, as soon as he discovered what had happened.

On Monday, too busy for piddly stuff like a misplaced prisoner, Benji turned the investigation over to his assistant, Donny. Although fresh out of law school, Donny was still pissed at being given such a menial task. He sat on it until late in the afternoon when he had nothing better to do.

Within fifteen minutes Donny was not only puzzled but intrigued, as every avenue of inquiry turned into a dead end. He entered all possible spelling variations of Ivan Demidovsky he could imagine, and although Ivan's old court encounters popped up, no data from the last six months appeared.

At four forty-five he gave Benji an account of his nonfindings.

"You tried," Benji responded as he grabbed his briefcase and headed for the door. Benji asked Donny to call his "friend" Anita and relay this report.

Oh, fine, now I'm your secretary too, Donny snarled silently.

"She's a reporter for the *West County News*," Benji called over his shoulder as he made his escape. "I can't remember the number. Thanks, Donny. Have a good evening."

A reporter. Donny thought that was interesting and located the newspaper's information online. After only a few minutes of him going through menus and punching numbers, a bright female voice admitted she was Anita.

She listened to Donny's remarkably thorough research in the matter. (He should come work for the paper, she said. Donny blushed.) She concluded that with no record of Ivan at the courthouse, a search of the prison records had to be made.

They batted back and forth the virtues of which one of them should make this request. Donny lobbed the task into Anita's court as a reporter. In any case, some drama was sure to ensue, and he relished the scenario already playing in his head.

Indeed, with exceptional speed, Anita's inquiry circled back to Benji's desk by early Tuesday morning. *No one* could find any information on Ivan Demidovsky other than the court minutes of his hearing, which identified Benji as the ADA. In a fury, Benji asked Donny what the hell was going on. Anita appeared at noon also asking … well, many questions, the most significant being, why was no one able to ascertain if Ivan Demidovsky was still in prison?

Nervous about a reporter—*especially* this reporter—putting pressure on this case, Benji personally called Claude, the administrator of the Martinsville prison. "We have evidence of a convict by the name of Ivan Demidovsky who's been in your facility, and we are unable to determine if he is still with you—or anywhere else, for that matter. Can you look into the possibility of an extra or missing prisoner and get back to me pronto? The media are onto this, and it would be a shame if *you've* lost someone."

Benji's own records of the Ivan case hid in a drawer—an imperfect filing system, he admitted—and the file took a few minutes to locate. The file confirmed his vague memory that the alcoholic Russian should be at Blackman County by now. Could he throw this information at Donny and get him to distribute it to the appropriate parties? A call to Blackman first might be wise.

The Blackman residence program had no record of a Demidovsky. Yes, no bed had been available at the facility back in November, so he should be on the wait list. But the wait list contained not a single name beginning with *D*, let alone this rather long one.

Anita was delighted with these results and reported them to Claire. A lost prisoner. Denied his rights. No representation. No transfer—a *court-ordered* transfer. No papers. Nothing. A forgotten prisoner. His only connection to the outside a few phone calls and a few letters to a ninety-two-year-old woman with dementia, apparently. No one had come looking for Ivan. The paperwork had slipped away ... Who knew how? There had been no follow-up, for no one had cared to follow up. No one, apparently, cared about Ivan Demidovsky's existence.

No one but Tidy. And she cared very much. So much so she wanted this man at her bedside when she died.

———

On Thursday, Judge Marian Truewell—Judge Letty was on leave following a surgery—reviewed the case of Ivan Demidovsky with ADA Worthington, who suggested the court had no reason to detain Mr. Demidovsky further. The Russian—right, Ukrainian—had more than served his time for a little pop on the cheek of some overzealous real estate agent, he argued.

"What about Judge Letty's ruling?" Judge Marian asked. "The punishment appears to be directed at this specific behavior. Sitting in a prison cell doesn't have the same effect as a year at Blackman."

"No," Benji admitted. He then recounted Tidy's court appearance and Judge Letty's consideration at that hearing. "So maybe some leniency, given the circumstances—"

"Oh, all right," Judge Truewell interrupted. "That's enough. If you can find him, let him go," she sighed and signed the court order in triplicate.

———

Claire and Julian waited outside the county courthouse. Benji ushered Ivan to them. A review of the prison kitchen list had turned up Ivan in cell block 10. The prison administrator kept his own counsel (so to speak), and since Benji didn't seem to care, the administrator had quickly replicated the paperwork necessary to show Ivan had been imprisoned—before he was released.

Julian had never laid eyes on Ivan, and thus Ivan's clean-shaven face, short haircut, and slimmer build did not surprise him. For Claire, however, a well-defined physique in the old black-and-gray clothing, which Ivan's weight loss made even more ill fitting, supplanted her memory of the thoroughly dejected man in bright red-and-yellow jail uniform. Ivan kept his eyes on the toes of his dull, scuffed shoes. He was embarrassed, Claire realized, and very shy.

Anxious to get rid of *his* embarrassment, Benji didn't waste time on introductions. "I understand Ms. Bourbon is awaiting his return. I would appreciate your seeing to this conveyance. If there's anything you can do to keep him out of the local pub, you'd be doing us a favor."

Honest to Pete, thought Claire. *Go write yourself a brief. Whose problem is this anyway?* "Yes," she said aloud. "Here is the information of his whereabouts, for the probation department."

Julian glared at Benji with disdain. He was disgusted that a system with stringent rules and paperwork could have failed so miserably because someone wasn't careful enough with the records. He was outraged over this mishap.

In Julian's car, conversation was strained.

"She okay?" Ivan finally asked from the backseat.

"She's very frail, very weak," Claire said, glancing at Julian, who kept his driver's eyes locked on the road.

"She dying?" he said softly.

"Yes, Ivan, I'm afraid she is. She is refusing to eat and only drinks a little coffee or water. She has chosen to stop her life, if you understand what I mean."

"*Da*, but iz sad."

"Of course. The end of anyone's life is sad. But I think Tidy has decided her time to pass on is now. She wants only to be comfortable and have your companionship."

Ivan turned his face to the side window to shield his emotions. "She in pain?"

"I'm quite sure she's not at the moment. You understand as well as anyone that if she was uncomfortable, she would tell us in no uncertain terms."

Ivan's face relaxed. He looked forward with his eyes to the road ahead and with his heart to seeing Tidy. They dropped him off in front of the green porch with Claire's instructions to call her if he needed anything.

Chapter 32

Ivan

"That you, Ivan?" Tidy's eyelids fluttered open; her weak, scratchy voice still delivered a hint of her southern background.

"Tidy, Tidy." Ivan knelt at the side of the bed, his head bent to hide his tears.

"Cut the waterfall, Ivan, and go make me some noodles. I want to smell those noodles again."

Ivan sniffled and made a hasty retreat, glad to have time to get his emotions under control while he cooked.

She didn't eat the noodles, much to Ivan's consternation, but she said that the aroma was heavenly and that one of her last wishes had been granted.

"What wishes, Tidy?"

"You coming home. That one's been granted. Smelling your noodles. That one's been granted too." She paused. "There's one more."

Ivan tensed. What else could he possibly do to make her live longer, happier?

"I want to see the iris—those purple flowers in the back."

Ivan shuffled his feet, looking at them as if they belonged to someone else. "Too soon. No flowers."

"Tomorrow, you go check. I want to keep going until the iris bloom." With that she closed her eyes and slept.

Ivan went back to his bedroom. Dust boles swished around the floor as he entered. Not part of Tidy's cleaning spate, the room hadn't been vacuumed in weeks and was dirty. But despite the room's relative neatness, he could tell it wasn't the same as when he had left. What had happened here?

He went to Tidy's doorway to ask, but she was snoring gently, her eyelids twitching slightly in her disturbed sleep. He would not wake her.

By the laundry machines he snatched up a broom and a rag and began cleaning. He stripped the bed, stuffed the washer, and vacillated between starting the machine or not, afraid the noise might rouse Tidy. He filled a bowl with hot water, found a sponge and soap, and wiped all the surfaces. He cleared the bureau drawers of sweater fluff, pieces of tissue, dust. The flurry of activity worked off pent-up energy and emotion.

He checked on Tidy again, watching her for a full two minutes for some sign of life—a tic of an eyelid, a soughing, an involuntary twitch of a leg. As she appeared to be in a very deep sleep, he decided to take a small risk and started the washing machine. In the kitchen, he compulsively improved on Tidy's scrubbing, beginning with the stove. He removed dried, blackened spots he recognized from his own cooking months earlier, whisked a few crumbs from the oven, labored over the grease in the sink, and swept the floor. Down on his hands and knees, he washed the tile with the sponge. Fortunately, it was a small kitchen.

After changing the laundry to the dryer, he opened the refrigerator to confirm its contents. While preparing the noodles, he had been alarmed to find only a half pound of butter, a pint of cream with an expired use-by date, three bagels (hard as rocks), and a nearly empty jar of marmalade. No greens, no chicken, no leftover potatoes, none of the usual foods for Tidy's refrigerator. There was no sign Miki had taken her to the store, but surely she had ordered Meals on Wheels, Ivan brooded. In his absence she often had no choice, she would sputter, because she was too tired to cook. But he found none of the telltale plastic meal trays—evidence of her giving in to the delivery—in the trash.

He inspected the pantry again. The canned goods had disappeared. The packaged rice mixes, the jars of pickles she loved, the Kit Kat bars (her treat to herself)—all gone. Together with the one bag of noodles he had cooked earlier, a jar of cinnamon and a nearly empty can of coffee were all that remained on the shelves.

He looked at the pan of congealed noodles on the cold stove. Why hadn't she eaten them? She loved these noodles. Ivan went back to her room, thinking perhaps she'd like them now. But not even the out-of-whack, thumping dryer drum stirred her. It was six o'clock, and Ivan knew she would sleep now for her eight or nine hours, wake up around three in the morning, stare at the ceiling until five, and then rise for her coffee. Her sleep pattern had been key to his nightly activity at Tony's Bar. He had to be back, tucked into bed well before she woke, or she'd throw him out. With bad timing on many a night, he'd ended up under the freeway bridge with Blackie, Rap, and the others. He shivered with the memory.

Back in the kitchen, he dumped the glop of cold, pasty, unappetizing noodles down the sink disposal. Thinking about food, however, caused his stomach to growl, and Ivan realized he hadn't eaten since this morning's soggy pancakes in jail. In fact, he was starving, and with the kitchen empty of edible foodstuffs, he wondered what to do. An easy answer to his hunger danced in his mind, but this solution to his growling stomach presented a couple of moral dilemmas.

Tony's Bar served small plates of food. Ivan had eaten lumpia or burritos there many evenings. He'd also drank there many evenings—until he'd barely been able to stumble back to Tidy's. But he wasn't supposed to drink anymore; how stupid to start again. After five months in jail without a single drop, he knew if he caught even a whiff of alcohol, he would succumb. On the other hand, he figured going to Tony's could be a test of his strength. If he could go to the bar and eat but not drink, he might be cured.

That dilemma aside, there was the matter of money. How to pay for his burrito and club soda—club soda, he hated the thought of it—since he hadn't a penny in his pocket? If Tidy were awake, she'd give him some money, but she wasn't awake.

Back in the living room, Ivan stared at her red vinyl bag on the couch; her black wallet with Velcro pockets would be buried in the bag. If she were awake, she'd give him the money from her stash in the wallet. She'd give him the money because some of it was, after all, his money. He'd pleaded with her to continue to cash his Social Security checks and to use this contribution to help pay her bills, just like always. And just like always she would have kept part of the money in her black wallet … to give him when he needed it. Tidy had apparently continued to receive his checks while he'd been incarcerated—a surprise. Perhaps this business of him being "lost" had something to do with it.

Ivan sat on the couch—not in Tidy's seat at the right end but on the opposite end. The red bag lay in the center. He gently turned the bag so that the opening gaped toward him. Rather than buried, the folded, Velcroed black wallet poked out from the top of the accumulation of junk she carried. He sat next to the bag for untold minutes. Eventually, with a last glance into her bedroom, he plucked out the wallet.

Ripping open the Velcro closure presented a problem; ripping Velcro made a lot of noise. He didn't like the idea of taking the wallet into the kitchen. To remove the wallet from the vicinity of the red bag seemed so much worse, but he did it anyway.

In the kitchen, his back to the door as if to muffle the sound with his body, he ripped the Velcro and counted $342 in the wallet. He took two twenties and quickly replaced everything else on the couch. He would tell her about the "loan" in the morning.

He checked the bolt on the front door and left by the back. Down the street, around the corner, and up another block, he came to Tony's. Inside his pals clapped him on the shoulder and yelled, "Hey, the Russkie's back." Ivan was momentarily overcome. In Tony's Bar, he had friends. No one judged him. In Tony's Bar he believed he was appreciated and understood. But then, he was their drinking buddy. Old sots cherished the company of other old sots.

He ordered a burrito and club soda. And didn't they razz him about that.

"Club soda! They turn you into some kind of teetotaler in the lockup?"

"Old maid. What's with you, man?"

As the evening progressed, his drinking pals brought him

up to date on the neighborhood gossip, including the latest with the old lady.

"That pal of yours ripped her off. Stole her car, credit cards."

"Unbelievable."

"Gutsy."

"Also pretty stupid. Kept the car, driving it around. Really dumb."

Confirmation of Ralph's information reignited Ivan's wrath. And now he learned everyone in town was gossiping about it. He was humiliated for Tidy.

"That's not the worst," Blackie said. "They couldn't pin the rap on him, so he's out."

Ivan was shocked. His bar pals were a little vague as to why Miki wasn't in jail. They figured he had a clever lawyer.

The initial air of fellowship and goodwill was sucked out of Ivan. His guilt about Tidy's abuse returned and deepened. He excused himself from the bar company and walked heavyhearted back to Tidy's.

———

Ivan stirred as the morning light penetrated his room. He lay in his familiar bed and marveled that he was no longer in prison. He listened casually and then intently for noises of Tidy in the kitchen. Nothing. She should be puttering around, getting her coffee. Concern gripped him as he pushed out of bed. He found his robe still in the closet and went in search of her.

He peeked into her bedroom. She lay in bed staring at the ceiling. "Tidy?"

"That you, Ivan? Come on in here. I've been thinking I

might like to get up today. Maybe go sit on the back porch and check on those iris."

"Why you not in kitchen, getting coffee?"

"I'm too weak to do that now, Ivan. I's hoping you'd get the coffee for me."

Ivan stared at her. What did she mean she was too weak? "I get coffee." He turned and went to the kitchen, questions pounding in his head. The woman, Claire, had told him Tidy was dying. He hadn't believed her—or hadn't wanted to believe her—but perhaps it was true. Why? She wasn't eating; maybe that was why. Was she taking her medicines? That was it. She just needed to take her medicines.

Suddenly the whole weight of Tidy's condition descended as a shroud. All of this had come about because he hadn't been here to care for her. She wasn't eating, because he hadn't been here to cook for her. She wasn't taking her medicines, because he hadn't been here to make sure she did. She was ill because he hadn't been here to take her to the hospital. He sat at the kitchen table, his head in his hands. Depression swept over him like an ocean wave.

"Ivan? Where's my coffee?"

He sprang from the chair and poured water into a pan. He heaped several spoonfuls of instant coffee into a mug and added the water once it had boiled. "Coming, Tidy." On a tray he carried the steaming mug of coffee with one teaspoon of sugar and enough cream for a chocolaty color—just the way she liked it. He put the tray on the bed beside her.

"You got to help me up here. I needs to go pee before I have any coffee." She pointed to the commode next to her bed.

He recalled his duty: empty the pot each morning. Other than the smell, the assignment wasn't onerous. Now she was suggesting something else. Did she want him to lift her up and help her get on the commode? The idea made him dizzy.

He had never touched her before except to steady her by holding her arm or to assist her out of the car by taking her bony hand. His face burned; his forehead grew damp. To help her out of bed and onto the commode was too intimate.

"Are you going to help me or not?" A sardonic tinge hung on the question, but the edges were softer than usual. "Come on, don't just stand there."

That was a command, and without another thought he leaned over and pulled her shoulders forward. Her bones, sharp and defined beneath her nightgown, poked his hand. With his other hand, he swung her legs to the side of the bed. Her nightgown lifted to disclose the lack of muscle and discolored, blotchy skin.

"Pull me up gently," she muttered. "I can hardly stand now."

He put his big hands under her armpits, raised her from the bed, shifted ninety degrees, and lowered her onto the open commode. He tried not to think about the feel of her body. If he let his mind acknowledge what he had done, he might be repulsed. He was wholly embarrassed.

"I can't pee through my nightgown, you ninny." She said it kindly, amused. She understood his awkwardness, his lack of experience. "Just pull it up in back."

He did as she instructed. His breath came in light gasps. Too personal, what she asked—too personal. Light-headed, he thought he might pass out.

"No need to listen to me tinkle. Take that coffee to the kitchen and warm it up while I do my business."

Ivan grabbed the mug and retreated. His head buzzed; the dizziness persisted. The fingers of his hands where he had held her armpits tingled. He couldn't think, didn't want to think.

At the microwave he punched the "beverage" button and stood in a stupor. The coffee wasn't really cold, but he put it in the microwave anyway. He didn't hear the microwave beeping to tell him to take it out.

"Ivan, I'm done now. Help me into the living room. I think I'll have my coffee on the sofa."

Abruptly the veil of his trance lifted, and Ivan was transformed. Like a dancer, he fairly leaped to the bedroom and swooped Tidy into his arms. Twirling around toward the door, he carried her like a bride over the threshold from the bedroom to the living room and, with gentle care, lowered her onto the couch.

"Wait," he cried, "I get pillows."

He gathered them from her bed and tucked them around her. He pushed the coffee table away and pulled the ottoman in front of her, elevating her legs. In the bedroom he whipped off the top blanket and brought it to cover her. He stood back to admire his work.

Tidy, at first startled by his dance, lit up with a smile in the comfort of her throne. "You're the best, Ivan. Now my coffee."

He brought the coffee and a piece of toast spread with the last bit of marmalade.

"You're looking mighty fine, Ivan. You lost weight, took all that hair off your face, got a decent haircut. Something good came out of being in jail this time. You're looking just about handsome."

Ivan turned toward her without expression. No one in his life had ever called him handsome or even "just about handsome."

"You'll be needing to get groceries—whatever you like, I'm not hungry. Get my wallet out of my bag. Take some money for groceries and extra in case you need gas for the car. Car's not been driven much lately, and I can't remember if it needs gas."

Ivan reached for the bag. This was the time to tell her about the forty dollars he'd borrowed last night, but he didn't. He counted out eighty dollars and put the rest back into the wallet. "You okay if I go now? Or I wait. You finish coffee, toast."

"I'm fine now. You go on. If I get tired, I'll doze here until you return."

Ivan sat in the car for a good three minutes before turning the ignition. These changed circumstances baffled him. Providing personal care for a ninety-two-year-old woman was not only beyond the scope of his experience; it was beyond his imagination. He went over the activity of the previous hour: putting her on the potty, lifting her nightgown. How had he become this care provider? His mother should be doing these things. He jumped at the thought of his mother. She hadn't crossed his mind in years. He didn't know if she was alive or dead—and she certainly wasn't here in California, lending him a hand.

He pictured Miki taking off in Tidy's car with her credit cards. He could do the same. When she was asleep, he could take the rest of the money and drive away in her car. He could drive away to … where? His shoulders sagged as he realized there was no place for him to go and no one in the world who would welcome him. His whole life—as sorry as it was—revolved in Oakmont … with Tidy.

In the grocery store—the supermarket over in Ridley—he chose the foodstuffs with care, everything Tidy relished. He'd make her eat because it would all be so delicious. He planned the menus in his head—borscht; spinach salad with the raspberry dressing she adored; more noodles, this time with some pork tenderloin; apple crisp with cream. More cream—for her coffee and the strudel. He wandered the aisles, right to left, inevitably coming to the liquor lane, where all reason collapsed. The depression of the early morning engulfed him anew. Tidy had been central to his life for so many years now; he couldn't imagine how he would be without her. What would happen to him when she died? His eyes passed over the wines, the beer, the whiskey and focused on the vodka. He rolled the cart in front of the array of clear liquor and snatched the cheapest bottle available.

Claire

Claire rang the doorbell in the early afternoon. The absence of Tidy's habitual yelling in response was a reminder of the change inside. In place of Tidy's usual vociferous greeting, a mute Ivan unbolted and opened the door.

"Hello, Ivan, how are things here today?"

To fill the silence, he swung the door wide for Claire's entrance.

"Ivan?"

"She okay. Tidy sleep much and no eat. I worry she no eat."

"I know, Ivan, but I think this is how she wants it to be."

"If you're going to talk," Tidy called, "get in here where I can hear you."

Claire and Ivan exchanged glances. Claire smiled. Ivan turned away. They both came into the living room, but Ivan started to retreat to his room. Claire stopped him. "Stay, Ivan; I'd like you to be with us for a moment." Ivan brought the desk chair for Claire and then stood against the opposite wall, not daring to look at either woman.

Claire expressed pleasure at seeing Tidy sitting up and looking a bit perkier.

"This man," Tidy said, gesturing toward Ivan, "is a tonic. He's good for me."

"He's doing a phenomenal job." Claire gulped. The issue of in-home care needed to be addressed now—no procrastination. "Tidy, I need to tell you I've asked a home-health nurse to visit, to monitor your condition." Tidy opened her mouth to protest, but Claire held up her hand to stop the words about to spew forth. "Wait, Tidy, let me finish. We *are* going to require some in-home care soon."

Tidy sat up slightly, looking sharply at Claire. "I don't need any nurse here. I've got Ivan."

Ivan's eyes flicked back and forth along the carpet, as if watching ants playing tennis.

"A nurse is coming this afternoon, Tidy—well, any moment now—to examine—"

"No nurse!"

"Tidy, the nurse isn't going to do anything, just check to—"

"I don't want no doctors, no nurses, *nobody* taking care of me but Ivan."

"Tidy, the nurse will only—"

The doorbell rang. Ivan ushered the nurse into the living room. Claire introduced everyone. Tidy sat still and silent, glowering. Ivan, sweating, glued his back to the wall, looking apprehensive and frightened.

The nurse, Susan, took Claire's chair, and Claire retreated to join Ivan. She patted his arm gently, trying to reassure him.

Susan asked Tidy a couple of questions, and Tidy answered, sharp and curt, "No comment."

Claire suppressed a slight smile. *There's our Tidy.* She

rescued Susan by coming forward and offering to help with the blood pressure cuff.

The medical essentials were recorded amid bitter comments from Tidy. ("What does it matter now?" "Of course my temperature's high. Too damn hot in here.")

"Are you in pain, Tidy?" the nurse asked, continuing in her assessment inventory.

"In pain? Yes, and you are the cause. Now I want you out of my house. No one but Ivan takes care of me. Get out."

Attempting to shout in her usual way caused Tidy to choke. She waved her arms, coughing. Ivan sprang for the kitchen and a glass of water. He sat on the couch, putting the glass to her lips, helping her take small sips to ease the convulsions.

The nurse rose, watching. Turning to Claire, she shrugged and made a silent exit. When Tidy stopped coughing, Ivan put the glass on the table but kept his arm behind her head to brace her neck. His other hand came back to her lap and grasped her fingers. Tidy sank into his support and closed her eyes. A tightness rose in Claire's throat.

"Too tired, Ivan. I'm too tired. Take me to bed."

Claire stared in astonishment as Ivan lifted Tidy from her throne and carried her to bed.

"Bring pillows, please," he said, and Claire did.

In bed, her blanket restored and tucked to her chin by Ivan's huge hands, Tidy fell asleep.

Claire motioned for Ivan to follow her to the kitchen. They sat at the table while Claire explained what would happen now that hospice care had been assigned—the nurse's visits, bathing, possibly more medicines. Ivan listened intently, clasping and unclasping his hands.

"You are doing a marvelous job of caring for her, and I

understand she doesn't want anyone else helping, but some of
these things will be easier for you, and her, if the nurse and her
aide can help."

"She get mad with other people."

Claire smiled. "Oh, I know. We heard that just now, didn't
we? But can you see how important it will be to have the nurse
and aide here to carry out certain tasks?"

"*Da*, yez, I can't do some of thez things."

"If you are comfortable saying that *you* want the nurse and
aide to help, you might ease her mind."

"Yez, I do this."

———————

That evening, snug in her bungalow, Claire pulled the photo
album out from under the magazines and puzzle books. She
turned the pages slowly. Her husband skiing, hiking, standing
in front of their first home, holding their infant daughter,
then hugging their daughter, all grown up, at her high school
graduation. She flipped on through the years, to the photo on
the balcony of their apartment overlooking Lake Como. He
didn't look ill; he appeared vibrant, full of life. In six months
he was dead.

As she closed the album, her thoughts went to Tidy and
Ivan. Ivan must be terrified, just as she had been, looking at
death for the first time. If only she'd known then what she
understood now.

Chapter 33

Ivan

After Claire left, Ivan returned to his room, reached under the bed, and pulled out the vodka. Sitting on the bed, he clutched the bottle before him with both hands, staring at the label.

Just one shot, he thought—to ease the pain behind his eyes, to relieve the turmoil in his stomach, to take away the ache in his heart.

Instead, he placed the bottle on his bedside table and retreated out the back door to the garden. The iris leaves had pushed further out of the ground. A few had some flower stems just appearing. Blossoms were still days away. It would be both a long time and a short time before the velvet purple petals appeared.

———

As the next week unfolded, Ivan began to manage Tidy's care with more ease, even the intimate chores. He changed her bed linens every two days and emptied the commode immediately on use; he cleaned the already clean surfaces of the bedroom furniture. Tidy did not object; he wasn't sure she noticed. He dusted the windowsills, vacuumed the carpet. The whole house smelled of freshness and Pine-Sol.

He sat by her bed and read to her from the newspaper. They chuckled together at the amusing behavior of politicians; Tidy made rude comments about the governor and tut-tutted the citizen complaints of bad roads, lax schools, and traffic congestion. They sailed around the world on the weather page, comparing temperatures in New Delhi, Moscow, Amsterdam, and Havana. "Wonder what it's like in Castro-land," Tidy mused. "Can't imagine how anyone lives there. Hot, humid, and Commie."

In the beginning he made the meals he had planned in the supermarket, but Tidy refused to eat. He cajoled and pleaded and begged, and she repeated she was not hungry. "The smells are delicious enough," she said.

After a few days, the drive to make her eat diminished. She sipped her coffee and occasionally sampled the oatmeal in the morning or the noodles and gravy in the late afternoon. But she reported it all tasted like cardboard, and she didn't care for cardboard. She said she didn't understand, because she knew he didn't cook up cardboard.

He said he was sorry, that he must have lost his touch in jail.

Ivan mentioned this to Claire during one of her visits. She explained to him that some elderly people who had decided to stop living would refrain from eating. It was one way to end life, she said.

"How she not want to live?" he cried. "She too beautiful to die."

Claire agreed but shrugged her shoulders, which to Ivan meant she didn't care. No, he knew that wasn't fair. He was confused by Tidy's dying and unable to process anything with clarity. He felt dumb, inadequate, useless, without the means to stop the dying. He was grieving, and she hadn't even died yet.

Susan came every day to check Tidy's vitals. Tidy's protests became weaker as her body began its process of shutting down. Ivan looked on dispiritedly as the aide bathed her. Tidy didn't mind the bath, she said; she always felt a little better when she was clean.

Julian

A few days after Ivan's return Julian turned up on Tidy's stoop, uncertain. Her accusation of theft had railed against his very high standards for financial propriety, but he could no longer use that as a reason for not visiting. There was something else too, and that something else drowned out the ideas that he'd grown up with, that he would never be good enough to do anything, much less to love.

He had ruminated over this visit and finally decided to chance an encounter. He needed to visit her before she died. Despite everything, he was aggrieved by the news that she had resolved to die. He supposed too that he wished absolution for the sins she'd pinned on him. And then there was the problem he carried in the nine-by-twelve-inch envelope tucked under his arm. Somewhat doggedly, he had trekked to her doorstep.

Ivan looked pleased to see him. Absent from Julian's mixed history with Tidy, Ivan wouldn't comprehend Julian's trepidation.

"How is she today?" Julian whispered.

"She's good—tired but okay." Ivan also spoke in a whisper. He stood aside for Julian to come in.

At Tidy's bedroom door, Julian found her sitting up in bed with pillows tucked around her. Like a rag doll, she tilted slightly to one side. Ivan pushed at the cushions to ease her upright again.

Her eyes rose to Julian's and did not leave his face. She waited without comment until Ivan had finished and left the room. "What do you want?"

Bad start, Julian thought, but he had come with a resolve and would not be deterred by her rhetoric.

"I came to say hello, Tidy. I heard you were not well, and I wanted to say I'm sorry."

Her eyes stayed locked on his. He continued standing in the doorway, wanting to disappear in an instant if this idea of his went awry.

"They tell me you are a good man."

"Someone told you that?"

"Claire, I think Claire. She says you and Emily are fine people and that I should be sorry I was so mean to you."

"Things were confusing back then, Tidy. Financial stuff can be bewildering and easy to—"

"You don't know how it was." There was a stir of anger in her voice. She subsided into the pillows. "Doesn't matter now. I'm going to die, and I'm glad." She hesitated a moment. "I wrote a note to call you, but I guess I forgot. It's a good thing you came."

Julian crossed the threshold into the room. "I was hoping you might say you still trust me." He paused, as if testing the breeze. "Do you remember asking me to help you with your will?"

Tidy's expression lapsed to the neutral place, allowing her

to search within herself, scouring for the memory she needed to respond to Julian. Julian had learned patience. This encounter had to work, or things would not go well when she died—whenever that occurred.

He crept further into the room to the chair by the bed. He stood by it for a moment, trying not to disturb her thoughts. Finally he sat. "You asked me to be executor of your will. Do you remember?"

"Don't rush me. I'm thinking." Her gaze remained steady in her middle space. Her fingers moved as if playing a piano in her lap. Staccato notes, all of them.

"It was before you stole—"

"I didn't steal from you, Tidy; I didn't. I would never do that to you."

Her eyes turned to hard black tacks, tensed, as she brought them to his face, her hands clenched. Then the tension dissolved, and she settled back into the bed linens. "Yes, I believe you speak the truth. That's what's wrong now: I can't make out what's true and what's not. It's why I shouldn't live anymore."

Julian's throat swelled; his breathing came in shallow rasps.

"I'm remembering about my last testament—how the wording should be."

"I have the paper with me, Tidy. We were not able to complete the process ..."

"What do you mean? I remember you writing everything down."

"I was not able to, ah, return to get your signature on the final copy."

"Why didn't you return? Said you would, and you didn't! ... Oh, oh Lord, yes, I did that awful thing. I said those bad things about you." She went still and quiet. Julian recognized the expression, as if she were watching a video, like a football replay on TV. She brought her eyes to Julian's face. "I'm sorry. I was wrong."

Now that he was within inches of his absolution, Julian didn't really want it. Tidy's confession would be too painful for him. If anything, he should absolve her. "Maybe we should bury the hatchet, Tidy."

Tidy snapped her attention back to Julian's face. "Ha! You mean let sleeping dogs lie."

Julian's mind spun. "Let bygones be bygones!"

Tidy chuckled. "You win." With an intake of breath, she choked and for a moment convulsed. Julian sprang from his chair. Tidy waved her hand to calm him as the coughing subsided.

Nervously, Julian returned to business. "I came here to be assured that you wanted these papers to be your last will and testament and, if so, to have you check them, read them, and sign them."

"Just show me where to sign. I trust you've written them the way I want."

In a flash Julian recognized he had overlooked a key element in this exercise. "Ah, Tidy, we need witnesses to your signature; otherwise the document won't be valid."

"You be the witness."

"I can't, because you've named me the executor. And *two* witnesses are required."

"Ivan'd be one."

"He's, ah, not qualified either."

"'Cause he's a jailbird?"

"No ..."

"Go get those bums down the street."

Julian waited a moment to be certain she was serious.

"Go on; go find them. They can't be far."

In fact, Julian had seen the two characters at the corner when he'd driven up. He wondered idly if drug dealers could be witnesses to a will. He'd need to ask them for some identification. How could he ask a couple of homeless drifters to witness Tidy's will? This was absurd.

But he went anyway. Out on the street, only the tall African American Julian knew as Blackie loitered. He strode down the sidewalk toward the street sign Blackie was leaning against. Julian knew if he hesitated, he'd never get through this. Blackie followed his approach, wary.

"I was hoping you could help me—that is, help Tidy—for a moment."

"We been hearing she's not so good."

Blackie's solemnity surprised Julian. "She's not well, and I'm trying to finish her end-of-life papers. I need two witnesses to her signature. Would you be willing?"

"It's that bad ... mighty sad. She's a good woman. Yes, I'll help."

"Is your friend around?"

"Rap? Some kind of friend." Blackie huffed. "I don't think he'd be worthy for this job. I'll find you a more respectable sort. We'll be at the door in ten, fifteen minutes."

"Thank you." Julian withdrew with relief, his hands clammy.

———

Tidy's signature quivered and dipped, lacking strength but not conviction. Mr. Nelson, from the corner store, had put up a "be back in ten minutes" sign and accompanied Blackie to

Tidy's door. They all hovered around Tidy's bed, watching her painstaking task, ready to do their part.

Ivan stayed in the living room, left out. Julian, worried about Ivan's confusion, sent him to the kitchen to make coffee, even knowing he wouldn't drink it.

Once the witness signatures were applied, their names spelled out, and yes, their driver's licenses proffered for identification, the men prepared to depart with hardly a word, unaccustomed to expressing final good-byes. Tidy wouldn't let them get away with it. "I'm saying good-bye now because I won't be around much longer. You two have been kind, and I thank you."

"You're welcome, Tidy." Mr. Nelson tightened his drooping shoulders.

Blackie, a man of fewer words, blew her a kiss. Tidy giggled.

With just Julian in the room, Tidy said, "I'm glad you're here to take care of these things. I don't want to die till I'm sure my requests will be honored."

"I promise, Tidy. Your wishes will be carried out."

"There's one more thing … I need you to write something for me."

The two spent a few more minutes, Tidy talking, Julian writing.

And then Tidy closed her eyes. "Okay, that's good. Now I'm tired."

Julian lingered a moment but realized he should leave; Tidy had dismissed him.

———

Julian delayed three days before telling Emily he had gone by to visit Tidy.

"You what?" She was incredulous. "After everything ..."

"I hoped she would forgive me ... us."

"And did she?"

"In a manner of speaking."

"What does that mean?"

"She didn't scream at me and tell me to leave." He smiled wanly.

"I'd like to visit her too," Emily said softly.

Julian sagged. "We need to go soon. Claire says she failing more each day."

———

Julian and Emily met at the peppermint stoop after work. Ivan smiled, if weakly, as he opened the door. "She be glad to see you."

"Let's hope so," Julian replied under his breath.

In fact, Tidy was pleased, smiling, especially at Emily. "You're a blooming rose."

Emily started and blushed. "How can you tell?"

"Tell what?"

"Oh, well, it's just ..." She glanced at Julian for help. He grinned but remained mute. He wanted to give Emily the privilege of telling Tidy. "We're going to have a baby."

Tidy chuckled. "That's good news. Important. You won't end up like me. No family."

Emily choked back a sob, her emotions out of whack with her hormones.

"Now I *know* it's my time," Tidy said. "I'm just a nuisance. Taking up space we need for your young'un. I'm glad I'll do some good for you."

Julian passed his hands over his eyes two, three times.

Emily's expression of concern didn't help. "Oh, Tidy. I'm sorry ... about family, but, well, we can be your family for now. We'll come visit ... that is, if it's okay with you ... May we?"

Tidy brightened. "Oh my, chile, of course. You come again ... tomorrow?"

"We'll see you then."

Chapter 34

Claire

Claire swung by Oakmont every two days, despite the extra time and miles since she had no other clients close by. Within days, Tidy said she was too weak to sit up on the couch, so Ivan would prop her up on the pillows in her bed. When she began to grumble of pain, Claire asked the nurse to leave some morphine and instruct Ivan how to administer it beneath Tidy's tongue. The drug would melt there, Claire explained to him, and then Tidy would be less distressed. Tidy soon stopped complaining altogether and slept more than she was awake.

Claire's previous self-imposed resolve not to be involved in the dying process softened as she continued to visit. She might have been reprocessing her thoughts about death, but she was careful to keep her observations clinical—changes in Tidy's speech, energy level, skin tone. And she talked with Ivan to help him understand the dying process. Yes, she told herself, the talk was for Ivan's sake, to help him cope with the meaning of death and dying. It had nothing to do with her own loose ends from her husband's death.

But she knew that wasn't true.

On one of these visits, she watched Ivan brush a tiny sponge across Tidy's lips to alleviate the dryness of dehydration.

"You are a wonderful care provider, Ivan."

He looked on her as if she had spoken in some other tongue.

"You have learned well from the hospice staff. You would be an asset in our program. I am often looking for someone to help our elderly ..."

"No, the dying is too much."

"I'm not talking about people who are necessarily at their end of life, Ivan. Many elderly people need assistance because they use a wheelchair or are unable to walk far or can't even wash themselves due to their impairments."

Ivan shrank into himself. Despite her observations to the contrary, she imagined that care providing embarrassed Ivan. "Many men in these circumstances are uncomfortable, too self-conscious to have a woman attend to them. You could be of great service to us as a care provider for men. You would be paid; you could get yourself off disability." Ivan directed his forlorn gaze on Claire's chin. "Your impairments wouldn't get in the way of being a care provider," she persisted. "You've proven that here." She wanted him to think ahead. *She* wanted to think of something else besides the woman dying in the other room.

Ivan looked skeptical but didn't argue.

Claire understood. He was overwhelmed with the present, and who could think of the future? She knew she was not one to preach about moving on when she, in many ways, was still stuck.

"We'll talk again in a few weeks, after ... after we've finished what we're doing here."

Julian

Julian and Emily appeared regularly too. They never stayed long, but Tidy, when she was awake, delighted in their visits.

During one such gathering, in company with Claire, Emily told Tidy that if the baby was a girl, she and Julian planned to name the child for her. Claire's gasp was audible. Even Ivan looked baffled. Tidy cackled, "Tidy McBain. Has a nice ring to it."

Emily, although momentarily horrified, recovered first. "Oh no, we were thinking about Teresa, *Teresa* McBain."

"Now that's a beautiful name, like the beauty I expect her to be," Julian said, beaming.

Emily and Julian's visits also provoked a ritual exchange, which made Julian twitchy.

"Juli, you taking good care of my money? You making sure he does, Emily?"

"Oh, yes," Emily said. "Julian's really an excellent accountant. He's keeping an earnest eye on your financial affairs, Tidy."

"He's not stealing from me now, is he?"

"I watch him like a hawk. No way he or anyone else can steal from you now."

"He stole from me once, you know. Why would he do that, steal from me?"

Despite Tidy's more mellow overall demeanor, Julian squirmed when she talked in this way.

"He took money from my bank account. Made me so mad." The remembrance riled her anew, but she soon tired with all the talking and bad memories. She shook her finger at Julian—a finger so thin, bony, and fragile Julian worried it might snap with the motion. "Young man, you stop your stealing."

Julian applied tolerance—tending to stoicism—to her mini
tirades. "I would never take anything of yours, Tidy. I like you
too much to cheat you."

The repetitions of his innocence pleased her. "That's good."
She smiled and closed her eyes. "I think I'm sleeping now."

Ivan

Ivan woke from a drowning dream, a lead weight, heavy, pushing
him down, down, hard to breathe, sucking in, gasping, rasping.
Tidy's breathing—labored, the nurse had called it—had awoken
him. The nurse had explained the breathing as a sign that Tidy
was moving toward death. Tidy's face showed signs too: gaunt
and waxy looking. Her fingers and toes were turning gray. Her
heart had difficulty pumping hard enough to push blood to
her extremities, the nurse had explained. Susan's information
about Tidy's changing condition helped Ivan to understand his
observations, but the specifics overwhelmed him. Only by her
breathing was Ivan certain she was still alive.

His fear that she might die in the night alone moved him to
wake up every hour to check her hoarse sucking of air. At times
long intervals interrupted the shallow rasping sounds, and he
was sure her last breath had left her. But after what seemed like
an eternity, her chest would rise, and she would emit a huff—a
breath, and another.

He slept in this fitful way on the couch, opposite the door to
her room, where he hoped he might detect any change in her.
One morning as his eyes opened, his body too tired to move,
he studied the sun streaming through Tidy's bedroom window.
Mid-May, he realized, and the day would be bright and warm.

A sudden thought roused him. From the kitchen he peered anxiously into the garden.

Overnight a half dozen iris had opened into full bloom: large purple bearded iris, with yellow inner standards and blue interiors; the exterior petals—the falls—a gorgeous deep, deep purple. He grabbed the kitchen shears and went outside to cut them. He was wrong; there were ten, not six. He found a large vase, arranged the sumptuous blossoms with care, and carried them triumphantly into her bedroom.

"Tidy," he whispered. "Tidy, the iriz here. Tidy, you hear me? The iriz here." He placed the vase on her bureau where she could easily gaze on the blossoms. He lifted her shoulders and adjusted the pillows to elevate her head. Her eyes opened with this movement and settled on the flowers.

"My last wish," she said, smiling. "They're mighty pretty. Thank you, Ivan."

He couldn't speak, his throat like a rock.

The coffee mug held only water now. He raised her head and let her sip. While she slept, he read the paper to her, softly, making intermittent comments about the content. He read *all* the temperatures, for all the places in the United States and in the world. It filled the space in the morning until the nurse and aide came.

He drank his coffee in the kitchen while the nurse and aide worked. The aide asked for clean sheets and nightgown, which he retrieved from the top of the dryer. "She'll feel better with a clean gown and sheets," the aide said. Ivan allowed the two women to do this task now. Tidy's ravaged body grieved him.

As they were leaving, the nurse said quietly, "It won't be long now."

He sat by Tidy all day.

Claire

Claire visited briefly midmorning.

"Listen to her," Ivan pleaded. "Breathing so bad. She going to die, but she don'."

"The ragged breathing is a stage of dying, Ivan, a natural phase of the dying process. She will breathe irregularly for a while."

"How long ... how long? Is so hard to listen."

"Yes, it is." Claire's own breathing came shallow and dry. A dizziness, perhaps caused by the noise inside her head, confused her. The rasping of her husband's last hours supplanted Tidy's soughing.

"She don' open eyes, don' say anything. Nothing."

Claire remembered what it was like. She had been paralyzed in these moments at her husband's bedside, until the hospice nurse had suggested she talk to him. The sound of her voice would be soothing, the nurse had said.

"She may not have energy left to talk or even open her eyes, but she may be able to hear you. Talk to her, Ivan. She would like that. And when she's rested, she may open her eyes again. It's possible."

Despite the passage of time, the anguish of her husband's last breaths remained raw and immediate for Claire. Unlike Tidy, her husband had been restless, moaning and gasping in his final hours. It had been painful to watch and listen to. She recalled how she'd stood at his bedside, willing a change. Without knowing why, she'd retold a favorite story. Her husband had become calm at the sound of her voice and died within an hour.

Ivan gestured to the flowers on the bureau. "The iriz, Tidy, you open eyes again for the iriz." To Claire, he whispered, "Iriz bloom; her last wish."

"They're beautiful. I'm glad spring came in time for her." Claire moved toward the front door, reminding Ivan as she left to call her when Tidy passed. She promised to come immediately.

"Thank you," he said, looking at the floor.

"You are wonderful to be with her for her end of life, Ivan. That's important to remember," Claire said. "With the medication Tidy is not in any pain. She's not suffering. When she's awake, she sees you and those lovely iris."

———

Claire walked down the street to her car. She knew that working with elderly people meant one had to expect death. Death was a part of life, as she had said to elders' families a number of times. She knew Tidy had had a long and productive life, but still she couldn't throw off this shroud of despair. Why couldn't she start the car and move on to her next client?

Because waiting for the last breath had been agony.

She turned the key but only enough to activate the CD player and the Bach *Well-Tempered Clavier* already deposited in the slit. Daniel Barenboim poured the notes into her car. She let the music consume her.

When the fourth prelude began, she started the car—and immediately turned the engine off. Without pausing to analyze why, she flipped to the phone listings in her notebook, pulled out her cell phone, and called Brian Moore. *Enough with boundaries and resolve.* There came a time when talking to someone who knew that you were processing life—and death—was important. She was relieved when Brian answered her call.

Ivan

Ivan stood for a long time by the door to Tidy's room as tears poured from his eyes and down his cheeks. He stared into the room, watching Tidy's chest rise and fall, rise and fall, rise and fall—and stop. He counted to fifty. He clenched his fist. *Pleez start again, Tidy, pleez.* And she did. A small shallow breath, and another, and another. Ivan melted in relief. He grabbed the newspaper from the bureau and settled into the chair by her bed.

"Tidy, Claire says maybe you hear me. I hope so. Iz better I talk to you.

"Iz a pretty day today, Tidy." He went to the garden section of the paper and read aloud an article about mulching roses. "I think I know about this, Tidy. I find some good—how they say?—manure and put by roses. Weed them. Water them. Help them grow—for you, Tidy." The tears started again. "I can't take care of you … I take care of them."

He went to his room to wipe his face and, from under the bed, removed the vodka. He cradled the as yet unopened bottle, took it to the kitchen, and found a clean glass.

His ears, tuned to the slightest sound, detected a rustling from Tidy's bed. He dropped the bottle and glass on the table and bolted to her bedside.

"Sit here and read to me," she murmured. Ivan looked on her in surprise. Her breathing was regular and less shallow. She was alert and talking.

"Bible's on the bureau. Read the psalm." Her eyes followed Ivan's hand as he reached for the Bible. The iris came in view, and she gazed on them while he started the twenty-third psalm.

He knew this was the one she wanted; she had often told him, "The twenty-third is the best part of the Bible."

"The Lord is my shepherd. I shall not want." He read laboriously. He knew from experience he needed to read every word correctly—no missing verbs, *t*'s carefully articulated at the end of words. "He makes me lie down in green pastures."

"In the old days, we'd go into the hills, out east county way—before they're all covered with houses. We'd stretch out in the grasses, look up at the sky—bright and blue. We knew God then."

Startled, Ivan looked up. He couldn't imagine Tidy lying in the grass, looking at the sky. She'd complain of the grass scratching her or the sun being too bright or the cow dung nearby smelling bad. He wondered why she thought lying in the grass was knowing God.

"Come on, keep going."

"He leads me beside still waters. He restores my soul." He paused again. Still waters. Even Ivan could guess what this meant.

"He leads me in the paths of righteousness, for his name's sake."

His eyes traveled to the next sentence, and he faltered.

"Go on; this part's the best," she whispered between her slight breaths.

His voice trembled. "Even though I walk through the valley of the shadow of death ..." His own breathing came in wheezy gulps.

"I'm not dead yet, Ivan; keep going."

"I will fear no evil."

"Nothing," she sighed.

"I will fear nothing," he repeated.

She smiled.

"For you are with me. Your rod and your staff, they comfort me." He paused again.

"You never understood that one. Pay no mind; I do."

"You prepare a table before me in the presence of my enemies." Another hesitation.

Tidy searched his face.

"Am I enemy, Tidy?"

"What're you talking about?"

"You always yelling at me, calling me names, sending me to jail."

"I don't send you to jail, Ivan; the cops do that. No, you're not an enemy."

With a breath of relief he went on. "You anoint my head with oil. My cup overflows." His composure broke completely, and a sob escaped.

"You stop that." Her voice was weak, but there was no mistaking the command, a clarion. "I won't have you bawling like a baby."

Ivan looked at her in surprise. Her eyes wide open, she peered straight into his.

"You're a grown man. Stop it right now."

He could not ignore her order; the tears evanesced.

"The last part, I need the last part." Her voice retreated.

"Surely goodness and mercy shall follow me all the days of my life, and I shall dwell in the house of the Lord forever."

"See, I'm just going to another house." The effort of their conversation had begun to take its toll. "Someday I'll be expecting you there too. I'll have a hankering for your noodles by then."

And she closed her eyes for the last time.

Another five hours swept the clock before her breathing stopped altogether. Ivan sat beside her and read the psalm again—and again—without the interruptions, although in the back of his mind he could hear her caustic remarks as he went along. He rearranged the iris in the vase several times. He sat as if in a stupor, listening to the slowing breaths, counting in the long pauses.

He counted to two hundred and realized he should stop.

He called Claire, who called Julian and Emily.

Chapter 35

Claire arrived first. She found a spot to park a half block up the street on the opposite side. As she climbed out of the car, activity at the peppermint stoop drew her attention. Even from a distance, there was no mistaking Bernie and Blackie. They bent toward the door, hesitated a moment, and retreated down the street. Claire squinted to bring into focus two coffee cans left on the porch, one with lilac branches overflowing the edges, the other gathering plum-colored calla lilies.

If Claire had been new to this case, she would have been astonished by the scene. But not now. She knew this neighborhood wanted to recognize in Tidy what she had been: an upstanding citizen loyal to the community, and when she had been better able, a caring and kind woman. And these two denizens of the streets wished to show their appreciation. Tidy had been marginalized by her fate of frailty, both physically and mentally. But she was not—and Claire would hold strong to this opinion—on the fringe, where Julian, and even to an extent Claire herself, had tried to assign her. Tidy had clung to her dignity, yearned for respect, and struggled for her independence to the end. *I'm proud of you, Tidy,* Claire thought, giving a thumbs-up to Tidy's spirit as she crossed the street.

Julian and Emily arrived not far behind Claire. Julian had a small pot of violets in one hand. He placed the posies on the now-immaculate coffee table—a colorful adornment to (in its present exposure) a rather drab table.

They sat in the living room, carefully avoiding the couch. Ivan served them tea and coffee and some strudel, which nobody ate. They talked about calling the mortuary and their plans for Tidy's interment in the graveyard behind the Baptist church, the church she had attended—when she'd remembered to go—enthusiastically, if not exactly faithfully.

Suddenly Julian jumped up and strode from the room and out the back entry. He was relieved to find the basement open. In a moment he rejoined the others cradling a cedar box in his hands.

"Mr. Browning," he said. "She wants him to be buried with her." The three looked at him, stupefied. No one spoke, but each had their private thoughts about Julian having this information and not telling a soul. Emily turned to face her husband with unabashed love. Ivan's eyes filled anew.

"He died a long time ago," Julian said. "But she never forgot him. He's been in the basement all these years."

"Does anyone know his first name?" Emily asked. "Or why her last name wasn't Browning?"

They all smiled.

"Curious, now that I think about it," Julian said. "I never found any reference to him. No papers in her files mention him."

"How did he die?" Emily asked. "Do you know?"

"Cancer," Claire said. "She told me when I first visited. There's only the photo of him. How I wish we had had a chance to ask ... Julian? When she showed you the ashes, did she talk of him?"

"No, before I could recover from the revelation of the ashes, we got into an argument about not having enough money in her checking account—again." *Endearing now,* Julian thought. *Why wasn't it endearing then?*

The others had similar thoughts.

He disturbed their musings by abruptly rising once more, this time heading for the front hallway. He transferred the coats on the wall to a chair in the living room and opened the hidey-hole. A red shopping bag with crossed candy canes crammed in against the file box startled him. He removed both and peered back into the storage hole, on the chance of other surprises.

In the far reaches of the space lay the pistol, unadorned, solitary, fastidiously couched on two folded kitchen towels. Julian gaped at the display, stunned.

Unconscious of the long moments he'd stood paralyzed in front of the storage space, Julian jumped at Claire's voice when she called, "Julian, are you all right?"

He swiveled on his feet, with a swift movement of his head to throw off the confusion. He returned to the living room with the bag and file box. "I'd almost forgotten this box, hidden in the small cabinet in the hallway. This bag, though, is strange; I've never seen it before."

Claire had; it had hung from Tidy's wrist on her first court appearance. Claire's throat went dry. She wasn't sure she wanted to know about the candy-striped bag.

Julian opened the file box and picked out an envelope labeled "correspondence." Holding it, he wrestled with his conscience, but his curiosity won out. He flipped open the envelope flap and pulled out the top sheet. He smiled. "'Dear Mr. Browning.' A letter ..." Julian's mouth felt cottony. "And at the end, 'With all my love, Tidy.' Her love letters," he said softly and quickly slipped the sheet back in the envelope.

Julian recounted to the others the task of helping Tidy write a new will and how she had sworn him to secrecy. From the file box he extracted a thin nine-by-twelve-inch envelope and placed it on the coffee table—to rest for a moment.

His attention went to the holiday shopping bag. He pulled out several plastic grocery bags containing odd-shaped objects. In the first he found a silver letter opener with a note that said "For Clare." He extended the gift to her.

She remained immobile, her eyes on the thin silver tool. She had never before accepted a gift from a client. One of her rules.

Sensing her conflict, Julian placed the silver piece on the table and lifted the second bag. The sound of pills in plastic vials was unmistakable. "These must be for you too." He handed Claire the bag. *Our Santa Claus has left such curious presents— and what kind of elf am I?* Julian thought.

Claire withdrew two large brown vials. "The Vicodin," Claire whispered. She peered in the bag and withdrew an empty window envelope. On the back Tidy had scrawled "See, I'm not so dumb."

"She hid them," Claire murmured. "All along she was hiding the pills, suffering with her pain, most likely because she couldn't remember where she had hidden the vials. They're full."

Claire's solemnity made Julian nervous. He rustled the last plastic bag to ward off the mood. It contained two silver candlesticks. The accompanying note said "For Juli and Emily. Thank you." The handwriting was cramped and wavy, written by a failing hand but not a failing mind. Julian sat in stunned silence. Emily wept quiet tears.

To ward off his own emotion, Julian shook the candy cane bag, hoping there was nothing left to discover. There was a soft swish from the bottom of the bag. Julian reached deep and extracted a small black box. The note taped to the box said "For Teresa McBain." This handwriting was in heavy block letters. Julian looked at Ivan.

"She make me do it. She didn't have strength."

Julian opened the tiny box, a pair of pearl earrings.

For a minute or two everyone sat with their gifts—except Ivan, who stared at the floor unmoving, unable to absorb what had just happened.

Julian cleared his throat, and everyone except Ivan lifted their attention to him. He told them about the gun remaining in the hidey-hole. "Her present for Jane Rios, perhaps."

Claire and Emily smiled.

Julian lifted the slim envelope from the coffee table and handed it to Ivan. "And this is for you, Ivan. Tidy was very particular—well, bossy—about the contents. She asked me to type up the … ah … document … but she signed it. These are her words, exactly. She asked me to give this envelope to you personally."

Ivan didn't acknowledge Julian's little speech. The others stole glances surreptitiously, sympathetic but concerned. With no warning or explanation, Ivan rose and, holding the envelope to his chest, retreated to his room.

In this privacy, Ivan withdrew the single sheet of paper from the envelope and read it, twice, and then reached under the bed for the bottle—still full. Holding it by the neck, he marched to the kitchen and began pouring the clear liquid into the sink.

Claire came in carrying the tray of coffee cups and uneaten strudel from the living room. "Ivan."

He tried to block his actions from her with his body, but she had seen what he was doing. Oddly, he drew strength from that knowledge.

The last of the vodka splatted from the bottle. "It's gone," he said, his voice strong. "She not here, but she know. I don' want her mad at me. I stop drinking for Tidy."

Claire nodded and gently touched Ivan's shoulder before returning to the living room. Ivan took out the letter to read it one last time.

> Dear Ivan,
>
> My time is coming; I can feel it. I asked them to get you out of jail for me. I wanted you here to take care of me at the end, to make my last days peaceful. My first wish, and it's been granted. I'm leaving instructions to give this letter to you when I die.
>
> My last will and testament is in the box in the hiding place. This will says that I'm leaving everything to you. I don't have anyone else, and anyway you are just like family, and I want to leave what's left to family. So that is you. You have been good to me, and you should have some reward.
>
> You can stay in the house or sell it. Might be best to sell it, the way the neighborhood is going to the dogs. But use the money wisely. Keep it in the bank. I am trusting that you won't use it to drink anymore. I will be mad if you do. I believe you are a good person, and you do not need to drink. Find yourself something useful to do. Ask

Clare; she might know of something. Or work at the church, to help like you have been helped.

Have a good life, Ivan.

Your friend, Tidy

Acknowledgments

In 2002, I trained to become a volunteer counselor for elders, visiting seniors in their homes to address changes, issues, and events in their lives that had emotional content. Years of intense learning followed. I extend a huge thank-you to the social workers, psychologists, family therapists, and adult-protection caseworkers who taught me what I needed to know to help my fellow elders.

Along the way I accepted as clients seniors who were victims of elder abuse. In this work I observed the anguish of elders having to confront someone they most likely trusted who had now abused them in some way. Again, I was constantly learning from these experiences—about the laws that protect elders and how difficult it is to prosecute the abusers. I am grateful to the attorneys of elder law and also the judges who hear elder-abuse cases for their patience with my questions about the law, court rulings, and their views on the state of elder abuse.

In addition, I thank the elders (and their families) who helped me understand the problems with growing old. These issues are never simple, and with increasing age they can become complex beyond belief. Letting me into their lives, even for a short while, allowed me to observe and learn.

I am grateful to my many friends and colleagues who agreed to read the manuscript at various stages of its creation and gave me so many helpful suggestions for improvement.

And finally, a special thank-you to my husband, Stephen Salmon, who not only read the manuscript several times but supported the project in every aspect of its creation.